SEALed with a Kiss

by

Patricia A. Graves

Milton Keynes, UK

AuthorHouse™
1663 Liberty Drive, Suite 200
Bloomington, IN 47403
www.authorhouse.com
Phone: 1-800-839-8640

AuthorHouse™ UK Ltd.
500 Avebury Boulevard
Central Milton Keynes, MK9 2BE
www.authorhouse.co.uk
Phone: 08001974150

First published by AuthorHouse 2/28/2007

ISBN: 978-1-4259-7589-0 (sc)

Printed in the United States of America
Bloomington, Indiana

This book is printed on acid-free paper.

I would like to give a special thanks to my sister, Sue Bradley. Without her support and encouragement this book would never have made it into print. She has a great sense of what readers like and she gives the very best advice. Thanks Sue for taking the time to read my many drafts and to make sure that I never go astray.

Prologue

Lieutenant Tyler Zackary Garrett stood *at ease* with the other seven men who made up SEAL Team Mega One. They were crammed into a tent that had definitely seen better days but was considered one of many hastily erected command posts located in the godforsaken desert of Iraq.

Lieutenant Garrett was the leader of Team Mega One. He and his SEALs had been stationed in Iraq for over eighteen months. They had completed more missions than he could count at the moment. All of their missions had been considered highly important to the powers that be—highly covert, and luckily for everyone, highly successful.

But now, after eighteen long months, it was finally time to go home. At least that's what had been promised to each man standing before Commander Jackson R. Pearl. That promise had been made six months ago when the men of Mega One had been asked to extend their tour of duty for first three, then four, and finally another six months. They were needed, they were asked to stay, and without question they had agreed. But now duffels had been packed, goodbyes had been said, and they were ready to go.

"I don't need to stand here and tell you how much the navy appreciates your dedication and all the sacrifices you have made."

Oh shit, thought Tyler, because from his fifteen-year career with the navy, he knew that this was never a good way to start a conversation.

"You have each given above and beyond the call of duty, and you have served your country well."

Double shit, was Tyler's next thought because he would bet a year's paycheck that he knew what was coming.

"You men are the best of the best, and you have earned your way home. You have earned the right to get on that helo tomorrow morning and head for Germany and then head on home to the good old U.S. of A."

Tyler suspected that he wasn't the only man standing before Commander Pearl with a sick feeling in the pit of his stomach. He suspected that every one of his men had already figured out that the likelihood of getting on that helo tomorrow morning was slim to none at all. He could feel the tension building in the stuffy, dirty tent and for a second he thought about putting a stop to the commander's little game. But Commander Pearl was on a roll and Tyler guessed that the man had probably spent the best part of an hour working on his speech, so why not stand back and just let things play out. After all, he could be wrong, and if he stepped in and interrupted the man in charge now he might really piss him off. And that he didn't want to do—not when there was maybe a one-in-a-million chance that he and his men would be going home tomorrow.

So forcing himself to keep his eyes focused straight ahead, he tried like hell not to read between the lines. But the next words out of Commander Pearl's mouth just confirmed his worst fears.

"I would never stand here and order any of you gentlemen to put away your gear and take on one more mission. I would not have the heart to issue such an order. But I can and will tell you this. We need four special ops men to take on a mission and I'm asking for volunteers. And I'm starting with Team Mega One. I'm starting with you because of your special and unique training in extraction. We have four marines who were ambushed while on a very sensitive reconnaissance mission, and we need to get to them. And we need to get to them now."

Commander Pearl paused for two seconds to let his words sink in before continuing.

"If any of you choose to volunteer, you need to understand that this will delay your going home by at least ten days. Maybe longer. There isn't another transport aircraft scheduled to leave this part of Iraq until the end of next week. And even that may be delayed. But if all goes according to plan, anyone who takes on this job will be first to board anything flying out of here that will get them home. On that you have my word."

"Do you have any idea what happened to the marines, sir?" Tyler asked the question that was on everyone's mind.

"Yes, Lieutenant, we do, because we heard it all. We were in limited, but as-needed communication with Colonel Bradley who was leading the patrol. He contacted us as soon as the ambush hit and we could hear our men take on fire from the enemy. Even though we had no trouble pinpointing their exact location, Colonel Bradley was confirming their coordinates when all of a sudden everything went silent. Before we were completely shut down the last thing we heard were the words *take cover.* That was three hours ago and we've heard nothing since."

"Can we track them?"

"It's obvious to us that all their equipment has been taken and most likely destroyed, because we've lost the ability to pick them up through GPS. But an Iraqi informant got word to us twenty minutes ago that all four marines are being held captive in a shithole of a village about two miles due east from where they were attacked."

"You said all four, Commander. Does that mean they're all alive?"

"According to our information, Lieutenant Garrett, all four marines are alive. One is wounded, but nothing too serious. We've been told that the terrorists plan to move them tomorrow to a more secure place, and then broadcast their capture. They want to strike up a deal with the U.S. government for their release, knowing full well that we do not negotiate with terrorists. And when that fails, which they are banking on, they plan to videotape and televise our marines' execution."

As far as Tyler Garrett was concerned, the outcome of the commander's request was a foregone conclusion. There wasn't a man on SEAL Team Mega One who would get aboard a helo and head home knowing that four comrades were being held captive—four comrades who needed their help. Sure the guys in trouble were marines, not navy, but when the chips were down a man in uniform was a brother in the armed forces.

"Why don't I give you and your men some time to consider my request, Lieutenant? I'll come back in say… thirty minutes."

"There's no need for that, Commander. I'll take in whoever else wants to go."

As Tyler spoke he looked over at the other seven men standing in line, more at attention than at ease. He looked from face to face, giving a silent signal to the single men on his team. It would be understood without having to discuss it that the men who had wives and kids at home should get the hell out of Dodge while they had a chance. The others would step forward and volunteer for this mission and get home when they got home. One week, two weeks…it really didn't matter as long as the married guys got home to their families.

As it so happened, there were three married men and five single men, including Tyler, who made up Team Mega One. The first man to speak up was Second Lieutenant Conner McKenzie, nicknamed of course, Mac. He was single, from a small town in North Carolina and was one of the most dedicated men to ever serve in the United States Navy.

"I'm in," was all he said as he took one step forward.

"Count me in too." William Bradshaw stepped up next to his colleague, Mac. He was the computer specialist on the team and he was divorced, with no other family to speak of. Tyler had known before he had even stepped forward that Billy would be going along.

"You guys will need me to tag along to watch your butts." Richard "Kid" Mueller was the newest and youngest member of Mega One. He had become good friends with all of the men over the last eighteen months, and Tyler was proud to have him along on this mission. Kid grinned and stepped forward.

"So there you have it, Commander. Four volunteers. Me, Mac, Billy, and Kid will go in and get the boys in green."

"Well now," came a slow, lazy voice from behind the men who had stepped forward. "The way I see it, you guys will probably be dropped from a helo, well after dark, somewhere close to the where the marines are being held. And if that's the case, you'll need a pilot who can fly anywhere, anytime, even with his eyes closed. And that would be me."

Lieutenant Joe Thornton didn't exactly step forward. He more or less shuffled forward. He was one of the original members of Team Mega One and was known to everyone as Flyboy. And the nickname was well deserved. When Joe sat behind the controls of anything with wings, he became a part of the aircraft. He always said, "If I can get the thing started, I can figure out how to fly it." And he had proven that statement to be true on more than one mission. Joe was considered the best pilot in the navy, and even though it wasn't necessary, Tyler was glad he wanted to take them in.

"And you'll need someone to fly shotgun." The sixth man to step forward was Scott Trent. He was married with two young kids that he hadn't seen in forever. But if Flyboy was going on this mission, there was no leaving Scotty Trent behind.

"Since I have more medical training than any of you guys and since there's a marine who's hurt, I think I'll lend you a hand." David Campenella stepped up and joined his teammates. It was common knowledge that David had completed three years of medical school before chucking it all in favor of marrying his high school sweetheart and signing on with the navy—all within the same month. Hence, his nickname: Medicine Man.

"Even with GPS I can't trust that you SEALs could find your way out of a paper bag. So I had better go along to make sure you make it back to the extraction pickup point." Second Lieutenant Brian Johnson was the last man to step in line.

In less than five minutes all eight men of SEAL Team Mega One had once again delayed their free ride home. They were a team and they stood together. And the only one who seemed surprised by this was Commander Pearl.

"Well gentlemen, as much as we could use each and every one of you on this mission, I am only asking for four volunteers. Four SEALs to find and extract four marines. Seems like pretty good odds from where I stand. So, four of you should feel free to catch that ride tomorrow and head on home."

"With all due respect, Commander, if I'm gonna drop from a helo into a dark desert that may or may not be infiltrated with terrorists, I'd just as soon have Flyboy as my pilot and Scotty as his wingman." Mac knew he was speaking up on behalf of everyone.

"And if I were that wounded marine, I'd sure as hell want Medicine Man there to patch me up." This came from Scotty.

"Your offer for a few of us to hitch a ride home is mighty generous, but we'd all feel a whole lot better if we stayed together. So thanks, but no thanks…sir." Second Lieutenant Johnson tacked on the "sir" almost as an afterthought.

Before anyone could say anything further, Tyler took the lead. "So, Commander Pearl, looks like you've got the entire team. When do we go?"

In point of fact, Commander Pearl had had no doubt that he was going to get the four volunteers he'd asked for. What he hadn't quite expected was the entire team. But in retrospect, he shouldn't have been surprised. SEALs had a dedication to one another that went beyond what most would call rational. They watched each other's backs and kept each other alive. And these eight men had been through hell and back as a team these past eighteen months, so sticking together now seemed par for the course.

"You leave at 2300 hours tonight and you'll be dropped one hour into the flight. Because the terrorists may be expecting some sort of rescue mission, you're going to be dropped five miles from the village. That means you'll have to walk to where the marines are being held. It'll be pitch dark and the helo won't be using any lights as you get close to your drop-off. You'll have less than five hours to get in, get out, and get back to the pickup spot. Flyboy and Scotty will be waiting to fly you the hell outta there before dawn, so be in place no later than 0500 hours. If you miss your designated pickup, you'll have to find cover until nightfall and we'll try again. We need to get everyone out under the radar."

"So what you're saying, Commander, is that the marines reconnaissance mission was off the record, so to speak? And our government would prefer that no one knows that four marines went missing and that we had to go in and get them out." Tyler put his thoughts into words because he believed that he and his men deserved to know what they were getting themselves into.

"Unfortunately that's exactly the case, Lieutenant Garrett. And that means if you get into any real trouble out there we can't send in any backup. You guys will quite literally be on your own. There are only three men other than yourselves who even know that the marines have been captured and that we're planning this rescue. Once you have accomplished your mission, even the rescue will be off the record. It'll be as if the mission never happened. This is as covert as it gets, gentlemen."

The commander's harsh reality of the situation really didn't change anything other than to strengthen the SEAL's resolve to get the job done and get it done quickly. This is what they were trained for, and each man on Team Mega One was exceptionally well trained.

"How many guards should we expect to encounter?" asked Tyler.

"That's hard to say. Our informant said the terrorist's cell that brought in the marines was fairly large—somewhere around twenty men—but that once the marines were put under guard, only about ten stayed behind. Looks like the rest moved on."

"How do we communicate?" Tyler's men stood back and let their leader ask all the questions.

"Communication will be with me and will be on an as-needed basis only. If you miss the dawn pickup, signal in. If not, we don't expect to hear from you. I'll just see you when you get back here."

"If officially there are no missing marines, and therefore no rescue mission, do we have orders to leave the guards unharmed?"

"That's the part I'll leave up to you and your men, Lieutenant. If you can accomplish the extraction without any bloodshed, all the better. But if you need to eliminate any resistance to get our men out, then you need to do whatever is necessary. Leaving bodies behind will certainly raise questions, but those are questions we'll handle if and when the time arises. This is your mission, Lieutenant Garrett, and I'll not second guess your methods."

That was good enough for Tyler and his men. They knew that they were walking into the worst possible scenario. They would be dropped in the dead of night with less than five hours to accomplish their goal, and any form of communication would be on an emergency basis only. With the grim words "there will be no backup on this mission" still ringing in his ear, Tyler didn't want their hands tied behind their backs if things got a little dicey.

"Anything else we need to know, Commander?"

"Nothing else I can think of, Lieutenant. Just be ready to go at 2300 hours."

"Come on, boys," Tyler said as each of his men turned to follow him out of the musty tent. "The sooner we get this over with the sooner we can all go home."

Chapter One

Six weeks later Tyler Garrett not only found himself back on U.S. soil, but he was in the second week of a long overdue, well-deserved fourteen-day leave.

The voluntary rescue mission in Iraq had actually stretched into another voluntary follow-up mission. The four captured marines had been rescued without a hitch, but then the SEALs were asked if they would pick up where the secretive reconnaissance mission had left off. And of course, all of the men of Team Mega One had said yes. They understood, without being told, that the information that the marines had been in the process of gathering was vitally important to the continued military success in Iraq. So off they went, together, as a team, delaying once again their long overdue trip back to the States. Now finally, six weeks later, they were all home, safe and sound.

The first week of Tyler's leave had been spent hanging out at his small two- bedroom beach cottage located in San Diego. He spent his mornings drinking coffee and leisurely reading the paper. During the afternoons he took long walks on the beach, or he just lay out on his tiny patio and did nothing more than watch the waves crash over the sand. His evenings were equally as quiet. He had a couple of dates during the week but nothing serious. Drinks, dinner, and back to his place, if he was lucky. On one of his dates he actually lucked out, because the young lady had willingly gone back to his place and didn't leave until the next morning. The sex had been good but not great, and Tyler had felt slightly saddened by the whole encounter.

Tyler Garrett never had to work very hard to get women to succumb to his good looks and his undeniable charm, and sometimes he missed the challenge of the chase. To his disappointment, he discovered early in his naval career that some women just wanted to go to bed with a Navy SEAL. And he suspected that was the case with the woman he had just taken to dinner and then to bed. And since it had been way too easy, Tyler didn't feel much of a need to even make the effort to give her a call. And truth be told, it really didn't matter all that much to him, because right now what he really craved was peace and quiet, and he got that by just lazing around his house.

But that's how he'd spent the first week of his leave, and now he found himself slipping out of his rental car, about to spring a surprise visit on his family. Because he had felt a real need to clear his head of all of the covert and dangerous missions he'd been on over the last eighteen months, Tyler had delayed going home for a visit. As soon as his feet had touched the ground in San Diego he had notified his folks that he was back in the States. But because he needed some time to himself, he had come up with one lame excuse after another as to why he couldn't just jump on a plane and head home to Austin, Texas (or more accurately, a small town about fifty miles outside of Austin). And because there were no more excuses, and because he really missed his folks and his little sister, here he was in Burns, Texas, walking up to the house he'd been raised in.

Tyler knew that his parents rarely locked their front door, but this time it didn't budge when he tried to turn the knob. He knocked and there was no answer. So he went around to where he knew someone would be: the landing strip located about a hundred yards from the house.

Tyler's family owned and operated a small, local flight school. They had a couple of small planes and one helicopter. His father and his baby sister were both certified flight instructors. The school was fairly well known in and around the surrounding communities and his family had done rather well over the years. They would never become rich and famous, but they made an honest and decent living—a living Tyler had walked away from at the age of twenty-one so that he could enlist in the navy and pursue his lifelong dream of becoming a Navy SEAL.

As Tyler walked slowly over to the landing strip, he was surprised that there was no activity to speak of. Everything seemed almost too quiet, and he felt an unwanted ripple of awareness. Maybe it was his training as a SEAL, but something seemed off and he felt uneasy with the all-consuming silence. Behind his aviator sunglasses he searched the area for signs of someone—anyone. And finally as his eyes landed on the familiar shape of his little sister, Katie, he drew in a deep sigh of relief.

Tyler was still quite a ways from where his sister was squirting down one of the planes, but she must have caught the reflection from his sunglasses because she suddenly looked up. Katie looked at the man walking directly toward her, recognized her brother in an instant, dropped the hose she was holding, and took off at a dead run.

"Oh, my God! Tyler, you're home!" Katie Garrett ran at full speed ahead and threw herself into her brother's open arms. She wrapped her own arms tightly around his neck and hung on to him as if she would never let him go. "Oh, my God! Oh, my God! You are really, really home!"

"Yes, little one, I am really, really home." As he spoke, Tyler tried to keep from laughing at his sister. She always had a flair for the dramatic and now was no exception.

"Why didn't you call? Why didn't you let us know you were coming? How come you didn't give us any notice?" She fired one question after another, all the time clinging to him for dear life.

"Let me breathe, Katie, and I'll tell you anything you want to know." Tyler planted a big kiss on the side of her face and gently pulled her arms from around his neck. He couldn't stop himself from laughing out loud.

"I just can't believe you're here. How long can you stay? Oh God, Tyler, Mom and Dad are going to have a fit when they find out you're home."

"So where are the folks anyway? The front door's locked and there was no answer when I knocked." As Tyler asked the question, he took his sister's arm and headed over to turn off the hose that Katie had haphazardly dropped to the ground.

"You won't believe this, but they're on a little vacation. They left this morning and won't be back for three days. They had no idea you were coming home, so they took off with the Keatings to the beach. I think we should call them and tell them you're home. They'll want to head back right away."

She started to take off toward the house but Tyler stopped her. "Hold on, Katie. I'll be around for the next seven days, so why don't we just let Mom and Dad enjoy their trip. We'll have plenty of time to catch up when they get back."

"Mom will kill me if I don't call her right away and you know it."

"Mom will not kill you, and don't worry. I'll tell them it was my idea not to call. God knows they hardly ever take a break," he added when he could tell she was about to interrupt. "And besides, when's the last time they left the business to take a few days off?"

"I don't know, Tyler. I really think we should call them."

"And I think you should come back over here and give me another hug." Katie flew back into his arms. "I really don't want to spoil their fun," he whispered as she tucked her head under his chin. "They'll feel obligated to cut their trip short because of me, and I'd feel bad if they did that. They deserve a little rest and relaxation. So how about you and I spend the next few days together and before you know it Mom and Dad will be home."

"I guess you're right. They never get away. And," she conceded as she pulled out of her brother's embrace, "they did seem pretty excited about the trip."

"Then it's settled."

Katie looked over at her big brother and she felt a sudden threat of tears. She swallowed hard but couldn't stop one tear from slipping onto her cheek.

"Why in the world are you crying, Katie bug?" Tyler's use of her childhood nickname just caused more tears to splash down onto her cheeks.

"Hey, what's the matter?" He reached for her and for the third time in less than five minutes she fell into his arms.

"I'm just so happy to see you. You were gone for so long and we hardly heard from you. We knew you wrote as often as you could, but we've all been so worried about you and we missed you so much."

Tyler felt a knot form in his own throat. "I've missed you too, sweetheart. And I'm home for a while now so there's no need to worry. And as you can see, I'm home without as much as a scratch. So no more tears, okay?" he asked as he tilted her head up to meet his eyes.

"Okay," she choked back.

Katie reached up and wiped her runny nose along her sleeve and then grinned at her brother as if she were ten years old. He grinned back and together, arm in arm, they headed back toward the house.

"So, what's to eat?

Two roast beef sandwiches later, Tyler still sat at the kitchen table, savoring every bite of his mother's homemade apple pie.

"It's so quiet around here. Did you cancel all the private lessons until Mom and Dad get back?" he asked between mouthfuls.

"Actually," Katie responded as she finished washing up the dishes, "the week was pretty quiet so there were just a couple of lessons to cancel."

"Then why didn't you go with them? You love the beach."

Katie pulled out a chair and sat down at the table across from her brother. She was having trouble again keeping back the unwanted tears. Tyler was ten years older than her and he was more than just her big brother. He was her idol. And she had worried about him every single second he was over in Iraq. She knew that his job as a SEAL was fraught with danger, and she lived in fear that one day he wouldn't come home. But he was home now, and that's all that mattered. So with a great deal of effort she forced back the tears that threatened to fall.

"I can't leave right now for two reasons. One is that I don't want to be away from Brandon, and the other is that I have a business commitment I can't get out of."

Tyler wondered how serious Brandon Wilson and his sister had gotten over the last eighteen months. "So things with you and Brandon are pretty serious?"

Katie blushed and the look in her eyes told him everything he wanted to know. But Katie, being Katie, held nothing back.

"I'm crazy in love with him, Ty, and he feels the same way about me. As soon as we have a chance to go see his parents in Dallas, he's going to make it official. He wants us to tell his parents first and then he'll ask Dad for my hand."

"So what's the holdup, Katie bug? Dallas isn't that far away." Tyler finished off his pie and thought about having another piece.

"Brandon's parents are always on the move. All they do is travel for his dad's job. They've been in Paris these past three months, and his dad's scheduled to go to China next. They promised to stop at home in Dallas before heading to China, so Brandon and I are sorta on call. As soon as they get to Dallas, we'll catch a flight out of here. Brandon thinks they should be home in about two weeks."

"And when will the wedding be?"

"Once we get everyone's blessing, including yours, we don't want to wait all that long. So I figured we would plan something for the next time you're home. I would never get married without you, Ty."

Tyler leaned over and gave his sister a light kiss on the cheek. "My blessing's a given. I like Brandon and I think you're good for each other."

"I think so too," she responded with a smile. "So when do you think you can make it home again?"

Oh boy, he thought. This was always the tricky part because there was never any way he could tell for sure when he'd be called away on a mission. Sometimes he might know weeks in advance, but more often than not he was sent out with less than forty-eight hours notice. But this was not the time to burst Katie's bubble, so he looked right at her and lied.

"I'll make arrangements for leave the minute you two set a date. And come hell or high water I'll be here for your wedding."

If Katie knew he was telling her only what she wanted to hear, she didn't let on, so Tyler quickly and wisely changed the subject.

"So what's the business commitment that's keeping you here?" He thought he detected a slight hesitation in her response to his question, but as soon as she started talking he wasn't so sure.

"Do you remember me telling you about my college friend Samantha James?" Katie didn't bother to wait for his reply. "She was assigned to be my big sister when I arrived at college. Even though she was a junior and I was a freshman, we really hit it off. We've kept in touch and she's coming for a visit starting tomorrow."

Tyler got up and took a beer out of the fridge. He leaned up against the counter, twisted off the cap, and took a long, deep swallow. "How's that a business commitment, Katie? Sounds more like pleasure to me."

Katie took a ragged breath and suddenly looked a little uncomfortable. She quickly dropped her gaze and started fiddling with the salt and pepper shakers on the table. Tyler narrowed his eyes and watched as she seemed to scramble for just the right words. He took another swallow of beer and waited…and waited, and waited.

"Well you see...," she began, "um…you see, Samantha is going to be here on business. She's um…she…"

Tyler usually had no trouble staying quiet. He always believed that silence was a great motivator to get someone else to talk. But even he couldn't stand to see his sister struggle with what she obviously didn't want to tell him.

"Out with it, Katie. What is it you don't want me to know about your friend Samantha?"

Katie finally looked over at her brother. "Okay, I'll tell you, but you have to promise me that you won't blow your top. I know how you can be."

He could feel a chill run up and down his spine, but he didn't let his apprehension show. Katie never had a problem telling him anything, so whatever it was she had to say had to be pretty damn bad. And he knew that if he so much as hinted at blowing his top, as she put it, she would clam up. So he stayed leaning against the sink, looking to the entire world like he was Mr. Cool and Calm. Which both of them knew was anything but the case.

"Of course I won't blow my top."

Katie didn't look convinced. "Not good enough, Ty. You need to promise me you'll not lose it when I explain about Samantha."

Tyler was not very good at making promises he might not be able to keep, but his curiosity got the best of him. "Okay. If it means that much to you, then I promise I won't lose my temper."

Katie knew that was as good as she was going to get, so she plunged right in before she lost her nerve. "Samantha is a freelance journalist and she's doing an article about flight schools. She's going to write us up in the magazine she's working for and we're going to get some great publicity. She gets her article, and we get free advertisement. She'll be here tomorrow to go through flight training, so to speak. She's staying here with me… um, with us. And I promised her lots of flying time. She should be here around ten tomorrow morning."

Tyler's body language had not changed from cool, calm, and relaxed, but he was seething inside, and Katie guessed as much.

"Don't you dare stand there and frown at me, Tyler Garrett. I know how you feel about journalists, but

Samantha is different. She takes her work very seriously and she's my friend."

Before he moved, he forced himself to pull a mask over his features. He also forced himself to sound like the voice of reason. He may hate journalists, but yelling at his sister now would do him absolutely no good. "If this Samantha woman is such a good friend of yours, surely she will understand that you need to reschedule her little business trip. Why don't you call her and tell her I'm here for a short visit and you'd prefer to give her flying lessons another time."

"She's not here for flying lessons, Ty. She's just going to watch me fly and then write about it. I've already gone over all the ground school requirements with her, so now all she needs is to observe the practical application."

"Whatever," he muttered before another swallow of beer. "So, since she's not coming here to learn to fly, there shouldn't be any problem having her come another time."

Katie got up from the table and got a beer of her own. She didn't really like the taste, but she needed something to soothe her nerves and opening a bottle of wine would take too long.

"Samantha has a deadline to meet and she's coming all the way from California. She lives in L.A. and she's already made arrangements to spend a few days here. There's no way I can ask her to change her plans now."

"Sure you can. It's real easy. All you have to do is pick up the phone and call her." Tyler's voice may have remained calm, but the look in his eyes told another story. And because of the defiant look he gave her, Katie didn't move. She just stood her ground and returned her brother's look, stare for stare. And the battle was on. Neither one gave an inch and neither one refused to glance away.

"If you won't do it," he said as he reached for the phone, "then I'll do it for you. Just give me her number."

Tyler was using his "I'm in charge and don't give me any shit" tone of voice. Katie suspected that he figured he could intimidate her into getting his way, and she decided that now was as good a time as any to show him how much she'd grown up while he was away.

"Don't treat me like one of your navy subordinates, Tyler, because it's not going to work. Samantha will be here tomorrow and that's the end of it. I love and adore you, big brother, but on this you will not win. So give it up." She tacked on a smile meant to melt his heart and Tyler knew in that instant that she was right. He was not going to win this one. She had dug in her heels and she wasn't going to budge. And being the good soldier that he was, he knew when to strategically back down.

"So when in hell did you grow up on me?" He couldn't quite stop his lips from turning up into a grin—a grin that more times than not caused a woman's heart to turn over and her pulse to start racing, a grin that soon changed into an all-out smile.

Relief flashed quickly in Katie's eyes, and just as she started to respond to his question there was a loud knock at the back door.

"Katie, you in there? Hurry up and open the door!"

The sound of Brandon's excited voice could be heard through the door. Katie shrugged her shoulders at the lift of Tyler's brow, and before she could do a thing the back door was flung open.

"Thank God you are here." Brandon was so focused on Katie that he didn't even see Tyler. "I just heard from my parents and they're home. They have a four-day reprieve before they need to head for China. If we leave first thing in the morning we can make our engagement official and then I can speak to your dad as soon as we get back from Dallas. The timing couldn't be better, sweetheart."

Tyler stood and watched as Brandon lifted his sister into his arms and planted a kiss smack dab on her lips. He swung her around in a circle and finally dropped her to her feet, planting another kiss on the tip of her nose. "I'll call the airport and you pack. If we're lucky we can catch the first flight out of here tomorrow."

The smile on Katie's face died and she glanced over at Tyler. And with his arms still wrapped around her waist, Brandon's eyes followed hers.

"Well, what do you know? You're home." Brandon didn't miss a beat. He let go of Katie and headed over to greet Tyler.

Tyler extended his hand to the young man that would soon become his brother-in-law. And in that instant he knew the truth of what he'd told his sister earlier: He really did like Brandon Wilson.

"Welcome home, Tyler."

"Thanks, Brandon. It's good to see you."

"Yeah, well it's great to see you. How come you didn't let anyone know you were coming?"

Katie had asked him the same question earlier. "To tell you the truth, I just got lucky. I was able to catch a hop on a military plane heading to Austin from Camp Pendleton. It was last-minute so all I had time to do was grab my duffel bag and jump aboard."

"How long are you staying?"

"Seven days. I may be able to extend my leave by a day or two, but not much longer than that."

As Tyler explained he was on leave for seven to nine days, the implication suddenly dawned on Brandon. And the young man's smile faltered. Tyler knew what was going on in Brandon's mind and he shifted his gaze over to his sister. As he studied Katie for a few seconds, he felt a quick pull on his heart. He felt really happy and excited for her, and the very last thing he wanted was for his unexpected trip home to ruin her chance to head for Dallas. Marriage and a family might not be in the cards for him, but he knew it was just right for Katie.

"Listen, you two."

"I've got an idea."

Both Tyler and Brandon spoke at the same time.

"You first, Lieutenant."

For some reason, Brandon always shifted back and forth between calling Tyler by his first name and addressing him by his rank. And Tyler figured that he reverted to calling him by his military rank when he was a little nervous or a little unsure of himself—like right now.

"No, you go ahead, Brandon. What were you about to say?"

Tyler sat back down at the table, stretched out his long legs, and crossed one ankle over the other.

"Well, I was just thinking." Brandon walked back over to Katie and draped his arm over her shoulder. "You obviously heard why we want to go to Dallas tomorrow and I think it'd be great if all three of us went together. My parents would love to see you, Lieutenant, and if you went along you wouldn't miss any time with your sister. We could leave in the morning and be back here the same day your folks return from the beach. How does that sound?"

The very last thing Tyler wanted was to go to Dallas. But he knew that if he refused to go along, Katie would never go either. And the look on Brandon's face was so hopeful that he didn't really have a choice. He was going to have to go to Dallas, like it or not.

"I can't go to Dallas now, Brandon, even if Tyler goes with us."

Both men looked at her as if she'd lost her mind.

"Of course you can, Katie." Tyler spoke before Brandon had a chance.

"No, I can't." She sounded so forlorn and it was clear that she was trying not to cry.

"We'll ask my cousin to look after the place while we're all gone, sweetheart. He can stop by every morning and every evening. That way everything will be fine until we get home." Brandon was sure that was just the solution.

"I still can't go. I have a commitment and I'll need to be here for the next few days. Oh God, Brandon, I'm so sorry."

It was clear that Brandon still hadn't connected the dots. But Tyler had no such trouble. And there was no way in hell he was going to let some journalist ruin his sister's future plans.

"Give me your friend's phone number, Katie. And this time don't argue with me. I'll just call and explain to her that you...I mean that we all have to fly to Dallas. She'll simply have to rearrange her plans."

"Oh that's right. In all the excitement I completely forgot that Samantha's coming tomorrow." Now Brandon sounded as forlorn as Katie.

Tyler rose from his chair in one fluid motion and was reaching out for the phone.

"It's too late, Ty. Samantha is already on a plane. She's landing in Austin around midnight."

"No problem. I'll call and leave a message for her at her hotel."

Katie pulled away from Brandon and went over and snatched the phone out of her brother's hand. "We've already discussed this and I'm not changing my mind. I made a promise to help Samantha with her article and I'm not cancelling on her at the last minute."

"Give me back the phone, Katie bug." As she slammed the receiver down into the cradle, Tyler decided to appeal to someone with hopefully more influence over his sister.

"See if you can reason with her, Brandon. I've already tried to talk her into cancelling her friend's trip out here, but she refuses to listen to me. Maybe she'll listen to you."

Katie crossed her arms under her breasts and stood and glared at her brother. Tyler felt an urge to laugh but decided that was not a good idea. Anyway, he was banking on the fact that Brandon could make her listen to reason.

"Actually, Tyler, I think your sister's right. She made a promise to her friend months ago and I for one don't want to ask her to break it. We'll make arrangements to see my parents as soon as they return from China. We've waited this long, so another four months won't make that much difference."

Tyler looked from Katie to Brandon and back again to Katie. And he felt a sick feeling in the pit of his stomach at what he knew he had to do. But Katie was his sister and he loved her more than anyone else on the face of the earth.

"Okay, you two, so how about a compromise?"

"A what?"

"You heard me. I said how about a compromise?"

"If I recall, Tyler, you're not very good at compromising. You either use your charm to get your way or you just bark out an order and then expect it to be followed. Lieutenant Garrett and the word *compromise* seem to be a contradiction in terms."

"Very funny," was his response, even though he knew that his sister was right. Compromising was certainly not his strong suit.

"What's your plan, Tyler?" Brandon decided that he had to be the one to ask, since Katie seemed highly suspicious of any compromise coming from her brother.

Tyler ignored his sister and turned his attention to Brandon. If he was going to sell his idea, he didn't think he could get away with looking Katie in the face. "How about you two take off to Dallas and do what you need to do before your parents leave for China. I'll stay here and take care of Samantha. I'll get her settled into the guest bedroom and fly her wherever the hell she wants to go. You'll get your parents blessing on your engagement, Samantha will get her damn article, and best of all you'll owe me one big time, Katie." He turned and grinned at his sister. "So, what do you think?"

"Well, I don't know about Katie, but I think it's a fantastic idea." Brandon was hoping some of his enthusiasm would rub off on Katie. "We'll leave first thing tomorrow and be back in three days, four days tops."

As Brandon spoke, Tyler shifted his eyes to his sister. He was watching her closely, trying to gage her response. And even if he wasn't much good at compromising, he was the very best at waiting.

"Come on, Katie. Tyler's got a good idea. Right?"

"You'd do that for me?" Katie didn't answer Brandon's question.

"I'd do anything for you. Even baby-sit your friend who just happens to have the most obnoxious career I can think of."

"But what about your leave? You can't expect me to believe that you'd like spending your free time flying a complete stranger around day and night. You do enough of that as a SEAL."

"I love flying. You know that. And most of the time when I'm aboard an aircraft I'm a passenger. Flyboy does most of the piloting when we're on flight duty. So don't worry about me, Katie."

"If I agree to this compromise of yours, will you promise me that you'll be nice to Samantha?"

"I'll be so nice and so charming that your friend won't even miss you. I may hate her profession but I have nothing against the lady personally."

Brandon stood silently and watched the exchange between brother and sister. Both he and Tyler knew that Katie wanted desperately to give in and go to Dallas, but they also knew that she had to be sure she was doing the right thing. So both men stayed quiet and let her think things over.

"You said that I'd owe you big time. Exactly what sort of payment do you have in mind?" She was teasing, and he knew it. But since it seemed she was on the verge of agreeing to go to Dallas, he played along.

"Oh I don't know, but rest assured I'll probably ask for something really, really big. Like if you two ever have a boy, I might expect that you would name him Tyler. Or, at the very least, I might *compromise* and let his middle name be Tyler." He emphasized the word *compromise*, and watched as Katie and Brandon tried not to laugh.

"I think we can live with that. Don't you, Brandon?"

"Sure thing." The relief in Brandon's voice was noticeable to everyone.

"Then why don't you go up and pack and let Brandon call the airport. After that Brandon and I will have a little talk out on the porch." Tyler reached into the refrigerator and took out two beers, one of which he handed off to Brandon.

"What kind of little talk?" Katie asked as she made her way slowly out of the kitchen.

"You know. The kind of talk a big brother has with the man who is about to marry his baby sister."

That comment stopped her dead in her tracks. "Tyler Garrett, don't you dare scare him off. And Brandon Wilson, don't you dare pay any attention to what my brother has to say. I love you both, but I will not have you ganging up on me. Is that clear?" This time Katie waited and waited.

Tyler slung one arm over Brandon's shoulder, his bottle of beer dangling from his other hand. "Come on, Brandon, my friend. Let's have our beer first and then you can call the airport. That is if you still want to go to Dallas after you hear some of my favorite stories." Katie watched in disbelief as the two men she loved most in the world waltzed right past her, completely ignoring her words of warning. "By the way, Brandon, did Katie ever tell you about the time she...."

As Tyler and Brandon made their way through the front door and out onto the porch, Katie let out a joyous laugh and then flew upstairs to pack, feeling that all was right with the world.

Chapter Two

Tyler sat on the top step of the front porch, watching as a small, four-door rental car pulled up right next to his. He took a sip of coffee and looked down at the complicated, high-tech watch he wore on his left wrist. It showed ten o'clock on the dot, and he was impressed that Katie's friend was right on time. But that was all he was going to allow himself to be impressed with, because even though he had told his sister that he didn't have anything against the woman personally, nothing could be farther from the truth. She was a journalist, and as far as he was concerned that meant that she was the enemy. She might not be a member of the insurgence or a member of a known terrorist cell, but she was the enemy all the same.

Tyler stood up just as the door to the driver's side opened. He watched as one long bare leg swung out of the car, only to be followed by another long, sleek bare leg. And to his dismay, the body that slid out to stand in shoes with sexy, three-inch heals, was a body to die for. Because Tyler had the advantage of wearing his aviator sunglasses, he took his own sweet time as his eyes traveled slowly from the toes of her *come fuck me* shoes, up to a face surrounded by flaming red hair and flashing green eyes. He studied the too-beautiful face and watched as her incredibly enticing lips turned up into just a hint of a smile—a smile that didn't quite reach her dark green eyes.

"If you are finished with your inspection, Lieutenant, perhaps you can tell your sister that Samantha is here."

Ah, the lady is full of surprises, Tyler thought, because she actually knew right off who he was. He took another long, slow sip of coffee and stepped down from the porch. And as he did so, it was Samantha's turn to make a full inspection of the gorgeous man walking toward her.

Samantha had seen pictures of Katie's Navy SEAL brother, but nothing could have prepared her for the real thing. Even at a quick glance, he was just so incredibly good looking. He stood an inch over six feet tall, had wonderfully broad shoulders, a flat- as-a-pancake stomach, and great jean-clad legs. And that was just from the neck down. His face was just as great as his body. Even with his expression cast in stone and his eyes hidden behind his shades, he couldn't disguise his handsome features. His face was tan, his nose perfectly formed, and he had the most delicious-looking mouth. His dark brown hair was longer than what she knew the military would approve of, and she wondered briefly if that was his *on leave* look. The man was way too sexy looking for his own good, and Samantha felt her mouth go dry as he stepped right up to her.

"I hate to be the bearer of bad news, Ms. James, but I'm afraid that you're stuck with me for the next few days. Katie and Brandon had to fly to Dallas this morning and they aren't expected back until Friday or Saturday."

Samantha suddenly wished that she hadn't taken off her sunglasses. She felt way too exposed to his close scrutiny and would have felt better had she had something to hide behind. Maybe it was because she couldn't see his eyes? Maybe it was his uninviting tone of voice? Or maybe there was just something about the way he stood and looked down at her. Whatever it was, she couldn't explain why she suddenly felt uncomfortable. But no matter how much at a disadvantage she felt, she refused to act intimidated, which is what she suspected he was trying to make her do. He was standing just a little too close, and she could sense his eyes traveling slowly up and down her body a second time.

"So, are you the official welcoming committee?"

Intimidated or not, she asked the question with a genuine smile, trying her best to get him to smile back. After all, as Katie's big brother she figured that he must have a smile hidden somewhere. But his smile never came, and instead she watched as a frown passed across his handsome face.

"I promised my sister that I'd look after you till she gets back."

Boy… that was anything but a welcoming comment, she thought as her own smile faded. "Well, I hope I'm not inconveniencing you too much?"

"It's only for three or four days, so it's no big deal."

Again she noticed his uninviting tone of voice. In fact his voice actually held a hint of annoyance. But because she didn't know this man, she decided to dismiss it from her mind. "Well it's a big deal to me, and I can't tell you how much I appreciate your willingness to help me out."

When he offered no response, Samantha wondered if she'd completely misunderstood the situation. In a flash she could hear Katie telling her all kinds of wonderful things about her big brother. Katie had used adjectives like *smart*, *fun*, *brave*, *generous*, and *friendly*. But the man Katie described to her over the years seemed nothing like the unfriendly man standing before her now. And she was more than a little confused. And she felt a wave of uncertainty. "You…um…. You are going to take me flying, aren't you? I mean, that's why I'm here and I can only stay in Burns for a few days. I'm due back in L.A. on Saturday. I was hoping to get in lots of flying time so I can convey the total experience to my readers. My article is going to be based mostly on my emotional reactions to flying, so I figured I'd need plenty of hours in the air." She knew she was babbling but she couldn't seem to stop herself. But Tyler had no such problem.

"Look, Ms. James. Let me tell you straight out. I can think of a hundred other things I'd rather be doing over the next four days, but I made a promise to my sister that I'd stay here and fly you around. But make no mistake, the minute Katie gets back I figure I've kept my promise and my obligation to you is over. So given that, you're thanks is really not necessary."

Samantha couldn't believe that anyone could be so blatantly rude. But only because he was Katie's brother and because she really needed this assignment, she drew in a deep, steadying breath and decided to try again.

"It must have been an emergency for Katie not to have called me."

He guessed that she was making a comment more than asking a question, but he decided to answer her anyway.

"Yeah, I guess you could say it was an emergency...of sorts."

She waited for him to elaborate but when he didn't she pushed for more information. She hated to give him the satisfaction of asking another question, but his lack of response was clearly meant to provoke her. And it was working. "I hope that Katie and Brandon are all right?" she asked as she lifted her eyes to stare up into his face. Even at five foot seven and wearing three-inch heels, she still needed to look up at him.

"They're fine." He purposely kept his reply vague and she felt a spark of irritation.

"Could you possibly be any more vague?" Her patience finally snapped.

"You have no idea just how vague I can be, Ms. James."

Samantha felt more than irritated. She felt a bubble of anger but decided that it would get her nowhere if she lost her temper now. For the life of her she couldn't begin to fathom why he'd taken such an instant dislike to her. She'd done nothing but show up, on time, as expected. He had no right to be so rude, and she came really close to telling him so. But unfortunately she needed him, at least until Katie got back from Dallas. So she swallowed what she really wanted to say and worked to keep her voice cool and calm.

"It may not be any of my business, Lieutenant, but I find it strange that Katie would take off to Dallas when you're obviously here on leave, and also knowing that I was arriving today." She tired to keep the sarcasm out of her voice, but some of it slipped through and she knew he caught it.

"You're right about one thing, ma'am. Katie's reasons for going to Dallas are none of your business. At least not until she gets home and tells you herself."

Samantha's eyes flashed a warning, which Tyler chose to ignore. "So until then," he continued in a slow Texas drawl, "the way I see it you have two choices. You can cancel this little trip of yours and reschedule with Katie for a later date, or you can accept that you're stuck with me and make do until Katie and Brandon get home. The choice is yours."

If given the choice she would get back into her rental car, slam the door in his face, and drive away without another word. But she was on a tight schedule and she had a deadline that wouldn't wait. And if she wanted to be considered for the next project that she really had her heart set on, then she had to be able to deliver on this one. So because she had no other option, this time she purposely sent Tyler her most *insincere* smile. Deciding that she'd had enough of his obnoxious behavior, she let the sarcasm flow.

"Why, it would be a pleasure to have you fly me around, Lieutenant Garrett. If I'm not mistaken, Katie has mentioned that you're somewhat of a hotshot pilot. My readers will love the fact that I'm being given the royal treatment by an honest to goodness Navy SEAL. What a plus. I just know my publisher will be thrilled as well." She knew she had made her point when a muscle twitched at the corner of his mouth—just a slight, barely noticeable twitch, but a twitch all the same.

Tyler almost came back with a rude comment about what she could do with her smartass mouth, but decided to save it for later. It was pretty much a given that they were going to challenge each other over the next four days, because the battle lines had already been drawn. And he was actually looking forward to the war, which should have surprised him but didn't. He needed something more than just flying around to occupy his mind until Katie and his parents returned, and fighting with Ms. Samantha James would do just fine. He was always up for a good fight, especially one that required a quickness of mind and sharper-than-average wits. And he figured that he would need both while doing battle with one of his sister's best friends.

"Well then, let's get your bags out of the car and get you settled in." He knew his sudden change of attitude would throw her for a loop, and he was right. She didn't quite know what to do. She stood routed in place and watched in disbelief as Tyler went around her, spotted her bags in the back seat, and retrieved them for her. "Why don't you grab your equipment and follow me on up to the guest room. I'll give you a few minutes to change into something more comfortable and then we can go for a little flight. Have you ever been up in a single-engine Piper?"

He walked past her with both her bags in hand and finally she felt like she had some movement in her legs. Not wanting him to think he had caught her off guard, she quickly grabbed her camera equipment from the car and chased after him into the house. He was halfway up the stairs when she caught up with him.

Tyler never slowed down. He kept going up the stairs, turned left, and headed into a room at the end of the hall. It just so happened that the guest room was right next to his, and for a second he wondered if he was better off putting her into his sister's room. But because she was right on his back and he didn't much feel like lugging her bags to the other end of the hall, he dumped her bags in the middle of the floor. Samantha nearly collided into him.

"I'll meet you out front in twenty minutes. That should give you plenty of time to change. And," he added as he made his way out of her room, "you'll want to wear some sunglasses." And with that he was gone.

Samantha stood in the middle of her room tying to figure what in the world had just happened. Since the moment she'd stepped out of the car, Katie's brother had been rude and unfriendly, and then in a blink of an eye he was carrying her bags into the guest room with almost a smile—*almost* being the operative word. He hadn't offered her so much as a real smile, a welcoming handshake, or any other words of encouragement, and she wondered how in the world she was going to put up with Lieutenant Tyler Garrett for the next four days. He might be the most gorgeous man she's ever laid eyes on, but he was quite possibly the most irritating as well. *And why does he want me to change my clothes*? she wondered. She looked down at her skirt and blouse and rather liked her outfit. The skirt was lightweight linen and was just a couple of inches above her knee. It was perhaps shorter than what she was used to, but it was so hot that she had decided earlier that a short skirt was okay without nylons. Her blouse was made of a soft white material that clung in all the right places. Her sandals were strappy and the heels were a little too high, but again she thought the shoes went well with the overall look. Deciding that she looked just fine and that she didn't need to change her clothes to suit Mr. Unfriendly, she grabbed her purse, her camera, and her sunglasses before heading out the door.

Samantha waited impatiently for Tyler on the front porch, but as promised he showed up twenty minutes later. Without so much as another word from him, a few minutes after that she found herself sitting in the passenger seat of a single-engine Piper, Cherokee.

Strapping her seatbelt tightly into place, she risked looking over at Tyler, who was completely ignoring her while he concentrated on writing on a form that was attached to a clipboard that he held in his right hand. And it flashed through her mind that he was left-handed. Something else flashed through her mind as well: that he looked so relaxed and so natural behind the controls of the plane while she was more nervous than she would have expected.

She'd never been in a small plane before, and she felt both anxious and just a little claustrophobic. Without realizing that she might be giving herself away, she wiped her damp palms down the front of her skirt—the skirt she now wished she wasn't wearing. As she'd climbed up into the cockpit of the plane, Samantha's tight skirt had made it awkward for her and she'd felt very unladylike. And now, sitting up front with Tyler, she was also much more aware of just how short her skirt actually was. The hem was hiked up around her thighs and no matter how hard she tugged, it wouldn't budge. Her legs were bare and much too exposed, and she silently cursed herself for her stubbornness and not changing into pants when she'd had her chance. But even she had to admit that it probably didn't really matter how short her skirt was for all the attention Tyler was paying to her. And sitting quietly, waiting for him to do whatever it is that pilots do, Samantha felt her anxiety level rising and felt even more claustrophobic.

"You'll feel better once we're in the air. You won't feel all closed in when there's nothing but blue sky surrounding you."

He hadn't even bothered to look over at her as he spoke; nor did he stop writing. And Samantha wondered how he could tell what she was feeling. But she didn't have time to give it any more thought, because in the next second he reached behind his seat, dropped the clipboard onto the floor, and turned in her direction.

"Before we take off I need to ask you a few questions."

As he spoke, she wished that he'd remove his sunglasses so that she could get a look at his eyes. But she'd rather die than to let him know that she was even the least bit curious about their color. "Okay," was her only response.

"Have you ever been up in anything other than a large commercial airliner?"

"No...and to tell you the truth, I haven't flown commercially all that much."

"Not a problem. Do you get air sick?"

"No...at least I never have." *Dear God, please, please don't let me get air sick in front of this man.*

"Are you nervous?"

She was tempted to sugar coat her answer but decided that now was not the time to lie. "A little."

Tyler sat completely still and continued to look at her.

"Okay, Lieutenant. Perhaps I'm more than just a little nervous."

"There's no need to be nervous, Ms. James. I've lost count of how many planes I've flown. This sweet little puppy is a piece of cake to fly, so why don't you just sit back and enjoy the ride."

She couldn't stop the next words that flew out of her mouth. "It's not actually the flying part I'm worried about. It's the takeoff and landing. I'm usually okay once we're up in the air. I know this will sound silly to you, but I've never quite gotten used to getting the plane off the ground and then setting it back down once we're up."

"Well, if it's any help, I've been trained to fly just about anything you can think of and I've even taken off and landed on aircraft carriers."

She knew he was trying to put her at ease, but until she was actually in the air, nothing was going to help.

"I know you're extremely well trained, Lieutenant, but trust me, even if Neal Armstrong were sitting at the controls right now, until we get through the takeoff, I'm going to be a nervous wreck."

"Well now, let's see if I can do something about that." Before she had a hint of what he was going to do, Tyler reached over and laid one hand over both of hers, which were clasped tightly together in her lap. One corner of his mouth kicked up into a half smile as he pried her fingers apart, one by one. "Now isn't that better?" he asked with a chuckle, and Samantha had to fight the urge not to yank her hands out of his. But then he started massaging her stiff and cramped fingers, and she felt the shock of his touch all the way to the tips of her toes. "My God, you really do need to relax. You're way, way too uptight about this little excursion."

Samantha could still hear some laughter in his voice. He was either teasing her or making fun of her, and she wasn't very happy with either one of those possibilities. So trying to regain her composure, she attempted to gently pull her hands away. But he just tightened his hold and kept on massaging.

"I wasn't kidding when I said this Piper Cherokee is a dream to pilot. I learned to fly in a plane just like this and I could fly this thing with my eyes closed."

"But you won't, right?" At the questioning lift of his brow she quickly added, "I mean, fly with your eyes closed. You'll keep both eyes wide open, right?"

This time his chuckle turned into all-out laughter. "Not even I'm that good of a pilot." As Tyler dropped her hands back into her lap, she immediately missed the warmth of his touch. It was crazy, especially since they didn't even like each other, but she'd liked the feel of his hand against hers. "Now, if you were going up with Flyboy he'd probably tell you he could get this baby in the air with or without his eyes open. And to tell you the truth, if he said he could fly blind I wouldn't bet against him."

Of course she asked the obvious question. "Who's Flyboy?"

"He's the best damn pilot in the United States Navy."

"Is he a member of your SEAL team?"

"Yeah, he is."

Tyler turned away, suddenly ready to get this show on the road. And even though she wanted to ask more questions about Flyboy and his team, he smoothly changed the subject.

"Okay, Ms. James, before we take her up, do you have any questions about any of the instruments on the cockpit control panel?" She noticed his swift change of mood. Now he seemed all business.

"Not really," she answered truthfully. "I'm not going to write all that much about any of the technical stuff. Unfortunately my editor wants this article to be more fluff than substance." Tyler looked slightly disappointed but didn't voice it. "Although, before we take off, I do have one small favor to ask." She sounded a little unsure and that immediately piqued his interest.

"Shoot."

"Even though you've made it perfectly clear that you'd rather be a hundred places other than out here flying me around, do you think we could call some sort of a truce and you could at least call me by my first name? Samantha or Sam will do just fine."

Ouch, he thought, *the lady sure knows how to play dirty.* Not wanting her to know that she'd hit a nerve, he pretended to take his time, thinking over her unexpected favor.

"I think I would rather call you Sam."

She was surprised but pleased by his response. "Then Sam it is."

"Yeah, well only if you stop calling me Lieutenant. Tyler or Ty will do just fine."

Finally, a breakthrough, she thought. "I think I would prefer to call you Tyler."

His only response was to send her a dazzling smile, right before he turned his attention back to the plane. And before she knew it, he had started it up and had managed to complete a perfect takeoff. At least she thought it was perfect because it was as smooth as silk.

"You can stop clutching so tightly onto the sides of your seat. The worst is over."

Samantha didn't even realize that she had a death grip on her seat, but it was no surprise that he hadn't missed it. She wondered if he learned his keen observation technique during his training as a SEAL. And instead of wondering, she decided to ask.

"How do you do that?"

"Do what?"

"You know."

"Trust me on this, Sam. I haven't a clue what you're taking about."

She liked how he called her Sam. "You seem to have this sixth sense about what I'm feeling, even when I'm not aware of it myself. And I was just wondering if you're training has anything to do with it."

"I guess my training has affected just about every aspect of my life," he answered matter-of-factly. "I've been in the navy for fifteen years, and ten of those years I've been a SEAL. We're definitely trained to watch, process, and record everything around us. Besides," he added with a grin, "you're pretty easy to read."

"I am not!" she protested even though she was pretty sure he was right on.

"Well let's just say that after knowing you less than an hour, I'd venture to guess that you'd never make it as an undercover cop, or a CIA agent, or a NARK, or a spy, or—"

"Okay, okay, Lieuten…I mean Tyler. You've made your point. A Bond girl I am not."

Tyler couldn't help it. With that comment, he couldn't stop himself from glancing over at her long, beautiful, bare legs—legs that seemed even that much longer because her skirt was hiked up so high. "Oh, I wouldn't go quite that far."

Earlier Samantha had wished that he would remove his sunglasses so that she could see his eyes, but now she was glad—really, really glad—that his eyes were covered.

"Shouldn't you keep your eyes focused straight ahead, or on the control panel, or at the very least on the gas gage?"

He laughed as he reluctantly drew his eyes away from her legs. She laughed along with him and as she leaned forward, focusing her own eyes on the expansive sky all around them, she drew in a deep, wondrous breath.

"Oh, my God, Tyler. This is absolutely beautiful. I had no idea it would be so incredibly beautiful." There was awe in her voice.

"Yeah, it's something, isn't it? You never get this perspective when you fly commercially. It takes sitting in the cockpit to truly appreciate the beauty of flying."

"How far are we going?"

"I thought we'd fly around for a while, just to give you a small taste of what it's like. Then we can go up again this evening if you want. If you think its beautiful now, wait till you see it at night."

"Is flying your favorite part of being a SEAL?"

He thought about her question before responding. "Not really. SEAL stands for sea, air, and land. We're trained to be experts in all three areas, and I guess it's all so much a part of the package, I don't favor one aspect of the job over another."

"I think I understand what you do on land and in the air, but what exactly does a SEAL do in the sea?"

"Lots of things." His answer wasn't meant to be flip, but it came out that way.

"I read somewhere that you guys are experts in underwater demolition. Is that what you do?" She was interested enough not to let the subject drop, even though he hadn't encouraged her to ask any more questions.

"Among other things."

"Here you go again, being as vague as possible. Is that part of your persona as a SEAL?" There was a hint of laughter in her voice.

"Yeah, well, like I said, I'm very well trained."

Samantha knew she would get nothing more out of him about his career as a Navy SEAL, so she gracefully let the subject drop—at least for now. And for the next few minutes a silence settled over them in the tiny plane.

The next hour seemed to fly by. Samantha had forgotten all about being nervous, and she was disappointed when he headed in for a landing. By the time he took the plane in she wasn't even clutching onto her seat. It didn't take a genius to figure out that he was a master behind the controls. He kept the plane nice and steady, pointing out all sorts of visible landmarks on the ground. He even took the time to explain some of the more complicated controls and some of the special terms associated with flight training. All and all, given how they had started out with each other, the trip had been better than she would have expected.

Tyler helped her out of the plane, having a hell of a time keeping his eyes off her legs. She had the most glorious legs, and a small part of him was pissed that she'd refused to change out of her short skirt. When he'd suggested she change clothes his reasoning had been twofold. He was a firm believer in always being prepared for the worst, and if for any reason at all he'd been forced into an emergency landing, climbing around in a short, tight skirt was anything but practical. His second reason was more of a personal nature. He didn't want to be attracted to this woman on any level. He wanted to keep his mind focused on what she did for a living, not on her long, inviting legs. And he'd figured right off the bat that he'd have a better chance of that if she would change into a pair of pants. But she hadn't and he'd had trouble keeping his eyes off of her for the entire hour, which now made him mad. And in typical Tyler Garrett fashion, he took his anger out on her.

"We'll pick up again later this evening. I need to go into town for a few hours, so do you think you can manage to keep yourself entertained while I'm gone?"

Samantha was completely blown away by his sudden change of mood and his curt tone of voice. Gone was the guy who went out of his way to make her relax in the plane. Gone was the pilot who also served as a rather charming tour guide. And back in place was Mr. Unfriendly. Completely out of nowhere, she was dealing again with someone who didn't want her around. But before she'd let him hightail it out of her sight, she wanted to get a few pictures of her hotshot Navy SEAL.

"Before you run off, do you think I can take a couple of pictures of you beside the plane?"

Tyler had already started walking away. He stopped at the sound of her voice but didn't turn completely around. He just looked at her over his shoulder.

"I need pictures to go along with the article."

"Take pictures of something else. I don't want my picture taken."

"But how can I write about you if I don't show my readers who you are?"

"No pictures of me, Samantha." He obviously expected no further argument from her, but her own stubbornness kicked in and she refused to let the subject drop, especially since he was being totally unreasonable.

"Oh come on, Tyler. One or two pictures won't hurt you."

This time he turned around to face her but didn't come any closer. He just reached up and slowly removed his sunglasses, piercing her with his gaze. And Samantha had to catch her breath. His eyes were a shade of gray that she couldn't quite describe—that is until they drilled even more fiercely into her. And then she had no trouble thinking of them as steel gray, hard and cold like steel.

"What is it exactly that you don't understand about me saying I don't want you to take my picture, Samantha?" His voice was as cold as his eyes and Samantha couldn't figure out why. What could she have possibly done in the last five minutes to put him in such a foul mood? They had gotten along quite well in the plane, but now his voice was bordering on nasty. And she was getting really tired of his unexpected and unexplained mood changes, especially since they were directed at her. Because she hated not to have the answers she wanted, she risked trying to find out.

"What in the hell is wrong with you anyway?" *Maybe that wasn't the best approach,* she thought as he narrowed his gaze. "If the fact that you're a SEAL is some deep dark secret, then all you have to do is say so, and I'll respect your privacy. But please don't talk to me like I'm some idiot that isn't capable of understanding that."

Tyler took one small step forward and then stopped himself. "It's been my experience that journalists are incapable of respecting anyone's privacy. All they're ever interested in is getting their story. And I don't have to explain anything to you other than the fact that I don't want to have my picture taken." With that he all but slammed his sunglasses back onto his face. "I'll be back later. If you want to go up again, fine. If you don't that's fine with me too. But," he added as he turned to walk away, "if we go up again tonight, you had better change out of that skirt and put on a damn pair of pants."

Before she could say another word, he was walking away. His stride conveyed his anger and his shoulders were stiff as a board. And Samantha was almost beside herself. She couldn't believe what had just happened. He was the most complicated, perplexing man she'd ever meant. How he could switch his moods so quickly was beyond her. And his insane comment about her skirt was even more puzzling. But as she stood alone on the runway, staring after his retreating back, she felt anger bubble up inside of her. *How dare he?* she thought as she stomped back to the house. *How dare he treat me this way?* "Well you will not get away with this, Lieutenant Tyler Zachary Garrett," she muttered to herself, "because the next time I lay eyes on you, you are going to get a piece of my mind."

But as Tyler kept walking, he couldn't have cared less what Samantha was going through. All he could think about was that day, two years ago, when he had lost not only a member of SEAL Team Mega One, but his best friend. And all because of a stubborn, irresponsible, selfish, pushy, son-of-a-bitch journalist.

Two Years Earlier

"Listen, Lieutenant Garrett, I don't want this guy here any more than you do. But our hands are tied."

"Well tie someone else's hands, Commander. This guy's been a pain in the ass since the day he got here, and I don't want to take him along on this mission. Afghanistan is no place for a rookie journalist. Christ, even the veteran journalists don't belong here half the time."

Commander Steven Wickline couldn't have agreed with his lieutenant more. But he had been given his own orders, which he now had to pass on to the new leader of SEAL Team Mega One.

"Sit down and listen to me for a minute, Tyler." The commander sounded as weary as he felt. "You know as well as I do who David Cushman's father is. As a United States Senator, he pulled enough strings in just the right places and now we need to make arrangements for his little boy to tag along on a mission. And because of the nature of your next op, I think it would be safer all around if he goes along with you and your men."

Tyler pulled out a chair and sat down. He was having a great deal of difficulty keeping his temper under control.

"No operation is foolproof, Commander, not even the one tonight."

"Come on, Tyler, for you and the members of your team, this one's about as foolproof as it gets."

Tyler knew that what the commander was saying was true. Tonight's mission was an extraction that would take place under fairly safe conditions. A few local healthcare professionals had been nabbed on their way into a hospital and were now being held for ransom. The Afghan government had asked for help in rescuing two doctors and two nurses, and the military had offered up Tyler's team of SEALs. The operation was simple. There were only a handful of ill-equipped, inexperienced kidnappers who were watching the place where the doctors and nurses were being held and the SEALs didn't expect much resistance. Team Mega One would get in, get out, and hand-deliver the healthcare professional back on the steps of their hospital within hours. The only hitch Tyler could think of was that they were being forced to take along a young, spoiled, raw journalist, who hadn't a clue what he was in for. Tyler tried another approach.

"Tell me something, Commander. I'd think the Afghan government would want to keep this thing under wraps. Why let a journalist tag along at all?"

"Yeah well, who would guess that our own government sees this as a golden opportunity to show off a bit. They think it's a good idea to let the kid film the extraction. It'll show you guys in action, putting yourselves at risk to rescue a few innocent Afghans. The politicians in high places think this will be great press. And the kid is screaming for some action. So I guess we kill two birds with one stone. And I need you and your team to make this work."

"I don't mind going in to get the doctors and nurses out, but I was not trained to be a babysitter. Nor were my men."

Commander Wickline couldn't suppress his grin. "But you'll do it for me anyway, won't you, Lieutenant?"

Tyler and the commander went way back. Commander Wickline had been the leader of Team Mega One until six months ago, and he had recommended Tyler to take over his role when he was promoted to commander and took on a wider range of responsibility. Tyler had no doubt that his mentor knew that he would get what he asked, and Tyler also knew when to toss in his hand. "Sure, Commander, we'll take the kid on the op. And if we're lucky," he added as he stood up, "maybe we can scare the shit out of the little bastard and he'll run back home to Daddy."

Commander Wickline stood up and extended his hand. "You won't be flown in on this one, Lieutenant. You'll be going by mobile transport. There will be back-up going along if you guys need it, but I doubt you will. Our sources tell us that the guys holding the hostages are pure amateurs. So God speed and good luck."

Tyler shook the commander's hand and left the operations center in search of his best friend, Second Lieutenant Kent Richards. He wanted to find Kent himself and deliver the bad news that they were now officially acting as a team of babysitters.

And as it turned out, as missions went, this one went off just as expected—at least up until the next morning, when Team Mega One arrived back at camp. Traveling in the last jeep in the mobile transport was Tyler, Kent, the kid journalist, and the driver. They had just escorted the hostages back to their hospital and were now heading back into camp.

Not to anyone's surprise, the kid David had been driving Tyler and Kent crazy all night. He had kept whining about the mud the SEALs had purposely smothered all over his face, telling him that he needed to darken his skin in order to be fully protected. They hadn't bothered to explain why they had used greasepaint instead of mud and the kid hadn't even thought to ask. He had just kept complaining. The SEALs had also put the fear of God into the young man. They had all shown up at 0200 hours, dressed in black with their faces darkened, black caps on their heads, and weapons strapped over their shoulders. Just looking at them dressed in black from head to toe and armed to the teeth, made the mission seem much more dangerous than it really was. But not one SEAL bothered to tell the kid that. They wanted him sweating bullets and were hoping to scare him just enough to get him out of their hair. And it had worked right up until the last jeep had pulled into camp. And that is when the nightmare really began.

The driver, Tyler, Kent, and David jumped out of the jeep. The driver took off in one direction and Tyler and Kent were headed in another when the kid's voice rang out.

"Hey guys, how about a picture of the two of you by the jeep?"

Tyler scowled, Kent grinned, and the kid grabbed onto his camera, which was hanging around his neck. "Just a couple of pictures for my article."

"No pictures of me," Tyler responded.

"Then how about you, Lieutenant Richards?"

"Me neither, kid. No pictures."

And that is when the whining started all over again. "Oh come on. I need a couple more pictures. It won't take but a second. I know now that you guys purposely tried to scare me out there last night and the least you can do is let me take a couple of pictures."

Tyler had no intention of giving in to the kid, whining or not, but Kent was a little more softhearted.

"Okay, two pictures by the jeep. But just two, understand?"

Tyler stood back and shook his head from side to side, a little disgusted that they were still catering to this kid. He was sick and tired of having the kid hang around just because his father was some damn senator. He'd done what he'd been asked and had taken the brat on the mission. But no more, he decided, and in about thirty seconds he planned to find the commander and tell him so.

Kent sauntered over to the jeep. "Where do you want me?"

"I just need one close-up and one with you and the jeep in the background." With that David snapped the close-up. Then he took several steps back. He looked through his viewfinder, wasn't satisfied, and stood back even farther. He was trying to decide the best angle to take the picture when all of a sudden a loud blast filled the air. And Tyler stood and watched in total disbelief and horror as his best friend was blown to pieces.

The force of the blast threw the kid to the dirt, but Tyler stumbled only once before he took off at a dead run.

The jeep was engulfed in flames and there was little to nothing left of Kent. Tyler was screaming obscenities at the top of his lungs, not even aware of the other soldiers that came out of nowhere. Tyler watched as the flames were extinguished, looking around frantically at the body parts of his best friend. Then with little or no thought of the consequences, Tyler turned toward David, who was still lying in the dirt, and all of his pent-up anger came rushing out at the kid. He headed toward him, ready to kill.

The only thing that saved David Cushman was the three SEALs that pulled Tyler off of him. If Tyler could have reached his weapon, which had dropped to the ground with the force of the blast, he might have actually blown the kid straight to hell. But as it was, the kid was rushed away from the scene and was sent home a day later in a flurry of excitement. The incident had been hushed up, and what was left of the body of Second Lieutenant Kent Richards was sent back to Washington to be buried. And in the days and weeks that followed, Tyler and the members of Team Mega One were left behind in Afghanistan to mourn the loss of their colleague and friend.

Present Day

As Tyler kept walking toward his car, he had to swallow back the bile that rose in his throat. Samantha's words had brought back all of the painful memories. Everything played back in his mind as if it were yesterday. He could see the military jeep, Kent smiling at the kid journalist, and then the blast that took his best friend's life. And his hatred for all journalists surfaced as strongly as if the accident had just happened.

Tyler was reasonable enough to know that his aversion to the all reporters and journalists wasn't fair, but he couldn't help it. Even though it had been determined that a member of a terrorist's cell had thrown the deadly grenade, he believed deep in his heart that Kent would still be alive today if it hadn't been for that spoiled brat kid insisting on taking a picture for his fucking article. And when Samantha had suggested she take his picture by the plane, something in him had snapped. And he needed to get as far away from her as possible.

Sure, she might be drop-dead gorgeous, and she might be smarter and nicer than he'd wanted to give her credit for, but she was still a journalist. And he considered that career choice to be the lowest of the low. And because of what she chose to do for a living, he was choosing to keep his distance. He would keep his promise to his sister, but nothing more. He would fly her cute little ass around, talk to her only when necessary, and never, ever forget that she was the enemy—an enemy with long legs, red hair that tempted a man to reach out and touch, and eyes that drew a man deep into their depths.

Boy, I'm in deep shit trouble, were his thoughts as he started up his car and headed into town, glancing up twice to see if he could catch sight of Samantha in the rearview mirror.

Chapter Three

Tyler didn't return home until almost seven o'clock. Once he headed into town, he'd decided to make the best of it. He went first into the town's only coffee shop and treated himself to a real down-home Texas barbeque lunch. It hadn't taken long for word to get around that he was home on leave, and within the hour the place had filled up with old friends and acquaintances. One hour easily stretched into two and before he knew it, it was already close to three o'clock. Not wanting to go home quite yet and face his house guest, Tyler decided to take a leisurely walk around town. And that's when he bumped into sweet Mary Lou Johnson.

Mary Lou and Tyler had what some would consider a history of sorts. They had been a hot-and-heavy couple during his senior year of high school, but the romance had faded almost the instant he left for college. Mary Lou was a year younger than Tyler and there was no way she was going to go through her senior year without a boyfriend on her arm. She liked having a boyfriend. She liked having a date for all the school dances, and she liked having sex, all of which she couldn't have if she and Tyler stayed together as a couple while he was away at school.

But Tyler, being Tyler, was smart enough to know that he liked those things as well, especially the part about having sex. And he figured his chances of having regular and frequent sex would highly improve if he went to college as an unattached male. So he and Mary Lou had a very amicable parting of ways.

During the past fifteen years, Tyler made it home on leave less and less, whereas in the early days of his navy career, he headed home to Texas whenever he could. And that meant that when he was home on leave he would usually hook up with Mary Lou. Somehow they would both find themselves between relationships when he ventured home, and they always just drifted together. They would spend all of their time between the sheets, discovering early on that they had very little else in common. But that was okay because it worked just fine for the both of them.

But as the years went by, and as Tyler visited less and less, his encounters with Mary Lou also became less frequent. When he would visit now, most times he never even bothered to look her up. Yet today, as luck would have it, he ran smack dab into her just as he was leaving the coffee shop.

"Well, I'll be damned. If it isn't Tyler Zachary Garrett, come home at long last."

Tyler couldn't help the grin that spread across his face as he stared at the woman standing before him. She was tall, blond, sassy and had a look in her eyes that told him she liked what she saw. And truth be told, so did he.

"Mary Lou Johnson," he drawled. "My God, woman, you are a sight for these sore eyes. You haven't changed one bit since the last time I saw you."

Her laugh was bold, loud, and husky. "And you're still the best bullshiter in all of Texas, Lieutenant Garrett."

Tyler leaned down and placed a kiss squarely on her mouth. "I was just thinking about giving you a call."

"Sure you were, sugar." She faked a pout and failed at it miserably. "But since I heard via the grapevine that y'all were in town, I thought I'd save you the price of a phone call and stop by to see for myself."

"So now that you've found me, what did you have in mind?" The instant the words were out of his mouth he wanted to take them back. He liked Mary Lou. He liked her a lot. They were old friends and sometime lovers. The old friends he had no problem with right now, but he really wasn't in the mood or the frame of mind to become her sometime lover. And a flood of relief washed over him at her easy response.

"How about you buy me a drink and we can catch up? I've been awful curious about what you've been up to these last…what has it been darlin'…four years since we've seen each other?"

"I'm flying later today so I can't drink, but I'll be happy to buy you one." That seemed good enough for Mary Lou.

"Then why don't we head on over to Bucky's Bar and I'll tell you all about my divorce?"

Uh oh, Tyler thought, but Mary Lou slipped her arm through his and he decided, *What the hell?* So off they went. As it turned out, Tyler had a great time. He drank sweetened iced tea and Mary Lou drank Coors beer, one after the other. And she was on quite a roll. Her stories about her divorce turned into stories about her marriage, which turned into stories about her love life, past and present. She was extremely entertaining and before either of them realized it, hours had flown by.

"I'm real sorry, Mary Lou, but I've gotta go."

She took one last swallow of her drink. "How about stopping by the house for a while, sugar? You know...for old time's sake?"

Tyler was surprised that he wasn't even tempted. "I really can't. I've got a customer waiting back at the house, and I'm already late as it is."

"Well now that surely is a pity," she said on a sigh, "cause I was just thinking that you look good enough to take home, and sexy enough to take a big bite out of."

Tyler figured he'd better get going while he still could. So he ignored her comment, scooted his chair back, and reached out a hand to help her up. "And you've probably had a little too much to drink. Come on, Mary Lou, I'll drive you home."

"No thanks, sugar. I think I'll stay around and have another." She lifted her empty beer bottle toward the bartender, signaling him for another. "Don't worry about me, Tyler. I'll have no trouble finding a ride home."

Tyler had no doubt about that. Already out of the corner of his eye he could see a couple of guys eyeing Mary Lou, just waiting for him to leave. "Well, it was sure good to see you, Mary Lou." He leaned down and kissed her lightly on her cheek.

"Keep in touch, sugar," was her breathy response. "And if you get lonely while you're home, you know where to find me." She breathed into his mouth as she turned her head and captured his lips with hers.

Tyler made his way out the door, tying to figure out why he wasn't the least bit interested in Mary Lou's offer. She still looked damned good, was unattached, and she was offering him sex with no strings attached. And he wondered if perhaps it was because he was tired, or maybe it was because he was getting a little too old for one-night stands. Because of his lifestyle as a SEAL, Tyler never saw himself settling down with one woman and having a family. Sure, some guys did. Even some of his teammates managed to have a navy career, a wife, and kids. But even so, he never got around to seeing himself in the role of husband and father. Being a SEAL was his life, and at thirty-six he figured he had probably three, maybe four more years as an active SEAL. After that he'd see what the navy had to offer. And if he stayed in the navy, which he thought he would, then maybe he'd think about settling down, but then again, maybe not. Totally out of character for Tyler, these were the thoughts that kept his mind occupied all the way back home.

As he pulled his rental car up to the front of the house, Tyler saw Samantha sitting on the top step of the porch, just as he'd done earlier that morning. She had changed into a pair of jeans, and a nice little pink tank top. Her hair was pulled back into a braid and she wore tiny gold earrings. She looked cool, calm, and sexier than hell. And he was surprised when Mary Lou's words came to his mind. Only this time the words were directed at Samantha, who he thought *looked good enough to take a big bite out of.*

Tyler dismissed that thought almost as quickly as it came. He refused to let himself think of her as sexy. He needed to keep his distance and he had already figured that the best way to do that was to keep her good and mad. As long as she was mad at him he could forget that she was a beautiful and desirable woman. As long as she stayed mad at him he could more easily keep away from her. Anger was going to be his best and perhaps only defense against thinking about what she might taste like. And in the next instant, he knew just how to go about getting her good and mad. But first he would need to keep her off balance, at least until he could put his plan into action—a plan that would ensure that she would get good and pissed off at him. Thinking about his hastily hatched plan, Tyler's mouth turned up into a grin just as he stepped out of the car.

Samantha became suspicious the second he slid out of the car with a devilish and all-too-cocky grin on his handsome face. She'd been sitting out on the front porch, dreading his return and his sourpuss mood. But the look in his eyes and the smile he was directing at her were anything but sourpuss—far from it. So of course, all her senses went on high alert. So she refused to give in and smile back. And besides, she was still ticked at him for his nasty mood earlier, and no matter how beguiling his smile, she wasn't ready to forgive him.

"Hey darlin', why don't we grab a quick sandwich and then I'll take you up for a look at the stars from the cockpit of a plane." He sailed right past her, grabbing gently onto her arm, and pulled her to her feet. And she had no choice but to follow in his wake. "There's still some roast beef left over and some nice, thick sourdough bread. It's too damn hot to cook, so let's make due with a cold supper."

He didn't ask her permission. He just kept pulling her with him right through the house and into the kitchen. "Pull out a chair and make yourself at home while I make our sandwiches. Do you like hot-and-spicy mustard?"

Samantha hadn't bothered to sit. Instead she stood, almost rooted to the spot, and tried her best to figure out what was going on. Because of the way he had left earlier, she had been prepared for him to return from town ready for a fight—a fight she'd been bracing herself for all afternoon. A fight that was obviously not in the cards. And she wondered why. "Okay, enough of this. Why are you being so nice?"

Tyler didn't as much as blink an eye. "Who, me? Now why in the world would you ask me such a question?"

Samantha just planted both hands on her hips and arched one eyebrow in an unspoken question.

"Would you believe that I'm just naturally a nice guy?" His eyes were actually laughing at her.

"No," was her one-word reply.

"Okay." His pause was purposeful. "Would you believe that I like your company?"

"Try again, Lieutenant." In reaction to his teasing tone, she smiled in spite of herself.

"Well, then, how about the truth. I happen to be hungry and I don't particularly like to eat alone." He turned away and started pulling stuff out of the fridge. "So either sit down or come on over here and give me a hand." Tyler plopped a piece of roast beef into his mouth and waited to see what she was going to do.

He looked so cute and so innocent that her suspicion level kicked up a notch. "Okay, I'll help. But don't think for a minute that you're off the hook for your earlier behavior." She walked over and joined him by the counter. "I'm only helping because I'm hungry too."

"You mad at me, Sam?" Even as he asked the question he knew what the answer was going to be, and he couldn't stop from thinking, *If you're mad at me now, just wait until later.*

"Of course I'm mad at you." She grabbed a knife out of the drawer and began spreading the hot-and-spicy mustard onto the bread. "You yelled at me for no reason at all, and then you went into town and left me here all alone for the entire afternoon."

"Does that mean you missed me?" He was making light of the situation and she didn't like it.

"In your dreams, Lieutenant Garrett."

Tyler just laughed as he piled their sandwiches high with all the fixings. "You want milk, tea, or beer?" he asked.

Samantha made a decision she hoped she wouldn't regret. She decided to bury the hatchet and be nice. "I think I'll have a beer."

He reached in the fridge and grabbed one bottle of beer and the carton of milk. And then he reached up and took a glass down from the cabinet. That is when Samantha noticed how his muscles stretched across his broad back and how good his shirt looked tucked into the waistband of his jeans. *God, this man is really a hunk.* But because he could also be one of the biggest jerks she'd ever met, she tried to ignore his strong, hard, sexy body.

"Grab the sandwiches, will you please?"

Samantha nearly stumbled when the word *please* came out of his mouth. But instead of commenting on it, she picked up the plates, walked over to the kitchen table, and sat down. Tyler pulled out a chair and sat down next to her.

"So what'd you do this afternoon?" he asked between bites, and she was surprised that he even cared enough to ask.

"I started working on my article. I wanted to jot down my first impressions of flying in the Piper while everything was still fresh in my mind."

"So what's the point of this article anyway?"

"Excuse me?" She wasn't sure she understood his question.

"Well, you said earlier that your editor wanted more fluff than substance. So I was just wondering what you're tying to accomplish and who's your target audience? You do have a target audience, don't you?" he asked when she didn't answer his first question.

"This may not be what you want to hear, but my article is pretty much filler. The magazine I'm writing for wanted something light and easy to read, and since the editor is fascinated with planes he hired me to do this article. And, of course, since I have a connection with Katie, it seemed like a good fit."

Tyler didn't respond for a while. He kept eating, his eyes watching the woman sitting beside him. He noticed that she almost looked embarrassed over this assignment, and he wondered why—not that he really cared one way or the other. But because of the silence that settled around them in the kitchen, he decided to ask.

"So how do you feel about that? Do you always write fluff? Or do you ever get around to writing any serious stuff?"

Samantha lifted her eyes to his and he could see an immediate change in her. Gone was any hint of embarrassment. She now had a stubborn, almost defiant look in her eyes. "Not that I need to explain myself to you, Tyler, but make no mistake about this. I plan to be a serious foreign correspondent and this current assignment is nothing more than a way for me to get there. The editor I'm working for now, Mr. Goldstein, is putting together a team of journalists who will go into remote, dangerous, and underprivileged areas to report on things that can and will make a difference. And I plan to be a member of that team. If I have to write hundreds of meaningless articles to get on this team, then I will write hundreds of meaningless articles. I want to be a part of something that really matters, and I would think that you, of all people, would understand that."

It was obvious that he'd hit a nerve. But because she had no idea how her speech had hit a nerve with him, he decided to tell her. "Like it or not, Samantha, I'm yet to be convinced that a journalist, any journalist, belongs in a remote and dangerous area. I'm trained for that type of environment, and you're not. Your desire to do something important and meaningful is admirable, but misguided. Work with the Red Cross or the Salvation Army if you want to do something worthwhile. But my advice to you is to stay away from a situation where you are out of your element. That can only get you and your fellow journalists in trouble."

He wasn't trying to be mean, just opinionated, and she felt her spine stiffen. "Well you can just keep your opinion to yourself, Tyler Garrett. If people like Peter Jennings and Tom Brokow listened to you, where would the world be today? We need good, solid, and honest reporting. We need people to take a risk and get to the heart of issues that can change lives. We need eyes and ears that will open the hearts and minds of every nation in this world. I'm sorry, Tyler, but I think you are dead wrong, and I plan to do everything in my power to prove it."

"Well," he said as he stood up and wiped his hands down the front of his jeans, "just think about this. While you're out there trying to prove your point, me and my men are the ones who are called in to save your ass when you get in trouble. Granted," he added when she started to open her mouth to speak, "you have one very cute ass, but not cute enough to risk the safety of my team."

Samantha stood so that she could look him straight in the eye. Sitting and being forced to look up at him put her at a distinct disadvantage. "I can see that you're way too pigheaded to even consider my point of view. And truthfully, I have no intention of seeing things your way either. So for the sake of argument, and so that we can make some sort of an effort to get along, can we at least agree to disagree?"

Something inside of Tyler appreciated the fact that she didn't back down from what she believed in. He might not agree with her, but it was clear that she felt passionate about her position. And even if he didn't like her point of view, he could respect her for sticking to her guns—not that he would ever tell her so.

"Why do I have this feeling that agreeing to disagree is going to be SOP with you and me, Sam?"

Samantha didn't even try to hide her smile. "Surely we can find something to agree on, Tyler? I bet we could if we tried really, really hard."

An unwanted thought passed through Tyler's mind. He felt certain that if he grabbed her and kissed her right now they would both agree on two things: one, that a kiss between them would be a really bad idea, and two, that a kiss between them would be really hot and would probably rock them both to the very tips of their toes. But Tyler never voiced his thoughts, because he had no intention of kissing Ms. Samantha James. Sure, she looked good enough to kiss the daylights out of, but that was never going to happen. He might be attracted to her, but he had enough control over his body and his mind not to act on that attraction—at least he hoped so.

"I think we can both agree that we need to get going. It's getting late and if you want to take a quick spin, we'd better get a move on."

"Quick and spin isn't exactly what I had in mind." She was trying to make a joke. "At least not when I'm in a plane."

Tyler had to look the other way. He knew what he was planning once he got her in the air, and he felt just a twinge of guilt. But damn it, he needed to get her good and mad at him so he could keep his distance. And that meant that he had to get her in the plane so that he could execute his plan.

"Come on, Sam. Let's go." He left her very little choice but to follow.

"Just give me one second and let me grab my camera. If I can't take pictures of you, maybe I can get some pictures of the stars." And before he could stop her she was off and running. "I'll meet you at the plane in five minutes."

She ran up the stairs and Tyler headed out of the house, turning off lights on his way. As soon as he got outside he took a big gulp of fresh air and felt instantly better. The air helped to clear his head. It also helped get rid of the intoxicating scent that seemed to surround Samantha. Whatever perfume she wore was driving him a little nuts, and he wasn't looking forward to being cooped up with her in the small confines of the plane. Shaking his head, he jammed both hands in his front pockets and stormed off toward the waiting aircraft. He was not going to let this woman get to him, and it made him mad that he was even thinking about how sweet she smelled. And he decided to put a stop to it here and now.

Tyler would have been shocked if he knew the real reason why Samantha had run off in search of her camera. Sure, she wanted to take some pictures of the stars, but what she really wanted was a chance to put on some fresh lipstick and make sure that the rest of her makeup didn't need a fast touchup. For some crazy and unexplainable reason, she wanted to look her best in front of Tyler. And that bothered her. But what really bothered her was how attracted she was to this impossible, strong-willed, arrogant, and devastatingly handsome man. *Not that anything would ever come of the attraction,* she reminded herself as she applied a light pink lip-gloss. He might be gorgeous but it was obvious that he didn't like her one bit, and she wasn't even all that sure if she liked him.

Being sexually aware of him and liking him were two different things. Besides, she wasn't into casual flings and on Saturday she would be on her way back home, never to see Lieutenant Tyler Garrett again. And that alone was reason enough to stay away from him. She would look, maybe even flirt a little, but not touch, she decided as she realized her five minutes were almost up. And with that thought firmly in her mind, she flew down the stairs, out the door, and headed toward the plane.

Like before, Tyler executed a flawless takeoff. He took it nice and easy, and Samantha was completely relaxed. The night that was spread out before them was so spectacular that she found herself actually holding her breath. They had spoken very little to each other, both of them absorbed in the beauty around them. Samantha had taken a couple of pictures, but she knew that the photographs would never do justice to the scene before her. And she just hoped that she could find a way to put into words what she was feeling.

"I guess we'd better head back." Tyler's words broke into her thoughts.

"I hate to go in, Tyler, but I guess it's getting late."

During the short flight, the inside of the cockpit had taken on a cozy and inviting glow. Sitting there trying to concentrate on flying, Tyler cursed under his breath as the enticing scent of Samantha kept on clouding his brain, which in turn caused him to question his determination to stay away from her. So he decided that if he was going to get her mad enough to keep her at a safe distance, he had to put his plan into action. And knowing it would be now or never, without a word of warning, he tilted the plane into a sweeping turn and Samantha felt her stomach take a dive.

Samantha had to close her eyes in order to help shake off the wave of dreaded nausea. When she felt calm enough to open them, she noticed that they were closer to home than she thought, because she could see the landing strip in the distance. She took a deep breath to steady her stomach when once again, without warning, Tyler started having a little fun.

"Did you know that a pilot can signal to another plane by tilting the wings just enough to cause a slight rolling from side to side?" And without waiting for her reply, he proceeded to demonstrate. And as the plane rolled from side to side, so did her stomach.

"Did you also know that with just the slightest movement of the elevator, I can pitch the nose of the plane up or down?" Before she had time to recover from wagging back and forth, he took the plane into an abrupt nosedive, right before bringing it back to level flight. And Samantha just about lost it. She had to swallow back the bile that rose in her throat, but when she looked over at her hotshot pilot, the bile in her throat turned to a knot of anger because he was doing this to her on purpose, and it was clear to her that he was enjoying every minute of her distress.

"Now if you're up to it, I can probably manage a barrel roll or some other fancy spins. What do you say?"

Samantha still couldn't find her voice, because she was afraid that if she tried to talk she might actually throw up. And she would rather jump out of the plane without a parachute than show her weakness and throw up in front of Tyler. But because she couldn't voice her objection, he took advantage of her silence and took the plane into another nosedive. Up again, down again, up again, down again, and up again, until she finally had to frantically grab onto the barf bag dangling from one of the controls.

As Samantha threw up into the plastic bag, Tyler steadied the plane and started his decent toward the runway. He was laughing and she was seething. And if she weren't so busy losing her supper, she would have given him hell.

Samantha practically jumped out of the plane the second it landed. She fled out of the cockpit and hit the dirt running. She wanted to get as far away from Tyler as possible. Still holding the barf bag in her hand, she heard his deep laughter ring out into the night and something made her stop in her tracks. With green eyes blazing, she turned slowly around to face him.

Tyler was bent over. He had both hands on his knees and was not even trying to hold back his laughter. He lifted his face just as she swung around to face him, and the daggers in her eyes should have wiped the smile right off his face. But they didn't. And instead he stood to his full height, still chuckling.

"Now listen to me for a minute, Sam." He tried to sound serious, but his smartass smile gave him away. And she finally lost her control. And since he had been impossible to deal with on and off for most of the day, she really let him have it.

"Don't you dare ask me to listen to you for even one second, Tyler Garrett! What you did to me up in that plane was unforgivable. Absolutely unforgivable!" He tried to interrupt but she kept on talking right over him.

"You not only scared the living daylights out of me up there, but you made me throw up!"

Tyler watched as she took one step closer to him and he thought she looked like she was ready to throw the barf bag right in his face. So he had to think fast. "Oh come on, Sam. Don't make such a big deal out of this."

What little control she had on her temper was now long gone. "You are out of your mind, do you realize that? What you did to me was a very big deal. What gives you the right to scare me the way you did? You may be some hotshot Navy SEAL, but right now you are nothing more than an irresponsible, dangerous, arrogant, inconsiderate, asshole pilot!" *There,* she thought to herself, *that should knock him down a peg or two.* But she should have known better, because her words barely seemed to faze him.

"Calling me dangerous, arrogant, inconsiderate, and even an asshole I can live with, Samantha, but irresponsible, never."

The fact that he wasn't taking this conversation seriously made her take another step toward him. "You had no right to scare me the way you did." This time she had lowered her voice but her words were spoken through clenched teeth.

"Oh, come on and admit it, Sam. You might have been a little air sick, but you were never really scared." Again he had the uncanny ability to read her like a book. "And anyway," he continued when she offered no response, "just think of this experience as a right of passage. And because of this, the next time you hit any turbulence, it'll seem like a piece of cake."

"Do you honestly think you can justify what you did to me up there?" Her words were full of astonishment.

"Sure. You might even consider that I did you a favor. Just think about how great this whole thing will play out in your article. Now, when we go up tomorrow in the chopper you'll—"

She couldn't stand to hear any more. "You can just go to hell!" And with those words, she spun on her heels and stomped back toward the house, depositing her barf bag in a trashcan along the way.

"It's no wonder you and Katie get along so well," he said as he kept up behind her. "You're both a bit of a drama queen."

Samantha just kept on walking. She refused to dignify his remark with a comment.

"Although, Katie's a whole lot tougher. She's a firm believer in the phrase 'Don't get mad, get even,' but I can see that you'd prefer to get mad and do nothing about it but walk away."

Now he was baiting her and she faltered as she started to walk up the porch steps. She thought for one brief instant that she would get a great deal of satisfaction out of turning around, slapping him hard across the face, and then walking away. But she had never struck anyone in her life and she wasn't about to start now, although the desire to feel her palm across his cheek was making her hand itch. Instead of giving in to this uncharacteristic temptation, she kept on walking. And he kept on talking.

"Are you going to pout all night?" She walked into the house, with him following closely behind.

"Leave me alone, Tyler." *Damn,* she thought, *I wasn't going to talk to him.*

"Not a chance," he responded as she started climbing the stairs, with him right on her heels. "So, what time do you want to go up in the morning?"

That comment finally got her attention, and she spun around so fast that she nearly knocked him down the stairs. "I have absolutely no intention of getting in a plane with you again. I'm not the crazy one here."

Tyler was standing one step down from Samantha and that brought them face to face. "No problem," was his unexpected, soft reply. "Because I thought we'd take the chopper up tomorrow. That'll give you a whole new perspective to write about."

She couldn't believe it. She couldn't believe that he actually thought she'd go anywhere with him again. And for a moment she was at a total loss for words, which ended up being a very bad thing—bad because they were standing so close to one another and all the lights in the house had been turned off—all except for a light at the end of the hall upstairs, and that light cast a dim, almost romantic glow around them.

Samantha and Tyler stood in silent combat. They were both watching each other, not sure who was going to be the first one to speak. In a matter of seconds the mood had shifted dramatically and Samantha suddenly became aware of how quickly her anger had dissipated. Standing this close to Tyler, looking into his intense gray eyes, she felt as if she were being drawn into a whirlpool. But somewhere in the far recess of her mind came a warning that she might actually drown in this whirlpool, if she didn't pull away. And the aching in her hand to slap his face turned into an ache of a different kind—an ache to reach out and touch. And that alone scared her even more than what she had just been put through up in the air. So running her tongue over her suddenly dry lips, she took a backward step up one more stair.

"I won't fly with you again. You're too reckless for me, Tyler. And I'm too scared to give you another chance."

Tyler wasn't buying it. She could tell just by looking at him. She could also tell that he had felt the same pull toward her that she had felt toward him. But he was so much better at hiding what was going on in his mind. At least that's what she thought right up until he finally spoke.

"Tell me something, Samantha. What are you really scared of? If you're so scared of a few bumps and turns in the air, then you'd never have agreed to write this article in the first place. So what is it really? Are you scared to go up with me as a pilot, or is there another reason you don't want to be alone with me tomorrow?"

His question was loaded and they both knew it. The sexual sparks were there, no doubt about it. As a matter of fact, the sexual sparks had been there on and off most of the day. And leave it to Tyler to bring it up—even in the most subtle way.

But Samantha wasn't stupid, and since she suspected that he already had an advantage over her, she wasn't about to hand him another one. So she refused to give him the answer that he expected.

"I'm only afraid of one thing, Tyler. And that's a pilot who's foolish enough to take unnecessary chances. Your stunts in the plane tonight were not only foolish but totally irresponsible. It amazes me that the navy allows you to fly. I'd hate to be a member of your SEAL team with you behind the controls."

Now they were back on solid ground: pissing each other off. And Tyler responded accordingly.

"Let me tell you what I think is foolish and irresponsible, Samantha. What is really foolish is a fluff journalist who actually thinks she can go off on some adventure, write about it, and manage to save the world in the process. And not only is that foolish thinking, but irresponsible as well. How in the hell do you expect to go off on an assignment out of the country if you're too damn afraid to even go up with me again? Because believe me, sweetheart, you'll encounter a hell of a lot more bumps, dips, and turns in an aircraft that's trying to make its way into some remote village that's not even on the map. Or tell me, instead of flying, do you plan to walk overseas?"

His sarcasm wasn't appreciated. And his criticism of her was even less appreciated. Earlier, in the kitchen, she had shared with him some of her dreams and ambitions, and now he was using that information for his own purpose and throwing it in her face. And she was spitting mad. And the itch to slap him was back, which was more welcome than she cared to admit. And because she hated being drawn to this man on a sexual level, she wanted to hold on to her anger.

"I'd tell you to go to hell again, but I'm not even sure the devil himself would have you!"

She didn't wait for his reply. She spun around, went up the last two steps, and practically ran to her room. She was so mad that she could actually feel steam coming out of her ears. And the only coherent thought she had was that she needed to get away. So she fled to her room, never looking back, leaving him standing alone on the stairs. But even in her escape, he seemed to get under her skin.

What made matters even worse was the deep laughter she heard from the top of the steps, just as she slammed her bedroom door, hoping to shut him out of her mind.

Chapter Four

Tyler stood at the bottom of the stairs, debating with himself whether or not to go knock on Samantha's bedroom door. It was already late in the afternoon and he hadn't caught a glimpse of her all day.

Because of his years of predawn training, he was never able to sleep in, and today was no exception. He was up, showered, shaved, and on his second cup of coffee before six. He had read the paper from beginning to end, cooked himself a breakfast of bacon and eggs, fooled around with the engine of a jeep that his dad had half torn apart, and was now at loose ends. So here it was, four in the afternoon, and he was not only bored but feeling a little guilty over the trick he had played on Samantha.

It was no surprise to Tyler that Samantha had avoided him all day. The only surprise was that she was able to keep it up for so long. After all, *enough is enough*, he thought to himself. He figured that she'd had ample opportunity to make her point, and now it was time to put her feelings aside and get on with why she was here in the first place. But the longer he'd waited for her to come out of hiding, the more obvious it became that he was going to have to make the first move, which really pissed him off—but not enough to stop him from climbing the stairs.

Tyler reached Samantha's door and before he could talk himself out of it, he lifted his fist and gave the door two solid bangs. There was no response. So he tried again, but this time he banged three times. Still no response. "Come on and open up, Sam. I know you're in there."

"Go away!"

"Open the door."

"No!"

Tyler took a deep breath. "Open the door, Samantha. I have something I want to tell you."

"I'm not interested in anything you have to say. So go away!"

"I'm not going away, so you might as well open this door." He tried to sound reasonable, but some of the impatience he was feeling came out in his voice.

"Then don't go away. You can stand there until hell freezes over for all I care."

Tyler had to close his eyes to keep his temper under control. To his way of thinking she was being totally ridiculous, and he didn't hesitate to let her know it. "Will you please stop acting like a friggin' three-year-old? You've been in there sulking all day and enough is enough, for Christ's sake. I came up here because I want to talk to you, and I want to talk to you now."

"So talk. No one's stopping you."

Tyler had to mentally count to ten. "I have no intention of talking to you through a closed door, Samantha. So I'm only going to say this one more time. Open this damn door!" *There, that should do it.*

"And I'm only going to say this one more time, Lieutenant Garrett. Go away!"

Tyler snapped. "We can do this one of two ways, Ms. James. You can either open this door now or I can kick the damn thing in. Either way, you've got about fifteen seconds to make up your mind."

There was a pause on the other side of the door and Tyler suspected that she was trying to figure out if he was bluffing or not. And her next comment confirmed exactly what he suspected.

"You wouldn't dare kick down this door, Tyler Garrett."

He couldn't help the smile that spread across his face. Sparing with her was ten times more fun than fooling around with some old jeep engine. "I'd advise you to step back, Samantha, because your fifteen seconds are just about up. And I don't want to explain to Katie how or why you got yourself hurt." He waited a heartbeat. "Five, four, three, two…"

The door was flung wide open and Samantha stood on the other side with both hands planted at her waist and a look on her face that was meant to kill. "I hope you're happy," she said, and her voice was dripping with sarcasm.

"Happy, no. Satisfied, hell yes." He made sure that his own voice mimicked her sarcastic tone.

"Well don't think for a second that I opened this door because you ordered me to. I only opened it because I'm a guest in this house and I don't want your parents coming home to find their home falling down around them." *God, could I have said anything more stupid?* she thought as she tried to keep a threatening look on her face.

But when it came to threatening looks, no one could top Tyler. "Give it up sweetheart. You know perfectly well that I wouldn't actually kick down this door. You opened it because your curiosity got the best of you. You're just way too inquisitive, and even though you're pissed as hell at me, you're also dying to know what I came up here to say to you."

"Nothing…absolutely nothing you have to say could interest me in the least." The green of her eyes flashed and her chin tilted up just an inch.

"You can't lie worth shit," was Tyler's taunting reply, and he watched as her eyes turned an even deeper green.

"And you are such a jerk."

Tyler's only response to her comment was to throw her a sweet, innocent smile.

"Tell me something," she asked. "How can Katie be such a wonderful, kind person and have a big brother who is such an overbearing, obnoxious jerk?" Before he had a chance to respond, she turned and walked back into the room. Tyler followed closely behind.

Samantha wasn't one to give in easily and she was still madder than a hornet at the arrogant lieutenant. Just the fact that he thought he could intimidate her made her see red. So she decided that her best defense would be to let him into her room but completely ignore him, which was going to be no easy task, especially since he looked so incredibly good.

The second Samantha had opened her door, she knew that she was in big trouble. One glance at the man standing before her had caused her pulse to race faster than a locomotive. He had on a pair of well-worn jeans, a blue denim shirt with the sleeves rolled up to his elbows, and a baseball cap turned backward on his head. His dark brown hair curled up slightly at the edge of the cap, and his sunglasses were tucked into the pocket of his shirt. He looked relaxed, confident, and just way too sexy. And she hated him for that. So resolving to completely ignore his overpowering presence, she went over to the small desk tucked into the corner of the room, plopped herself down in the chair, and began to type on her laptop, acting for all the world as if he didn't exist.

She typed and he waited. She typed some more and he waited some more. And as expected, his patience finally gave out.

"I want to talk to you."

She just kept on typing.

"Did you hear me?"

She just kept on typing.

"I didn't come up here to watch you type, Samantha. I want to talk to you."

She just kept on typing.

This time when Tyler didn't say anything, Samantha thought she'd won and that he might actually go away. But her inner victory was short-lived, because in the next second she could sense more than hear him walking up behind her. Because she could be every bit as stubborn as the pigheaded Navy SEAL, she refused to act like she was aware of his presence. She kept her eyes focused on the computer screen and her back straight as an arrow, and her fingers flew across the keyboard. Seconds seemed to tick by and Samantha was congratulating herself on how well she was blocking him out. But then he did the unexpected, and for a brief second she stopped what she was doing, frozen in place.

Tyler simply placed both of his hands on the back of her chair, leaned forward, and brought his eyes level with the computer screen. He was so still and so close that Samantha could actually feel his warm breath against her neck. But what actually caused her pulse to skip was the smell of his clean hair, fresh soap, and the masculine scent of someone who was all man.

"Is this your article?" His mouth was almost touching her ear and she felt a tingle throughout her entire body. And for an instant all she could do was nod, because with him leaning in so close she didn't think she could speak if her life depended on it. As Samantha did everything in her power to keep breathing in a slow, steady rhythm, Tyler was taking his sweet time reading over her shoulder. If Samantha could have thought clearly, she would have admitted that his sudden change of mood had confused her once again. Instead of demanding that she stop typing and give him her undivided attention, he seemed content to read on and watch as her fingers began to falter over the keys.

"You know, if you come up with me in the chopper, you'll have a whole lot more to write about. It's a completely different flying experience—one you don't want to miss."

When she didn't respond, he moved in just a little closer. "I promise I'll behave myself. No surprises, Sam. You have my word."

No matter how much Samantha wanted to give him the cold shoulder, at the feel of his breath against her skin, her resolve to ignore him was starting to melt away. And she wondered if he knew exactly what he was doing to her senses. Was he purposely speaking in a low, almost husky voice? Did he need to be this close to her? Did he have to smell so good that her stomach felt like she had swallowed a handful of butterflies? Was he trying to distract her on purpose, or was she just way too sexually susceptible where he was concerned? All of these questions kept flying through her already muddled mind.

And truth be told, Tyler's mind was a little muddled itself. The second he leaned in over her shoulder, he was taken in by her sweet, intoxicating perfume. Her soft, flowing hair had accidentally skimmed lightly against his cheek, and he felt a burning need to bury his face into its silkiness. Her blouse was unbuttoned just enough so that when he lowered his eyes, he could catch a glimpse of her white, lacy bra. Because he was finding it hard to concentrate on anything but the swell of her breasts, he forced his mind off of her body and reminded himself why he had come into her room in the first place.

"Come on, Samantha. Why don't you admit that you're not really mad at me anymore? And anyway, you know you want to give me another chance. So why don't you give it up and come along like a good girl."

Now he was teasing her, and she wasn't about to let him get away with that. So without thinking, she swirled around and jumped up from her chair. And the next thing she knew, she was suddenly face to face with Tyler, gazing into eyes that could almost hypnotize her into submission. She was so caught off guard by their closeness that she stood perfectly still, unable to move. And all Tyler did was watch her with eyes that went from teasing to something she couldn't quite read, although she suspected that there was reckless abandon as well as an open invitation behind his long, dark lashes.

As the room seemed to close in around them, this time Samantha could feel his breath against her mouth. The heat from his eyes was enough to take her own breath away, and she felt an uncontrollable urge to lean forward the scant inch it would take to bring their lips together. She was losing ground way too fast, and Tyler was loosing ground right along with her.

Tyler leaned down just enough so that his mouth was almost touching hers. He was careful to move slowly, so as not to cause her to draw away. And as he waited to see how she would react, he was drawn to the sudden awareness that flashed through Samantha's eyes—an awareness of him, her own attraction to him, and that he was about to kiss her. And even though his better judgment told him that kissing her would be a big mistake, the man in him just couldn't let this opportunity pass him by.

"Will you slap me if I kiss you?" He asked in a low, seductive voice, and she wasn't sure she heard him correctly.

"Excuse me?" Her own voice was barely above a whisper.

"I'm asking permission to kiss you, Samantha."

Oh my God, she thought, *Oh my God. I really, really want to say yes.* But even as her mind screamed yes, her common sense told her she had to tell him no. For her own sake, she just had to tell him no.

"I don't think … um … I don't think that's a very good idea." She could hardly choke out the words.

"As usual, we disagree," he drawled without skipping a beat. "Because I think kissing you right now would be a very good idea." Tyler was smart enough to let that comment hang in the air. It had to be her decision.

Samantha knew that he was waiting for her to give him the go-ahead, just as she knew that he would not force a kiss on her. And without any warning whatsoever, she wanted to feel his mouth on hers so badly that it scared her to death. And only because it scared her so much, she couldn't bring herself to give in to what she wanted. So she chickened out.

"Please don't kiss me, Tyler."

Tyler was certain that if he ignored her plea and kissed her anyway, she would give in and most likely kiss him back. He could see just a hint of an invitation in her eyes and he could feel the air crackle between them. But because he wanted her to tell him with words that she wanted his kiss, he didn't make another move.

"Please…don't," was all she could manage.

Dismissing an unwanted twinge of disappointment, Tyler fought through the fog in his head and noticed two things. He noticed the uncertainly in her voice and he noticed that she didn't actually say she didn't want him to kiss her. But either way, he figured he was better off backing away. After all, he'd been telling himself for two days now that he needed to stay away from this woman on a physical level. And he would be foolish to let one little kiss get in his way. One little kiss was certainly not worth it. Or at least that's what he told himself as he stood to his full height, breaking the spell between them.

"You were right the first time, Sam. Kissing you would not be a very good idea."

Surprisingly, Samantha found that she was stung by his words. Sure she wanted him to back off, but her pride was bruised that he did so with little or no discouragement. He didn't even try to talk her into a kiss, and her ego took quite a hit. But she would never in a million years let on that his lack of pursuit meant a thing to her. *If he doesn't want to kiss me enough to coax me into it, then I don't want to kiss him either.* At least that's what she told herself. And to prove her point, she sat back down and simply shrugged her shoulders before she turned her attention back to her computer, which she shut down with one quick command.

It was quite a struggle but Samantha was finally able to get her body under control. She had to swallow back the lump that had formed in her throat, forcing herself to appear calm and totally unaffected by a kiss that didn't happen. Giving herself another ten seconds, she finally felt like she could look at Tyler again without blushing down to the tips of her toes. And with a confidence she didn't really feel, she said the first thing that came to mind.

"You promise that if I go up with you, you won't pull any reckless stunts in the helicopter?" She spoke as she turned again in her seat, facing him with an accusing look in her eyes.

"I said I'd behave myself, didn't I?"

He sounded way too cool, which didn't sit right with Samantha. She hated to admit it, but she wanted him to be every bit as shaken up as she was by what had almost happened between them. But instead he looked and sounded like he couldn't have cared less that she had asked him not to kiss her, which was starting to make her mad at him all over again.

Because Samantha didn't like looking up at him, she stood. Even standing toe to toe, she realized that she was at a disadvantage. Tyler just always seemed to get the best of her. And that was a situation she hoped to change, one way or another.

"You should know that if you purposely make me air sick again, or if you do anything to scare me, I'll find a way to make your life a living hell for as long as I'm here."

"And you think my life isn't already a living hell with you hanging around day in and day out?" His lopsided grin told her that his words weren't meant to hurt. He was just trying to tease her along. And for some crazy reason, all of her anger at him fled in that instant and she wanted to play back.

"I probably shouldn't trust you as far as I can throw you. And I should probably have my head examined. But who knows when I'll get another chance to go up in a helicopter. And because I really need more information for my article, and because I'm such a forgiving person, I've decided to give you a chance to redeem yourself."

"I don't exactly remember asking you to forgive me, Samantha." Without realizing it he took a step closer to her.

"Sure you did, Tyler. When you asked if you could kiss me, I figured that it was going to be an *I'm sorry* sort of kiss. Right?"

She wanted to get the whole issue of that *almost* kiss out of the way. She wanted to get it out of her mind, and she figured that the best way for her to do that was for her to say out loud how little it would have meant to her.

"If you think that's the sort of kiss we were going to share, then you don't know me at all." All teasing was gone from Tyler's voice.

Samantha opened her mouth to say something but nothing came out. And she knew then that her reason for binging up the *almost* kiss was about to backfire.

"Just so that I'm perfectly clear. If and when I kiss you, Samantha James, it will not be an *I'm sorry* sort of kiss. It will be a kiss that will bring you to your knees. It will be hot, long, slow, and wet. I will taste you with my mouth and then I will taste you with my tongue. When I kiss a woman, I don't play around. So don't fool yourself into thinking that when I kiss you, it will be something simple."

Tyler's words left her unable to think and unable to move. He had taken her breath away at his description of his kiss, and she wasn't sure she would ever get that image out of her mind. Standing there, watching him, she could actually feel his lips touching and taking control of hers and his tongue slipping into her mouth. And because the feeling was so real, she could also feel a blush rising to her cheeks—a blush she knew that Tyler was also aware of. And that was the reality that finally caused her to fight for control of the suddenly out-of-control situation.

"I…I think we may have gotten somewhat off track." She tried to sound calm but gave herself away when she absentmindedly ran her tongue over her lower lip.

"And I think we've been off track from the moment you stepped out of your car."

She started to ask him what he meant by that remark but thought better of it, because suddenly the only thing she could think about was how much she needed to get out of this room. She just knew that if they stayed in her bedroom, talking about missed kisses and being off track, she would lose even more ground with him. And that she simply could not afford. So out of pure desperation, she decided it was time to get going while she still could.

"If we want to take off while the sun is still shining, I guess we'd better get a move on. And since I've already decided to trust that you'll behave, I guess I'm about as ready as I'm going to be." She was pretty sure that her unexpected change of topic caught him off guard, but she never would have known it by his quick, almost indifferent response.

Tyler narrowed his eyes and studied her for a couple of long seconds. "Okay, Sam, let's go." And in what was typical Tyler Garrett fashion, he didn't even give her another glance before he turned toward the door. "You coming?" he asked over his shoulder, and Samantha knew better than to lag too far behind. So she grabbed her purse and her sunglasses, following him down the stairs, out the door, and to the waiting chopper.

* * *

Tyler was as good as his word. He took things nice and easy, from takeoff to landing. He explained the workings of the helicopter, answered all her questions, and made sure the ride was as enjoyable as possible. The only problem was that like the night before, he couldn't get away from her damn perfume. Her scent seemed to wrap around his senses, playing havoc with his brain cells—or what was left of his brain cells, which he was starting to think wasn't much. Tyler was convinced that both his right and left brain compartments were completely saturated with thoughts of sex. He thought about having sex in the air, sex on the ground, sex in a car, sex in the kitchen, and sex in a bed. He thought about having sex in all these places, at any time, day and night. And as he thought about having sex with Samantha James in all of these places, he felt himself getting so hard that he had to shift in his seat in order to try to make himself comfortable.

"Are you all right, Tyler?"

He pretended like he hadn't heard her.

"Are you all right?" she persisted. "You keep fidgeting?"

If she only knew was his disgruntled thought, and he felt a spurt of anger toward the woman causing his discomfort. But because they had been getting along so well, he decided to give her a break and keep his pent-up frustration to himself.

"I'm fine," was his muttered comment.

"You sure?"

"I said I'm fine." His tone of voice was harsher than he had intended, but *damn it,* he was anything but fine.

"Sorry," she replied. "It's just that you seem…I don't know…you just seem a little distracted."

And that did it. He had to get out of the cramped helicopter or he was going to do something he might really regret—like put the damn thing on autopilot, grab her around the neck, pull her as close to him as possible, and kiss the hell out of her.

"If you've had enough, Sam, I wouldn't mind calling it a night." He had to shift one more time in his seat.

Tyler wasn't really asking her whether or not sure was ready to go in and Samantha knew it. He was trying to be somewhat polite, but she knew that he was simply stating the obvious, and that was that he was ready to call it a night.

"It's such a beautiful evening that I really hate to go in. But I guess I'm ready to head back if you are."

With that Tyler glanced at the watch he wore on his left wrist. "It's actually later than I thought. We've been up for almost two hours."

"You're kidding." She couldn't believe that the time had gone by so quickly.

"By the time we land and I get this thing back in the hanger, it'll be close to seven. How about we go into town and grab a bite to eat. Have you ever had real Texas barbeque?"

Samantha was surprised by his invitation. She had fully expected him to land the plane, get her settled back at the house, and take off on his own like he had done the day before.

"Actually, I haven't. The couple of times that I've visited Katie, we've eaten with your parents. We'd make plans to go into town, but would never quite get there."

"Well since its Wednesday, it's rib night at The Horse Shoe Bar and Grill. The drinks are cheap and the barbeque is the best you'll find anywhere in the state. So how about it? Wanna go?"

Samantha felt her spirits lifting. "Sure. Sounds like fun."

Tyler didn't offer up a response. All he did was glance briefly over at Samantha, and then he took the chopper into a full, smooth, easy turn.

Less than an hour later, he was opening the door to The Horse Shoe, stepping aside to let Samantha in.

"If I remember correctly, it can get pretty crowded in here on a Wednesday night." Tyler spoke into Samantha's ear at the same time that he slipped his arm around her waist to lead the way. And it didn't take but a second for her to realize that his words were an understatement to say the least, because the place was packed. There were people everywhere and Samantha wasn't sure where Tyler was headed. It looked to her like every seat in the place was taken, even at the bar. But he kept his arm around her waist, maneuvering them through the crowd.

As they made their way around tables and chairs, several people offered up a greeting. "Hey, Tyler." "Good to see ya, man." "How's it going, Tyler?" Tyler didn't stop to chat. He just smiled back, drawled a hello, and kept on moving as though he had a destination in mind. And magically he found the only empty table in the place.

Tyler pulled out a chair for Samantha and she was a little surprised by his display of good manners. She took the chair he offered, looked up to smile her thanks, but noticed that his attention was suddenly directed elsewhere. As her eyes followed his across the room, her smile froze on her face, because he was focused on a woman who was threading her way through the tables, heading straight for him. It didn't take a genius to figure out that this woman was a waitress at the bar. She wore a short, tight skirt that left little or nothing to the imagination, with an even tinier white apron. She had midnight black hair that hung down to the middle of her back, blue eyes that sparkled, and a smile to die for.

Samantha glanced one more time at Tyler and she felt a knot of disappointment curl into her stomach as the corners of his mouth turned up into a sexy grin—a sexy grin that was an open invitation if she ever saw one.

In what could only be described as *slow motion*, the lovely woman reached their table, stepped up and wrapped her arms around Tyler's neck, plastered her body up against his, and kissed him right in front of God and everyone. And Samantha watched in stunned silence. But what was even more stunning was the fact that not one person in the place seemed to think that the amorous greeting was inappropriate. As a matter of fact, no one seemed to be paying them the least bit of attention. It was obvious that it was only Samantha who was incapable of looking away.

Finally, after what seemed like forever, Tyler finished the kiss and he was laughing as he pulled himself out of the woman's arms.

"How in the hell have you been, Carolina?" With that Tyler turned toward a stunned Samantha. "Samantha, I'd like you to meet an old friend of mine, Carolina Avena. Carolina, this is a new friend of mine, Samantha James."

Carolina reached out and reluctantly took hold of the hand that Samantha extended. "It's nice to meet you."

"It's nice to meet you too, Carolina."

Tyler pulled out his own chair and sat down.

"Sam's a friend of Katie's and she's here from California to write an article about flying. Katie and Brandon are in Dallas for a few days, so I'm helping her out until they get back."

"How nice," was Carolina's mumbled response as she turned her attention away from Samantha, almost dismissing her out of hand. It was disgustingly obvious that she was only interested in Tyler. Her body language said it all. And the look in her eyes said that without question she was ready, willing, and more than able.

"So how long are you in town, Tyler?" Carolina had moved in so close to Tyler that the only place left for her to go was to sit on his lap. And after watching the way the woman was drooling over him, Samantha wouldn't put it past her to do just that.

"It depends."

"On anything in particular?" This time Carolina's hand found its way to Tyler's shoulder. And it stayed there.

"I'm not sure how long I can stay."

Samantha was immediately struck by how vague Tyler's answers were to Carolina's questions. She knew firsthand that he could be the master of evasion, but she couldn't help but wonder why he was being so vague now, especially since he seemed so glad to lay eyes on the beautiful woman—or at least that's what one would have surmised by that kiss they'd just exchanged.

"Well, no matter how long you're in town, promise me that you won't be a stranger? My number's in the book, so give me a call before you head back to San Diego. It'd be fun to spend some time together while you're home."

Samantha held her breath waiting for Tyler's response. But to her surprise, all he did was flash another one of his sexy smiles.

"I gotta get back to work, so don't forget to give me a call. I'll be mighty disappointed if you don't." With those parting words, Carolina ran her hand slowly along Tyler's shoulder, gave Samantha one last fleeting glance, and then turned to make her way back toward the bar.

"Sorry about that." At the sound of Tyler's voice, Samantha had to force her eyes away from the retreating woman. "Carolina and I go way back. She was married to a buddy of mine, but they got divorced about…oh, I think it's been about five years now."

"Well she is certainly friendly enough." Samantha tried to keep the displeasure out of her voice but it didn't work. And of course, Tyler didn't miss it either.

"Meaning?" was his one-word question, and she suddenly wished that she'd kept her mouth shut. After all, it was none of her business how friendly Ms. Carolina Avena was. She was Tyler's friend, not hers, and she told herself that she didn't care one bit if he called her or not. She refused—absolutely refused—to feel jealous where this man was concerned. So she decided that her best bet was to act like she hadn't heard his question. But she should've known that Tyler wouldn't let her get away with it.

"Come on, Sam, out with it. What did you mean by that comment?"

Before she could stop herself, Samantha said exactly what was on her mind. "You know perfectly well what I'm referring to, Tyler Garrett. Your friend Carolina is quite the kisser, which seemed like a pretty friendly gesture, if you ask me."

"Now, if I didn't know better," he drawled, "I might actually think that you're just a tad bit jealous." Tyler leaned back in his chair, balancing on only two legs.

"Get over yourself, Lieutenant. *Jealous* is hardly the word I'd use to describe my reaction to that kiss. The word *bored* comes to mind, as well as *annoyed*, *embarrassed* and slightly *disgusted*." *God, I hope I sound convincing*, she prayed, because jealous was exactly what she had felt.

"My, my. One little kiss and yet so many adjectives. Sure you don't want to add another word or two to that list of yours?"

As usual, he was doing what he did best: turning the tables on her by making fun of the situation. But this time she wouldn't let him get the best of her.

"No need. I think I just about covered it."

"And I think you are only fooling yourself, sweetheart."

"Meaning?" This time it was her turn to ask the one-word question.

Tyler let his chair fall back on all four legs, and then he leaned in close enough to bring his face just an inch or so away from Samantha's. His gray eyes searched her face for a brief second, and when he spoke his voice was low and seductive. "I could take your observation that my kiss with Carolina seemed boring as a direct challenge, my dear Samantha. And if I do that, then you're going to be in a whole lot of trouble. I don't take challenges lightly, and if I decide that I want to prove you wrong, I'll have a lot of fun in doing just that. And when I'm finished with you, I think you'll be adding an entirely different list of words to describe your own reaction to my kiss."

As expected, Tyler words sent a chill of anticipation throughout Samantha's body. She was held spellbound by the look in his eyes as he spoke. His words were direct, arrogant, and borderline rude. And she loved how they made her feel, because she had to admit that never in her life had she responded this way to another man. Even though she knew that he was being purposely outrageous, every fiber of her being was aware of his closeness, the intensity of his eyes, and the promise of a kiss that was yet to come.

And that in itself was a challenge all its own—a challenge in a new game with rules that were constantly changing. But this was a game that she couldn't afford to lose—a game that called on everything she possessed to stay cool, calm, and collected, even if she was feeling anything but. Luckily, before she was forced to reply and quite possibly lose the game with the first words out of her mouth, another waitress came by, this time with menus in hand.

"Well, Tyler Garrett. Welcome home."

The spell was broken. Tyler leaned back and Samantha drew in a deep, ragged breath. Both of them knew that the challenge was still on the table and that the interruption had only postponed the outcome—an outcome that Samantha was scared to death to accept but even more scared to let go by.

"Monica, darlin', let me introduce you to a friend of mine from California." It didn't escape Samantha's notice that this time Tyler had introduced her as his friend, as opposed to Katie's friend. And without thinking too much about what that might mean, introductions were made, menus were passed out, and orders were taken, all within a matter of minutes.

Tyler ordered ribs for both of them, with a glass of wine for Samantha and a bottle of beer for himself. Then he seemed to settle back to enjoy the rest of the evening, which ended up going by in somewhat of a blur.

Just as their food arrived, so did a couple of friends, who without being invited to do so, pulled up chairs and joined them. And a minute after that, more friends of

Tyler's showed up. And before Samantha knew what was happening, their table was crammed with five other guys, along with more bottles of beer and even more platters of ribs.

The night turned out to be so much fun that Samantha didn't even mind the crowd. Tyler's friends told great stories and they teased her constantly about being a Yankee from California. They talked football, football, and more football, arguing about which two teams were going to make it to the Super Bowl. Bets were made on the Dallas Cowboys and the Houston Texans, and only when Samantha spoke up did a silence descend over everyone sitting at their table.

"I'll put fifty bucks on the Oakland Raiders making it to the Super Bowl this year. They made a couple of good draft choices, and they have the best wideout in the NFL. Their QB had a great season last year, and he should be even better this year. Their running game has improved and at the end of last season their defense ranked in the top ten."

Tyler and his friends couldn't have looked more surprised even if they'd tried. They were actually speechless, which was saying quite a lot, at least for Tyler.

"What's the matter?"

The six men just sat at the table looking from one to the other.

"Oh, come on guys. Doesn't anyone want to take my bet?"

Finally Tyler found his voice. "Are you crazy? First of all, in case you've forgotten, you're in Texas right now, not back in California. And second, how can you possibly think, for even one minute that the Oakland Raiders will make it to the Super Bowl? And third…if—and this is a big if—if any team in California could make it to the Super Bowl, it would be the San Diego Charges, not the Oakland Raiders."

Samantha sat up straight as a board. "Nobody—absolutely nobody—maligns my team and gets away with it." As she spoke, she looked around the table at the men who were nodding their heads in agreement with Tyler's *stupid* statement.

"Is that so?" Tyler spoke up for everyone, using what she now knew to be his "I'm in command of this situation" tone of voice. And she knew that if there was ever a time for her to stand up to him, that time was now, especially since it was all in jest.

"You cannot intimidate me when it comes to football, so don't you even try. I have the greatest respect for the Cowboys and the Texans," she quickly added because, after all, she was in Texas, "but my money is still on the Oakland Raiders. So, Mr. Garrett, I would suggest that if you disagree with me, then you can put your money where your mouth is. And I believe that I have a fifty-dollar bet on the table. So either take the bet, or keep your opinion to yourself. It's your call. " She was so pleased with her little speech that without thinking, she reached over, grabbed Tyler's beer bottle, and took a long, slow drink.

Tyler's reaction surprised her. He threw back his head, laughed out loud, and then dug into the pocket of his jeans. "Fifty bucks says that the Raiders will not be in the Super Bowl." He plopped the bills down on the table.

"Any more takers?" he asked, and three other guys at the table added their money to the pot. "You confident enough to cover all these bets, sweetheart?"

Now that was a challenge that Samantha could not pass up—not in a million years.

"I'll take those bets," she responded with more confidence than she actually felt. But she wouldn't be able to live with herself if she backed down now. "Two hundred bucks it is." She scrambled around in her purse and thanked her lucky stars that she had enough cash to cover the bets.

"Here, Jeremy, you hold onto this for us until the end of the season. And when the time comes, you can pay us all back our fifty, plus our winnings from Ms. James." This time it was Tyler's turn to take a long, slow drink from his bottle of beer.

"Well I'll be damned." Jeremy scooped up the money. "The end of football season is a long ways off. Are you two sure you want me to hold onto this much dough?"

"Absolutely," Samantha and Tyler answered simultaneously.

"As a matter of fact, you can get my home address in L.A. from Kate and mail me my winnings at the end of the season."

"In your dreams, sweetheart."

Before Samantha could respond to Tyler's wisecrack, the argument over the Dallas Cowboys and the Houston Texans started up all over again. And Jeremy ordered another round. "Beer or wine, Samantha?"

"I think this time I'll have a beer."

She could tell by the guys' smiles that she had won them over. She was certain that they were taken off guard by her knowledge of football, and now here she was kicking back and drinking a beer. Not in her wildest dreams would she have imagined that she would care if Tyler's friends liked her or not, but as the evening progressed she realized that it did matter. She wanted them all to like her, so all in all, the evening was turning out to be even better than she would have expected.

Another round of beers turned into another, and then another, and suddenly Samantha knew that she had passed her limit a couple of beers ago. She had no idea what time it was, but she was feeling both a little drunk and a little sleepy. She had wanted to keep up with the guys, which was now proving to be her downfall. And as she turned to Tyler to see how he was holding up, she felt a slight ringing in her ears.

Tyler had been keeping an eye on Samantha, wondering when she was going to feel the affects of all the booze she was drinking. He had a feeling it was important for her to fit in with his friends, and being a lightweight drinker was not something she'd easily admit to. So instead of cutting her off, as he'd been tempted to do, he'd kept a silent watch over her. But now, looking into her bleary eyes, he knew that it was time to take her home.

"You about ready to go, Sam?" Even as Tyler asked the question, he was getting to his feet. "It's almost eleven. So, if you're ready."

Trying not to be too obvious, he reached down and helped her up from her chair. He had to hide his grin as she leaned against his arm as if to steady herself. "Say goodnight to everyone, Sam?"

"Goodnight, everyone." She felt a little lightheaded, so she kept a firm grip on Tyler's arm. "It was really nice meeting all you guys."

The guys at the table all smiled as Tyler led her away. "Hey, Samantha," one brave soul called out, "when you get tired of soldier boy, you give me a call. I'll be happy to show you around town anytime. Anytime at all."

Samantha giggled and Tyler looked back over his shoulder and frowned. Kevin was grinning from ear to ear, and Tyler felt an unexpected urge to go back to the table and have a few quiet words with his good friend. And surprisingly, *screw you* came readily to mind. But Tyler knew that Kevin was only joking, and when his buddy tilted his beer bottle in Tyler's direction in the form of a salute, the prick of jealously that he'd felt at Kevin's words quickly fled. Well, almost.

"Come on, Sam. Let's get outta here." Tyler all but dragged Samantha out the door, through the parking lot, and over to his car. He opened the passenger door and helped her inside, before going over and sliding in behind the wheel. Without so much as glancing in her direction, he started up the car and headed home. All Tyler wanted was to get home and to get away from the woman sitting beside him. He needed to distance himself from her and he needed to do it fast, because she was just a little too sexy right now for his peace of mind. She was way too relaxed, a little sleepy, and just this side of tipsy: all in all, not a good combination. So without any further conversation, he focused all of his attention on getting himself back to his house without giving in to his unwanted desire to reach over and touch her.

"I really enjoyed meeting your friends tonight." Her voice broke through the silence in the car. "They seem like really nice guys."

Tyler's only response was one word. "Yeah."

"I guess you've known them most of your life."

"Yeah." Another one-word reply.

"Did you all go through high school together?"

She prepared herself for another vague response.

"Yeah."

"Do you keep in touch with them when you're away, or just see them when you're home?"

Tyler's impatience was obvious. "If you're finished with twenty questions, Sam, why don't you close your eyes for the rest of the drive home?"

Samantha knew a dismissal when she heard one, but she wasn't quite through with her questions. She didn't feel like closing her mouth or her eyes. In fact she was suddenly wide awake and feeling a little reckless—so reckless that she wanted to see if she could throw Tyler for a loop, even though she sensed that she was playing with fire.

"So, is Kevin single?"

Tyler nearly lost control of the car. "What?" He was clearly astounded by her question.

"I figured that he's single since he offered to show me around town, but I thought I should make sure. With some guys, being married doesn't stop them."

Samantha didn't really care one way or another if Kevin was married or single, but the beer she drank made her brave enough to have a little fun with Tyler. Anyway, he was being withdrawn and uncommunicative, which she didn't like. So she thought she would see if she could push his buttons.

"I think he may like me a little, and I think he's kinda cute."

Tyler slammed on the breaks as he came up to a red light. "Kevin Branch is a big fat flirt, Samantha, and my advice to you is to stay the hell away from him."

Samantha smiled in the darkness. Finally she seemed to have hit a nerve with Mr. Cool. And since she thought that she might have the upper hand for the first time since laying eyes on the man, she wasn't about to let up. "I wasn't asking you for advice, Tyler. I asked you whether or not Kevin is married or single."

The red light turned green but Tyler stayed put. He sat looking over at Samantha as if she'd suddenly lost her mind.

"You have the green light." She tried to sound sweet and helpful but her voice came out a little slurred. She was still feeling the effects of all that beer.

Tyler had to shake his head to clear his mind. He was stunned that she was sitting in his car, full of booze, looking all soft and kissable, and asking him about another man—so stunned that he actually sat through the green light.

"Oops. You missed the light."

He heard Samantha, but only when another car came up behind him did Tyler seem able to pull his thoughts together. And with a clear mind also came strong words of warning. "You may not have asked for my advice, but let me give it to you again anyway. Kevin is my friend, and yes, he's a nice guy. But it goes without saying that he is also single, uncommitted, horny, and looking for an easy one-night stand. So unless you're looking for the same thing, then I'd advise you to stay away from him. Because believe me, sweetheart, Kevin can charm the pants off of most woman without even trying."

For the king of one-word responses, Samantha thought that Tyler had just given quite a speech. But before she could tell him to mind his own business, the driver behind them honked his horn. Tyler had almost sat through another green light.

"I have to admit I'm really not into one-night stands."

"Yeah, well, that's pretty much what I thought." The car behind them honked again and Tyler shot through the light. "That's why I was trying to offer up a little friendly advice."

To Samantha's way of thinking Tyler sounded way too smug, and she was sorry that she'd confessed something so personal. She had never had a one-night stand and to be honest, she had no plans to have one now. But that was a piece of information she would just keep to herself—at least for the time being—because she wasn't finished having a little fun.

"But sometimes I wonder if I've missed out on something really big. Since most everyone I know has had a one-night stand at some point in their lives, it must be worth trying. And the fact that it's for only one night has a certain allure all its own. At least with a one-night stand there would be no expectations. It would be just sex, and nothing more. So what do you think? Do you think I should take Kevin up on his offer to show me around town, even if it might lead to a one-night stand?"

"Are you nuts!? How in the hell can you ask me such a thing!?" Tyler's voice came out louder than he intended.

"You don't need to yell. I'm just asking you a question."

"You're not just asking me a question. You're asking me the most stupid question I've ever heard. In this day and age how can you even think there's some allure in having a one-night stand? I refuse to even dignify your question with an answer." Tyler's need to reach out and touch Samantha had only intensified in the last couple of minutes, but now he wanted to reach over and throttle her.

"So are you telling me you don't approve of one-night stands?"

For the life of him he couldn't figure out why she wouldn't close her eyes and go to sleep.

"I'm telling you that I've had enough one-niters to know what I'm talking about when I strongly advise against them." He sounded completely exasperated. "Meaningless sex only leaves you with an empty feeling and even more unsatisfied the next morning. Trust me, Samantha, it might seem like a good idea at the time, but it's not. Sex is much, much better with a partner that you care about. I've had both and I speak from experience. One-night stands aren't worth the time or the effort."

Instantly Samantha wasn't having fun anymore. Hearing Tyler talk about having other lovers made her sorry she'd brought the subject up. Sure, she knew he wasn't a monk, but she didn't need or want to know just how many women were in his past. She'd wanted to have fun and shake him up a bit, but somehow the whole thing had backfired and he'd gotten the upper hand. He'd managed to make her teasing about Kevin and one-night stands sound irresponsible and juvenile. And to make matters even worse, she realized that she had somehow developed a little crush on the handsome Navy SEAL—nothing serious, mind you, just a little crush, but enough of a little crush that she didn't need him lecturing her on safe sex, risky behavior, and empty feelings on the morning after.

"All right, you win, Tyler. You've convinced me that pursuing anything with Kevin along the lines of a one-night stand is probably not a good idea."

"Probably?" Now it was his turn not to let the subject drop, and she didn't like his tone of voice.

"Okay, okay. You want me to say it, I'll say it. Pursuing anything with Kevin is not a good idea. In fact it is a very bad idea. In fact it's just about the worst idea I've ever had. And as you've already pointed out, it's certainly the most stupid idea I've ever had. There! Are you happy now?"

"Happy has nothing to do with this, Samantha." The smugness was definitely back. "It's just that you're my responsibility until Katie gets home, and she would skin me alive if I let you go off and do something… er…something so out of character."

She sat straight up like a jack-in-the-box. "You were going to say 'do something stupid,' weren't you? You were going to call me stupid again!" This time her voice came out louder than intended.

"Don't be ridiculous. I have not called you stupid any time tonight."

"Oh yes you have. You said that—"

"Samantha." He interrupted her with a low, intense, no-nonsense tone of voice. "I might want to call you lots of things, but stupid is not one of them. You may be stubborn, frustrating, and a general pain in the ass, but stupid you are not. So, unless you want to start another argument that you cannot win, why don't we change the subject?"

He waited for her to challenge him and to start another argument. But when she stayed silent he glanced over at her. And what he saw made him chuckle to himself. There she was with her head laid back against the seat, her eyes closed, and finally sound asleep.

Ten minutes later Tyler pulled the car into the driveway. He got out, went around to the passenger side, and opened the door. "Come on, sleepyhead. We're home." He reached in and lightly shook her shoulder. "Open your eyes, Sam."

Maybe it was his gentle touch. Or maybe it was his soft, coaxing tone of voice. Whatever it was, Sam felt warmth spread throughout her body when she opened her eyes and looked up into his.

"Give me your hand."

Samantha did as she was told. She put her small hand in his and her heart fluttered when his fingers closed around hers. His hand was warm, a little rough, and felt really, really good—so good that she didn't even try to pull away once he had helped her from the car.

Even in Samantha's slightly drunken state, she was surprised that Tyler didn't let go, as she had expected him to. Instead of dropping her hand like a hot potato, he kept it tucked snugly in his. Again her heart skipped a beat.

In complete silence, Tyler led Samantha up the porch steps, into the darkened house, and up the stairs. He kept a tight hold on her hand, escorting her to her bedroom.

They stopped right in front of Samantha's closed bedroom door, but she made no move to go in. Instead she leaned against the door, appearing content to do nothing more than stand there and gaze at Tyler.

"Get some sleep, Sam."

It took a full second for his words to register, and when they did he could see a flicker of disappointment in her eyes. But because she was just sober enough not to want him to see that disappointment, she did her best to recover.

"You too, Tyler."

She sounded a little sleepy and way too sexy, which wasn't good for Tyler's peace of mind. So he dropped her hand and took one step away from her. "I need to run a few errands in town tomorrow. I wanted to take you up in the Cessna in the morning, but when I checked it out earlier, there was something in the engine that didn't sound quite right to me. I'll pick up some parts in town, but we may not be able to go up tomorrow as planned."

He was trying to keep his mind off the drowsy look in her beautiful eyes. He was also trying not to notice how she was leaning back against her door, as if she needed it to help keep her in an upright position. *God, it would be so easy to kiss her right now,* he thought as he turned away and took a step toward the protection of his own room.

"Good night, Samantha." He really needed to get the hell away from her.

"Don't you want to kiss me goodnight?"

At her softly spoken question, Tyler stopped dead in his tracks. *Oh God* was his only thought as he dropped his head, closed his eyes, and prayed that he hadn't heard her correctly. He knew that there was nothing wrong with his hearing, but he seemed incapable of giving her a response—mostly because he didn't know how in the hell he wanted to respond.

"One little goodnight kiss couldn't hurt. Could it?"

Tyler stood rooted to the spot, knowing that if he turned around and looked at her he would be a dead man. No matter how many times he told himself that she was bad news, he knew that he would never be able to stop himself from kissing the daylights out of her if he turned around. So taking a deep, ragged breath, he acted like he hadn't heard her whispered words. But Samantha was either too drunk or too stubborn, because she spoke up again just as he took another step toward his room.

"I'll bet Kevin would kiss me goodnight."

Tyler stopped and then turned slowly around to drill her with a hard, warning look in his eyes. And when he did nothing more than just watch her, she stopped teasing him about Kevin and said what she was really feeling.

"But I don't want Kevin to kiss me, Tyler. I want you to kiss me goodnight."

Samantha's words were soft and sweet, spoken with an invitation that he just couldn't resist. All night he'd tried to ignore the *come and get me* look in her eyes, but now he decided that he'd be a fool to deny himself any longer. With his gaze locked with hers, Tyler walked back to stand directly in front of her. In slow motion he reached out and placed his hands on either side of her head, with his palms and fingers flat against the door. Barely an inch separated their bodies, but he didn't take that little step closer. Instead he just bent his face down toward hers, his lips stopping a breath away from hers.

And in a flash both of them knew that the game was over. The teasing and the taunting had come to an end. Tyler eyes told her as much, and his mouth, so close to hers, told her he was going to kiss her, and nothing—absolutely nothing—was going to stop him. At least Samantha prayed that nothing would stop him.

Letting out the little breath she had been holding, Samantha slowly lowered her eyes, just as Tyler finally closed the gap between their lips. And in the very next instant, Samantha wondered if her life was ever going to be the same again.

Tyler's kiss was so warm, and so sensual, and so coaxing that Samantha nearly melted into a heap. He had done nothing more than touch his mouth to hers, kissing her softly at first and then adding a little more pressure. His hands were still plastered to the door and his body was still an inch away from hers. All he was doing was leaning down and kissing her, using only his mouth to bring her more pleasure than she thought was possible. And without realizing it, she sighed and then leaned even more deeply into his kiss.

Tyler had only intended to give her a quick goodnight kiss. His plan had been to give her what she'd asked for by allowing himself one quick taste of her. But as soon as his lips touched hers, his good intentions went right out the window. And just as he'd suspected, he was a dead man.

Samantha tasted so sweet and she was so responsive that Tyler felt himself giving in to his basic need—the need to taste and feel the inside of her mouth with his tongue. With a great deal of effort he kept his hands flat against the door. He also made sure that he didn't let his body get any closer to hers. But that was all the self-control that he could muster at the moment. And because he couldn't stop himself, he swept his tongue lightly over her lips right before parting them. And then he slipped his tongue inside her mouth so that he could taste and feast upon her sweetness.

Samantha's knees were so weak she nearly slid down the door. The touch of Tyler's tongue turned her into molten lava and she was amazed that she was able to remain standing. With the liquor left in her system, Tyler's wonderful mouth on hers, and him still only touching her with his lips and tongue, she felt more off balance than she'd ever felt before. And she loved every second of it.

But before she could get lost any further in his glorious kiss, Tyler surprised her by lifting his mouth ever so slowly from hers. He took in one deep breath and then laid his forehead against hers. Without saying a word, he kept his eyes closed and worked hard on getting his mind and his body under control.

Samantha wasn't quite so lucky. She was working equally hard at getting her emotions under control, but it wasn't exactly working. Her breathing was strained and she was having trouble getting her heartbeat to slow down to what would be considered normal. She was far from under control, and her brain didn't help when it betrayed her by thinking how badly she wanted to kiss Tyler again.

But in the same instant that she had that thought, she knew that she wasn't going to get the chance, because Tyler had lifted his head and was pushing himself away from her.

"Consider yourself warned, Samantha." His voice was dangerously low, and his eyes were impaling her with his message of warning. "Because if you were sober right now, I'd give you an entirely different kind of kiss and my hands would be all over that sweet little body of yours. And unless I'm reading you completely wrong, it would take all of about ten seconds for us to end up in your bed."

Samantha was so blown away by his words that she could do nothing more than stand and stare up into his eyes. She knew she should say something, anything, but her brain couldn't come up with a coherent thought. And to make matters even worse, she was still dazed by his kiss.

"So don't play with me, Samantha James. You wanted a goodnight kiss, and you got it. But unless you can handle something more, leave me the hell alone. I'll be your friend while you're here, but I will not be some guy you can casually kiss just because you've had too much to drink and happen to be in the mood."

He let his words sink in before continuing. "I know I said earlier that I'd advise you against having a one-night stand, but after getting a taste of you, I'd be willing to make an exception where you and I are concerned. So unless you want to have sex, I'd suggest that you not try to seduce me into kissing you again."

He waited a couple of long seconds to see what she had to say for herself. When she still didn't offer any response, Tyler finished with a terse, "Understood?"

Samantha nodded her head. Her throat was so dry that she couldn't speak even if she'd come up with something to say. She got the message loud and clear. It would have been hard not to, because Tyler Garrett made sure of it.

He was not into kissing her if it didn't lead to something else.

Tyler could tell that she understood him perfectly, because her eyes were so expressive. All the softness was gone and in its place was a keen awareness and an acceptance that he wasn't in the mood to play kissing games with her. He wanted her. Both of them knew that. And if he'd leaned into her as he'd been tempted to do, his body would have communicated that to her as well. But the simple fact was that she was leaving in a few days and he didn't have the time or the inclination to wine and dine her into bed. So to his way of thinking, they were both better off as casual friends and nothing more.

As Samantha worked at pulling herself together, Tyler turned on his heels and headed back toward his room. He opened his door, walked inside, and shut the door behind him without so much as looking back at her. And for the first time since he had bent down to kiss her, Samantha let out a sobering breath.

With fingers that were shaking, she opened her own bedroom door and stepped inside. She brought one hand up to her cheek, feeling warmth spread through her fingers. She was flushed and hot, and even if a gun had been pointed to her head, she would've been hard-pressed to say why she felt as if she were on fire. Was it because of Tyler's words of warning? Was it because she was mad as hell at his insolence? Or was it because of the kiss she had felt all the way to the tips of her toes?

Somehow Samantha suspected that her body was still flushed because she couldn't seem to let go of *the kiss*—the kiss that seemed to invade not only her body but her mind and soul, the kiss that she desperately wanted to sample again, the kiss that was uniquely Lieutenant Tyler Zachary Garrett.

With a deep sigh of resignation, Samantha got undressed and crawled into bed. She replayed his kiss over and over in her mind, and then she replayed his words of warning. She didn't like what he had to say, and she wanted to show him that he couldn't just kiss her like he did and then tell her to stay the hell away from him. She was a big girl, not some child who didn't know what she was doing. She could handle Tyler, any time and any place. And she refused to let his words scare her off.

So with a sense of determination, she decided that she would flirt with the sexy Navy SEAL if and when she wanted to. She would not take his orders like some underling. She would do as she pleased and not let him get the upper hand. She was perfectly capable of flirting and keeping things under control. She liked to flirt, so why not have some fun for the remainder of her trip? "After all," she muttered right before she drifted off to sleep, "it's about time someone put that man in his place, and it might as well be me."

Chapter Five

Tyler had been gone that morning when Samantha had gotten up. The coffee pot was on; the newspaper was strewn about on the kitchen table. But there was no sign of the man himself—not so much as a note. He had disappeared to God knows where, and if it hadn't been for his words the night before that he needed to go into town, she would've guessed that he had purposely made himself scarce.

Samantha would never admit it to herself but she was grateful that she didn't have to face him before she even had a chance for a cup of strong black coffee. She had just a twinge of a hangover—nothing too serious, but serious enough that she knew she'd be better off facing him after a cup of coffee and a couple of aspirins. She needed her wits about her whenever she was around him, and especially today, when she felt even more off balance than usual.

Sometime during the night, after waking up for the third time, Samantha finally figured out what was keeping her from being able to stay asleep. Well, not exactly *what* was keeping her from sleeping, but *whom.* And of course the *whom* was Tyler Garrett.

On and off during the night, Samantha wondered how Tyler was going to treat her after their kiss. She had already dismissed his words of warning, convincing herself that a little bit of flirting with him would be good for both of them. It would help to loosen them both up, and keep the real sexual frustration at bay. Innocent flirting was natural between men and women, and she would not let his outrageous words of the night before put her off. She didn't really believe for a second that Tyler had meant what he said anyway. Well, at least she didn't think he'd meant everything that he said. The part about making an exception and having a one-night stand with her he probably meant, but the part about not wanting to have anything to do with kissing her again without taking her to bed…she doubted that he meant that.

But even with all that resolved in her mind, she was still concerned about how he was going to treat her. And that made her thankful that he wasn't waiting for her in the kitchen when she got up.

Samantha was able to take her time getting dressed. She had a light breakfast, worked on her article, and waited for Tyler. She was upstairs working and was so engrossed in her writing that she didn't even realize what time it was until the phone rang. The answering machine kicked on and she could hear Tyler's voice.

"Pick up if you're there, Samantha."

Samantha scooted back her chair, got up, and ran downstairs to grab the phone. "I'm here," she said a little breathlessly.

"Have you been out running?" He could tell she was trying to catch her breath.

"No. I was upstairs working, and I hurried so that you wouldn't hang up." She took another deep breath. "What's up?" She tried desperately to sound as casual as he sounded.

"I just wanted to let you know that the part I needed for the Cessna wasn't in stock, so I had to order it. And since we won't be able to go flying today, I thought I'd hang out with Kevin this afternoon. I'll be back in time to take you to dinner. How does Mexican sound?"

"Great. I…um…I love Mexican food." Her response was a little unsure, because the last thing she expected was this friendly chit-chat.

"Good. I should be home by six." And with that he said a quick goodbye and hung up.

And Samantha was now more confused than ever. All day she had thought on and off about the kiss last night, yet on the phone Tyler never let on that it had even happened. She couldn't quite believe that he'd just forgotten about last night, especially after he'd kissed her and left her standing in the hall, having issued what could have been either a threat or a challenge; Samantha wasn't sure which. But either way, since he wasn't coming home until later, she'd just have to wait until dinner to see if he would even bring up the kiss they'd shared last night. And as Samantha made her way back upstairs, she promised herself that if he said nothing and could so easily dismiss their kiss, then so could she.

Tyler took Samantha to a small but lovely Mexican restaurant. The drive over had been more pleasant than she'd expected because he'd actually shown up at six in a surprisingly good mood. But even given his apparent good mood, as they headed over to the restaurant Samantha couldn't relax. She kept waiting for him to bring up *the kiss.* Yet as the miles went by, and he didn't so much as hint that he might bring it up, Samantha finally decided to put their reckless kiss out of her mind and relax and enjoy her evening out.

Because it was such a nice night, once they reached their destination, Tyler found them a table outside and pulled out a chair for Samantha. An instant after they were both seated, a waitress appeared.

"Can I bring you something from the bar?"

"I probably shouldn't, but I'd really like to try one of their margaritas." She sounded like she was asking Tyler's permission.

"Go ahead, Sam." Before she could change her mind he turned to the waitress. "The lady will have a margarita and I'll have a beer."

Samantha looked around the quaint patio and they settled into an easy silence until the waitress brought their drinks. She sat down an oversized margarita in front of Samantha and a large, cold beer in front of Tyler. And he laughed again when he saw the look on Samantha's face.

"Don't worry, Sam. You don't need to drink it all. Just drink what you want."

"Okay," was her whispered response.

When the waitress asked if they were ready to order, Samantha asked if Tyler would order for both of them. To her delight he ordered crab enchiladas, rice and beans, and a side of spicy guacamole. The chips the waitress brought to the table were still warm. And without waiting another second, Samantha dug into the chips and salsa.

Between sips of the cold, delicious margarita and the warm chips and spicy salsa, Samantha's senses were already on overdrive. She was enjoying every sip, every bite, and every glance at the man sitting across from her. Their conversation was easy and comfortable, and Tyler kept her entertained with stories about his years in the navy. He told her about training as a SEAL, about his first mission, and about his long absences. Even though the subjects were serious, he managed to keep it light and easy, at least until Samantha asked her next question.

"Have you ever been seriously hurt on a mission?"

The shadow that seemed to pass through his eyes actually told her what she wanted to know. Tyler answered her anyway.

"Yeah. I was seriously injured about five years ago."

"What happened?"

"It's classified."

"Then tell me the part that's not classified."

"It's not a pretty story, Sam."

"Tell me anyway." She sensed that she should let the matter drop but she didn't want to. She wanted to hear his *not so pretty* story.

"Why do you want to know?"

"Why don't you want to tell me?" She thought her best defense would be to throw his own question right back at him.

Tyler actually smiled. Then he grew quiet. And Samantha knew that he was trying to decide whether or not he should tell her the story.

"You may be sorry you asked."

"Why don't you let me be the judge of that?" She simply refused to back down.

Again Tyler grew quiet. Then he sat back in his chair and looked out into the distance. Samantha found that she was actually holding her breath, waiting to see what he was going to do.

"I was injured on a mission that went bad." His soft voice startled her but she didn't move an inch. She wanted to be able to take in every word.

"I wasn't team leader five years ago, but I was a member of Team Mega One. We were in the Middle East, but I can't tell you where. Suffice to say, we were in a shithole of a place, getting ready to do what we do best. We were being sent in to rescue a contractor who'd just negotiated a deal with our government to build electrical companies in several towns. Because of the size of the project, he had to live in the area for close to a year, so his wife and his six-year-old daughter joined him. Without going into great detail, one day he and his daughter were kidnapped right off the street, and held for ransom. So that's when Uncle Sam sent us in to get them."

"What happened?"

Tyler's eyes found hers and for a second she thought that he might not go on. One second he was studying her, perhaps sizing her up, and the next second he seemed to be miles away. And it wasn't until he spoke that Samantha realized that he was already back in the Middle East, in that shithole of a town, on a mission that somehow went bad.

* * *

Five Years Ago
Beirut, Lebanon

"Five minutes to jump."

Tyler, Mac, Lucas and Medicine Man were geared up, standing in the open doorway of a helo, ready to parachute out. The method of jumping that would be executed on this mission was what the SEALs refer to as HALO: high altitude/low opening freefall. It was in the dead of night and they had all volunteered for this mission. Only four members of the team were needed on the ground, and they stepped forward to volunteer without a second thought. Flyboy was at the controls of the helo. They would be dropped about five miles outside of Beirut. Ditching their parachutes, they would make their way to the far northern outskirts of the city where intel had informed them their hostages were being held.

"You ready to go?" Mac always liked to be the last man out.

"Yeah. I'm ready." And on the signal from the copilot, Tyler went first. Lucas and Medicine Man followed. Mac was the last to jump.

As each man hit the ground, he rolled, got to his feet, and unhooked his parachute. Within seconds they were on their way to rescue their hostages. The walk took them just under two hours. It took them another hour to scope out the building they needed to infiltrate. They were told that there'd be plenty of guards to deal with, but so far none had been spotted. So the four of them stayed put for an hour, watching and waiting. But finally time was running out. Second Lieutenant Conner McKenzie was in charge of this mission, so on his command the four SEALs went in.

Tyler was point man. He went first and slipped into the building without any trouble, completely unnoticed, and without leaving any bodies behind. "I'm in." He spoke into his transmitter.

"Status report." Mac wanted to know what the rest of the team was up against before he sent the other men in.

"It's almost too damn quiet in here." Tyler was slightly suspicious because he'd gotten into the building so easily and still there wasn't a guard in sight. Suddenly the hair on the back of his neck stood up. "Something's not right, Mac. Are we sure the hostages are in this building?" As Tyler spoke into his transmitter, he moved silently along the room, making his way to a long, narrow flight of stairs.

"Affirmative," was Mac's response. "According to intel, our contractor and his daughter are being held in a room at the top of the stairs."

Tyler looked up into the darkness. "I'm at the foot of the stairs now. Do you want me to go up and take a look?"

"Negative. Lucas is coming in to join you. The two of you can go up together."

"Roger that," was Tyler's reply.

In a few short minutes Lucas joined Tyler at the bottom of the stairs.

"How come this seems too easy?" Lucas was feeling the same apprehension that Tyler felt. Getting into the building unnoticed was nothing unusual, but both men didn't like the fact that there wasn't a guard in sight. That was unusual.

"We're both in, Mac, and it's way too quiet. What's the order?"

Mac wasted no time in responding. "Our orders are to go in and to bring the hostages out. Proceed with caution."

That's all Tyler and Lucas needed to hear. They would continue up those dark stairs, even though every instinct was telling both men that something wasn't right. But they were trained to follow orders without question, so up they went.

At the top of the stairs Tyler motioned for Lucas to check out the two closed doors on the right. Tyler turned and went to the left, where he would check out two other closed doors. Lucas moved to the first closed door on the right; Tyler stood next to the first closed door on the left. Together they raised their weapons. On the silent count of three the SEALs opened each door and stepped inside with rifles at the ready. Within a second both men were back out in the hall. Tyler proceeded to the next room, as did Lucas. Again, weapons were drawn and ready. And again, on the silent count of three, both men opened a door and stepped inside. This time, though, when Lucas stepped back out into the empty hall, Tyler motioned him into his room.

In the stuffy, decayed room, lying on a small cot, was the little six-year-old girl. Her eyes were closed, her color was as white as a ghost, and her breathing was labored. Tyler and Lucas went over and knelt down by the cot. Tyler reached out and laid two fingers against the little girl's neck, trying to gage her pulse rate. He looked over at his teammate with a worrisome look in his eyes. In silent communication Lucas opened a first aid kit and went to work checking out the little girl. Tyler called in to Mac.

"One hostage found. Daughter is in bad condition, but is alive. Father is not here."

"Shit!" Mac's expletive came over the transmitter. "Where the hell is the father?"

"Except for the little girl, this building is completely deserted."

There was a slight pause. "I don't like this, Tyler. You and Lucas get the hell out of there."

"Negative, Mac. Lucas is still working on the little girl. We need…" He looked over at Lucas, who held up two fingers. "We need two minutes."

"Fuck two minutes. Get the hell out of there, now! That's an order."

"We're on our way out."

"Roger that," came the reply from Mac. "We've got you covered."

As Lucas stuffed his medical supplies into his backpack, Tyler scooped up the little girl. Together they left the room, went cautiously down the stairs, and headed out the door. Unfortunately they were about five seconds too late. Just as they crossed the threshold and took a couple of long strides in the direction of where Mac and Medicine Man were waiting, a thunderous explosion tore into the night. Without any warning whatsoever, the building that they had just come out of went up in flames, throwing Tyler, his little hostage, and Lucas high into the air and down onto the ground with a resounding crash.

And seconds after that, bullets started flying. Tyler, who acted purely on instinct and training, cradled the little girl in his arms and did his best to break the fall. He stayed down on the ground just long enough to find where Lucas had landed. Tyler had been the first one out of the building and it was no surprise Lucas had taken the worst of the explosion. He was laying face down less than a yard from where Tyler had landed.

Lucas wasn't moving. Tyler had a terrible feeling that he was dead but he couldn't reach him to find out. He needed to get Emma to safety. As bullets whizzed over his head, Tyler got to his knees, never letting go of the little girl.

"I've got you!" He could hear Medicine Man yelling over the sound of gunfire and he took it on faith that he could get up and run. The *tat, tat, tat* of an automatic machine gun being fired provided Tyler and Emma all the cover they needed. He got to his feet, and ran in the direction where he knew Mac was. He'd just reached the outskirts of the town when he saw Mac out of the corner of his eye. He laid Emma down on the ground. Because he'd lost his weapon in the explosion, Mac tossed him an M16. He clicked off the safety and turned to fire, just as a bullet caught him in the side. It took him to the ground. And as he hit the ground, he felt a ringing in his ears and a searing pain in his side. He knew that he should try to get up but he couldn't move. He was aware that the fighting was still going on, even though the sounds around him seemed very, very far away. And then, without warning, everything went pitch black, as if someone had simply turned off a light switch.

Present Day

"And when I woke up I was in a hospital in Germany. Along with a bullet wound in my side, I had several broken ribs, a dislocated shoulder, and one hell of a concussion."

"What happened to the little girl and to Lucas?" Samantha had a bad feeling about what his answer was going to be.

"Both were killed by the explosion. Emma—that was the little girl's name—was so weak that she didn't have any strength left to survive the impact of the explosion. Lucas suffered a serious head injury and by the time Mac and Medicine Man got to him, and got us both to the waiting helo, Lucas was dead. I have a sketchy memory of the trip back to the helo because I kept slipping in and out of consciousness, but I do remember thinking that this was the most fucked up mission I'd ever been on. It was a real setup, right from the beginning. In retrospect we were obviously expected, and the kidnappers thought they could kill two birds with one stone. They almost got rid of not only the little girl, but me and Lucas as well. We went in and lost one hostage, one teammate was killed, and we left without finding the other hostage. It was what we call a real clusterfuck."

"How long did it take you to recover?"

The far-away, distant look finally left his eyes and he seemed able to focus on Samantha again.

"Physically I recovered pretty quickly. But for the first time since I joined the navy I actually thought about calling it quits."

"Because of little Emma?"

Tyler drew in a deep breath. "Because of Emma, Lucas, and the fact that we never did find the father. I was also sick and tired of being sent on a mission with bad intel. That wasn't the first mission we'd been on where the information was less than reliable, but it was the first mission where bad intel cost us lives."

"What made you decide to stay in the navy?"

"Lots of things."

"Like what?"

Tyler gave her a look that said *enough already,* and luckily for her, before he had a chance to say those words, they were interrupted by a pretty waitress. Samantha had been so intent on Tyler's story that she barely noticed that she had polished off not only her ultra-sized margarita, but every bite of her dinner. It was only when the waitress asked if she could bring them dessert that she even remembered where they were.

"Just coffee for me, please."

"Make that coffee for two."

The waitress returned in less than a minute with two steaming cups of coffee. Samantha took a long sip, sighed her content, and then rested her chin on the palm of one hand. She watched Tyler as he drank his coffee, his eyes on her face. She noticed that as he watched her his eyes became warm and inviting. And because she felt as though they had crossed some sort of a bridge in their relationship, and because he had just shared such an important life experience with her, she asked him the one question that had been bothering her from the first day she had met him.

"Why do you have such an aversion to journalists?"

Tyler's hand froze halfway to his mouth, his coffee cup suspended in mid air. In a flash the friendliness was gone from his eyes, replaced by a hard, cold, distant look. The soft gray of his eyes was now a stormy, cloudy gray. For a brief second Samantha was sorry she had asked the question. But that passed quickly, as her curiosity got the best of her. And even under such a daunting look, she refused to withdraw the question. Instead she took a different approach.

"I sense that you have a very good reason for the things you said the other day, and I'd like to hear it. I don't want to pry, Tyler, but I can't help but wonder why you hate my profession so much."

He was able to pull a mask over his features, giving away nothing of what he was feeling.

"And don't try to deny that you hate what I do for a living," she added when she suspected what he was about to say.

"Don't push your luck, Samantha. I've already told you more about my past than I tell most people."

"I realize that, Tyler. And I'm flattered that you told me about your mission five years ago. But I think we are on our way to becoming friends, and I'd like to know what happened in your past to make you feel the way you do about journalists."

When he offered no response, Samantha decided to see if she could wait him out. So she took one sip of coffee, and then another, and then another.

With a steady hand and a purposeful gaze, Tyler set his own coffee cup down. His eyes were latched onto Samantha's face, and he spoke, deciding that *if* they were on their way to becoming friends, then she could probably handle the truth. Anyway, he had just told her one very personal story, so what would it hurt to share another.

"It happened two years ago, in Iraq. Because of a fuc… um, because of an irresponsible, spoiled-brat, out-of-his-element journalist, I lost not only a member of my team, but one of my best friends." It had been a long time since Tyler had said the words out loud, and when he did he felt the all too familiar knot in his stomach.

"Will you tell me about it?"

As soon as she asked the question, there was a stillness that settled around them, and they could have been the only two people left on the planet.

"I know you'll probably find this hard to believe, but I'd really like to understand what happened. And as I've just proven to you, I really am a good listener."

There was something in her voice that touched in Tyler a need to tell her the story. He rarely spoke of the turn of events that took Kent's life, but now he wanted to share that day with someone—someone with red hair, green eyes, mile long-legs, and a mouth that begged to be kissed. So before he could talk himself out of it, he sat back in his chair, took a deep breath, and continued talking.

Samantha never once interrupted Tyler, because she sensed that if she did he might draw away. His eyes never left hers and his voice cracked only once. She could see the raw pain etched in every feature of his face and she could hear the anger in his words. And through it all she kept quiet, knowing that pity would be the last thing he'd want from her. She knew that he might accept her understanding, but pity he would never accept. So she swallowed her own sorrow as he told his story, her only act of comfort to reach across the table and take one of his hands in hers.

"And two years ago I vowed that I'd never again have a damned thing to do with a journalist. They will throw me out of the navy before I'll take another journalist on one of my missions."

Samantha noticed that after the telling of the story, the only thing left seemed to be the anger.

"I'm so deeply sorry about what happened to your friend, Tyler." Samantha spoke softly, her eyes conveying the true depths of her own feelings. "But please don't judge all of us by what happened in Iraq. I'm not some over-eager, irresponsible journalist, and I'd like to think that I would have put the safety of you and your men before any story."

His only response was to pull his hand away from hers. And she realized that they weren't going to discuss this topic any further. He'd told her why he felt the way he did and it looked like he had no intention of changing his mind or his feelings about journalists. But because she felt cheated and because she wanted to change his mind, she had one more thing to say on the subject.

"Again, I'm asking you not to use what happened in Iraq against me. No matter how much I'd like to deny it, I'm drawn to you, Tyler. I'm drawn to your character, the path you have chosen in life, your dedication to your family, and your unrelenting loyalty to your SEAL team and your friends. I'm even drawn to your stubbornness and your temper. So given all that, can't you give me a chance and decide whether or not you like me because of what you know about me, and not about what you think you know about me? Like I said," she added on a whisper, "I think we are on our way to becoming friends."

The story about little Emma, the story about Kent, and now this entire conversation had just gotten way too serious. Tyler didn't want to give himself a chance to change his mind about Samantha. He didn't want to let his guard down and admit that what she said made perfect sense. In fact, he wanted more than ever to keep her at arm's length and he felt a twinge of regret that he'd shared so much with her. But since he couldn't turn back the clock and take back his words, he decided that the next best thing was to try to shift the topic of conversation.

"We're both better off if I don't change my mind about you, sweetheart. Because if I did, it's a sure bet that I'd do my best right now to try to convince you to spend the night with me tonight. In my bed."

Bam, just like that they were back on familiar ground, talking about sex. Samantha was smart enough to see right through his little game, but even so she realized it would do her no good to try to pursue a serious conversation with him.

"You know what I think, Tyler Garrett? I think that you plan on making outrageous comments just so you can keep me off balance. And you know what else I think? I think that if I took your offer seriously and said yes to your suggestion of spending the night together, you would probably run for the hills."

Tyler laid his arms in front of him on the table and leaned forward. "Try me," was all he said in a dangerously low voice, but it was enough—enough to convince Samantha that he wasn't fooling around.

"You're impossible! You know that, don't you?"

One side of Tyler's lips turned up into an almost smile. "And you're in way over your head."

"I wouldn't be so sure about that if I were you. I'm much more capable of handling you than you give me credit for." She flashed him a smile of her own.

"Then prove it, Samantha. Let's head home right now. You can go into your bedroom or you can go with me into mine. It's your call."

Samantha wanted so badly to say the words *your bedroom,* but she knew that she just couldn't. No matter how much she was drawn to Tyler, she knew that going to bed with him would be a mistake—not a physical mistake, she told herself, but a mental mistake. And risking her heart and her peace of mind over this complicated man was something she wouldn't do—not now, not tomorrow, and not ever.

So making sure she rose from the table with as much grace as possible, she met his eyes dead on when she gave her answer. "I think I'd better sleep in my own room tonight." Samantha would never know how she found the resolve to sound so calm and unaffected.

If Tyler were disappointed, one would never know it. He simply laid his napkin down beside his empty coffee cup, pushed back his chair, stood, and threw a wad of money on the table. Then without a word, he took hold of Samantha's arm.

"We can dodge the attraction between us for tonight, Samantha, but what's really brewing between us won't be that easy to dodge. Not in the long run."

Samantha was caught off guard by his unexpected words, and she couldn't come up with a clever response. She also couldn't deny that what he'd just said was right on target. So not wanting to say something that would backfire, she wisely remained silent as she walked with him through the restaurant and out to the car.

It wasn't until they were back in the car, heading for home, that Samantha finally found her voice.

"It would be a mistake for us to go to bed together." She just had to get this settled once and for all.

"I know."

"I'm only going to be here for another few days. And since neither one of us is looking for a long-term commitment, ending up in bed right now would not be a good idea."

"I agree."

"So it would probably be wise if we stayed away from any further sexual comments and sexual innuendoes, don't you agree?"

"Okay."

"After all, we're both mature adults and it should be easy for us to stop flirting around with the idea of having sex, and to keep our relationship strictly platonic. Right?"

"Right."

"I mean...we have...um, we have been flirting around with the idea of having sex, haven't we?"

"Yes."

"Okay then. We're both agreed that we will put an immediate stop to thinking or talking about having sex with each other. Agreed?"

"Agreed."

"Oh, and one other thing. Absolutely no more touching. We definitely need to keep from touching each other. Agreed?"

"Agreed."

It suddenly dawned on Samantha that she'd done all the talking and that Tyler was back to giving his infamous one-word answers.

"Don't you have anything else to say?"

"Not really."

Okay, so now he was giving her two-word answers. *Not good enough*, was her thought, right before she pushed the issue.

"And why not, Tyler? At least on this issue, I would have thought you'd have a lot more to say."

Through the reflection cast by the lights on the dash she could detect a slight clenching of Tyler's jaw. And because she was finished with babbling on, she sat back and waited for him to speak. She didn't have long to wait.

"What is it exactly that you want me to say, Sam? I agree with every word you said."

"Just like that?" she asked. "You have nothing to add?" Her stubbornness was taking over her common sense.

"Oh, I have plenty I'd like to add, but I seriously doubt that you want to hear it."

"Try me." She threw his earlier words back in his face.

Tyler knew that he should just keep driving and keep his mouth shut. But he wasn't in the mood to listen to his own inner voice, so he said exactly what was on his mind.

"Okay, you want it straight, I'll give it to you straight." He waited one second to give her time to brace herself for what was coming. "You're one hundred percent right that sleeping together would be a big mistake. You're also one hundred percent right that neither one of us wants a long-term, permanent relationship. But you're dead wrong about everything else. You think that because we're…as you put it…mature adults, that we can just dismiss away the sexual tension. Well, think again, sweetheart. The sexual tension is here to stay and will be here until you get on a plane and head for home. So why don't you do us both a favor and stop talking nonsense about neither one of us thinking about sex. I'll agree to all your other terms. I'll not talk to you about sex. I'll leave out the sexual innuendos. I'll even stop touching you. But you cannot control my mind, sweetheart, so don't even try."

Samantha should have been madder than a hornet at his words but she wasn't because she knew that he was right. They had enough sexual sparks between them to set off a bomb, and that wasn't likely to just go away. In fact, it was liable to get even worse now that they'd both agreed not to act on their sexual attraction.

But even though she might have agreed with Tyler, she would never give him the satisfaction of telling him so. He knew he had hit his mark, so there was no use in debating the matter with him. Anyway, he said it all when he told her that she couldn't control his thoughts, which really meant that he would think about having sex with her if he damn well pleased, and she knew that it was silly for her to think otherwise.

And truth be told, that was just as well. Because she knew that no matter what she'd said, she was going to think about having sex with Tyler—and she was going to think about it a lot. But since she also believed that she would never act on those thoughts, she foolishly believed that she was safe. And she wasted no time in telling him so.

"As usual, you've made your point. You think what you want and I'll think what I want. And as long as we both keep our thoughts to ourselves, there shouldn't be a problem."

"If that's what you want to believe, Samantha, that's fine with me."

Samantha was starting to feel frustrated. She had done her best to sound like the voice of reason, but somehow Tyler managed to make her sound like the irrational one. And to top if off, he seemed to have no problem making his point, while she seemed incapable of getting through to him. So she decided that since she had already said everything there was to say, her best bet was to say nothing further, at least for the rest of the drive home.

By the time Tyler parked the car, Samantha was wound as tight as a drum. She was acutely aware of every move he made and every breath he took. Even in complete silence he seemed able to dominate her thoughts. So she wasted no time in getting out of the car. And as she took off toward the house, he was right behind her. And in her hurry to get away, just as she reached the front porch, she took the first step and stumbled. Before she hit the ground, Tyler's hands grabbed her from behind and hauled her back against him. Trying to steady herself, Samantha leaned into the hardness of his body.

For what seemed like a lifetime they both stood completely still. Samantha stood there, aware of every contour of Tyler's hard body. And Tyler stood and took in the unique scent of the woman he held against him. When she made no move to pull away, his hands tightened their hold on her waist one second before he turned her around to face him. And before either of them had a chance to so much as catch their breath, the spark between them ignited into an all-out flame.

Tyler didn't wait; nor did he ask permission. He simply pulled Samantha into his arms, lowered his mouth to her waiting lips, and kissed her like he had promised. And she kissed him right back.

The long-awaited kiss they shared was an open-mouthed, lustful, hot, devouring kind of kiss. It was neither gentle nor persuasive. It was long, wet, and thorough. Tyler's tongue swept into Samantha's mouth and she responded without caring about the consequences. Her own tongue touched, played with, and teased his. They had both waited so long, and the desire was so strong that neither wanted to waste time in a sweet get-to-know-you kiss. Instead, by silent agreement, they both sensed the need to take the kiss to an even deeper level. So in an attempt to deepen the kiss, Tyler shifted the slant of his mouth while he ran his hands up and down Samantha's back.

Allowing herself to react to his kiss and his touch, Samantha let her own hands wander. Surprising both of them, she reached around, tugged his shirttail from his pants, and laid her hands seductively along his lower back.

As he continued to drink in the sweetness of her mouth, Tyler took them both up one porch step and then another. Stumbling together, they somehow made their way into the house, never breaking the contact of their lips. As the front door shut behind them, Tyler's hands found their way to the front of Samantha's blouse. And in less than a heartbeat her blouse fluttered to the floor; his shirt followed.

The sudden touch of skin against skin brought a long, soft sigh from Samantha, and Tyler needed no further encouragement. He lifted his mouth from hers just long enough to find the most sensitive spot at the side of her neck. His mouth was scorching her with deep pleasure as he continued to lead them through the darkened house.

It was a miracle that they made it as far as the stairs. Tyler's hot open mouth trailed wet kisses along her throat before he allowed himself to nibble seductively at her lips. Samantha was completely lost to the feel of his mouth and she couldn't stop as her hands began caressing his bare shoulders, his wonderful board chest, and his strong, bare back. Tyler reached up and tangled one hand in her hair, while his other hand stayed at her waist. He knew that he needed to get them both up the stairs and into one of the bedrooms, and if he let his hands roam over her now as he longed to do, he would never make it that far.

With a restraint he didn't know he possessed, he took them up one stair at a time. It was a slow but seductive process, and halfway up the stairs Samantha lost both of her shoes. But she didn't mind, because she was so totally focused on the man kissing her senseless and backing her slowly up the stairs.

Finally, with Tyler's mouth once again taking control of Samantha's, they reached their destination. As he backed Samantha into her bedroom, he managed to close the door by kicking it shut with the heel of his boot. And that's when he decided it was now his turn to let his hands do a little wandering of their own.

Releasing his hold on her hair, Tyler's finger's skimmed down Samantha's neck, down through her shoulder blades, to rest at the back clasp of her bra. With his other hand he pulled her up against his body so that she could make no mistake about how badly he wanted her.

Samantha melted against Tyler. She had never in her life felt such overwhelming sensations. Her entire body was on fire and she felt like she was going to faint from the sheer pleasure of what Tyler was doing to her. One minute his mouth was on hers, sweeping his tongue along her lower lip, and the next minute his mouth was sucking lightly on the skin beneath her ear. She could feel his erection pressed against her and she felt fear and excitement at the same time.

"I want to feel you beneath me, Samantha." He chocked out the words and his hot breath caused a ripple of desire to crash through her. "I want to touch and taste every inch of you." Again, she felt a wave of desire.

This time, even through her cloud of desire, the fear she had refused to acknowledge seemed to find its way to the forefront of her mind. And as he continued to whisper into her ear, she realized exactly what they were about to do. And fear began slowly to take over the reckless desire.

As Tyler continued to tell her what he wanted to do with her, her brain latched on to the fact that they were no longer playing a game. In another minute or so, Tyler would have her out of her clothes and flat on her back in bed. With that thought came the realization that no matter how much she wanted him at this moment, she wasn't really ready to become his one-night stand.

With one quick twist, Tyler's hand expertly released the snap of her bra. As his hand slowly, ever so slowly, started to make its way to her easily exposed breast, he kept whispering to her about how he was going to enjoy undressing her, and she knew that her time was running out. But as his warm hand slipped under her bra and cupped her breast, she was more confused than ever. And she allowed herself to get lost in his touch.

But just before he bent down to pick her up and carry her over to the bed, something in the far recess of Samantha's mind told her that if she was going to stop, she had to do it now. She didn't know how she felt about Tyler Garrett, but she did know that he was right when he'd said earlier that she was in way over her head. So forcing herself to take a deep, sobering breath, and with a shake of her drugged head, she took a tiny step back.

Tyler immediately misunderstood her step out of his arms. His mind automatically figured that she was anxious to get into bed so that they could get down to what they both really wanted. And as she took a step back, he took a step forward.

"Tyler…I…"

She couldn't find the right words and he wasn't helping any by looking so unbelievingly sexy. He was walking toward her with gray eyes so full of passion that they almost looked like sparkling diamonds. His hair was messed up, he was bare-chested, and his body was primed for action. He looked so gorgeous that for a second Samantha felt her resolve faltering—but only for a second, because in the next second her common sense came to her rescue.

Tyler didn't pick up on her sudden change of mood. He thought that she was just having a little fun at playing hard to get, so he kept on advancing, and she kept up her retreat. It wasn't until the back of her knees came into contact with the bed, that she came to a halt—but not Tyler. He took one more step, reached out and took hold of her, and dragged her back into his arms. Samantha started to tell him no the same instant his mouth found hers. And the word no was swallowed by the onslaught of his kiss.

Before she lost even more ground and caved in to his power of persuasion, she had to put a stop to his kiss. She had to pull out of his arms and stay out of his arms so that she could think straight. So mustering all her willpower, she placed both of her hands against his naked chest, and applied just enough pressure to cause him to lift his mouth from hers.

"We can't do this, Tyler." Her voice was barely above a whisper.

"Sure we can." His voice was low and hoarse.

"I mean it, Tyler. We can't do this."

"I mean it, Sam. Sure we can." He was so sexually aroused that he failed to take her seriously.

Before he could pull her back into his arms, Samantha stepped away. "I…I know I let things get out of hand, but I'm…"

He reached for her and wrapped a hand around her neck. "Come back here, sweetheart. I'm not finished with you." As he started to lower his head, she pulled away again, and this time Tyler realized that something was amiss. So he stopped and took a long, good look at her.

And what he saw caused him to stand there and watch her with narrowed eyes.

As an eerie silence descended over the room, and as the minutes ticked on and on Samantha finally reached back with shaking fingers and refastened her bra.

"What's going on here, Samantha?"

Samantha called on all her inner strength, and she refused to look away when she gave him her answer. "I've changed my mind."

"You've changed your mind?" His voice was low and cautious. "Just like that, you've changed your mind?"

Even though she felt like a complete fool, she couldn't allow herself to back down. If she did, she would fly back into his arms and never let go.

"I'm not ready for this. I thought I was, but I'm not." For a second she thought she might actually cry, but Tyler didn't seem to notice.

"Well why don't you come back over here, and let's see what more I can do to make you ready?"

Samantha held her ground. "Please don't joke about this Tyler. I'm really not ready for this."

"You're kidding…right?"

His tone didn't have a hint of understanding, and what little desire she still felt left her in a flash. "I think you should leave now, Tyler."

"For Christ's sake, you're not kidding. Are you?" Now his words were full of disbelief.

"No. I'm not kidding. I'm not ready for you." She had to drop her eyes from his penetrating gaze.

Tyler stood and stared at her. Only when he realized that she was dead serious did he let his eyes wander from the top of her head to the tips of her toes. As he brought his gaze slowly back up, his eyes rested on the swell of her breasts peaking out above the lace of her bra.

"Well don't you think you could have realized that before we both lost half our clothes?" Suddenly she remembered that she was standing before him without her blouse. "And couldn't it have crossed your mind that you weren't ready for this before we made our way up the stairs and into this bedroom?"

She looked around in a panic, as if realizing for the first time where they were. "Please, Tyler, let me try to explain."

"Do you really think at this moment that I give a damn about an explanation? I can't believe this. I can't believe that we're in your bedroom in a state of undress, that we've just kissed the hell out of each other, and now you're standing there and saying that you've simply changed your mind."

"But Tyler…" Her words stuck in her throat as he closed his eyes and ran his fingers impatiently through his hair. So she tried again. "Tyler, if you…"

"I told you I'm not interested in your explanation."

Again, Samantha's words of reason were lodged in her throat. She wanted to explain but it was obvious that Tyler was in no mood to listen. But because she was so confused and because she thought he was being totally unreasonable, she felt a sudden need to strike back. "You sound just like an immature, frustrated adolescent."

Those words did it. His eyes snapped open and his desire for her was instantly washed away to be replaced by anger—an immediate, cold, controlled anger. "Don't even go there with me, Samantha. Not now."

"And to top if off, Tyler, you're not being fair. If you will just give a minute, I will..."

"You want fair, Samantha, well here's fair. After allowing your hands to pretty much roam all over me for the last ten minutes, and after the foreplay we just participated in, I think fair would be for me to get laid."

Her mouth dropped open at his rude, blunt words.

"Don't look so shocked, sweetheart. Up until you chickened out, we were both about to get—"

"Don't use that word again!" She almost screamed at him. "I hate that word!"

"Get laid, have sex, make love. Call it whatever you want, it's all the same to me."

"I don't believe that, Tyler Garrett. Not for a second do I believe that you mean that." Her voice was low and calm—almost too calm.

"Well, believe it." He voice was low and anything but calm. It was cold as ice.

"And you know what else," he added when she failed to respond. "I should have paid more attention to the head between my shoulders and stayed the hell away from you. You may be tempting as hell, but in the long run you're nothing but trouble. And your kind of trouble I can do without." With that said, he drilled her with a look that was meant to kill, walked right passed her, and headed for the door. "Nothing but trouble." And those were the last words she heard as the door slammed loudly behind him.

Chapter Six

Tyler sat at the kitchen table the next morning, staring blankly into his bowl of cold cereal. He pushed his Cheerios around with his spoon, not really interested in eating. But he'd already been up for three hours and his stomach was telling him he was hungry. He hadn't slept for shit last night and he didn't have enough enthusiasm to cook something hot, so cold cereal was his only choice.

Taking a sip of his fourth cup of coffee, he felt an unwanted caffeine rush and thought about dumping the rest down the drain. But because the coffee tasted better than the cereal, he took another long sip. Just as he was setting down his cup, the kitchen door swung wide open and in walked Samantha.

Samantha didn't so much as blink an eye. She waltzed right into the kitchen as if she owned the place. "Good morning." Her smile was just a little too bright and she sounded a little too good natured, which made Tyler suspicious. "Isn't it a beautiful day?"

Instead of responding, he took another sip of coffee.

"I don't know about you, but I had a wonderful night's sleep. And I'm absolutely starving this morning. I think I'll whip up an omelet."

She sounded way too friendly this morning and Tyler wondered what she was up to. So he decided that his best line of defense would be to remain silent and see if he could figure out where she was heading with her inane chatter.

"Oh, I see you've already had your breakfast." She eyed his bowl of Cheerios with a look of disgust. "Too bad you didn't wait for me. I've have made an omelet for both of us."

Tyler knew a bald-faced lie when he heard one, but he said nothing as he watched her sashay over to the fridge and take out eggs, cheese, and other assorted goodies.

"I can still make you one if you'd like?" she asked with a phony smile, and he almost snapped out his response.

"No thanks." He replied a little more tersely than he wanted.

Samantha left her ingredients sitting on the counter and poured herself a cup of coffee. "You don't look very well this morning. Are you feeling all right?" Actually, she thought that he looked absolutely gorgeous, but she'd keep that thought to herself until the day she died.

"I couldn't feel better if I tried." He got up from the table and walked over to the coffee pot, even though another cup of coffee was the absolute last thing he wanted. When he reached the counter where Samantha was standing, he nonchalantly brushed her aside with a gentle bump of his hip, pretending that she was in his way of reaching the coffee pot. He could feel her seething.

"Well, forgive me for saying so, but you don't look like you got nearly enough sleep last night." Another bald-faced lie, but what would he know?

"I slept like a baby. No reason not to." He eyed her over the rim of his cup and Samantha had a sudden urge to throw the rest of her coffee right in his face. But instead of violence, she chose words to fight with.

"Then there must be something else wrong with you, because you look like hell this morning."

This time Tyler didn't bite. Instead he sent her an "I know exactly what you're up to" look and sat back down at the kitchen table.

For a few seconds they seemed to be at a standoff. Tyler stayed purposely quiet, wanting to see where Samantha would go next. The battle of wits between them was intriguing and he was anxious to see her next move. He didn't have long to wait.

"Are you still mad at me?" Her voice was as sweet as sugar as she joined him at the table and sat down with her cup of coffee. And Tyler's suspicion grew. He now had a pretty good idea what she was up to, so he decided to give her as good as he got. It would be a cold day in hell before she could outsmart him.

"I'm not mad at you, Sam. Whatever made you think I'm mad?" His voice was sweet as pie, and he could tell he'd surprised her with that response.

"Oh, please. Do you need me to spell it out for you?"

He narrowed his eyes but his voice remained as sweet as can be. "Yeah. I guess that's exactly what I need."

She took a sip of coffee. "I guess I figured you were mad at me when you stormed out of my room last night and slammed the door." Now she tried to sound sweet *and* innocent.

"Not at all," he replied without skipping a beat. "You asked me to leave your room and I left. What's to be mad about?"

This time it was Samantha's turn to feel suspicious because Tyler wasn't acting at all like himself. She was also feeling frustrated because this conversation was not going according to the plan she'd concocted. She'd actually been up half the night tossing and turning, and finally at dawn she began plotting exactly how she would handle him this morning. Since she believed that keeping him off guard was the key to success, she forced herself to flash him a fake, sweet smile.

"Well, I guess I thought you were still mad because we didn't…I mean, because we almost…because I put a stop to…"

"Hey, we enjoyed a few hot kisses last night and almost tore each other's clothes off. No big deal."

Tyler had to pick up his coffee and take a sip in order to hide his grin. It was painfully clear that Samantha was trying to get a rise out of him and failing at it miserably. But Samantha, being Samantha, wouldn't give up.

"So you mean to tell me that you weren't mad that we didn't make love last night?" She was finished with beating around the bush.

"It's real easy, Sam. If you'd wanted to make love last night, that would've been fine with me. But you didn't, and that's fine with me too." He was lying through his teeth, but he was determined that she'd never know it.

"So the slamming of the door had nothing to do with you being mad?" *Let him talk his way around this one,* she thought.

"Actually the slamming of the door was an accident."

Samantha had to grit her teeth. He was way too calm. She wanted to be the one to be cool, calm, happy, and carefree this morning. And he was ruining everything with his "I don't give a damn" attitude. So she decided to try again.

"Well, just so we understand each other, Tyler, a woman always has the right to say no. And that's all I did last night. I exercised my right to say no."

A slight muscle twitched at the side of Tyler's mouth. She was finally hitting a nerve.

"Does a woman also have a right to be a tease?"

Samantha nearly spilled her coffee down the front of her blouse. She just couldn't believe her ears. She couldn't believe that in this day and age he would actually ask her such a question. And as far as she was concerned, the gloves were now off.

"Did you just call me a tease?" Her voice was lethal.

"If the shoe fits."

Samantha jumped up out of her chair. If she had a gun, she was certain that she'd shoot him. But since there was no weapon readily at hand she decided to take one more stab at being the voice of reason. "I think an apology is in order, Tyler Garrett." She was amazed at how calm she sounded.

"I agree, Samantha James. And because I'm such a gentleman, I will graciously accept your apology."

The scenario that Samantha had planned so carefully in her head had now spun completely out of control—all because of the arrogant, cocky, unpredictable Navy SEAL sitting so casually before her. And when he made the mistake of smiling, she lost it.

"I have nothing to apologize for and you damn well know it!" She was practically screaming. "And you need to apologize to me!"

"No way."

Samantha was seeing red. "I want an apology, Tyler Garrett. And I want it now!"

"Well we don't always get what we want. Now do we?"

He was referring to last night and she knew it. And that made her even more furious. "I said I want you to say you're sorry!"

"And I said no way."

Samantha took what she hoped was a threatening step toward him, but he didn't flinch. Instead he calmly picked up his spoon and scooped up a spoonful of soggy Cheerios. She tried another attack. "If you won't apologize to me then I want you to take back what you said."

"No."

"I mean it, Tyler. Take it back."

"No."

I swear that I can't be held accountable for what I might do if you won't take back what you called me. So take it back!"

"No."

Samantha watched as Tyler shoved the Cheerios into his mouth and something in her just snapped. And in the next breath, three things happened at once.

Just as Tyler swallowed his Cheerios, Samantha reached over, grabbed what was left of his bowl of cereal, and without thinking about the consequences, she reached out and dumped everything right over the top of his head. Tyler reacted within a split second. He scrambled to his feet, causing his chair to crash to the ground, screaming loud obscenities directly at Samantha. In the very next second, just as Samantha started screaming back, the kitchen door was flung open. And there, with stunned expressions on their faces, stood Katie, Brandon, and Tyler's parents.

The scene in the kitchen was something to behold. Samantha was holding an empty cereal bowl in her hand and Tyler was standing in the middle of the floor with soggy Cheerios on his head and milk dripping down onto his clothes. He looked like he was ready to kill and the only thing that stopped him from reaching out and taking Samantha over his knee was the look on his parents' face.

Because no one as much as moved a muscle, a long silence settled over the room. Katie and Brandon's eyes kept darting from Tyler to Samantha, not sure what to make of the situation. Tyler's father looked like he was having trouble keeping a straight face. And as the seconds turned into minutes, it was Tyler's mother, Rebecca, who finally stepped forward and broke through the uncomfortable silence.

"So my dear, I see you've finally met my son."

* * *

"Come on, Samantha. I can't stand it. You've gotta tell me what happened between you and my brother." Katie and Samantha were closed up in Katie's room and had been since the fiasco in the kitchen.

"Please don't ask me again, Katie. I'm too embarrassed to talk about it."

Katie was sprawled on her bed and Samantha was standing over at the window, looking out at Tyler and his father in the yard. Tyler had cleaned up, changed clothes, and was now having what appeared to be a serious conversation with his father. Samantha could only imagine what they were discussing—or more likely, *who* they were discussing.

Samantha had to close her eyes whenever she thought about the horrible scene in the kitchen. She felt a sick feeling in the pit of her stomach and she wondered if she would ever get over the embarrassment. She kept replaying the sight of Rebecca stepping forward at the exact same moment that Tyler's father, William, had lost it and burst out laughing. Brandon's laughter had quickly followed. Tyler's mother had taken hold of his arm just as Katie gabbed onto Samantha and dragged her out of the kitchen and into the safety of her room. That had been over an hour ago, and Katie was still trying to get answers out of her.

"I don't see why you should feel embarrassed. Tyler was the one standing there with the bowl of cereal poured over his head." Katie couldn't stop her squeal of laughter. "My God, I think that might be about the funniest thing I've ever seen."

Samantha groaned. "Please don't, Katie. It's bad enough that I have to face you with what I did, but I'm not sure how I'm ever going to face your parents."

"Are you kidding? We all know that Tyler can be bossy at times, and knowing you, my guess is that he probably deserved it. He did deserve it, didn't he?"

This time Samantha sighed. "You're not going to let up, are you?"

"Not until you give me a hint at what happened. You don't have to tell me everything, just why you dumped the cereal over his head."

Samantha forced her eyes away from the two compelling men in the yard and walked over to the bed. She sat on the edge, took a breath to steady her nerves, and told Katie as little as possible.

"Your brother called me a name and then he refused to take it back. I asked him more than once to apologize and he flatly refused. So before I could stop myself, I grabbed the cereal bowl and let him have it."

"What did he call you?"

This was exactly what Samantha was afraid of. "That's not really the issue, Katie. He was wrong and refused to apologize. That's the real issue."

Katie had a stubborn streak, just like her brother. And when she wanted answers she wasn't easily dissuaded. "Yeah, well, I can see that, but come on, Samantha, it must have been really bad for you to react the way you did."

"It was bad. Really, really bad." Just thinking about the entire episode caused Samantha to blush.

"So what did he call you?"

Samantha lifted her eyes to her friend and thought, *Oh, why not. Tyler will probably tell her anyway.*

"Your brother had the bad manners to actually call me a tease. And when I demanded that he take it back, he had the audacity to look at me and say 'no way.'"

Katie nearly swallowed her gum. "He called you a—"

"Please don't say it, Katie. Hearing it from your brother was bad enough." Samantha actually felt a little better now that everything was out in the open—well, almost everything.

"My God, why in the world would he call you a tease?"

Samantha felt her blush deepen and she was certain that Katie didn't miss it. But since she'd already gone this far, she figured she might as well go a little further.

"Well, he kinda kissed me last night and I kinda kissed him back." She let it go at that.

Katie scooted up and sat on the edge of the bed next to her friend. And with a sympathetic look, she spoke her mind. "You know, Samantha, Tyler has always had a way with women. He's never lacked for female company, and well, it's hard for me to believe that he'd call you such an awful name just because you guys shared a kiss. And if he did, then I'm really disappointed in him."

Samantha couldn't even look over at Katie. The last thing she wanted was for Katie to misunderstand the situation and blame her brother entirely. Sure, Tyler was dead wrong for saying what he'd said and not apologizing, but she knew that she'd played a part as well, and it was time for her to fuss up.

"I...I guess that maybe...maybe we did a little more than just kiss." Katie could tell that this was killing Samantha, but she stayed quiet, letting her tell her side of the story. "It's just that before I knew it, we were in my bedroom heading into a situation that was way out of control. So I pulled back before it was too late. And just like a typical man, Tyler was *not* a happy camper when he stomped out of my room. And this morning when I tried to have a reasonable conversation about last night, your big, fat, jerk of a brother called me a tease. And when he wouldn't take it back, I lost my temper. And that's when you opened the kitchen door." Samantha let out the breath she wasn't even aware she was holding.

"Whoa, that's quite a story."

Samantha finally found the courage to look over at her friend. "It's a story I'm not particularly proud of."

"Oh come on, Samantha. It's a great story. All except for the part where Tyler called you a name and you lost your temper, I love it that you and my brother hit it off. Who knows, maybe you two will patch things up, fall madly in love, and we'll become sisters-in-law one day."

Samantha finally started to laugh. That scenario was so ludicrous that she couldn't help it; she laughed until she hurt.

"What's so funny?"

"Everything you just said." Samantha was still laughing. "Your brother and I have been fighting since the minute I got here. We seem to barely tolerate each other. I won't even bore you with the terrible trick he played on me the first night he took me up in the Piper Cub. Suffice to say, I almost killed him. And all of that is what makes what happened between us even worse. Patching things up is about the only thing we might be capable of."

Katie wasn't fooled—not for a second. "So, how do you really feel about my big brother?"

Since all of her defenses were down, and because she was such a lousy liar, Samantha answered her honestly. "I have a terrible crush on him, Katie. Even after last night and even after the fight this morning, I still have a crush on him. Now how pathetic is that?"

The smile on Katie's face said it all. "Please don't look at me like that. I'll get over this silly crush soon enough. I'll be leaving tomorrow and I'll probably never see Tyler again. So you can wipe that stupid smile off you face."

"You know what, Samantha? I think you and my brother are made for each other. He's always had it way too easy where women are concerned. He's much too good looking for his own good, and he's never had to put much effort into getting any girl. And then, out of the blue, you come along and give him hell. You're just what he needs and whether you want to believe it or not, I think he's just what you need too."

Samantha was appalled at Katie's words—not so much what she said but how much she wanted to believe them. And because that scared her more than she'd admit, she dismissed them out of hand.

"Don't be ridiculous, Katie. Your brother is the last thing I need. But what I do need right now is to figure out a way to face your parents."

Katie jumped off the bed. "You don't need to worry about Mom and Dad. They love you, Samantha, and they won't get involved. Trust me, they'll just let you and Tyler work things out."

Samantha walked back over to the window. She was both disappointed and relieved that Tyler and his father were nowhere in sight. "Even if I can face your parents, I'm not sure about your brother. Granted, he deserved what he got, but if the look on his face was any indication of how he's feeling, it might be better if I tried to catch a flight home today."

"Oh no you don't, Samantha James. You can't leave today. Mom is planning a family engagement dinner for me and Brandon tonight, and it would mean the world to me to have you there."

With those words, Samantha whirled around. "You're engaged?"

"Yeah. Did I forget to mention it? Brandon and I went to Dallas to get his parents blessing and then we headed up to the beach where Mom and Dad were staying so that Brandon could ask Dad's permission to marry me. Isn't that romantic? Anyway, of course Dad said yes, and that's how we all ended up back here together."

Samantha dismissed away her own misery and ran over to give her friend a long-overdue hug. "Oh my God, Katie. I'm so happy for you and Brandon. Congratulations, sweetie."

Katie returned the hug and managed to force a reluctant Samantha to agree to stay another night. "Trust me, Samantha, dinner will be great. And if I know Tyler, he's already forgotten all about your little disagreement. It's no secret that he's demanding and autocratic, but that's just his officer training kicking in. By the time we sit down to dinner, everything will be fine. Just you wait and see."

They were already thirty minutes into dinner and Samantha was still waiting to see a sign—any sign—that Tyler had forgotten about their encounter in the kitchen. However, as the meal progressed she became more and more convinced that he'd never actually forget about their fight, because it just wasn't in his nature.

Samantha had tried all through dinner to act carefree and unaffected, but it was difficult. Tyler was seated next to her and more than once his arm brushed against hers. It was a tight fit around the table, with very little space between the two of them. As she sat this close to him, her mind drifted back to the dinner and the confidences they'd shared last night. But since so much had happened between them since last night, their cozy dinner now seemed like a lifetime ago.

"Pass the peas, will you, son?"

Samantha was brought back to the present as Tyler reached over and handed the bowl of peas to her to pass, looking directly at her for the first time all evening. His gaze locked with hers and she was momentarily distracted, trying to read into his gray eyes. But the brief connection was broken as Tyler's father reached over to take the dish from her hands.

Conversation around the table was never lacking. Rebecca and Robert talked about their brief vacation at the beach, and of course everyone talked about the wedding that was yet to be scheduled. Katie talked nonstop and Samantha just prayed that no one took notice that she had barely said a word.

As for Tyler, he sat quietly next to Samantha, and for that, at least, she was grateful. But just because he was uncharacteristically quiet didn't mean that he'd put aside their differences, and she strongly suspected that forgiveness was going to be a long time coming. To make matters even worse, as the evening went on, she could almost feel the tension in him. He was anything but relaxed, and like her, he had spent most of his time pushing his food around on his plate, not really eating much of anything.

"Tyler, dear, don't you like the ham?"

Leave it to a mother to notice that her son wasn't eating was Samantha's thought as she forced herself to eat a forkful of ham. The last thing she wanted was to focus attention on her own lack of appetite.

"The dinner's great, Mom. As always."

"Well, eat up, dear. You skipped lunch and you didn't have much for breakfast."

Everyone at the table stopped eating, as five forks were suddenly suspended in mid-air. Rebecca's reference to the disastrous breakfast was obviously said without thinking.

"Oh my goodness. I really am sorry. It just slipped out."

All eyes were turned toward Samantha and Tyler, and surprisingly, the silent one finally spoke up and saved what had turned into an awkward moment.

"It's okay, Mom. Sam and I've already made up, and there's no hard feelings between us. Right, Sam?" He kicked her gently under the table. It was obvious that he wanted to put his mother at ease, and she couldn't fault him for that, so she played along.

"Um…right…no hard feelings." Samantha looked down at her plate because she didn't want anyone to see through her lie.

"Actually, Sam's apology was so unexpected and so heartfelt, that putting our argument behind me was the very least I could do."

Samantha nearly choked on the sip of water she'd just taken. She couldn't believe that he didn't leave well enough alone, and she was amazed at how easily he'd lied to his parents just to suit himself. For an instant her fingers itched to take her fork and stab him right where he sat. But as she gathered her wits about her, she decided that she could do him more harm with words. And this time she had no trouble lying.

"Tyler's right, Mr. and Mrs. Garrett. I simply had to apologize to him for losing my temper at breakfast. Especially since Tyler had the courage to seek me out earlier and admit that he'd been totally unbearable this morning, and completely wrong. I know it took a lot for him to beg for my forgiveness and I never hold a grudge. So as your son said, our stupid little argument is forgotten." It was her turn to kick him gently under the table.

Before Tyler could respond, his mother spoke up. "Well that's wonderful, Samantha. We're all glad you've patched things up. So are you two going dancing with Katie and Brandon after dinner?"

Samantha didn't think things could get much worse, until she looked up and caught the laughter in Katie's eyes. She tried giving her friend a look of warning, but it was too late, because Katie apparently had a plan of her own.

"Oh that'd be great. Brandon and I are headed to The Western Connection to celebrate our engagement. Why don't you guys come along?"

Samantha's stomach sank. She knew that Katie meant well, but the last thing she needed was to force Tyler into taking her dancing. And before she could politely decline the invitation, Tyler did it for her—and not so politely.

"Sorry, Katie bug. I've got other plans."

"Oh come on, can't you cancel them, Ty? It's Samantha's last night here. She leaves first thing in the morning."

"You don't need…"

"No, I can't…"

Samantha and Tyler spoke at the same time.

The situation was getting worse by the second, and Samantha gave up all pretense of eating. She put down her fork and turned to tell Tyler not to bother to change his plans, but he beat her to the punch.

"I can't go dancing with you tonight, Katie." He was speaking to his sister but his eyes were on Samantha. "I've got a date."

Now things were as bad as they could possibly get. Tyler sounded arrogant, smug, and way too pleased with himself. And the slight hold Samantha had on her nerves snapped. She had been willing to forgive and forget, but the son of a bitch sitting next to her obviously wasn't. Why else would he make a date when he knew it was her last night in town and then throw it in her face? And in front of an audience, no less. *Well, two can play this game Tyler Garrett.* And before she could talk herself out of it, she let him have a taste of his own medicine.

"Well I'd love to go with you, Katie, and since I'd hate to be a third wheel, maybe I'll give Kevin a call and see if he'd like to go along."

She knew she hit her mark when the smirk on Tyler's face disappeared and was replaced by a look of total disbelief. Now was the time to push her luck.

"I took a few country-western dance lessons a couple of years ago, and I bet it'll come back to me. I hope Kevin won't mind that I'm just a beginner? I'd hate to step all over his toes."

Katie was fast on the draw and thought her brother deserved to be put in his place. "Are you kidding? Kevin's a great dancer and I'm sure he'd love to teach you a few good moves."

If looks could kill, Katie would be dead in her chair. Tyler's gray eyes turned the color of hot melted steel, and he trained those eyes right on his baby sister.

"Then it's settled." Samantha's voice was light and airy, but for some reason she felt like crying. "You go on your date, and I'll go with Katie, Brandon, and Kevin."

Samantha would have sworn that she could feel Tyler stiffen beside her, but she wasn't sure, because he was such an expert at covering up. And because he was so good at hiding his feelings, he seemed totally relaxed when she risked peeking over at him through her lowered lashes. She continued to watch as he reached over, picked up his glass, and drained his wine in one long drink. Even though it seemed like a lifetime, it was really only a couple of heartbeats until Tyler's mother broke the uneasy silence that seemed to settle over the room.

"If everyone's done, I'll go get dessert."

Tyler pushed back his chair, stood up, and flung his napkin down, all in one fluid motion.

"I hate to rush off, Mom, but I don't want to be late. I told Mary Lou that I'd pick her up right after dinner." He sauntered over to his mother, leaned down, and gave her a peck on the cheek. "I'll save dessert for later."

Samantha felt her stomach drop down to her toes at his last words, and she wondered if she was the only one to get the double meaning. She knew that he wanted her to think that his dessert was going to be *his date*, and she could have killed him on the spot for planting that thought in her head, although the truth was that the thought had already crossed her mind. The moment he'd mentioned he had a date her mind betrayed her by conjuring up images of Tyler with another woman. She knew herself just how charming he could be when he put his mind to it, and she didn't doubt for a second that he would lay it on thick tonight. After all, he was probably still mad at her for not only saying no the night before, but for dumping his cereal on top of his hard, stubborn head. And she wouldn't put it past him to think that the best way to get back at her would be to sleep with another woman. And with that depressing thought, Samantha felt unwanted tears build up behind her eyes—tears she absolutely, positively refused to shed.

As Tyler stood behind his mother, his wicked eyes rested on Samantha. "In case Katie doesn't have Kevin's phone number, I'll leave it for you by the phone. I don't think he's in the book."

And with those words, he delivered the final blow. Blinking back the tears, all Samantha could do was to sit in silence as he turned to blow his sister a kiss goodbye. "I'll see everyone tomorrow."

Well so much for having won this round was Samantha's regretful thought as she watched Tyler head out of the dining room. He was the real winner, and she knew it. He had a date with someone named Mary Lou, and even though she said she'd go along with Katie and Brandon, she really had no intention of going dancing. She had said she'd go and she'd purposely brought up Kevin just to see if she could rattle Tyler's cage a little, and for an instant she had. She knew she had. But as usual with Tyler, he managed to get the upper hand in their battle of wills.

Samantha glanced over at Katie and she received from her friend a smile of such understanding that she felt like crying right there in front of everyone. And suddenly she just wanted to flee to her room, pack, get into bed, and wait for the sun to come up so she could leave. She'd gotten everything she'd come to Texas for and a whole lot more. She had enough first-hand information to write a pretty decent article for her editor. She had faced her fears of flying head on, she had met Katie's big brother, and she had even fallen a little bit in love. What else could a girl ask for?

Swallowing the lump in her throat, and forcing her tears not to fall, she looked around the table at the family she had come to care so much about and knew that it was time for her to go home.

Chapter Seven

Samantha slipped out of bed before the sun came up, hoping to make her way as quietly as possible out of the Garrett house. Since she had said her goodbyes to Katie, Brandon, and Mr. and Mrs. Garrett the night before, she saw no reason to wake them up before the crack of dawn. And she certainly saw no reason to wake Tyler, especially since she wasn't even sure if he'd made it home from *his date.*

Even though she'd deny it until the day she died, she had stayed awake until after 2:00 a.m., waiting and listening for Tyler's car. She had tossed and turned, telling herself over and over again that she didn't give a hoot if he came home or not. But as the hours ticked by, she felt more and more forlorn over the fact that she'd not heard his car pull up to the house.

In the silent, stillness of the night, Samantha had even gotten up once to look out the window to see if his car was in the driveway, just in case she hadn't heard him drive up. And when she'd realized that it was after 2:00 a.m. and his car was nowhere in sight, she finally gave up. Feeling lost and more than a little disappointed, she had crawled back under the covers, berating herself for falling for the handsome, unpredictable, irritating, charming, stubborn Navy SEAL. She had buried her face in her pillow, trying desperately to stop the unwelcome tears. Never in her life had Samantha fallen for someone so quickly. And never in her life had she fallen for someone so hard.

No matter how mad Tyler made her, she simply felt more alive with him and more attracted to him than any man she'd ever met. The sad bottom line was that no matter how hard she tried to talk herself out of it, Samantha was intrigued by Tyler. Sure, he was drop-dead gorgeous, but she was attracted to the whole package. She liked his sense of humor, his sharp-as-a-tack brain, and the fact that she had to be on her toes whenever she was around him. She even liked what he did for a living.

Samantha had never been drawn to men in uniform, but her mouth watered as she envisioned Tyler decked out in what she thought were called dress whites. She could easily picture him looking official, arrogant, and more handsome than anyone had a right to. And her heart skipped a beat when she admitted that he made her anxious and nervous, and best of all, he made her feel excited all the time. To put it in the simplest of terms, Samantha wanted Tyler. And she believed that right up until the moment that she'd dumped his cereal over the top of his head, he'd wanted her too.

But like most men, Tyler was easily distracted, and he'd proven that point when he'd wasted no time in finding himself a date—a date who was probably more than willing to jump right into bed with him. Thinking about that very real possibility made Samantha start to cry. As one tear turned into another, and then another, she tried to push away thoughts of Tyler with another woman.

Lying alone in bed, just thinking about how close they'd come to making love, she could almost feel his hands on her body and she was certain she'd never be able to forget the taste of his mouth. She hated—absolutely hated—imagining him touching and kissing someone else. But she'd made her decision not to sleep with him and now she had to live with it, even if her heart was a little bit broken in the process. With thoughts of broken hearts, Tyler making love with someone other than herself, and her trip home, she had finally cried herself to sleep.

Now, with the dawning of a new day, just as the sun started to rise, Samantha let herself out the front door. She closed the door softly behind her, stepped off the porch, and stopped dead in her tracks because there, as big as day, was Tyler's car. As she walked over to her own car and slipped in behind the wheel, she realized that sometime during the wee hours of the morning he had finally made it home. *Not that it matters now,* she thought as she started her car and headed for the airport. They had parted on bad terms last night and nothing could change that now. Because here she was on her way to catch a plane to L.A., never having had a change to say goodbye and unlikely to ever see Tyler again.

During the hour-long drive to the airport, Samantha tried to clear her head of all thoughts of Tyler. Instead, the more miles she put behind her, the more tempted she was to turn the car around, head back to the Garretts', and give him the kind of goodbye he'd never forget. But because she knew she didn't really have the nerve to do such a brazen thing, and because she was terrified that he'd reject her, she kept on driving straight to the airport.

Samantha checked her luggage, printed out her boarding pass, and still had over an hour before her flight left Austin. She thanked the young woman behind the ticket counter and turned to make her way over to the security checkpoint, which was pretty much deserted this early in the morning. She had not taken more than ten steps when she looked up and nearly stumbled over her own two feet. Because there was Tyler, standing just inside the door of the terminal, watching her with his penetrating gray eyes. And just like that, she felt the breath knocked right out of her.

Never once looking away, Tyler walked slowly toward Samantha. She noted right off the bat the serious look on his face and the determination in his eyes. Taken completely off guard, her mind was reeling and she called on every ounce of willpower to pull herself together. This was neither the time nor the place for him to see how flustered she felt.

Tyler reached Samantha, gently took hold of her arm, and led her out of the way of the other passengers heading toward security.

"I'm glad I caught you." His words were as unexpected as his presence, and Samantha spoke without thinking.

"Why are you here, Tyler? What do you want?" That wasn't at all what she'd wanted to say, but she couldn't seem to stop herself. He looked so good and she was so miserable that she felt an unexplainable urge to strike out at him.

"I need to talk with you, Samantha."

"What about?" Her voice was a little friendlier but a lot more cautious.

"What time does your plane leave?"

"I have just over an hour before we board."

She wasn't sure if he even noticed, but he still had a gentle hold on her arm.

"Can we step outside for a while? I need to say something to you and I think better when I'm outside."

Without waiting for permission, Tyler led her out the door. He spotted an isolated bench along the wall of the building and headed in that direction. As they sat down Samantha was aware of her heart pounding loud enough for the entire world to hear. As she sat quietly, waiting for Tyler to speak, she tried to still her wildly beating heart.

"So you were actually going to leave without saying goodbye."

It didn't get past Samantha that Tyler wasn't asking a question but simply stating a fact, so she decided to do the same. "I left without saying goodbye to you because I didn't think you'd really care."

Her unexpected brutal honesty made him slightly uncomfortable, and he sat looking out into the distance, contemplating how he was going to respond. But he didn't contemplate all that long, because Tyler, being Tyler, decided to be just as honest, even if it put him at a distinct disadvantage.

"I care, Samantha." He let those three little words sink in before he continued. "You may not believe this, and I guess my recent behavior's proven otherwise, but I've grown rather fond of you over the past few days. Fond enough that I didn't want you to leave without the chance to say goodbye."

Fondness wasn't exactly what she was looking for from him, but she'd take whatever she could get. "Then I guess this means that you're not mad at me anymore?" Before she flew away, never to see him again, she wanted a chance to clear the air between them.

"Yeah. Well… about that…" To Samantha's astonishment, Tyler actually sounded embarrassed. "That's another reason I'm here. I figure that I owe you an apology… big time."

Samantha's mind instantly latched on to the fact that Tyler Garrett was a man full of surprises. She never expected to hear the words *I owe you an apology* come out of his mouth, and she waited with baited breath for him to continue. But when he just sat there, saying nothing more, she decided that he might need a little prodding.

"Go on," was all she said.

Tyler glanced over at her and smiled. "You're not going to make this easy for me, are you?"

She smiled back. "Not on your life."

Tyler took a deep, uncomfortable breath and plunged right in. "I'm not going to apologize over the fact that you and I almost made love, Sam. But I will apologize for the things I said to you. I acted like a real bastard, and I'm sorry I called you a…" He started to say *tease* but stopped when he remembered her reaction to that particular word. So with a look of apology in his eyes, he simply said to her, "I'm sorry. My behavior was inexcusable the other night. You were right when you said a woman has the option to say no, and I've always respected that. I was completely out of line, and I couldn't let you get on that plane today without setting the record straight between us. And since

I couldn't sleep worth shit last night, when I heard you leave the house, I decided to follow you to the airport."

Whatever she had expected him to say, this wasn't it. She had expected more of a reluctant apology from him and not one so heartfelt. So for a long moment she was speechless.

"So, is all forgiven?"

How in the world can I not forgive him? her brain screamed. *And how in the world can I not ask him to forgive me in return?* "All is forgiven, Tyler." She looked up into his eyes. "That is, if you'll accept my apology for overreacting yesterday morning, and dumping your cereal all over you."

As Tyler laughed out loud she felt some of her stress drain out of her for the first time since spotting him standing at the terminal door.

"Dad's still laughing about that. He thought it was hilarious, and for some unexplained reason, I think that little scene in the kitchen actually made his day."

Samantha cringed, remembering the looks on everyone's face as they stood taking in that *little scene* in the kitchen. "Your parents will probably never allow me back in their house."

"Sure they will. They think you're terrific. And besides, you're coming back for Katie's wedding, right?"

"Right," she responded. And just the mention of Katie's wedding somehow triggered something else, and she spoke without thinking. "How was your date?" That was the absolute last thing she'd planned to ask him, and she was astounded at herself for letting it slip out.

"My what?"

Samantha wasn't sure who was more shocked by her question: herself or Tyler. But since it was too late to back down now, she shifted toward him and asked the question again, but this time with a lot more bravado. "I asked about your date last night. You said earlier that you didn't sleep well, and I was just wondering if that had anything to do with your date?"

Tyler tried to hide his surprise at not only her question, but the sudden change of topic, but Samantha caught the look that flashed through his eyes anyway. The only thing she wasn't sure about was whether it was a look or surprise or a look of amusement. But either way, she watched him as he thought about her question and took his sweet time answering her. Finally he turned toward Samantha.

"My date lasted all of about thirty minutes, Sam." As he spoke his eyes roamed leisurely over her face, finally resting on her lips. "I met an old girlfriend for a quick drink. We had a beer, a few laughs, and then I called it a night."

"But you didn't get home until after two!" *Oh my God*, she thought as the words tumbled out. She could have cut out her tongue for letting that slip, and she tried to do some quick damage control. "Not that I care when you got home last night. It's just that I didn't fall asleep until well after two, and you still weren't home."

To her surprise, Tyler's lips curved up into the most beguiling grin. "Were you waiting up for me, Samantha? How sweet."

"Don't flatter yourself." Her heartbeat had finally returned to normal and she felt some of her spunk returning. "I just couldn't sleep, that's all. And I was feeling a little restless, so I got up and looked out the window. And that's when I noticed that your car was still gone. It's really none of my business when you got in and I only asked about your date to be polite." She drew in a deep breath, proud that she was back in control of her emotions.

"Well, it wasn't much of a date. Like I said, it was over before it even started. Less than an hour after I entered the bar I was headed over to Steve's for a poker game with the guys."

"Why are you telling me this?" Her question was spoken as softly as the look in her eyes.

"Why do you think?"

"Believe me, Tyler, when it comes to you I hardly know what to think."

His eyes drifted back down to her lips, and it was with a great deal of effort that he lifted his gaze to take in the confused look on her face.

"It's pretty simple, Sam. Last night I was still pissed as hell at you, and I wanted you to think I had a date—a real date. But once I got to the bar, I realized that the last woman I wanted to be with was Mary Lou, so I drank one beer and then got the hell outta there. I knew you were probably dancing the night away with Kevin, and since Steve had a game going, I headed over to his place. We played porker until almost three."

Samantha felt a sudden warmth spread through her at Tyler's confession that he didn't have a real date last night. And because time was running out, she knew that it was her turn to tell the truth. And since she would be catching a plane, she figured that she really didn't have all that much to lose.

"I wasn't dancing the night away with Kevin. I wasn't dancing the night away with anyone. I begged off and headed up to my room to pack. I guess it was just a coincidence that I couldn't fall asleep and noticed that you were out so late."

Tyler watched her for what seemed like a lifetime before he spoke. "I don't really believe in coincidences, Sam. I do believe in fate, though, and I can't help but wonder if fate didn't have a hand in bringing us together." He paused for a brief second. "What do you think?"

Samantha didn't want to play word games with him any longer. She didn't want to remember their last time together and feel sorry that she'd held back. So with a silent prayer that she wasn't making a mistake, she spoke what was in her heart—or at least some of what was in her heart.

"I don't know much about fate Tyler. But this much I do know. I know that you may very well be my one regret in life. I feel something for you, and I wish I'd had the courage to follow through on those feeling. I will always wonder what it would have been like to make love with you. And I'll probably always regret that I didn't get to find out."

If the look on Tyler's face was anything to go by, her words had blown him away. But even as surprised as he was, he was an expert at pulling off a quick recovery.

"I wouldn't want you to leave Texas with any regrets." His voice took on a low, sexy tone. "And I'd hate like hell for you to leave with regrets because of me."

Samantha thought about her plane leaving in less than an hour. "I guess it's too late to change things now, Tyler."

There wasn't really anything more she could say. But this was not the case for the man of few words. "It's never too late, Sam." As his stare met hers head on, she clasped her hands together on her lap.

"Well, unless you plan to get on that plane with me right now, and join the mile-high club, then it really is too late." She tried to make light of the situation, but he wouldn't let her.

"As tempting as that would be, I think I've got a better idea. Why don't you go in and reschedule your flight, and then you and I can go find a hotel room right now?"

Samantha suspected that he was deadly serious, and for the life of her she couldn't think of a thing to say. Tyler took her silence as a sign of encouragement.

"You'll need to see if you can get a flight out tomorrow, Samantha. Because once I get you in bed, I won't let you out until the sun comes up again. I've already thought of a hundred different ways I want to make love to you, and I plan to try out as many as possible. Just say the word, and I'll find us a room."

"My bags are already checked." She barely choked out the words, because her mind had already latched on to a hundred different ways she wanted to make love to him.

"I'm sure we can get them back."

This was it. Tyler was calling her bluff. She didn't doubt for a second that he'd find a way to retrieve her bags, find them a room, whisk her away, and make love to her until, as he put it, the sun came up again. And even though everything inside her was screaming out to say yes, she still wasn't sure what to do. She was just as scared to say yes as she was to say no, and all she could do was look into his eyes and try to figure out how she was going to make the right decision.

As Tyler watched Samantha struggling with the battle going on inside her brain, he remained quiet. He had said what needed to be said, and now it was up to her. He would not coax, urge, or try to talk her into spending the day and night with him. Samantha was a grown woman who knew exactly what he was offering her. He had offered to take her to bed. He had offered to make love to her every way possible. He had offered to spend the next twenty-four hours with her. Those were the things he could freely offer her, and nothing more. And because he wasn't prepared or willing to offer anything more than sex, the decision to stay had to be hers, without any further encouragement from him. He needed to know that if she said yes, it was because she wanted to be with him as much as he wanted to be with her. So even though he thought about pushing her a little harder, he sat quietly, watched her, and waited.

"Do you remember the other night when we almost made love, and I stopped because I told you that I wasn't ready for you?"

Even as she asked the question, Tyler knew exactly where this was heading. But he answered her anyway. "I remember."

"You'll never know how tempted I am to take you up on your offer to go off with you right this minute. I want to be with you, Tyler, even when I know that there'll be nothing between us beyond tomorrow. I want to be able to throw caution to the wind and have you be my first and last one-night stand. But..." She stopped and took a long, deep breath. "But even though I want to, I just can't." She dropped her eyes and stared down at her hands, clasped together tightly in her lap. "Even though I'd like to be very sophisticated about the whole thing, the truth is that I'm still not ready for you."

If Samantha had looked up into Tyler's face just then, she would have seen a world of understanding. Instead of forcing her to lift her face to his, as he wanted to do, he reached over and took hold of one of her hands.

"And as much as I'd like to try to talk you into it, I'm not going to."

She finally lifted her eyes, titled her head, and looked over at him. His words and the fact that he'd given up so easily had taken her by surprise. And with what seemed to be her habit whenever she was around him, she spoke without thinking.

"Why not?"

Tyler stared at her for all of three seconds and then he burst out laughing. "Make up your mind, Samantha." His laughter turned into a seductive chuckle. "You want me to turn on the charm and try to talk you into bed, then just say so. I'd be more than happy to give it another shot."

Samantha smiled, in spite of the fact that she knew she couldn't lead him on any longer. As badly as she wanted to stay, she was going to get on the plane and head home.

"I may live to regret the fact that I'm getting on that plane today, but I'll never regret for one second that I had the chance to meet you."

The laughter left Tyler's eyes in a flash. "So you're going?"

"I'm going," she whispered. When he didn't say anything, she added, "And I hope that we can be friends."

"We already are friends, Sam."

She waited, expecting him to say more, but he left it at that. And when Samantha realized that she really couldn't think of anything more to say, she knew it was time to leave. She gently pulled her hand out of Tyler's warm grip, stood up, and looked down at him still sitting on the bench.

"Goodbye, Tyler."

He didn't say a word. He just sat and looked up at her with those startling gray eyes. With her heart lodged in her throat, she gave him a wobbly smile and started to walk away.

"Samantha."

The sound of his voice stopped her in her tracks and when she turned around Tyler was walking toward her. And for the second time in less than an hour, she saw a look of determination in his eyes. Tyler was standing in front of her in two seconds flat, and before she had a chance to say a word, he dragged her up against his body, wrapped his arms around her, and brought his mouth crashing down on hers.

The kiss was quite scandalous for so early in the morning, especially given the fact that they were in a very public spot. Even though they were at an airport, and people always kissed at airports, this was the kind of kiss that drew attention. But it was obvious to anyone passing by that the two of them couldn't have cared less. They were so focused on each other that the kiss was the only thing that mattered, at least to Samantha.

The instant that Tyler's mouth found hers, Samantha was more than ready to change her mind and stay. He was just so persuasive, knowing exactly how to kiss a woman. His lips were warm and inviting, and she responded without a care in the world. So what if people were walking by, probably disgusted by such a public display of affection? The only thing she cared about at the moment was Tyler and the way he was making her feel, which was as if she were the most desirable woman in the world.

As Samantha wrapped her arms around his neck, wanting to get as close to him as possible, Tyler placed both of his hands at her waist. And with a sigh of regret, he lifted his head, breaking the kiss, but not the contact.

"I'll tell you what." His voice was a little raspy. "You ever decide that you're ready for me, you look me up. If you want a chance to finish what we've started, I'm not that hard to find. Just show up at the base in San Diego, and if I'm in the country, I'll probably be at the base. Just ask the soldier at the guard shack to find me. It's up to you, Sam. When and if you're ready, you know where I'll be."

Samantha felt dazed. She was still trying to recover from his very public kiss, and his words were a little hard to process. She was so caught up in a swirl of emotions that she didn't realize for a second that Tyler had already started to walk away. Watching as his long strides took him farther and farther away from her, she felt an overwhelming desire to run after him, even though she knew it wouldn't do her any good. Tyler had kissed her one last time, told her rather abruptly that the next step—if there was going to be a next step—was entirely up to her, and then he had walked away, leaving her more confused than ever.

Not surprisingly, Tyler seemed able to walk away without as much as a backward glance. Samantha, on the other hand, seemed unable to move. With trembling fingers, she reached up and touched her lips. Her mouth was still wet from his kiss. Her body was still warm from his touch. And her eyes followed him until he was so far away that she couldn't make out his shape any longer.

Finally, after several long minutes ticked by, and she knew for sure that he wasn't coming back, Samantha gathered her wits about her and headed back inside. She made her way through airport security, found her gate, boarded the plane, and took off for home, never once seriously considering that she might actually look Tyler up. They had their chance and it passed them by. Call it fate, call it karma, call it bad timing. Whatever label she chose to put on it, they just weren't meant to be together. They were two different people with little or nothing in common. They were two ships that just so happened to pass in the night. There was no reason to even think she'd try to find him in San Diego. And she found it hard to believe that he really wanted her to. It was obvious that she simply needed to accept that she was better off never setting eyes on Lieutenant Tyler Garrett again. And luckily for her, she had a long flight home to convince herself of exactly that.

Chapter Eight

Six Weeks Later

"May I help you, ma'am?"

"Yes…I'm here to see Lieutenant Tyler Garrett. He said to stop by the base if I was ever in town. And…well… I'm in town."

"Your name, please."

"Oh, of course. You need to know who I am. My name is Samantha. Samantha James."

The young navy ensign picked up a clipboard and scanned it. "Your name is not on today's visitors list, Ms. James. Is the lieutenant expecting you?"

Samantha turned ten shades of red. This was exactly what she had dreaded. But since she was already here, she'd feel even more foolish if she turned the car around and fled. So she did her very best to sound like springing a surprise visit on Tyler was an everyday event.

"I'm sorry. I probably should have called first. I thought I could just stop by to say a quick hello. I'm sorry to have bothered you. I'll just come by another day after I've—"

"It's no problem, ma'am. If you'll just give me a moment, I'll see if Lieutenant Garrett is on base."

Samantha finally drew in a deep, calming breath. She was a nervous wreck. She had questioned her decision to come here a thousand times and now she was embarrassed. Why hadn't she thought to call ahead? If he wasn't around then a phone call would have saved her from coming all this way. Even now a part of her hoped that Tyler was out of the country so that she wouldn't see him. Another part of her, the part that rules her heart, prayed that he was here and that he'd be happy to see, or at least not *unhappy* to see her.

"Lieutenant Garrett is here, ma'am, and he said to tell you that he'll be right out."

Samantha's heart turned over in her chest.

"If you'd like to park your car in the visitors' parking lot to your right, the lieutenant should be here in about five minutes."

The guard checked Samantha's ID before he handed her a visitor's pass. She slipped the pass around her neck, and the gate sung open to allow her access onto the base. She parked her car in the small visitor's lot, turned off the ignition, and got out. She desperately needed some fresh air, and the late afternoon San Diego breeze was just the answer. Samantha leaned against her car, turned her face into the sun, and closed her eyes. She felt a flicker of fear trickle down to the tips of her toes—the fear that she had made a mistake by coming here.

In the past six weeks, Samantha had done little else but think about Tyler. As soon as she'd gotten home to L.A., she'd tried her best to put the Navy SEAL out of her mind. If she let herself, thoughts of Tyler would consume her, so she got through her days by working hard and keeping her mind busy. She would make herself keep going at full speed all day until she'd fall into bed totally exhausted. Desperate for undisturbed sleep, she'd lie down each night with the hope that this would be the night she'd sleep like a baby. And that's when the memories would come back in full force.

The memories that kept her awake each night were always the same. She would get into bed and almost immediately her mind would start to replay the first time Tyler kissed her, the time they'd almost made love, Tyler's laughter, his anger, the look on his face when she'd said she thought Kevin was cute, his stormy gray eyes, and his goodbye kiss. She would think about him over and over again until well after midnight, when she would finally drift off to sleep. And every night she would fall asleep recalling his words: *"You ever decide you're ready for me, you look me up. If you want a chance to finish what we've started, I'm not that hard to find. It's up to you. When and if you're ready, you know where I'll be."*

Those were the words that Samantha had carried around day and night for the past six weeks. She would find herself stopping in the middle of her day, wondering if Tyler was out of the country or at the base. She kept trying to picture his surprise if she showed up in San Diego. She thought about him and *finishing what they had started* so often that she was starting to go out of her mind. The fact that she missed and wanted Tyler Garrett was simply not going to go away. Finally she had swallowed her pride, packed a small weekend bag, and headed for San Diego. And now here she was, standing at his naval base with her heart lodged in her throat.

With a deep, sobering sigh, Samantha opened her eyes. And if she thought her heart was lodged in her throat before, seeing Tyler walk toward her now almost caused her heart to stop beating. Samantha had to force herself to breathe, because never in her life had she seen a man who was so compelling.

Tyler, dressed in a navy uniform, was almost more than she could take. He had on summer navy whites with black and gold lieutenant stripes on the shoulder and an officer's cap pulled down low, the brim almost hiding his eyes. The uniform outlined the contours of his body, making him look intense and sexy. His long strides were purposeful, and he had a glorious, broad smile on his face. He looked like every woman's fantasy man, and Samantha couldn't take her eyes off him. She also felt totally incapable of speech.

"My God, Samantha. What the hell are you doing here?"

In typically Tyler fashion, he strolled right up to her, saying exactly what was on his mind. There was no, *How are you Sam?* There was no, *It's great to see you*— just a blunt question that caused her to rethink the wisdom of her decision to come.

But as the dashing SEAL stood before her, she thought she saw something else. It was the smile on his face and the look in his eyes that were telling her that perhaps he was glad to see her. And she decided to take a chance—a chance she hoped she wouldn't live to regret.

"I came to see you, Tyler. I came to see if you're still interested in finishing what we started six weeks ago?"

That was exactly what Samantha had *not* wanted to say. While driving to San Diego she had made up a story to tell him about how she was in San Diego on business and just thought she'd stop by to say hello. She was going to let him make the first move and seduce her into staying the weekend. Of course she had decided to stay all along, but he didn't need to know that. She'd wanted him to pursue her, charm her, and beg her to spend the night with him. But as usual, the first words out of his mouth made her forget her carefully laid plans.

As Samantha's words sunk in, Tyler just stood looking down at her. His smile faded, his eyes narrowed, and the look on his face was impossible to read. As they stood watching each other, Samantha felt a slight urge to flee. But her need to stay and see this thing through was stronger than her need for flight, so she stood her ground and waited.

With the breeze blowing through her hair, she lifted her face and her hand at the same time. Her face lifted so that she could study the man before her and her hand lifted to shade her eyes from the sun. And still she stood her ground and waited.

Finally, he spoke and broke the silence.

"You sure, Sam?"

"I wouldn't be here if I weren't." Even though her words came out cool and calm, she was dying inside.

"I'm only asking because I'd be lying if I told you I'm not surprised to see you."

Samantha was more confused than ever. He'd told her six weeks ago to look him up if and when she was ready for him, yet now he acted as if he'd never issued such an invitation. She didn't know what to say.

"Tell you what. Why don't we have dinner tonight and then we can talk about why you're here?"

Now Samantha's need to flee took over everything else. He didn't really want her here and that was getting painfully obvious. So before she did or said anything more to add to her embarrassment, she needed to make a clean getaway.

"Listen, Tyler. I can see that my coming uninvited was a mistake. Why don't I go, and—"

"Are you kidding!?" He took a step closer. "Don't you dare think about leaving. I'm really glad that you're here and I trying my damnedest not to take you in my arms right now and show you just how glad I am. But," he added as his gaze swept over to the guard house, "I'm afraid we've got an audience and when I kiss you I plan to do it in private."

The relief that she felt was overwhelming. "Are you sure?" Now it was her turn to ask.

"Samantha James, if you try to leave this base, I swear I'll put you under military arrest."

"Can you do that?"

"Try to leave and just watch me." His smile was back and it was dazzling.

"Something tells me you could and would do just that, Lieutenant. And since I'd rather not spend the weekend in the brig, I guess I'd better stay." The smile she gave him was equally as dazzling.

Tyler's laughter was carried away with the breeze. "Come on, Sam. I need to let the guys know I'm taking off for the weekend."

He reached out and took hold of her arm, and the warmth of his hand spread through every inch of her body.

"Did I come at a bad time?" She still wasn't totally convinced that she could just show up unannounced and off he'd go with her. With Tyler, nothing was ever that simple.

"Your timing couldn't be better. The team's been home for a couple of weeks, and we were just killing time and having a cup of coffee."

She knew she wasn't supposed to ask but she did anyway. "Have you been on a mission?"

"Sort of."

She was never sure what to expect with Tyler, especially since she knew his missions were top secret.

"Have you been out of the country?" She just couldn't help herself.

Keeping a gentle hold on her arm, Tyler led her in the direction of a large white brick building. "No, not this time. But we were out of town for training."

Again, not much information, but just enough to spike her interest. "I didn't realize you still train. After fifteen years, I guess I thought you'd know how to do it all."

"No one ever knows how to do it all, sweetheart. When we're not on a mission, we train, and we train, and when we have some free time, we train some more."

Before she could respond, they reached the entrance to the building he'd probably come out of when the guard at the gate called to tell him she was on base. He opened the door to allow her to go through. Together they walked down a long hall, around a corner, down another hall, and into a large conference room.

As the door opened and Samantha and Tyler walked into the room, conversation came to a screeching halt.

One by one, the men sitting around the table looked in their direction. And one by one, six pairs of eyes took in Samantha, from the top of her head to the tip of her toes and back up again.

Samantha knew that she looked good, because she'd spent hours getting ready to face Tyler. She had applied just the right touch of makeup, her hair hung long and loose down her back, and her white sundress fit her to perfection. It was a soft, white islet design with a short flared skirt that showed off her best feature, her long legs. Her legs were bare and tanned, and she wore white high-heeled sandals. Her toes were painted a light summer pink, and her lipstick was an exact match. She was dressed to kill and she couldn't help but smile when the men in the room showed their appreciation.

"All right, you guys, enough. Put your tongues back in your mouths and let me introduce you to a friend of mine."

Tyler placed a proprietary hand at her waist and led her into the room. "Everyone, this is Samantha James. Samantha, these lazy bums are the guys that make up SEAL Team Mega One."

Samantha was completely blown away. Never in her life had she seen such handsome, appealing, athletic-looking men all in one room. Looking from one SEAL to the other, her heart went pitter-patter.

"Sam, here's a quick intro. The ugly mug sitting at the head of the table is Mac. To his left is Billy, and to his left is Kid." Tyler kept up the introductions, leading her around the table, one at a time. "This is Scotty, this is Medicine Man, and this cocky son of a bitch is Flyboy.

And that's everyone on the team, except for Brian, who's on a personal leave."

Her head was reeling as the men offered her a greeting and a smile. "Please have a seat, ma'am." Flyboy was already on his feet, pulling out a chair for her. "And we'll get you a cup of coffee." He sent her a dazzling smile.

Samantha sat and Tyler latched onto an empty chair, squeezing it in beside her. It didn't escape her notice that he seemed a little possessive, which pleased her more than she wanted to admit.

"What do you take in your coffee, ma'am?"

"Nothing, thank you. I drink my coffee black."

"I'll get it."

"I'll get it."

Flyboy and Mac spoke at the same time, both of them fighting over the coffee pot.

Mac was a half-second faster. But Flyboy was a whole lot smarter, because he grabbed the just-poured cup of coffee away from Mac, leaned over Samantha's shoulder to place it in front of her, and continued to flirt outrageously. "You are a woman after my own heart, Ms. James."

Samantha turned her head to offer him a smile of thanks. Flyboy winked, Tyler scowled, and again she felt a flutter in her heart. And then, without thinking, Samantha blurted out her excitement at meeting the pilot she and Tyler had talked about in Texas. "I understand that you're the best pilot in the navy."

Flyboy's eyes twinkled with pure delight. "Yes ma'am, I most certainly am. And at the risk of not sounding modest enough, I must say I can fly anything, anywhere, anytime."

"So I've heard. I've even been told that you could probably manage a take off and landing with your eyes closed."

Flyboy and the other SEALs looked from Samantha to Tyler and back to Samantha. "Did Panther tell you that?"

It took Samantha a moment to realize that Flyboy was talking about Tyler. Like most of the guys on the team, he had a nickname—a nickname she would ask him about later.

"Yes. He said you're the absolute best."

Surprisingly, Flyboy let out a hoot of laughter. "Well now, that's saying quite a lot coming from the lieutenant here."

"Did Panther also tell you that I taught Flyboy everything he knows about flying?" This came from Kid, the youngest member of the team.

"The hell you did, youngster. Whatever Flyboy learned he learned from me." Mac obviously wanted to get into the act.

"Give it up, Mac. You couldn't fly your way out of a paper bag." Now it was Billy's turn to speak up.

"Are you kidding me? I could fly circles around you and we all know it."

"Care to put your money where your mouth is?"

Samantha listened with pure glee as the men started arguing around the table. She was having the time of her life. Here she was, surrounded by the best-looking men on the face of the earth, all arguing among themselves in an effort to impress her. *What girl wouldn't love this?* she thought as she felt Tyler's hand settle on her arm.

"We're outta here." Tyler shouted over the voices that were still raised in dispute over who was the best flyer on the team.

"But I'm not finished with my coffee." Samantha raised her own voice of protest as he stood and tried to urge her along.

"I'll get you another cup later." He tugged and she reluctantly let him pull her to her feet.

"Ah, come on, Lieutenant. Let the lady stay and finish her coffee." Flyboy was at it again. "We haven't settled who's the best pilot on the team, and I for one want that cleared up once and for all."

"There's nothing to clear up." This came from Medicine Man, who until this moment had stayed quiet. "Everyone here knows I'm the one who taught you everything you know about flying." And with those words, the men started in on each other again—only this time the disagreement was even louder.

"I'll see you guys at 0500 on Monday." Tyler yelled out the command. "And don't call me over the weekend, and stay the hell away from my house. I don't want to hear or see any of you unless it's an emergency. Understand?"

Heads nodded, okays were muttered, and there was even one "yes sir" in there. And as Tyler and Samantha headed out of the conference room, the argument ensued.

"How long will that go on?" she asked around a bubble of laughter.

"Not long. Everyone knows that Flyboy's the best, and fighting over the issue was pretty much for your benefit."

"How sweet." She peeked over at Tyler as she spoke and wasn't disappointed when another scowl crossed his face. *Could he be a little jealous?* She hoped that was the case.

"Sweet has nothing to do with it, Sam. You're a beautiful, desirable woman and the guys are…well, let's just say that they're guys. And anytime you take a room full of testosterone and throw a lovely woman into the mix, the end result is one huge pissing contest."

"I don't care what you say, Tyler Garrett. I think those guys are sweet. And don't you try to talk me out of it."

His only response was an exaggerated groan.

"Oh stop being such a jerk. There's nothing wrong with being called sweet, even if the adjective is used to describe a room full of really buff guys."

"I think I'll keep that little tidbit between you and me," he chuckled. "*Sweet* is not exactly an adjective that's normally used to describe a Navy SEAL."

"Then what is?"

He smoothly changed the subject just as they reached her car. "My jeep's back at my house. I rode in with Mac this morning. Do you want to drive or want me to drive?"

Even though Samantha was thrilled that Tyler seemed pleased to see her, she just had to ask one more time. "I know I've caught you off guard by showing up here unannounced, so you need to be honest and tell me if my being here is not convenient for you."

Tyler gave her a low, sexy smile. "I'm pleased as hell that you're here, Sam, and there's no one I'd rather have show up unannounced. There's no doubt about that."

He couldn't have said anything better, and since that's all she needed to hear, Samantha reached into her purse and threw him her car keys. "You drive."

She waited until they left the base before she asked the question again. "So, what sort of adjective is normally used when describing a Navy SEAL?"

Again there was that low, sexy, chuckle. "Well, to be honest, you'll usually hear people refer to us as determined, strong-willed, authoritative, autocratic, and…well, you get the picture."

"It sounds to me like you're describing yourself, Tyler. Or do those characteristics apply to all Navy SEALs?" There was laughter in her voice.

"Point well taken." It surprised her that he didn't seem the least bit put off by her observation. "And believe it or not, we all pretty much fall into the same category of adjectives. Oh, and did I forget to mention that we are always referred to as very, very smart and very, very sexy?"

Samantha couldn't stop the laughter. He was being so charming and so cute that she just couldn't help herself. "By the way," she added with a smile, "where are we going?" She suddenly realized that she'd let him take control and hadn't a clue where they were heading.

"I thought we'd go over to my place. We can have a drink out on the deck and then decide where we want to go to dinner. Is that okay with you?"

"That sounds wonderful." She was actually breathless with anticipation.

"I live right around the corner. Since I never know when I'll be needed to report for duty at a moment's notice, I lucked out and found a house close to the base."

He turned onto a street that resembled a typical beach community. The houses were all small, very close together, and had tiny alleyways in between each one of them. The narrow street afforded the view of the back of the houses, as the front of the houses faced the ocean. To Samantha it was the perfect place for the man driving her car to live. And she felt a pang of envy as he turned her car into the driveway and parked next to a brand new Jeep.

Tyler turned off the ignition, climbed out of the car, and hurried over to open her door. He reached in to help Samantha out. "You car's safe here in the driveway. Mine stays here and no one bothers it. The neighbors all look out for each other."

Samantha was so taken with the sun, which was just starting its descent, that she hadn't noticed at first that Tyler had tucked her small hand in his. But as she drew in the beauty of the sunset, she also drew in the feel of his warm hand against her skin.

"If we hurry, we can catch the rest of the sunset off the deck, with a glass of wine."As he pulled her along, she noted that he must have noticed how entranced she was with the view spilling out before her.

In record time Tyler had ushered Samantha into the house and onto the deck overlooking the ocean. He excused himself just as she drew in a deep breath, and before she knew it he was placing a cool glass of wine in her hand. He had a cold beer for himself.

"It's so beautiful here, Tyler. The sunset is breathtaking."

"Here's to beautiful and breathtaking" he whispered as he touched the tip of his beer bottle against the glass she held in her hand. "And I'm not referring to the sunset."

As he whispered those few words, Samantha drew her eyes away from the sunset. She tilted her head toward Tyler, and the look in his eyes told her that she had heard him correctly. He was calling *her* both beautiful and breathtaking, and because her mouth was suddenly drier than a desert, all she could manage was a long, slow swallow of the refreshing wine.

The corners of Tyler's eyes crinkled as he grinned down at her. But all too soon he turned away, leaned his forearms on top of the deck's railing, and took a long, slow drink of his own. "I don't think I'll ever get tired of this view. Sometimes when I'm out of the country in some godforsaken place in the Middle East, I close my eyes and think about standing out on this deck, and watching a sunset just like this."

His eyes were focused straight ahead, and for some reason Samantha suspected that he'd just shared something very private with her. "Does it help?" she asked quietly.

"Yeah. It does." He took another taste of beer. "Especially when I'm gone for months at a time."

"I can see how you'd miss this place. It's really lovely. How did you ever come across it?"

"Are you trying to find out, without asking me point blank, how I can afford a house on the beach on what I get paid?"

At first Samantha thought he was serious, and she was appalled that he'd think she would care or ask about such a thing. Then, before she could answer, he dipped his head and kissed her lightly on her temple. "Just kidding."

It was the kiss that rendered her speechless. Even though he barely touched her with his lips, she felt her pulse start to beat like a drum.

"Aren't you the least bit curious how I can afford this place?"

"Should I be?" She had finally found her voice.

"Believe it or not, most people I meet are not only curious about how a career Navy SEAL can afford a beach house, albeit a small beach house, and some are even rude enough to ask."

"Well I'm neither curious enough nor rude enough to ask." The truth was that she was just as curious as most and was dying to ask, but she'd never let him know that.

"Did Katie ever tell you about our grandparents?"

Samantha was so taken aback by the sudden change of topic that she almost asked him where in the world had that question come from. Instead she answered him, suspecting that the off-the-wall question was leading somewhere.

"She told me once that both of you were very close to your grandparents and that they died the year before she went off to college. If I'm not mistaken, I think she told me they both died in a boating accident."

"Did she tell you that when they died, they left Katie and me a big chunk of money?"

Ah, now she knew where this was heading. "No. We never talked much about money."

"Yeah, we never did either. That's why it was such a surprise to Katie and me when we found out my grandparents had a bundle of money, and they left most of it to us. Katie used her share of the inheritance to go to college, and I plunked mine down on this house. It came on the market right before housing in San Diego went through the roof, so I really lucked out." Samantha reached out and laid her hand on Tyler's arm. "The place is in pretty good shape, although I've been thinking about doing a little remodeling. But the problem with that plan is I'm away so much of the time."

Reminding her of what he did for a living reminded her that there was something else she'd wanted to ask him about. But she stayed silent for a few seconds, wanting to see if he'd continue talking to her about his life. When it became obvious that he'd said all he was going to say, she plunged right in.

"I couldn't help but notice that some of the guys on your team referred to you as Panther. How in the world did you get that nickname?"

"I was afraid you'd get around to asking me about that."

There was no way she was going to let him get out of answering her. "Come on, Tyler, out with it. Most of the guys seem to have nicknames, and I can figure out how they came up with most of them. Flyboy is pretty obvious, as is Medicine Man. But you'll have to help me out on this nickname of yours."

He was quiet for so long that she thought he might actually refuse to answer her, which of course just made her all the more curious.

"It's really no big deal, Samantha." He startled her when he started speaking. And because she didn't want to give him any reason not to continue, she stayed silent and sipped her wine.

"I picked up the nickname after a mission we were on...oh, I don't know...about ten years ago. We were called in for a hostage extraction, which is what Team Mega One specializes in. We infiltrated a small village tucked away in the Costa Rican jungle, in the dead of night. We got out four hostages and made our way immediately to the extraction point, where the helo would pick us up. Afterwards, when we were all packed safely into the helo, one of the women hostages told me that because we were all dressed in black, and because of the way I moved, I reminded her of a panther. She said I looked and moved just like a black panther: sleek, silent, and stealthy. Well, that's all the guys needed to hear. It started out as a joke, with everyone calling me Panther. But somehow, even after the joke wore off, the nickname didn't. I've been called Panther ever since. Along with a few other choice names I'd rather not share with you right now."

Samantha's mind was suddenly on overload. He'd given her so much information about himself all at once and she had tons of questions. Why was he in Costa Rica? Who were the hostages? How long was he there? Who was the woman who called him a panther? She doubted that he'd actually answer any of those questions, but she decided to give it a shot anyway.

"Why would a team of SEALs be sent into Costa Rica to rescue some hostages? Wouldn't the Costa Rican officials deal with a kidnapping?"

"They would if this were a regular, run-of-the-mill hostage situation. You know, the kind you read about in the papers all the time. But this particular village, where the hostages were being held, was a cover for a small terrorist cell. And this was a cell that naval intel had been targeting for a long time. So the chance to extract four individuals who might be able to give the intel guys some useful information about their abductors was the opportunity they'd been waiting for. So, navy intel contacted us. We went in, got the hostages out, and handed them over to the Pentagon."

"How long were you there?"

"Not long." *Uh oh*, she thought. One and two-word answers were always an indication that Tyler was getting ready to close the lid on a particular subject.

"So who were the hostages?"

"I can't tell you that, Sam."

"Okay, but can I ask you just one more question?"

"You can ask." His response implied that she might not get an answer.

"The woman. The one who said you reminded her of a black panther. A sleek, silent, stealthy panther. Did you ever see her again?"

"Why would you think I'd see her again?"

She'd gone this far, so there was no backing down now. "Because her description of you was right on the money, and sexy as hell. And I have to wonder about a woman who would come up with such a tantalizing description. Trust me Tyler, her words, though accurate, were meant to seduce. And knowing you as well as I do, my bet is you didn't miss the subtle invitation." He threw her a look that said, *You've got to be kidding.*

"So, did you see that woman again?"

"No. I did not. And that's the end of this subject."

She loved it when she could make him squirm, which wasn't very often. But because she got the answer she was hoping for, she let the matter drop.

"It's getting kinda late." The sun had gone down and the night had settled in around them. "We can go somewhere for dinner or if you want I can throw a couple of steaks on the grill."

It took Samantha all of two seconds to make up her mind. "I'd rather not go out, Tyler. I'd rather stay in with you." She didn't even try to pretend that she was talking about dinner. She'd come to San Diego with a packed overnight bag, and they hadn't really broached the subject of why she was here. As much as she enjoyed getting to know a side of Tyler that she suspected he kept locked away, what she really wanted was to get to know him in bed. And if she didn't do something about it soon, she was pretty sure she'd go stark raving mad. "Steaks on the grill would be very nice, but that's not really why I'm here."

She watched as Tyler took in the full meaning of what she'd just said. She'd laid her cards on the table and now it was up to him.

"I need to ask you one more time, Sam." He had moved closer to her and his voice had taken on a husky sound. "Are you sure about this?"

They both knew exactly what he was talking about. She was so glad it was finally out in the open, and she wasted no time in letting him know exactly how she felt.

"I'm here because I want to be with you, Tyler. I'm a big girl and I'm not asking for anything from you beyond this weekend. I've tried to get you out of my head these past six weeks, and nothing I do is working. So, I came here hoping that you still want to be with me." She waited a few seconds before adding. "No strings attached."

Tyler eyes left her face and he stared out into the darkness before turning back to her. For a brief second he was amazed at how beautiful she looked bathed by the light of the moon. "I've wanted to make love to you from the moment I set eyes on you, Samantha, and that hasn't changed. And right now I think I'd give up ten years of my life to spend this weekend with you. But even though you say you don't expect anything more from me, I'm not sure that's fair to either one of us."

"I don't understand, Tyler." And she really didn't. "What are you saying?"

"I'm only saying the same thing I told you six weeks ago in Texas. I'm simply not interested in any more one-night stands. I've had enough of those to last me a lifetime, and I don't think it's something you're cut out for either."

She could hardly believe her ears. "Are you saying you want us to have more than just this weekend? That you want there to be something more between us?" Her heart was beating a mile a minute and she felt as though her life depended on his answer.

"All I'm saying is that you deserve more than just two days of sex. You deserve a chance at a long-term, committed relationship."

"And what about you? Don't you think you deserve the same?"

He finished his beer in one long swallow. "Even if I thought we could work on having that type of relationship, the reality is that we could spend the next two days together and then I could be gone, without you even knowing it, for weeks, or even months. Are you prepared to deal with that, Sam? Because if we decide to take whatever this thing is between us to another level, you need to know exactly what you're getting into. My job takes precedence over anyone or anything. I get a call and I go. It's as simple as that. Other women in my life haven't been able to put up with what I do for very long.

They always say they don't want more, but in the end, when I can't give them what they need, the relationship falls apart."

That was quite a speech and Samantha didn't even need to think about her response. It came right from her heart. "I'm not most women, Tyler."

Her whispered words touched a spot in his heart that he thought was immune. And as he thought about her straightforward response, he studied her for a while, letting his eyes sweep over her upturned face.

"Be careful what you wish for, Sam. You might be sorry."

"I'm willing to take that risk."

"Are you?"

"Yes."

He thought about that for a moment."Then you want to give this thing between us a try? Starting with this weekend? Even though I can't promise you where it will end up?"

"Yes." Again, her answer was simple and to the point.

"Because," he added with what sounded like a note of caution in his voice, "once I get you into the bedroom, you are all mine. And you'll be lucky if I let you out of my bed before Monday. What I told you in Texas still stands. I have thought of at least a hundred different ways I want to make love to you, and I plan to keep you in bed until we try out as many as possible."

Her breath caught in her throat and her words came out on a sigh. "Since I'm planning on *not* leaving your bed all weekend, there shouldn't be any problem."

And that was all Tyler needed to hear. Without hesitation, he took her wine glass out of her hand and set her glass and his beer bottle down on the railing. And then he leaned down and swept her up into his arms. She wound her arms around his neck at the same instant that his mouth came down to take possession of hers. And Samantha believed that she would have fallen to the ground if he hadn't been holding her in his arms. The kiss was that incredible.

Samantha signed into Tyler's mouth and he slipped his tongue between her parted lips. As she lost herself in his sampling of her sweet, moist mouth, he turned with her in his arms and headed into the house. His tongue took its time tasting, his arms tightened around her, and he never faltered in his determination to get her into the bedroom. Never lifting his mouth from hers, he walked into the house, through the living room, and turned toward the hall. Tyler stopped just long enough to lift his head to change the angle of the kiss. He looked down at her just as she lifted her soft, dazed eyes. Her mouth was moist from his kisses and her breathing was as ragged as his. He took her mouth again. And as she returned his kiss with a sweep of her own tongue, he started back down the hall. Tyler finally reached his bedroom door and had started to push it open with his foot just as the doorbell starting ringing.

At first Samantha thought there was a ringing in her ears, but then Tyler stopped dead in his tracks and she knew that something was wrong. As the ringing continued, he slowly lifted his head. He stood with her in his arms and shifted his gaze toward the ringing coming from front door. The doorbell rang again.

Without saying a word, Tyler lowered Samantha to her feet. The doorbell rang again. Tyler looked down at Samantha and ran a hand through his hair. The doorbell rang again. "I'll be right back," he whispered, and she noticed that his words were a little raw. Before she could stop him, he left her standing alone in the darkened hallway and made his way to the front door. She walked over and stood at the end of the hall and watched as he flipped on the hall light. The doorbell rang again. Since it was in Samantha's nature to satisfy her curiosity, she walked over and joined Tyler, right before he opened the door. And that is when all hell broke loose.

In less than one second, six large, loud Navy SEALs came barreling into the house. They had all changed out of their uniforms into casual clothes and they held a variety of pizza boxes in their hands. One of the guys carried two six packs of beer and another had an extra large bottle of red wine. They came in uninvited, full of mischief, and obviously prepared to stay, at least through dinner.

"Hey, Panther. Hey, Miss James. We thought you might like a little pizza."

"Who wants beer and who wants wine?"

"Hey man, its dark in here. We need a little light."

Once the guys were in the house, they started making themselves right at home, which Samantha suspected they did quite often. But this time Tyler wasn't going to let them get away with it. "Stop right there!" He barked out what sounded like an order, but no one paid him the least bit of attention. "Don't you even think that you're staying for dinner. I want you to take your pizza and get the hell out of my house." Still, no one was listening. "I am not going to say it again. Go home!"

"What kind of pizza do you want, Lieutenant?"

Samantha couldn't keep it in one more second. The scene before her was hilarious. It was so obvious that the guys showed up just to give Tyler a hard time, and they were having a ball. And when Scotty looked around in all innocence and asked Tyler what kind of pizza he wanted, she lost it and doubled over in laughter.

"This is really not funny, Samantha." Tyler sounded so exasperated that she started laughing all over again.

"My God, Tyler, will you look at them. They think they are at home."

As Tyler looked around, he finally saw some of the humor in the absurd situation. In less than two minutes, his teammates had managed to turn his house upside down. Pizza boxes were strewn all over the kitchen counters. Men were sprawled all over the furniture and on the floor, with a slice of pizza in one hand and a beer in the other. The lights had been turned on all over the house, and everyone was talking at once—everyone, that is, except for the two people the guys had come over to have dinner with.

"I think we're outnumbered," Samantha murmured right before she walked into the kitchen and selected a slice of cheesy pizza.

With one more glance at the motley crew gathered in his living room, Tyler went up and snatched a beer right out of Mac's hand. "You had all better be gone in one hour. Do you hear me? One hour. If this house is not cleared out in the next sixty minutes, I swear the first chance I get I'm going to volunteer every one of you for a mission somewhere in Iceland." He tried to sound threatening but even he couldn't quite stop the beginning of a grin. But because he wanted them to think he was dead serious, he drilled each man with steel-cold eyes and then took a drink of Mac's beer.

"Hey, give me back my beer."

Tyler passed the bottle back to Mac just as Samantha came out of the kitchen. She had piled a couple slices of pizza onto a plate and had helped herself to a beer. She handed both off to Tyler as she folded her legs under her and sat down on the floor.

Tyler just looked around and knew that he didn't stand a chance. So with reluctant resignation, he handed her back both the plate and the beer and leaned down to whisper into her ear. "Keep an eye on these guys for me. I'm going to change out of my uniform."

Samantha nodded around a bite of pizza and resisted the urge to turn and watch him leave the room. She loved watching him walk and secretly agreed that he moved just like a panther.

"So, Miss James, how long have you known the lieutenant?"

It came out like a casual question from Medicine Man, but she knew better. These guys were not only here to give their leader a hard time but to look out for him as well. She was an unknown, and they were a group of guys who didn't like dealing with unknowns. So this little impromptu dinner had more than one purpose, and she found that she didn't mind a bit. As a matter of fact, she was looking forward to the challenge. *So let the interrogation begin*, she thought as she met their looks head on.

"I met Tyler six weeks ago at his parents' home in Burns, Texas. And please, won't you all call me Samantha."

"That's right. Panther went home on leave. Do you live in Burns, Samantha?"

"I live in Los Angeles. I'd gone to Burns to visit Katie, Tyler's sister."

"Ah, so you're a friend of Katie's?" Billy asked the question around a bite of pizza.

"Yes. We went to college together."

"Cool." This came from Kid, the youngster. "Although I gotta say, Samantha, I've been to Burns once with Panther, and there's not a whole lot to do there."

"Well, actually, this last visit with Katie was more of a business trip for me. I went to get some firsthand information on flying for an article I was writing."

"Ah, so you're a writer?" Flyboy threw the question over his shoulder as he walked into the kitchen to grab a beer.

"Yes, I write. But I'd rather be referred to as a journalist." The second the words were out of her mouth, she wondered if these men felt the same way about journalists that Tyler did. She didn't have to wait long to find out.

"Holy shit, Samantha. You're a journalist?"

It was now or never. If she wanted to win these guys over, she had to be up front and completely honest with them. There could be no holding back. She knew it and they knew it. And since she truly believed in what she was about to say, that made it a whole lot easier.

"I think I know how you all feel about journalists, and I'll tell you exactly what I told Tyler. There are good journalists and bad journalists in this world, and I'll always do my very best to be one of the good guys. Believe me, we had words over what I do for a living more than once. And in the end, I asked Tyler not to judge what I do because of what happened to Kent, but to give me a chance and judge me on my own merit. And I'm here now because he's decided to do just that."

"Did Tyler tell you about Kent Richards, or did Katie tell you what happened?" There was a hint of disbelief in Flyboy's voice.

"Tyler told me." She didn't explain any further.

"Then that's good enough for us."

Just like that she could tell that she'd passed their test. And it wasn't hard for her to figure out why. If Tyler had told her something as personal as the story about Kent's death, then she knew his men would figure that she might be someone special in his life. At least that's what she hoped they thought, because she liked and respected these men and wanted them to like and respect her in return.

"So, how long are you staying in San Diego?"

Samantha didn't have a chance to respond, as Tyler came back into the room, sat down beside her, and draped an arm over her shoulder. "Enough with the twenty questions. I want you guys to drink your beer, and eat your pizza so you can go home."

Samantha laughed, the guys completely ignored him once again, and Tyler finally gave up. And as everyone ate, drank, and relaxed, one hour started to slip into two. The time passed quickly, with each man trying to top the other by telling the most outrageous stories. They told tales on each other, making sure that they didn't pass up an opportunity to pick on Tyler. Every man on Team Mega One had some sort of anecdote about the leader of their pack, and Samantha laughed so hard that at times she would almost topple over. But when ten o'clock finally rolled around, Tyler did something that truly amazed her. He got up, walked quietly over to the front door, and opened it. He didn't say one word. He just stood there and waited until each of the men on his team got the message and started to file out.

"Goodnight, Samantha."

"Night, Sam."

"See ya around, Samantha."

"It was a pleasure to meet you, Samantha."

When the last man finally walked out, Tyler closed and locked the door behind them. Samantha, needing no further encouragement, got up, walked over, and joined him in the tiny entryway. She had kicked off her shoes sometime during the last hour, and now she stood before him in her pretty white sundress, barefoot and incredibly sexy.

"I'm sorry." His words were soft.

"Don't be," she whispered back. "The guys are pretty terrific."

"The guys are in a shitload of trouble with me. And they'll all pay, come Monday." She could hear the amusement in his voice.

Samantha reached up and drew the backs of her fingers over his five o'clock shadow. "Those guys care about you, Tyler. And they were only here to check me out."

He reached up and took hold of her hand, brought it around to his mouth, and kissed the tips of her fingers. "Those guys were only here to give me a bad time. And come Monday morning they'll wish they'd stayed the hell away."

"What are you going to do?" She asked with a shiver, as his mouth found its way to the palm of her hand. His lips rested against her palm.

"I think my team may have fallen a little behind in their underwater demolition training." His tongue touched and played seductively with her palm. "So I think that some additional training is in order." His free hand trailed slowly up and down her arm. "Yeah, I think the guys are in need of about eight long, hard hours of underwater training."

Samantha laughed softly but was distracted by the feel of his lips against the palm of her hand and the feel of his fingers against her skin. She took a small step toward Tyler, sighed, and leaned in to kiss him lightly on his cheek. He kept the palm of her hand against his lips and he breathed in her scent. She lingered, letting herself enjoy the feel of his warm breath, until he took his mouth away from her hand.

"So, where were we?" His voice was low and raspy.

At the sound of Tyler's voice and the look in his eyes, another shiver went through Samantha—a shiver of excitement and anticipation. And because she couldn't seem to form a coherent thought in her head, she responded to his question without words. Keeping her own eyes focused on his, she lifted slightly trembling fingers to the buttons on her sundress. With slow but deliberate movements, she began to unbutton her dress.

As Samantha's fingers moved down the front of her dress, so did Tyler's eyes. He stood absolutely still, watching as each button slid through the next buttonhole, providing him with a brief glimpse of satiny, smooth skin—skin that he was dying to touch and taste. But because he sensed that it was important to Samantha that she be the one in control, he kept his hands at his sides while he let his eyes drink in the sight of her.

Samantha may not have had much experience when it came to men, but she was no fool. She knew, just by watching the man standing before her, what an effort it was for him not to reach out and touch. And she gloried in the fact that she was the cause of the little twitch in his tightly locked jaw. She also didn't miss the fevered look in his eyes.

After she slipped loose the last button, she then reached up and slid the straps of her sundress off her shoulders. With just a slight swish of her hips, the dress slid down her body, pooling at her bare feet. And there she stood, in the most scant, laciest bra she ever wore, with equally scant lacy panties.

Tyler, still standing ramrod still, closed his eyes for one second so that he could clear his head. He needed to get a grip on himself. Otherwise he was going to throw Samantha down on the floor and make love to her right there in the entryway. When he felt like he was getting his mind and his body somewhat under control, he risked opening his eyes. And that's when he lost it. She just looked so inviting and so tempting that he gave up trying to get a grip. And before she had a chance to do or say a thing, he reached out and pulled her into his arms.

Tyler's lips found hers and he forgot that he wanted to be gentle and seductive. He crushed her tightly against his hard, throbbing body as his tongue found its way almost roughly into her mouth. He tasted, savored, and ravaged her mouth. And surprisingly, she tasted, savored, and ravaged him right back. Samantha reached up, wrapped her arms around his neck, and leaned into him as closely as she could. She felt as though she wanted to crawl right through his skin because she just couldn't seem to get close enough.

Tyler managed to let go of her only long enough to reach out one hand and turn off the light. Then he placed both hands on her waist and lifted her up. She responded by wrapping her legs around his waist. They accomplished all of this without breaking the kiss.

With Samantha's arms and legs wrapped around him, Tyler headed straight for the bedroom. He made it there in record time. Lifting his mouth so that they could both take a long-overdue breath, Tyler put one knee on the mattress and laid her down on the bed. He followed with his body covering hers. Samantha closed her eyes as desire shot through every inch of her. Feeling the length of Tyler's hard body pressed into hers almost brought her over the edge.

Tyler lifted his weight off Samantha by resting his forearms an either side of her head. He allowed himself the luxury of watching her as she struggled to regain control of her breathing. His own breathing was deep, ragged, and way too fast. Like his heartbeat, he needed to slow himself down.

"I've never wanted a woman so badly in my life." His words were spoken as he dropped his head and placed his hot open mouth at the side of Samantha's neck. She felt desire like a bolt of lightening and tightened her legs, which were still wrapped around his waist. He reacted by placing slow, wet kisses down her exposed throat. At the same time that his mouth explored her throat, one of his hands started doing some exploring of its own.

Keeping his weight balanced on one forearm, he let his fingertips trail slowly up Samantha's arm, lightly across her shoulder, and down to her breast. His fingers lightly skimmed over her lacy bra, letting his mind fill with the scent of her. And in that instant, Tyler knew that he had to taste her again.

He lifted his mouth from her throat, captured her lips, and proceeded to kiss her in a way that was almost vulgar. His tongue slipped in and out of her mouth, imitating the act of making love. His hand settled over her breast. He let his lower body sink deeply into hers. He pressed himself against the center of her. He was ready, and he wanted her to know it.

Samantha was so attuned to his every move, his every touch, and his every groan that she reached between their bodies with one hand and tore apart the buttons on his shirt. Some came through the buttonholes and others scattered as they were torn away. She needed to feel his skin. She needed to run her hands over his chest. She too was ready, and she wanted him to know it.

Somehow Tyler broke contact between them just long enough to shrug out of his shirt. As his shirt hit the floor, he was pulled back down by Samantha, who brought his mouth down to hers. And this time she initiated a kiss that all but blew his mind.

Because he simply couldn't stop himself, his hands were now all over her body. He had unfastened the front clasp of her bra and he cupped her warm, round breast in the palm of his hand. She arched into his hand. And while he was pleasing her with his touch at her breast, her hands were touching every inch of his bare skin. She skimmed her hands slowly up and down his back. And when she felt his body react to her touch, she let her nails follow the path her hands had taken. Their kisses were long, hot, and carnal. They were lost in each other and were giving in to their building desire more and more by the second.

Tyler didn't so much as lift his head as he kissed his way across Samantha's chin, down her neck, and over her collarbone, finally reaching his destination.

As they both touched and took from one another, they were both so caught up in their foreplay that neither one heard the cell phone that was ringing on the nightstand. It rang once, twice, and on the third ring Tyler snapped his head up, closed his eyes, and shook his head as if he were in a fog. On the fourth ring, he whipped his head around, reached out to turn on the bedside light, and grabbed up the phone.

At first Samantha had trouble adjusting to the sudden light in the room. Within seconds her eyes adapted to the brightness, and then all she could do was watch in a haze of desire as he spoke into the phone. "Lieutenant Garrett." His voice was so raspy he sounded like he was in dire need of a drink of water.

"What time?" He asked, and almost instantly he sounded more like himself.

Samantha was amazed that he could pull himself together so fast, when she was having a difficult time finding her sense of balance. She was still wrapped all around him, wanting desperately to pull him back down into her arms. But something in his eyes told her that this phone call was all business. And as soon as she realized that, she felt a sick feeling deep in her stomach.

She continued staring at Tyler as he listened intently and took in whatever information was being given to him. The look on his face was no longer that of a lover. He looked serious, intent, and focused. Instinctively Samantha knew that their time together was over, at least for tonight. Whoever was on the phone was commanding all of his attention. With an inward sigh of regret, she unwrapped her legs from around his waist and dropped her hands from his shoulders. He held the cell phone to his ear with one hand while still balancing himself on his other forearm. His eyes were latched on to Samantha's face.

"Will you contact the others?"

His green eyes had lost their drowsy, sensual look. His eyes were now clear and alert.

"Yes sir, I'll be there at 2300 hours."

Samantha knew that in military time 2300 hours was eleven o'clock at night, which meant that she had less than an hour left to be with him.

Tyler snapped shut his cell phone, pulled himself off of Samantha, and rolled onto his back. Staring up at the ceiling, he reached for her hand. "I have to go."

She noticed right away that he didn't offer any type of an apology. He didn't say "I'm sorry, but I have to go." He didn't say "I hope you'll understand, but I have to go." He didn't even say "I don't want to, but I have to go." He simply stated "I have to go." Since she wasn't sure what to say, she squeezed his hand.

They lay side by side for a few minutes, holding hands, both lost in their own thoughts. Finally, when Samantha couldn't stand the silence any longer, she turned onto her side, wanting to look at him when she spoke.

"I understand." She wanted to say more but those were the only words that came out.

"Do you?" He released her hand, sat up, and swung his legs over the side of the bed.

She reached out to touch him, but he stood before her hand reached his wonderfully bare back.

Tyler walked over to a closet and reached up to take down a duffel bag. Next he pulled out a backpack. Both were fully packed. As he took down his gear, Samantha re-hooked her bra and sat up in bed, bringing her knees up to her chin. She wrapped her arms around her legs and laid her cheek on top of her knees, never taking her eyes off of him. She watched as he opened a drawer and pulled out a pair of camouflage pants, and an olive green T-shirt. Without any shyness on his part, he stripped out of his jeans. And then he stepped into the pants, pulled on the drab green T-shirt, and tucked it into the waistband. Next he slipped a belt through the belt loops around his waist. He went back over to the closet and pulled out a pair of lace-up boots. He walked back over to the bed, sat down with his back to Samantha, and put them on, tucking the pants down into the boots. In less than a minute he was dressed and ready to go.

Samantha was so mesmerized watching him getting dressed that she forget that she was still in her bra and panties, sitting on his bed, acting as if she had all the time in the world. As the reality of their situation hit her, she bounded from the bed, ready to run in the direction of the entryway to retrieve her sundress. She rounded the bed and started for the door when unexpectedly Tyler's hand reached out to stop her. His fingers grabbed her around the wrist, pulling her back from her dead run. Even though she felt self-conscious that he was fully dressed while she was half naked, she didn't even try to stop him as he pulled her to him and onto his lap.

He pulled her down, wrapped his arms around her, and laid his head in the crook of her neck. He took a long, deep breath and she wondered if he was trying to take her scent with him. As Tyler continued to hold her, she wrapped her arms around him. Her fingers found their way into his hair, stroking and loving the feel of it between her fingers. She felt her heart swell and tears building.

Too soon Tyler lifted his head, leaned back, and looked into her moist eyes. His own eyes narrowed for just a second as he noticed she was trying to blink back tears. But wisely he didn't comment about it, and neither did she. Instead he leaned forward and kissed her softy on her trembling lips.

"I've only got a few more minutes, Samantha, and then I've got to go."

"I know." Her voice cracked.

"I don't know when I'll be able to see you again."

"I know."

"I don't even know when or if I'll be able to call you."

"I know." She realized that he was all but telling her that he was being sent out of the country on one of his mysterious missions.

Tyler bent his head and kissed her again. But this time he kissed her on the tip of her nose and Samantha thought that was even more romantic than if he'd kissed her fully on the mouth. Without saying anything further, he lifted her from his lap and headed into the small bathroom.

With a heavy heart, Samantha went in search of the sundress she had slipped out of less than an hour ago. She found it in a puddle on the floor of the entryway. She put it back on and felt a little better now that she was dressed. She found her shoes in the living room and slipped those onto her feet. Just like Tyler, in less than a minute she was dressed and ready to go.

He came out of the bedroom with his backpack slung over one shoulder and his duffel in his hand. He also had some sort of high-tech weapon slung over his other shoulder. He looked so soldier-like that Samantha said the first words that came to mind.

"Oh my God, Tyler. You look like you're ready to jump right out of a plane in some very faraway place." As soon as those words left her mouth, she realized how real that possibility was.

"Listen, Sam." He sat his duffel down as he came up to her. "It doesn't make sense for you to make the drive back to L.A. tonight." It didn't get past her that he ignored her comment about his jumping out of a plane. "Why don't you stay here? Just because I have to leave, doesn't mean you have to. You can spend the rest of the weekend enjoying the beach if you want, and head back as you'd planned on Sunday."

"I…I don't know." She was still trying to get her mind around the fact that after they'd come so close to finally making love, he was up and leaving her. Sure, she knew it wasn't his fault, and he'd warned her that this could happen, but her mind was still a little muddled over the whole thing.

He reached up and touched her cheek. "I wish you'd stay. I like the idea of thinking about you sleeping in my bed. Even though we didn't get quite that far, at least I'll know that for a couple of days anyway, you were curled up under my sheets."

There was no way in the world Samantha could tell him no, especially since she wanted to stay in the worst way. She felt that if she stayed in his house, and in his bed, she would always have a part of him with her—a part of him that she would tuck away in her memories.

"I'll stay, Tyler. Thank you for offering."

He took her hand, turned it palm up, and dropped a key into it. "Here's the house key. Just lock up when you leave. And if you don't mind, would you take the key to my neighbor to the right? I'll pick it up when I get back."

She closed her fingers tightly around the key. "Okay." That was all she could manage, because tears were threatening to fall again.

Tyler picked up his duffel bag. Then he reached out and took hold of Samantha's hand. They walked over to the front door.

"This is how it is, Sam. It will always be like this."

"I don't care." She made herself hold back the tears. There would be plenty of time for tears after he was gone. "I'm not going to give up on us."

"You may change your mind after you've had a chance to think about it."

"I won't." She was firm in her resolve and she wanted him to know it.

"You mean you'll wait for me?"

"Yes…if you want me to."

Tyler had never asked a woman to wait for him in his life. He never wanted that kind of responsibility. He wanted to be able leave on a mission without thoughts of anyone left behind. So he was surprised with the words that came out of his mouth.

"I want you to. I want to see you when I get back. I want to know that you're waiting for me to come home."

Samantha reached up and laid her hand against his cheek. Then she leaned in and kissed him. Her kiss was slow, sweet, and full of promise. "I'll be waiting, Tyler. I promise."

Tyler stared down into Samantha's upturned face until he heard someone honk a car horn. "That's Flyboy." He whispered against her parted lips. "He's picking me up." Not out of character, when he lifted his head everything about him became all business. "I'll let you know when I'm home. It could be days, weeks, or months. But I'll call you as soon as I'm back." He had instantly turned into Lieutenant Garrett, leader of SEAL Team Mega One. His manner and expression were quite serious.

Samantha stepped back as he opened the door, but before she let him go, she reached out and touched his arm. "Please stay safe, Tyler."

He nodded.

"Every day I'll ask God to watch out for you."

He didn't respond. He just watched her for a brief, fleeting second, the look in his eyes a look that Samantha couldn't quite place. Then he reached out and touched her lightly on her cheek one last time.

Samantha thought for a moment that he was going to say something. But instead he dropped his hand from her cheek and took one step out the door. He took another step and then stopped. He stood still, with his back to

Samantha, looking out into the night. Then he set his duffel bag down on the ground. Taking a deep, sobering breath, he looked at her over his shoulder, right before he turned around, walked back over to her, grabbed her around the waist, pulled her up against him, and kissed her goodbye like there was no tomorrow.

Chapter Nine

Two Months Later

"Welcome to the Nigerian border, Lieutenant Garrett."

Tyler shook hands with the commanding officer.

"Sorry to drag you and your men away from…where in the hell have you been anyway?"

"We've been back in Iraq these past two months."

"I thought you'd completed your tour of duty in that God-awful country."

"Yeah, well, we were needed to help out on a couple of rescue missions. Then, there was an investigation into a botched operation, so we were all held up another month."

"Who screwed up?"

"Intel."

"Figures."

Tyler and Commander Westinghouse made their way into the mess hall. It was right before dawn, so the place was deserted. They helped themselves to coffee and sat at the end of a long table. The makeshift marine base located on the border of Nigeria was fairly self-contained. It sat on ten acres and at any given time it housed over two hundred marines and navy personnel. All military personnel assigned to this base were *just passing through.* The base was considered temporary, even though it had been set up over a year ago. It had an airstrip, officers' quarters, and a command center.

"Do you know why you and your team are here, Lieutenant?"

Tyler took a sip of coffee. It tasted like shit but it was hot and had the hit of caffeine he needed. "All I was told was that we were needed for a special op that is at the highest security level."

"And I guess I don't need to tell you what that means."

"It means that we were never here."

Commander Westinghouse looked over at the SEAL, wishing that he had a better assignment for the young man. He knew that the mission he was about to send Team Mega One on was the kind that got men killed. It was fraught with too many unknowns, and lately the intel they received was less than totally reliable. But because of the nature of this mission, and because of who was being held hostage, he needed the expertise of the men on Tyler's team. He also needed absolute certainty that this op would be kept top secret and that there'd be no leaks after the mission was accomplished. And he knew that Lieutenant Garrett and his men had a reputation for completing dangerous, highly covert missions and keeping their ops under wraps.

"I don't have a lot of time to fill you in. Suffice it to say, now that you're here, this mission is scheduled for tomorrow. Are your men ready?"

"My men are always ready, Commander."

That was exactly the answer Commander Westinghouse had expected. "Then let's go over the details now. You'll need plenty of time to put your extraction plan together, because this extraction's going to be handled a little differently."

Tyler didn't ask what the commander meant by *differently*, because he knew that he'd find out soon enough.

"Okay Lieutenant, here's what we've got. Three days ago a group of Nigerian rebels kidnapped four doctors who had gone into a small village to perform surgery on kids with special needs. The doctors belong to an organization I'm sure you've heard of. They're all part of a network of healthcare professionals called Doctors Without Borders. They go into underprivileged areas in third-world countries, set up MASH-type surgery centers, and usually stay a couple of weeks."

"I've heard of them, Commander," Tyler interrupted. "They do some pretty remarkable work. But they usually go into places under the radar, and if I'm not mistaken they're usually well protected. What do the rebels want with them?"

"Good question, Lieutenant. And it's the first question we asked ourselves. But soon it became obvious that it's not the doctors the rebels were after."

Now the commander really had Tyler's attention. "How many hostages are being held?"

"Six."

"Okay. The rebels have four doctors, and two others. Who are the other two?" Tyler waited. He wanted to move this thing along, especially since the commander had already inferred he'd need most of the day to work out his extraction plan.

"It seems that this visit by Doctors Without Borders had some high-powered publicity behind it. There's a senator in Washington who's been trying to get the Senate to provide funding for the humanitarian projects of Doctors Without Borders. Our government is hesitating to make a financial commitment, so the senator figured some good publicity would help his cause. So he decided to send a couple of journalists along with the doctors to report on the conditions they work in and the success of their patients."

"Let me guess." Tyler interrupted again. "Now we also have two journalists who had no business being in a village in Nigeria being held hostage."

"That's it exactly, Lieutenant. And we need you and your team to go in and get them out."

Tyler was still trying to put all of the pieces together. "But what makes this rescue so top secret? There are four doctors, and two journalists. I don't get it."

"If you're finished with your coffee, let's walk over to my office and I'll fill you in on the rest."

Tyler shoved his coffee aside, scraped back his chair, and stood up. The commander led the way.

"There are two things that make this a top-secret mission, Lieutenant Garrett. First, one of the journalists being held happens to be the son of the senator who's trying to get the special funding. I'm pretty sure you know who I'm taking about. His name's Senator Cushman." Tyler's stomach tied up in knots at what he knew was coming. "As a matter of fact, I think you know the senator's son. I understand he went on a mission with you in Afghanistan two years ago. His name is David Cushman."

Tyler spoke through clenched teeth. "Yes, I know him."

"What we know from two undercover CIA agents who have infiltrated this group of rebels, is that the rebels found out the kid was coming to Nigeria, so the abduction was planned before he even got here. We're still not sure why they decided to nab the other journalist and the four doctors, unless it was to give them even more bargaining chips."

"What are they asking for?"

They reached the command headquarters and headed straight for the commander's office. There they each poured themselves another cup of awful-tasting coffee.

"That's reason number two why this mission is top secret. The rebels made an audiotape and sent their message directly to Senator Cushman, in Washington, D.C. They're demanding twenty million dollars, and they want it in two installments. When they receive the first ten million they'll let the doctors go. When they receive the balance, they'll let both journalists go."

"Does the senator have the money?"

"Actually, he does. But he's smart enough to know that while the rebels might let the doctors go, his son and the other journalist won't be as lucky. Once they're free, they'll have the power of the press at their fingertips, and that the rebels can't risk. So Senator Cushman called in favors from some very influential people. These influential people called us, and we called in you and your team."

Tyler figured that wasn't all there was to this mission. "Do we know what they plan to do with the twenty million?"

"The two undercover agents were very clear on that. It seems that the rebels have a pipeline to some very costly military weapons. Sale on the black market is going to the highest bidder, and twenty million bucks ought to buy them a lot of firepower."

"Shit! Sorry, sir. But it makes me crazy to think about military weapons falling into the wrong hands. "

"No need to apologize, Lieutenant. Those are my sentiments exactly."

"Where're the hostages being held?"

"Luckily, they're all together in a village about fifty miles east of here. It's fairly sophisticated, as villages go. The hostages are being held in a building made of cinderblock, and it's locked up tight as a drum. It's deep in the jungle, hard to get to, and fairly well guarded."

Commander Westinghouse opened his desk drawer and pulled out a bottle of whiskey. He splashed some into his tepid coffee and offered up the bottle to Tyler, who shook his heard. Six in the morning was a little too early for him to indulge.

"When you say the village is fairly well guarded, what are we up against?"

The commander took a long, hard drink. "Remember I told you that the exaction on this mission will be different?"

Tyler didn't answer. He knew the question was rhetorical.

"This village is operated by a group of rebels who have a legion of followers. The group inside is fairly small, so you shouldn't have any problem getting in. The problem will be in getting out and making it safely through the jungle to the extraction point. Once it's noticed that the hostages are gone, they'll put the word out and call on all the rebel troops around them. And when they do that, a group as large as the one you'll be leading will be way too easy to spot."

Tyler figured it out in a second. "So we're going to split up once we get the hostages out."

"Exactly. Once you have all six hostages, it'll be best if you all go in different directions. We'll arrange for different pickups over the next two days. You work that out with your men and our pilots."

Tyler wanted to get to work. He needed to bring his team up to date and work out the extraction plans.

"Here's a map of the area and a drawing of the village. The drawing is pretty crude, but it's the best the CIA guys could smuggle out." Commander Westinghouse handed over the documents. "We've also identified some other villages scattered throughout the jungle, with people who are willing to work with Americans. You and your men will need to hide out until extraction, and some of these people will help."

"Will the CIA guys be of any help?"

"No. Unfortunately they can't blow their cover. They need to stay entrenched with this band of rebels until they can get to the guys at the top."

"No problem. We'll get the hostages without their help. I just hope they won't get in the way. I'd hate to kill one of them by mistake."

"Don't worry, Lieutenant. They won't be anywhere near the building when you go in. They're leaving this op to you guys."

"Good." With that Tyler stood and started to salute when the commander waived him off.

"Feel free to talk to my soldiers who've been in contact with the CIA agents. They can give you even more details about the village you'll be infiltrating. You can find them around here at camp. "

Tyler nodded and then turned to leave.

"Here's one other thing you'll need, Lieutenant Garrett. It's a list of the names of the hostages."

Tyler took the list and barely gave it a glance. He'd been dismissed and would look it over more carefully later. So tucking the documents under his arm, he wasted no time in finding his men. He headed back to the mess hall, where he found all of them having a hearty breakfast. He poured himself his third cup of really bad coffee.

"Hey, Panther. You get our orders?"

Tyler pulled up a chair and sat down, spreading out the map and the drawing of the village where the hostages were being held. While the men ate, he laid out the mission, leaving nothing out, and emphasizing the fact that this mission was top secret because David Cushman was one of the hostages.

"We also have help, if we need it, from some of the surrounding villagers. Once we separate, we'll all need someplace to hold up for a least a day or two."

Tyler took out the list of names. "We'll slip in right before dawn. Six of us will take the hostages in different directions, and two of us will act as decoys. After we've got the hostages out, we'll all be picked up at different places within forty-eight hours. I want everyone to study this map and file an extraction plan with the pilots who'll be assigned to this op."

Mac was the first to speak up. "Tell you what, Panther. I'll volunteer right up front to take the kid journalist out safely. Because of the way you feel about the guy I don't want you to be tempted to leave him behind."

No one believed for even a second that Tyler still didn't blame David Cushman for Kent's death two years ago. But everyone at the table also knew that Tyler would put his own feelings aside and do his job. And that's why Mac felt comfortable making a joke.

"Who's the other journalist?" Scotty's question reminded Tyler of the list of names he held in his hand. His eyes slowly scanned the list, and when he spotted the last name his heart stopped. He thought that it had actually stopped.

"Jesus. What's wrong?"

Tyler's eyes were glued to the list and his hand clutched the paper so tightly that Flyboy had trouble pulling it out of his grip. Everyone went completely silent while Flyboy scanned the names. Without a word he passed the list to his teammate. Each man read the names, passed the list on, and lifted his eyes toward Tyler.

"We'll get her out of there, Lieutenant."

Mac's words were meant as words of reassurance, but Tyler didn't even hear him. He didn't hear anything but the words "I'm not going to give up on us." He'd repeated Samantha's words to himself over a thousand times during the last two months, and now here he was, getting ready to go into the jungle of Nigeria to rescue her. He felt sick to his stomach.

"She'll be okay, Panther. She's seems tougher than she looks."

Tyler glanced around the table at the concerned looks on the faces of the men he trusted most in this world. And instantly he knew that he had to push aside the panic he was feeling and start acting like their leader. Samantha needed him, but she wasn't the only one. The were six hostages being held in this jungle village, and SEAL Team Mega One would go in and get *all* of them out.

"We'll leave here at 1500 hours tomorrow and make our way to the village. We'll be driven by jeep for part of the way. We'll be dropped off about ten miles from the target. If all goes according to plan, we should reach the outskirts of the village, where the hostages are being held, in twelve hours from the time we leave base. Make sure we have four M16s with night-vision pocket scopes, and four M16 A2s with long-range optical scopes. We'll split the weapons up between us. We'll also need plenty of ammo. Kid, you and Brian find the guys who've talked with the CIA agents. I want a better layout of the village and I want to pinpoint the exact location of where our hostages are held. I want to coordinate our extraction plans and I want to talk with each of the pilots. Get some rest today if you can. Once we're on foot, it'll be one hell of a trek to get to the target destination. We'll meet back here two hours before departure tomorrow."

The leader they knew was back in charge. He'd put his personal feelings aside and dealt with the mission—all aspects of the mission. And he'd done it in a blink of an eye.

Tyler watched as the men in his command left the mess hall. He knew that they were fully prepared and ready to go. They were now in their element. They would go in and get the job done, because that's what they were trained to do. They would get Samantha out of the predicament she'd gotten herself into; Tyler had no doubt about that. He also had no doubt that once they were all home, safe and sound, Samantha would be in more danger than she could possibly imagine—because he was personally going to throttle her. Seeing her name on the list of hostages had given him the scare of a lifetime, and he wasn't going to rescue her and not give her a piece of his mind. *Yep,* he decided as he made his way out of the mess hall, *once I get my hands on Samantha James, I am going to throttle that woman, right in front of God and everyone.*

1300 Hours
Two Hours before Departure

"I want to see each extraction plan."

Seven men dropped papers onto the table and shoved them toward their leader.

"Once we separate, we won't see each other again until we reach base camp. We'll be on our own with our hostages until we're picked up at different extraction points within forty-eight hours. I understand that we'll have navy pilots from here, and a couple taking off from a carrier in the Indian Ocean assigned to this op." Tyler had talked personally with the pilots assigned to this base. He'd also talked with the pilots on the carrier by radio. He didn't want to leave anything to chance.

"Let's go over our plan."

1400 Hours
One Hour before Departure

"Once we get to the target destination, we'll talk through our insertion plan one more time."

The SEALs had changed into full jungle combat gear, which consisted of jungle fatigues, jungle boots, and floppy bush hats. They were now applying black greasepaint to their faces, necks, and hands.

"Billy, you and Kid are the assigned decoys on this mission. You'll also be the last extracted."

The two men simply nodded and checked their automatic weapons.

"From talking with the guys who've been in contact with the CIA agents and checking the coordinates on the map, it'll take us at least five hours to reach the village on foot. That'll put us in contact with the target at 0300 hours. We'll wait and watch the village for a while before we go in, but we can't wait more than one hour. We need to get the hostages out and make our way through the jungle while it's still dark."

The sound of each man checking his M16 was all that could be heard.

"Finish checking your weapons, and make sure you have enough MREs and enough water for two days."

Backpacks were strapped on and weapons were slung over shoulders.

"Let's move!"

2200 Hours
Drop Off
Foot Patrol

"Okay, Lieutenant Garrett. Our orders are to drop you and your team off here. This is as far as we go."

Tyler and his men picked up their gear from the floorboard of the jeeps they were traveling in. In seconds backpacks were in place, weapons secured, and they were ready to go the next leg of the mission on foot.

"Good luck, sir."

Tyler was already so into the mission that he barely heard the young soldier. His mind was only focused on what lay ahead and the job that needed to be done.

The SEALs gathered around their leader as the jeeps pulled away.

"This jungle is full of rag-tag rebels, so stay alert. Mac, you take the point. Brian, you take the rear."

The men lined up in patrol formation and headed out.

"We have five hours to target point."

0300 Hours
Target Point

"The building holding our hostages is the one about fifty yards to the left."

Mac had the map out and had easily located the building that the CIA agents had marked.

Tyler looked through his night-vision binoculars. He slowly scanned the village.

As he lowered the binoculars, the men gathered around him.

"Okay, Brian, you go in. I only spotted two guards at the front of the building. Make your way to the east side. According to intel, that's where you'll find a small window, and you should be able to see the hostages once you're in place. Report in on their situation, and stay put."

Brian slipped night-vision goggles in place. He clicked the safety off on his M16, handed his backpack off to Scotty, laid belly-down on the ground, and began to crawl into the village. The other SEALs spread out with their weapons ready. They also lay down on the ground to watch and to wait.

Each man had a pair of night-vision binoculars focused on the village. They could keep track of Brian and keep track of any unwelcome activity. So far so good. They kept trained eyes on Brian until he reached the building and disappeared around the east corner.

"In place." Brian spoke in a low whisper into his transmitter, which carried his words right into the ears of each team member.

"Have you located the window?" Tyler's also spoke in a whisper.

"Roger that."

"Status report."

Brian looked through the dirty window and luckily between the moonlight flickering through the window and his night-vision goggles, he could make out the hostages inside. He scanned the room, counting. *One, two, three, four, five.* He stopped, scanned the room, and counted again. *One, two, three, four, five.* "Shit." His expletive alerted the other men.

"We have a problem here, Lieutenant."

"Report."

"I count only five hostages. And it's impossible to tell who's missing."

"Are you sure?" Even though Tyler knew the answer, he'd felt compelled to ask.

"I'm sure, Panther. There are only five people in this building."

"Shit." This time it was Tyler's turn to swear. "Okay, Brian, stay put. We'll stay on watch until 0400, and then we'll execute. Check in again in fifteen minutes."

"Roger that, Lieutenant."

Brian hunkered down and the men of SEAL Team Mega One kept a watchful eye on the village. There was enough moonlight to see by, so Tyler put away his binoculars and scanned the grounds with his eyes. No one said a word. They just waited.

After fifteen minutes, Brian checked in and Tyler knew that they only had another thirty minutes before they had to go in. With or without the sixth hostage, they would go in and get the five out. Their orders were clear and they would be carried out.

As the time ticked quietly away, the men's attention was drawn to a door opening in another building across the compound. Rifles were lifted and aimed in the direction of the door. Two rebels came out the door. They were followed by another rebel, who was practically dragging one of the hostages. The hostage stumbled but was roughly jerked upright by a pull on the arm. It was only when a soft cry of pain could be heard in the silence of the night that Tyler realized just who the hostage was. And he felt as if he'd been punched right in the stomach. It was all he could do not to go charging in after her. But he stayed right where he was, feeling the knot in his stomach tighten with each breath he took.

As Tyler and his men watched, Samantha was hauled up against the rebel. His arm snaked tightly around her waist, trapping her own arm tightly against her side. Tyler's body stilled. The rebel brought his other hand up and snatched hold of Samantha's other hand, trapping it in his grip. He wrapped her hand around her back, now clutching both of her hands in one of his. Now that he had both of Samantha's hands trapped behind her back, the rebel took advantage of the situation, and allowed his other hand to wander.

First, the dirty rebel laid his filthy hand over Samantha's breast. His eyes seemed glued to the alarm that crossed her face, and he laughed out loud. Samantha squirmed but to no avail, because he just laughed that much louder. As he leaned down and breathed against her face, he pinched her nipple hard enough to cause her to cry out. The rebel laughed again and Tyler felt a blinding rage well up inside him. But he knew that he couldn't act on this rage. He had to stay focused on the mission and he had to stay perfectly still. In the long run, Samantha's life and the life of five other hostages depended on him staying in control—no matter how much it cost him.

Samantha tried to pull out of the rebel's grip but he didn't give her struggles a second thought. Once he was finished with molesting her breast, he reached down and latched onto the zipper of her jeans. She struggled even harder. The rebel simply ignored her and started pulling her zipper down.

Tyler's control finally broke. No way was he going to lie there and watch the bastard molest and possibly rape Samantha. No fucking way. So with a clear and determined mind, he lifted his weapon, aiming directly at the rebel's head. Mac, lying next to Tyler, lifted his own weapon, aiming at the head of the second rebel. Flyboy lifted his weapon and aimed at the head of the third rebel. If things got too nasty, they would take the rebels out with one clean shot between them.

Samantha started to weep and without taking his eyes off of her, Tyler whispered into his transmitter. "On the count of three." Mac and Flyboy were ready.

But before Tyler could count off, the two other rebels decided that they weren't going to stand around and wait for their comrade to have his fun. One of them grabbed onto his hand, yanked it away from Samantha's zipper, and pulled him away. She staggered back and a brief argument between the three rebels ensued.

Tyler, Mac, and Flyboy never lowered their weapons. They were still aiming dead-on and ready. But luckily for the three asshole rebels, the SEALs didn't need to pull their triggers. Because the two rebels had obviously convinced their friend that it was wiser to leave Samantha alone.

As Tyler and his men all looked on, Samantha was suddenly being pushed and pulled in the direction of the building holding the other hostages. All M16s were following their movements, with each man never taking his eye away from the scope of his weapon.

It was Mac who alerted Brian. "Sixth hostage coming in now. Three rebels."

"Roger." Brian kept his body crouched down low against the building, but his weapon was at the ready, just in case one of the rebels wandered over to where he was hiding out.

Tyler could hear the men's exchange through his earpiece, but his eyes and his rifle never left Samantha. He was focused on every step she took. He had to swallow back the bile that rose in his throat at the sight of her being handled so roughly. And it seemed to him that it was taking forever for her to get across the compound.

As he watched, Samantha stumbled again, but this time she fell on her knees in the dirt. The rebel closest to her grabbed her arm, yanked her to her feet, and then without warning he slapped her across the face with the back of his hand.

And in that instant Tyler had to call on all his willpower and all of his training not to pull the trigger. His finger actually twitched around the sensitive trigger of his weapon. His body stiffened as he saw and heard the slap across her cheek, and he took long, deep breaths. He felt a hated and a rage beyond anything he'd ever felt before in his life. And he felt fear—fear for Samantha and the fact that he had to wait until she was safely in the building with the other hostages before he could go in and get her.

Just hang in there, Samantha. Just hang in a few more minutes. We're coming. His mind screamed the words he couldn't voice out loud. He forced himself to calm down and bring his anger under control as he watched Samantha tugged the rest of the way and into the building. All three rebels went inside as well, leaving two guards outside the door.

"Report." Tyler's command was directed at Brian.

"Sixth hostage accounted for. Three rebels inside."

All they could do now was wait—wait and see if the rebels would come out, leaving the hostages alone, not that it mattered. The SEALs would go in and get the hostages out. And if three rebels stayed inside the building, that just meant that there would be three more bodies left behind.

With less than fifteen minutes to extraction, the door to the building holding the hostages opened and all three rebels came out. They spoke briefly to the two guards and then headed back toward the building they had dragged Samantha out of. The two guards stayed in place.

Tyler took his eyes off his scope just long enough to check the dial on his watch. Fifteen minutes to wait and watch. In fifteen minutes he would go in and get Samantha.

0400 Hours
Extraction

"Once we're within the perimeter, voice communication is on an as-needed basis only." Tyler spoke softy into his transmitter.

"Medicine Man, you, me, Mac, and Flyboy will go in first and make our way toward the back of the building. Scotty, you follow, taking up position on the west side. It's clear that the guards are posted at the front entrance of the building only, so we'll stay clear. Kid, you and Billy cover our six, and lay low in case we need fire support. As soon as we reach the target building, we'll call in. And remember that the entire village is considered our kill zone."

Each man took his M16 from his shoulder. The automatic weapons were at the ready. Almost invisible, blending with their surroundings, Team Mega One went silently about its job. It took less than ten minutes for each man to get in place.

"Call in." Tyler's voice came over the transmitter.

"Mac, in place."

"Billy, in place."

"Kid, in place."

"Flyboy, in place."

"Scotty, in place."

"Medicine Man, in place."

"Brian, in place."

"Roger that."

The SEALs who'd made it to the back of the cinderblock structure immediately went to work. The drawing they had been given of the village had sketched out this building with only one entrance at the north end and two windows in the back, built up high, toward the roof. Those windows were for ventilation only, but unlike the small window that Brian had used, these windows were large enough for the men to get through. The plan was that Tyler and two of the SEALs would make their way to the top of the roof and enter the building through the windows. Scotty and Brian would stay in place on the east and west side of the building, keeping watch. Flyboy would stay in the back of the building, doing the same.

Once the SEALs got inside the building, they would round up the hostages and make sure everyone was in good enough shape to walk. After that it would start to get risky. On Tyler's command, Scotty and Brian would move into position and take out the guards at the front of the building. They had counted two guards, so that wasn't a big problem. Two SEALs could take out two guards with one hand tied behind their backs. The problem was going to be with getting six untrained hostages out of a village without being noticed.

Silently, Mac removed a rope from his backpack. The rope had a hook on the end, which would be used to latch onto the thatched roof as quietly as possible. Mac stood back and tossed the rope. It worked on the first try. All six men lifted their weapons and waited, ready to kill if necessary, in case the noise had alerted the guards. When there was no commotion from the front of the building, they continued on. Once the rope was in place, Mac wrapped the other end around his waist. Within minutes he had scaled up the side of the building. He tossed the rope back down to the other SEALs. Medicine Man went next and Tyler followed.

Blending in with the night, Tyler, Mac, and Medicine Man easily dislodged the makeshift windows. Like their ascension up the wall, this time they wrapped the end of the rope around their waists and used it to scale down into the building. Like birds of the jungle, they gently glided inside.

Tyler was the first in. And when his feet quietly hit the floor, he was sickened by what he saw. He could make out the hostages through the moonlight streaming in through the window that he had just come through. They were all spread out on the cold, hard floor. Their hands were bound behind their backs, their legs were tied at the ankles, and they all had dirty rags tied over their mouths and over their eyes. Taking a deep breath, he stood in complete silence until his other two teammates made it into the room.

"We're in." Tyler was alerting the other members of the team.

The three SEALs inside the dusty, filthy building went over to the hostages, quietly waking them one by one. Blindfolds and gags were removed first. "I'm Lieutenant Conner McKenzie, with the United States Navy SEALs, and we're here to take you home" were the softly spoken words.

As Mac and Medicine Man made their way from one hostage to the other, Tyler made his way to Samantha. Even though all the hostages were now awake, the SEALs moved silently so that the noise inside the room was barely audible. Tyler knelt down and very gently touched her shoulder. "It's me, Sam," he whispered. "It's Tyler. And we've come to take you home."

He helped her into a sitting position and then he removed her blindfold. Next he removed her gag. In the semi-darkness Tyler was barely discernable. But because his own eyes had adjusted to the moonlit room, he could see Samantha pretty well. And at the sight of her his heart turned over.

"Are you all right, Samantha?" Even though he desperately wanted to pull her into his arms and comfort her, he needed to do his job right now, and that was to assess her condition and get her the hell out of Dodge.

"Is…is that really you, Tyler?" Her words were low and raspy.

"It's me and the team. We've been sent in to get you out, but we can't do that until we know if you're able to move on your own. So you need to tell me if you're hurt." His words were barely above a whisper.

Tyler watched as giant tears spilled out of her eyes. "I…" She stopped and chocked back a sob. "I can walk." She could barely talk, but for right now she'd told him all he needed to know.

"I'm going to untie your hands and feet."

As he spoke, he took out a knife from a sheath on his belt. Then he cut the rope binding her feet. Next he reached behind Samantha and cut the rope wrapped tightly around her hands. Before Samantha could even register that she was finally freed, Tyler slipped the blade of the knife between his teeth and placed both of his hands on her shoulders. Slowly, just in case her arms were bruised from being yanked around and manhandled by the rebels, he helped maneuver her arms from behind her back. He spoke around the knife he held between his teeth.

"Just take it nice and easy, Sam. Your arms might be a little sore, but nothing appears to be dislocated."

Samantha didn't respond. Even in her terrified, tired, muddled mind, she knew that it was imperative that she and the others stay as quiet as possible.

Tyler removed the knife from between his teeth, placing in back in its sheath. "Let me see your hands."

Samantha put both of her hands in his for him to inspect her wrists. And his blood turned to ice when he saw how red and raw the ropes had left her tender skin. Without another word, he looked up and caught Medicine Man's eye. He signaled to him and Medicine Man came over with a roll of bandages and an open jar of salve. Medicine Man handed the jar to Tyler.

While Tyler kept hold of one of Samantha's hands, he dipped two fingers into the jar, scooping out the thick, healing salve. Gently, under the watchful eyes of Medicine Man, he spread the salve gently over her raw, exposed skin. Then he took a bandage from Medicine Man and carefully wrapped it around her wrist. Tearing it with his teeth, he tied and secured the bandage. He repeated the process with her other wrist.

When he was finished, Tyler gently squeezed Samantha's hand. Then he looked around the room, noting that everyone was patched up and ready to go. They couldn't wait any longer; their time was running out.

"You need to listen to me very carefully, Samantha, because we need to get out of here and we're all going to do this together. Understand?"

"Yes." The tears had stopped but her voice was still cracking.

"In about ten seconds we're all going to walk through that front door. And then you need to stay as close to me as you possibly can. You also need to do exactly what I say, when I say it. No questions asked. Can you do both of those things?"

"Yes."

As quietly as possible, the SEALs told each hostage the same thing that Tyler had just told Samantha. As Tyler looked around he was given the sign from Mac and

Medicine Man that everyone was well enough to walk and ready to move.

"Take them out." Tyler spoke into his transmitter to Brian and Scotty. He had just given them the command to take out the guards.

"Roger that" came the response.

As the SEALs quietly gathered their group of civilians together, outside two guards were eliminated without so much as working up a sweat. In less than a minute the words *mission accomplished* were conveyed to the men in the room through the transmitters they each had in their ears. Time was now of the essence.

"Let's go."

On Tyler's command, the door to the small room that had served as a prison of sorts was slowly opened. Tyler stepped up to the door and his watchful eyes looked out and scanned the area. He waited and watched just long enough to make sure that it was safe for them to leave. Tyler slipped out first, followed by Samantha and two other hostages. Next Mac slipped through the door, followed by the other three hostages. Medicine Man was the last to leave. The group backed up against the wall of the cinderblock building. The SEALs communicated in silence by using hand gestures. When they were joined by Scotty, Brian, and Flyboy, each SEAL took one of the hostages and made his way into the night, all heading out of the village toward where Kid and Billy were providing cover.

It was a slow escape, with each person walking in a bent position, the group staying as low to the ground as they could. Several times they were forced to stop, drop to the ground, and wait. On Tyler's command they would get up, stay low to the ground, and do their best to keep moving. The SEALs and their hostages spread out so that they would not be easily spotted and so that they would blend as much as possible into the surrounding darkness.

Just as intel had reported, the village was fairly quiet, other than the two men standing guard at the only entrance into the makeshift prison house and the three rebels who had been with Samantha. Everyone was asleep at this time of night, believing that no one would dare enter their camp and attempt to rescue the hostages, risking the wrath of the rebels. Just as expected, the rebels overconfidence and their inflated egos worked in favor of Tyler and his men. Slipping into the village and slipping out was proving to be a piece of cake. But every man on the team knew that this was going to be the easy part. Once word got out that the hostages were on the loose, the tough part of the mission would begin—and that would be getting all six hostages out of the Nigerian jungle safe and sound.

As quietly as possible, six SEALs and six civilians finally made their way out of the rebel camp. They joined up with Kid and Billy.

"Listen up." Tyler knelt down on one knee, his men following suit in a tight circle. "It looks like everyone is in good enough shape to travel, so let's move. We'll split up at my command. Kid and Billy, stay behind and keep watch on the village, but get the hell out of here before dawn."

Without another word, the SEALs and the hostages all moved farther into the jungle. Because of the elation and excitement of being rescued, no one had a problem with keeping a fairly brisk pace. Also, because everyone seemed lost in their own thoughts, no one spoke for about thirty minutes; they just kept moving. Working their way through the terrain, the SEALs training kicked in and they once again walked in formation. As soon as Tyler thought it was safe, he stopped.

"Okay, it's time we split up. You all know your orders. Get to your extraction point with your hostage and stay out of sight as much as possible. We'll all see each other in forty-eight hours back at the base."

In what Samantha would later think of as a surreal moment, the band of SEALs vanished into the jungle with the hostages, all heading off in different directions. Tyler watched his men disappear before he reached out and took hold of Samantha's hand.

"We need to keep moving, Sam. Are you up to it?"

"Yes." Somewhere in the far recess of her mind, it registered that the only word she seemed capable of saying was *yes*. She'd hardly muttered another word since he'd removed her filthy gag.

"We have about an hour's walk ahead of us before we can stop. Do you need anything?" They were moving through the dense jungle as he talked to her. And because she sensed his urgency to keep moving, her only response was "No, I'm fine."

Tightening his hold on her hand, Tyler kept up a pace he thought she might be able to keep up with. He knew that as soon as the sun came up it wouldn't take the rebels all that long to discover the bodies of the two guards and realize that the hostages were missing. And he wanted to be as far away from that village as possible when the alarm went out. So keeping her close to his side, he kept moving.

Samantha called on all her strength not to pull away from Tyler and flop down on the jungle floor. She was actually a little battered and the trek through the terrain was harder than she would have expected. Her legs were so tired and her body cried out for the chance to lie down and get some sleep. She hadn't slept more than a few hours each of the three nights she'd been held captive, and now she could barely keep her eyes open. But her fear of being recaptured overrode her weariness, so she made herself put one foot in front of the other. Plus, she wasn't sure she could get Tyler to stop and let her rest even if she wanted to. He was just so much the Navy SEAL right now.

Samantha felt a desperate need to talk with the man who had risked his life and the life of his men to rescue her and the others. She wanted more than anything to be able to stop walking, wrap herself in his arms, and to talk to him. She wanted to hear his words of reassurance that everyone was going to get out of this mess safely. She needed to hear his deep voice tell her that everything was going to be okay. But instead of acting on what she wanted, she just held tightly onto his hand and kept on going. Right now he wasn't the man that she'd fallen a little in love with; he was Lieutenant Tyler Garrett, leader of SEAL Team Mega One. And if she thought for one minute that she could forget that, all she had to do was take one look at him.

If this were any other time or any other place, Samantha would be totally enthralled by the man who had come to rescue her. Dressed in jungle fatigues, wearing all his survival gear, and with a dangerous-looking weapon slung over his shoulder, he looked strong, rugged, and devastatingly handsome. But this was not a role they were playing, and she was not only tired to the bone, but she was scared to death. So she drew in deep breaths to try to steady her raveled nerves and tried to keep up with him as best she could.

After a long, grueling hour, they finally stopped on the outskirts of another small, isolated village. Keeping hold of her hand, he knelt down on one knee, taking her with him. She let out a deep sigh of relief as she sat on the ground, thankful for the brief respite.

"I need to check some coordinates." He was still so focused on the task at hand that he hadn't even bothered to look over at her. But she didn't care. She was finally able to sit down and rest. And that's all she cared about at the moment.

Samantha watched through tired eyes as Tyler swept his backpack off and laid it on the ground. He unzipped the pack, reached in, and took out what looked like a map. Tilting the paper up toward the moonlight, he studied it for only a second. Then he took out what looked like a very complicated compass, glanced at it, and then stuffed both the map and the high-tech compass back into the bag.

"This is where we spend the day. We've got someone in the village who's willing to help us out. We'll pass the day in one of the huts, catching up on our sleep before we head out again as soon as the sun goes down."

"Do you think I could have a drink of water?" She hated to interrupt, but her throat was so dry and she needed a drink so badly that she didn't think she could move another inch without some water.

Tyler finally allowed himself to take a good, long, hard look at her. He'd been on "mission autopilot," his only focus to lead his men and the hostages as far away from danger as possible. But now, at the sound of her ragged voice, he narrowed his eyes to take in Samantha, realizing that she looked like she was about to fall flat on her face.

Without a word, he released the water container that was hooked onto his belt, unscrewed the cap, and handed it over. With shaking hands, Samantha took the military canteen and lifted it to her mouth.

"Take small sips at first, Sam."

As her eyes found his over the top of the canteen, she did what he said. She drank small sips of water. The cool liquid felt exquisite going down her dry throat and she signed her pleasure. She drank enough to satisfy her thirst and handed the canteen over to Tyler. He took one long swallow and then refastened the canteen to his belt.

Tyler noticed that she looked like she couldn't put one foot in front of the other. But he couldn't afford to coddle her right now. They needed to get into the village just a few yards away and find a sanctuary in one of the huts. The sun was just about to come up and he knew that any minute now an alarm would go out throughout the jungle—an alarm that would put all the rebels in the area on the hunt for the missing hostages.

"It's not far now, Samantha. Do you think you can make it a few more yards?"

Samantha suddenly realized that she wasn't sure if she could get up and walk any farther. She felt as weak as a kitten. Once she had sat down, all of her strength seemed to desert her, and she didn't seem to have any reserve to call on. The last thing she wanted was to let Tyler down, but for a moment all she could do was to stare up at him with tears that came out of nowhere. She was appalled that she couldn't move and even more appalled that she couldn't stop crying. She was falling apart at that moment and there didn't seem to be a thing she could do to stop it.

Tyler reacted in a split second. He slung his backpack over his shoulders, reached out, and scooped Samantha up into his arms. In one fluid movement he was on his feet, carrying her tightly against his chest.

"Just relax, sweetheart. As soon as we get settled, I'll be able to take a look at how you're doing. It'll just be a few more minutes."

Tyler walked and talked and Samantha clung to him. She wrapped her arms around his neck and buried her face into the curve of his shoulder. She was ashamed at how she was acting, but for the first time in three days she felt like she was going to get out of this mess alive. But until they were safely hidden away inside one of the village huts, she was not going to let go of her protector.

Tyler walked into the village with Samantha in his arms and was met by a man he knew was a missionary. The man had obviously been on the lookout for them.

"Lieutenant Garrett?"

Tyler nodded. He would have liked to shake the man's hand, but his arms were full of Samantha.

"Your commander sent word to expect you. I'm Father Dominick."

"Do you have a place for us to spend the day?"

"Come with me, Lieutenant."

Tyler knew that he could trust the missionary because he'd already been told at base camp that the man's name was Father Dominick and that he was trying to get the people in the Nigerian jungle to not only accept Jesus, but to turn away from the rebels who had control of the jungle. According to Commander Westinghouse, Father Dominick had been successful with the people in this small village and that was why he'd been willing to offer them a refuge for the day. He was willing to take the risk of providing a hideout for Tyler and Samantha because he believed strongly in supporting the United States and the troops.

The sun came up as Tyler followed Father Dominic through a maze of huts and hastily constructed cinderblock buildings. He stopped when they reached the small church.

"I'm going to give the two of you my room in the chapel. It's a small room to your right. If the rebels come looking for you and start searching around, there's a trap door in my room that leads down into a small tunnel that will take you out into the jungle. It's not much of an escape route, but it will give you a way out and a head start, if nothing else.

"Thank you, Father. We appreciate everything you're doing for us."

"I am not only a man of God, Lieutenant, but I'm also a citizen of the United States. Even though I choose to live here with these poor village people, I love our government and I have the utmost respect for our military. These rebels are full of evil and they are destroying everything and everyone that stands in their way. So I feel privileged to be able to help you out."

Tyler was at a loss for words. The old missionary man was as brave as the men he served with, and Tyler felt humbled by him. Thanking the man with his eyes, Tyler started to turn away and head into the chapel.

"Is she all right?"

Tyler stopped but before he could answer, Samantha lifted her head from his shoulder. "Yes, Father. I'll be fine." To prove her point, she dropped her arms from around Tyler's neck, and urged him to let her stand on her own two feet. He reluctantly let her go but kept one arm firmly around her waist.

Father Dominic reached out and gently touched Samantha's arm while his eyes latched on to Tyler. "What can I get you?"

Tyler didn't want to be rude, but all of his instincts were telling him to get inside. He needed to check out Samantha's condition, get some food into both of them, and then get as much sleep as possible. He planned to head out as soon as the sun went down, because they had a lot of miles to cover before they reached the next village that was considered a safe destination. And the conditions were not going to be easy. They would be on foot, walking at night, watching out for rebels who he knew would be looking for them.

Tyler and Samantha stepped into the chapel and Father Dominic followed. "I brought food for us, Father, but we could use some more water, if you have some to spare."

All Tyler had in his backpack were Meals Ready to Eat, but he didn't want to ask Father Dominic to provide them with food. He suspected that food was not all that plentiful in this village and he didn't want to take from them what little they had.

"There's a large jug of water in my room, Lieutenant. Please help yourself."

As Tyler turned toward the small room on the right, something dawned on him. "Do your people know we're here?"

"No, Lieutenant. Even though they would never give you and the lady up to the rebels, the people of this village are not good liars. If the rebels ask, they'll be able to say they never saw you and it will be the truth."

"And what about you, Father? If asked about us, how do you handle the lying?" Even though Tyler absolutely trusted this man, he felt that he had to ask the question.

"I have already worked that out with God."

The statement was simple and to the point, and Tyler realized that not only did he trust this man, but he liked him as well. And the last thing he wanted was to put Father Dominic or his people in jeopardy.

"If your people don't know we're here, then let's keep it that way. When Ms. James and I are ready to leave, we'll make use of your tunnel and slip out. Okay with you, Father?"

Father Dominic reached out his hand. "Go with God, young man."

Tyler clasped the man's hand in his. "God bless you and your people, Father. And thank you."

"Yes, thank you, Father." As Samantha added her own words of thanks, she wanted to reach out and hug the wonderful old man. But Tyler didn't give her the chance. He tightened his hold around her waist, turned, and led her into the private room.

The second they were in the room, he closed the door behind them and pulled her into his arms. She proceeded to melt against him.

Tyler bent his head and laid his cheek against her hair. "Are you okay?" She nodded into his shoulder and he allowed himself to just hold her for a while.

Samantha wrapped her arms around Tyler's waist and clung to him for all she was worth. Even though she felt safe in his arms, she couldn't stop herself from trembling. And he felt it. "Are you sure you're okay?" Again, she nodded into his shoulder. "Let me check you out just to be sure." Before she could protest, he led her gently over to the small bed tucked against one wall of the room.

Samantha sat on the edge of the mattress and Tyler knelt down in front of her. He shrugged out of his backpack and started rummaging though it. As shc watched in silence, he brought out what looked like a first aid kit and sat it down next to him on the floor. Then he sat there for what seemed like forever and just looked at her. His troubled gray eyes searched her face, and then traveled slowly down her body.

"Did they hurt you Sam?" He could hardly choke out the question for fear of the answer.

"Just a little."

He blinked his eyes to fight down the uncontrolled anger. "Did they…did they?" He couldn't bring himself to actually ask the question, but since Samantha knew exactly what he was asking her, she answered him.

"I wasn't raped."

As she whispered those words, she dropped her eyes to her hands clasped tightly in her lap, and Tyler let out a deep sigh of relief. The knot in his stomach was still there, but he couldn't dwell on his own anger now. He had to make sure that Samantha was all right. He reached out and lifted her face up so that her eyes looked directly into his. And then, with a cautious and gentle touch, Tyler began to run his hands along her slender throat, down her arms, along her ribcage, over her hips, and down her legs. Satisfied for the moment, he continued his scrutiny. He reached out and brushed her hair out of her eyes, tucking it behind both ears. His eyes narrowed and he visibly flinched when he noted a purple bruise at her left temple, a cut on her cheekbone, and a slightly swollen lip. And Tyler knew beyond a shadow of a doubt that if he ever found the men responsible for this, he would kill them without a second thought.

While looking at Samantha's bruised and battered face, his anger was overwhelming—so overwhelming that he had to force himself to deal with the task at hand instead of letting loose with a string of curse words. Calling on his ability to mask the emotions he was feeling inside, he got up and poured some water into a bowl and carried it back to the bed. Crouching down in front of Samantha, he took a clean cloth out of the small first aid kit and dunked it into the water. He took the damp cloth and held it in his hand for a moment while he looked into her tired eyes. Then, without a word, he started to tenderly clean the dirt and dried blood away from her face.

Samantha sat quietly, not moving a muscle while Tyler took the dampened cloth and gently worked on her face. He rubbed away at the dirt and blood as gently as possible. His thumb stroked the uninjured corner of her lip before he moved the cloth to her neck. When he finished with her neck, he rinsed the cloth and started cleaning the dirt and grime from her hands. He was so serious and so focused on what he was doing that she couldn't stop herself as she reached out and laid a hand along his cheek. At the touch of her hand, he stopped what he was doing and looked up.

"I'm so tired," she whispered.

Tyler dropped the cloth into the bowl of water. "Do you want to eat something or do you want to sleep?"

"I need to sleep, Tyler. I've hardly slept for three days."

At her softly spoken words, he let his eyes roam over her face one more time. And when he couldn't stand to look at her bruises any longer, he reached out and took both of her hands in his, with her palms up.

"Are your wrists sore?"

"A little."

His head was bent, and they both seemed unable to take their eyes away from her hands in his.

"I'll get you a couple of aspirins. If you take a couple, that should help you sleep."

Reluctantly, Tyler placed her hands back in her lap. She watched quietly as he looked through his first aid kit. He retrieved a bottle of aspirin, spilled a couple into his hand, and gave them to Samantha with the canteen. He skimmed the back of his fingers gently down her cheek, urging her to take the pills.

Next Tyler reached down and slipped off Samantha's shoes. Then he got up from his crouched position, took hold of Samantha's hand, and bought her to her feet. He pulled back the threadbare blanket on the bed and helped her lie down. She sank into the mattress, stretching out as she lay on her back. Her hair fanned out against the pillow and she closed her eyes. Tyler lifted the blanket and covered her. And for a long minute, he stood and looked down at her.

As Samantha fell into an immediate, exhausted sleep, Tyler went over and picked up the bowl of water. He took the wet cloth and worked at the grease paint on his face, neck, and hands. When he finished he removed his jungle boots, unhooked all the gear from his belt, and went over to join Samantha. He needed to catch as much sleep as he could before they started out again.

Since she was dead to the world, he didn't think she'd mind if he crawled in beside her in the only bed in the room. He knew that he could stretch out on the floor and sleep, because he was trained to sleep anywhere, anytime. And over the years he'd slept in a lot worse places. But right now he didn't want to lie on the cold, hard floor; he wanted to lie down next to Samantha. So as quietly as possible, he pulled back the blanket and slipped into bed. Laying on his back, he pulled the blanket back up. He closed his eyes and tried to force his body to relax.

"I've never been so scared in all my life."

At the sound of her voice, Tyler opened his eyes. He was surprised that she wasn't sound asleep. He knew that it would be awhile before he'd be able to drop off himself, and since they had almost twelve hours before dark, he thought they could both put sleep off for a little while longer.

"Do you want to talk about it, Sam?" He knew that she'd have to tell the story sooner or later, but he'd leave it up to her as to when she would be ready.

"I'm not sure I can." Her voice was barely above a whisper.

Tyler reached out and took hold of her hand. "Why don't you try."

There was a minute or two of silence. Then she squeezed his hand and turned onto her side, facing him. He responded by turning onto his side, facing her. They were just inches away from each other.

"It was such a nightmare, Tyler, and everything seemed to happen so fast. The men who took us just came out of nowhere. You probably know that I was there to cover a story for Doctors Without Borders?" He nodded and she continued with her story. "It was in the middle of the day, and the village that the doctors were working in was suddenly surrounded by rebels who came storming in and started rounding everyone up. They were pushing, shoving, and shouting at everyone. They pointed rifles at us, threatening to shoot if we didn't do what they said. And they seemed to know exactly who they were looking for."

"What made you think that?" He hadn't intended to interrupt her, but he couldn't help himself from asking.

"The rebels made the doctors, nurses, and journalists all stand together in the middle of the village. They walked around us, looking from one to the other, stopping only when they laid eyes on David Cushman. As soon as they spotted David they grabbed four doctors, me, and David. With guns pointed at our backs, we were loaded into jeeps and driven to the village where you and your men rescued us." As she talked her hand clutched even tighter onto Tyler's.

"Then what happened?" His voice was low and coaxing.

"As soon as we reached their camp, they herded us into the room where you found us. They tied us up, gagged and blindfolded us, and then left us alone. We couldn't see or talk to each other and they left us like that all night. And all we could do was lay there and wait for them to come back."

She drew in a ragged breath, and Tyler could tell that she was reliving the fear she had felt then. "It's all right, Samantha. I'm here with you, and you're safe now."

Her eyes found his and somehow she was able to draw on his strength and continue telling him about her ordeal. "The next morning, after a terrifying night, they came and got us one at a time. When it was my turn, they took me inside a different building and started asking me all sorts of questions about David and his father."

"What kind of questions?"

"A man I heard them refer to as Miguel asked me to tell them everything I knew about David and his family. He specifically wanted to know about David's father, Senator Cushman. And when I told them I knew very little about any of them, that's when Miguel lost his temper. He leaned down into my face and ordered me to tell him what he wanted to know. When I told him again that I knew very little about David, and nothing about his family, that's when he hit me." She closed her eyes for a second. "One minute I was sitting in a chair and the next instant I was knocked to the ground."

This time Tyler's hand tightened around hers. He felt a blinding rage take hold of him as he pictured Samantha being hit hard across her beautiful face. He released her hand and reached out and lightly touched one finger to the cut at her lip. His touch was light and brief. As her eyes looked into the turbulent gray of his, his hand slid slowly down her neck, his fingers resting against her skin.

"After that, I was dragged back to join the others. And that's when the nightmare continued. They only time we were not tied, gagged, and blindfolded was when we were allowed to eat, pay a visit to the crude bathroom, or when they brought us back to the other building for another interrogation."

Tyler's thumb caressed her throat. "Were the questions always the same?"

"Yes," she murmured. The slow back-and-forth movement of his thumb was so comforting. "They kept asking me about David. They wanted to know how close he was to his family, and they kept asking if I knew how much money his father had. And I kept telling them that I hardly knew the man, and that I knew absolutely nothing about his father. Miguel would finally lose his patience with me and he would strike out at me again. I actually lost count of how many times he hit me." She stopped for a second, struggling with what she wanted to say next. "This morning, sometime before dawn, Miguel was so angry that he told me if I didn't come up with the right answers I would be dead by this time tomorrow. He said he'd give me one more day to think about it. And then I was dragged back and tied up again."

One large tear slipped down onto Samantha's cheek, and Tyler reached over and wiped it away. "Lying on that filthy floor, tied and gagged, I finally resigned myself that I was going to die in this remote, awful village. And it's funny, but once I accepted my fate, some of the fear left me. It wasn't that I was afraid to die anymore. What I was terrified of was how I was going to die. I tried not to let my imagination run away with me, and before I gave in to the building panic, you came to rescue me." Her voice finally broke and a flood of tears fell from her eyes.

Tyler reached out and pulled her into his arms. "It's all right, sweetheart. It's all right." He spoke softly into her ear as she cried against his chest.

"I was so scared, Tyler. So scared."

"Shh." His hand rubbed gently up and down her back. "Shh, now. Everything will be all right." And as he tried to soothe her, she clutched onto his shirt and cried her eyes out.

"I knew I was going to die." She buried her face and cried some more.

"I know, sweetheart. I know."

"You saved my life. You and your men saved us all."

"I would never let you die, Samantha. Never."

Samantha couldn't seem to stop the tears. And for the moment she didn't even try. It felt so good to let herself go and find the comfort she was seeking in Tyler's arms. So she gave in to her need and let the tears soak the front of his shirt.

Once she was all cried out, she lifted her face and looked up at him with tear-drenched eyes. "Can I ask you something?" She wanted to ask him the question that had been nagging at her since the SEALs had split up.

"Sure." His voice was soft and soothing.

"Now that we've all been rescued, is there any reason why the rebels would even bother looking for us? Surely they must realize that David, being a senator's son, is safe by now, or is at least well on his way to being safe. So why look for any of us when it was obvious it's David they were going to ransom."

"You got a look at them, right?"

Now Samantha knew why they were running from the rebels. "You mean they're afraid we can identify them?"

"Believe it or not, Sam, what these bands of men are doing is illegal. Even in the jungle of Nigeria kidnapping is against the law. So it stands to reason that they'll expect you to give a statement to the authorities as soon as you can. And they can't allow that to happen. They never had any intention of letting any of you go. Once they got the information they needed, they would have..." He paused for a second. "They would have carried out their threat to kill you. Their strength lies in the fact that there are never any people that can actually identify them. And they will do anything in their power to see that you don't get the chance. So they'll come after us. You can count on it."

That was exactly what Samantha didn't want to hear, and she was having trouble processing everything he'd just said.

"Right now I'm so tried. My mind and my body are just so tired."

Being careful not to hurt her, Tyler bent his head and lightly touched his lips to hers. At the same time he drew her closer against his body. "Just close your eyes." His words were spoken against her slightly parted mouth. "Close your eyes and try not to think about anything but sleep."

Samantha responded to his softly spoken words by snuggling as close to him as she could. She wrapped one arm around his waist, laid her head under his chin, and closed her eyes. He kept on talking to her, rubbing his hand up and down her back, urging her to relax. Slowly, little by little, she felt herself give way to her utter exhaustion.

As he continued to whisper to her, she allowed herself to feel safe, warm, and secure for the first time in days. And as his voice drifted farther and farther away, she finally drifted further and further into sleep.

Chapter Ten

"Wake up, Samantha." Tyler gently shook her. "We need to go."

Samantha opened her eyes to find Tyler leaning over her. The first thing she noticed was that he was fully dressed, gear and all.

"You need to get up, Sam."

The urgency in his voice didn't get past her, and without hesitation she threw back the blanket and swung her legs over the side of the bed.

"A small band of rebels are here in the village, and we need to leave before they decide to check out the church."

Samantha reached for her shoes.

"I've been watching them from the window for the last five minutes, hoping they'll move on, but it doesn't look like they're going anywhere. They've started searching some of the huts."

Samantha was on her feet, instantly awake. She noticed that the curtain was back in place over the window.

"Father Dominic is doing his best to keep them at bay, but we can't take any chances. Even though it's not quite dark yet, we need to go now."

Samantha had noticed that Tyler had very carefully put everything back in its place, and other than the rumpled bed, it didn't look like anyone had used the room.

"Let's straighten the bed and get the hell out of here." He voiced her exact thoughts.

Together they made up the bed, Samantha's hands shaking like a leaf. The thought of the rebels right outside scared her to death.

"I'm ready." She was desperate to get out of the village and put as must distance between them as possible.

"Listen to me for a minute." Tyler had on his Navy SEAL face, and Samantha stopped and paid very close attention. "I had a chance to check out the tunnel while you were sleeping, and I can't risk us using a flashlight to make our way through in case the rebels find the trap door before we're out. Any light would give us away in a second. So it's going to be pitch black down there."

All Samantha could do was nod her head.

"It's also going to be slow going because we'll need to crawl on our hands and knees."

Again, all she could do was nod her agreement.

"I want you to go down first and make as little noise as possible. I'll follow right behind."

"Do you know how long the tunnel is?"

"No. But it can't go all that far. It's only meant as an escape route."

"Okay." Samantha made her way over to the trap door. She wanted to get going.

"There's one other thing, Sam." She had lifted the trap door but stopped at the sound of his voice. "As soon as we're down there, no matter what, I want you to keep going until you come to the end of the tunnel. When you reach the end, there'll be a hatch in the jungle floor for you to push up and out of."

At his words, Samantha felt a bubble of pure, unadulterated panic. "But you'll be right behind me. Right?"

"Listen, Samantha. I have every intention of staying as close to you as possible. But if for some reason the rebels make it into the tunnel right after us, I may need to stop long enough to keep them from following us out."

"What do you mean you may need to stop? How in the world can you stop them from following us out?"

Tyler stepped over to Samantha. "I'm trained to do whatever it takes to get you to safety, Sam, so you have to trust me."

"I'm not worried about my safety, Tyler, I'm worried about yours. If you stop down there to fight the rebels you'll never get out. That's what I'm worried about."

"Don't worry about me. I know what I'm doing."

Suddenly Samantha felt as if she were in some sort of a dream. This just couldn't be happening—not after he'd just rescued her. No way could he even hint that both of them might not make it out of the tunnel alive. She refused to accept what he was trying hard not to say.

"If you need to stop down in that tunnel so that you can deal with the rebels, I'll stay with you."

"No, you won't. If I stop I want you to keep going. And if I don't catch up to you in five minutes, then I want you to get the hell out of the tunnel and find a place to hide in the jungle. Do you understand me, Samantha? This is not negotiable." He slapped something into her hand. "Keep this on you at all times. It's a GPS tracking device. If something happens to me, it'll allow the navy pilot whose supposed to pick us up to track you down. If we miss the extraction pickup, they'll start searching for us."

As she tucked the tracking device into the pocket of her jeans, her panic turned into a fear that bordered on a feeling of terror. "Please don't make me go on without you, Tyler."

His only response was to unsnap his water canteen from his belt. He hooked it through Samantha's belt and snapped it into place. Next he unbuttoned her blouse and stuffed a couple of MREs inside. "This shouldn't weigh you down too much. If you need to hide out in the jungle, stay put. You'll have enough food and water until someone finds you."

Before she could say another word, Tyler checked his M16, grabbed hold of Samantha, and led her down the trap door. She almost fell onto her hands and knees because she was shaking so much. Not only was she terrified beyond belief of the possibility that she might be separated from Tyler, she was also terrified of what might lie ahead of her in the dark. But because she was even more terrified of what she knew was behind her, she reacted on pure instinct and started crawling.

"Keep up a steady pace, Samantha, and take regular, even breaths. Don't let the darkness freak you out."

His voice already sounded too far away. But she would rather die than let Tyler down, so she did as she was told. She breathed in the musty air and kept on crawling, and crawling, and crawling. The going was slow and it seemed like she'd been down in that tunnel a lifetime, though in fact they'd only been crawling for about five minutes.

Samantha risked looking over her shoulder and she was relieved to see that Tyler was right on her heels. It was impossible to tell how far they'd gone in the dark, and she just hoped and prayed that they'd soon be safely out of the tunnel. But just as she repeated her prayer one more time, the worst possible thing happened.

Both Samantha and Tyler heard voices in the distance and she knew that the rebels had just found the trap door. Her heart almost stopped beating as fear enveloped her. All she could think about was that Tyler was going to force her to go on without him and that he would stay behind to keep her safe. And in that instant she knew what she'd been afraid to admit to herself: that she was truly, madly in love with him. It was suddenly so clear to her. She had fallen in love with Tyler Garrett and she loved him unconditionally. She loved everything about him. She loved who he was, what he stood for, and how he lived his life. She loved him whether or not he felt the same way about her. And she also knew that she'd never be able to leave him in this tunnel alone, fighting to save her life.

Before she had time to dig in her heels and refuse to go without him, Tyler surprised her by slamming her down onto her stomach. As she drew a dusty breath into her lungs, she felt his hard body slide up to cover hers.

"I think we're far enough away so that they can't see us, but even if we're not, we should blend into the darkness enough so that they can't make us out."

"Thank God." Samantha didn't even realize that she'd spoken out loud.

Tyler shifted his body just enough so that all his weight wasn't on Samantha. With the backpack and his weapon slung over his shoulder, he knew that he must weigh a ton. But he also knew that his fatigues would blend into the darkness much better than what Samantha was wearing, so he stayed put.

"What I said earlier still stands, Samantha." He was whispering into her ear. "If they head in here after us, you go. Don't stop until you reach the hatch and make your way into the jungle and find a place to hide. I'll catch up and find you as soon as I can."

They both knew that if he stayed behind to delay the rebels that he wouldn't be coming out. He'd die protecting her. She knew it and he knew it. And she almost died right then and there just thinking about that possibility.

The tunnel acted like a funnel, and they could hear the voices of at least two men arguing about whether or not they should go more deeply into the tunnel. One wanted to check it out and one didn't. Realizing that he may need to make a split-second decision, Tyler reached over and latched onto the strap of his weapon. He figured that he could slip his weapon off his shoulder, turn around, and eliminate at least two of the rebels before more men came down the trap door. That alone would give Samantha enough time to make her getaway.

Tyler's breathing was as steady as a rock, and he was mentally preparing himself for the battle ahead. He started to slip off of Samantha so that he could turn himself around, when he stopped dead in his tracks because suddenly a ray of light came right at the two of them, breaking through the darkness.

Tyler didn't as much as move a muscle. Inside he was cursing up a storm that he was in such a compromising position. If he moved they might be detected, but if he didn't move he couldn't turn around so that he could at least fire his weapon. With all of his senses on full alert, he let his body sink a little more into Samantha, hoping to protect her if bullets started flying.

They stayed completely immobile for several long seconds. It wasn't long before Tyler realized that the beam of light was really meager, not making its way to them. If the rebels didn't come any farther into the tunnel, they should be safe and able to make their way out into the jungle, he thought. Tyler preferred jungle survival to being stuck in this dark tunnel any day of the week, and he listened intently as the rebels continued arguing over whether or not they wanted to go any farther.

"I think you can see, Commander Gomez, that I was telling you the truth." Father Dominic's voice came at them loud and clear, through the darkness. "I'd never put my people in danger by hiding anyone fleeing from you and your men." Father Dominic was obviously addressing the leader of the rebels. "That trap door has been here for as long as I can remember, and it's never used. I can only imagine what kind of jungle creatures have made that tunnel their home."

Samantha shuttered at those words because as she had crawled along she had wondered the same thing. But given the choice, she'd choose unknown jungle creatures over the rebel creatures without giving it a second thought.

The pathetic beam of light was still pointed down the tunnel. Tyler stayed still and Samantha kept praying. And finally, with luck and God on their side, the light went out.

"If we find that you have lied to us, Father, you can mark my words that we'll be back." The rebel's words were less of a threat and more of a promise, and Samantha prayed that Father Dominic and his people would not come to any harm because of the two of them.

The sounds of men making their way up the rickety trapdoor steps was enough to make Samantha want to cry out in relief. Next was the sound of the trapdoor being slammed shut.

"Stay still, Sam. We need to make sure they're gone."

Staying still was no problem for Samantha. She was so scared that she wasn't sure she could get her limbs to move.

"Am I hurting you?" Tyler spoke into her ear at the same time that he slightly adjusted his weight.

"No." Her words were barely above a whisper.

They stayed as quiet as church mice for the longest five minutes of Samantha's life. The only sound that could be heard was her labored breathing.

"I think it's safe for us to go on." Tyler lifted himself off of Samantha and reached out to help her back up on to her hand and knees. "Are you ready to go on?"

"I…yes, I'm ready."

"Like before, Sam, just keep going at a nice, even, steady pace. The exit can't be that far way."

Suddenly Samantha was desperate to get out of the dark, nasty tunnel. She wanted a breath of fresh air so badly she could hardly stand it. So without another word, she took off crawling, but this time she crawled a little faster than before. What seemed like hours were actually only minutes. Five, ten, and then fifteen minutes ticked by before Samantha came to the end of the tunnel. She stopped, turned halfway around, and sat down on her bottom, waiting for instructions from Tyler.

In the dark, Tyler stopped right behind her. Neither one of them could see a thing, but Samantha could tell that Tyler was reaching up, feeling along the ceiling of the tunnel, searching for the hatch that would lead them to fresh air.

"Got it."

Samantha felt her heartbeat kick up a notch. She hated the dark, cramped tunnel, but she felt a ripple of fear at what might be waiting for them in the jungle. Luckily, she didn't have time to think about what lay beyond the hatch door, because Tyler was talking to her.

"I'm going to go up first. Do you think you can manage to trade places with me?"

It was hard going in such close quarters, but with a few bumps and grinds Tyler and Samantha were able to change places. Tyler then slipped his backpack off his shoulders and handed it off to Samantha in the dark. His weapon he kept firmly in one hand. "Let's get the hell out of here."

With that, Tyler cautiously lifted the hatch. And because God was still on their side, darkness had finally fallen. Grateful for the cover of night, Tyler stood just long enough to look around. When he felt it was safe he pulled himself out of the tunnel. He reached down for his backpack and then he reached down for Samantha.

As soon as they were both out of the tunnel, they packed the hatch back down, making sure it disappeared into the jungle floor.

"I want to get farther away from the village before we stop to eat. Are you okay with that?"

Samantha was already on her feet, ready to go. "Yes. I'm ready."

Tyler had extracted the complicated-looking compass from his backpack. He spent a few seconds getting his bearings and then he stuffed it into the pocket of his fatigues. "This way." And before Samantha knew it they were off. Tyler led the way, with Samantha following close behind. Because of all the overgrown foliage, they were forced to walk one behind the other. The dense foliage also made the going pretty rough. But Samantha wouldn't complain. She was safe from the rebels, at least for the time being, and she was with Tyler, the man she now knew she loved more than anyone else in the world.

They walked for well over two hours before Tyler found a place he decided was safe for them to rest. It was a small clearing, barely discernable to the naked eye. Tree branches hung low over the clearing, creating a hiding place of sorts. Tyler pulled back a large fern and made it possible for Samantha to make her way into the safe haven. He stepped in behind her, dropping the fern back in place. Between the low-hanging tree leaves and the surrounding ferns, they were swallowed up in a nice little cocoon.

"How in the world did you see this place?" Samantha was amazed by their hiding place.

"It's not that hard to find, if you know what you're looking for."

"Do you think the rebels can find us here?"

"We're not going to stay long enough to find out. We still have a lot of ground to cover before we reach the next village where we can spend the day. But I thought you could use some food and a little rest."

There was just enough moonlight streaming in through the tops of the trees. "Is it safe to sit down?" As inviting as their little nest was, Samantha was still scared to death of the jungle.

"I came prepared," was Tyler's reply, and she watched in awe as he removed a blanket out of his backpack. He spread the blanket on the ground and encouraged Samantha to sit.

"What all do you have in that thing?"

"My survival gear. I've got a couple of blankets, a first aid kit which includes iodine in case we need to sterilize the water, MRE's, night-vision goggles, extra ammo, and lots of other goodies." He sat down next to Samantha.

"How much does it weigh?"

"Not that much."

Samantha wasn't fooled for a minute. That backpack of his had to weigh a ton, but she suspected he was used to it because it was just another part of his training.

"Do you think you can get those MREs out of your blouse?" His words broke into her train of thought about his training. But before she could register what he'd asked her, he leaned over and started unbuttoning her blouse. And as she sat and watched, he removed the Meals Ready to Eat that he'd stuffed into her blouse earlier.

"You're in for a treat." He looked over the MREs he held in his hand. "Tonight we've got pot roast and… chicken casserole. So, what is your pleasure?"

For the first time in days Samantha actually smiled. "I think I'll have the pot roast, if you don't mind."

Tyler smiled. Then he tore open the package and handed it to her. "Pot roast for the lady. It's the best the navy has to offer." He sent her a smile right before he opened his own meal-in-a-bag.

"Just squeeze and eat."

Samantha watched as Tyler squeezed the contents of his package into his mouth. She did the same. And she was surprised that the stuff tasted so good. But it did taste good and she was ravenous, so she didn't waste a single bite. As they sat on the blanket, eating in silence, Samantha thought that if anyone had ever told her that she'd be sitting on the jungle floor somewhere in Nigeria, eating MRE's, running from the rebels with Tyler Garrett, she would have laughed in their face. Never in her wildest dreams could she have imagined that she'd be here. She had aspirations that she'd be able to write about such an event, but not about participating in one herself. And it wasn't the first time that she wondered how Tyler could do this for a living, day in and day out.

"Is this how it always is, Tyler? Are you always in this much danger when you and your team go in to rescue someone?"

Instead of answering her, he unhooked the water canteen from her belt and handed it to her. She took several long swallows before handing it back to him. Tyler brought the canteen up to his mouth and Samantha watched as he drank. And she was both amazed and a little embarrassed that she thought he looked sexy just drinking out of a canteen. *God help me*, she thought as he handed her back the canteen.

"You need to drink more, Sam. I don't want you getting dehydrated out here."

Samantha took another long drink. "So, have you decided that you aren't going to answer my question?" She handed him back the canteen and he seemed to take an inordinate amount of time screwing the cap back on. Finally he lifted his gray eyes to her.

"It's not a question with a simple answer."

"Okay." She wasn't going to be put off. "So give me the complex answer. I can handle it."

It took him less than a heartbeat to realize that she probably could handle just about anything. So far she'd shown him that she was a real trouper, and he figured that the truth couldn't hurt. So he didn't try to sugar coat his response.

"There are varying degrees of danger, Sam. But to answer your question, yes, we are always in some sort of danger. Since Team Mega One specializes in hostage extraction, we're rarely needed unless the mission is extremely risky and covert. We are always sent in to hostile environments and there is always the possibility that one or more of us won't come out alive. We know that going in, and we go in anyway, because that's what we're trained to do. And that's how we live our lives."

Samantha had been hoping for a different answer. She'd been hoping that he'd tell her that the situation they found themselves in now was not the norm. She had been hoping that he'd tell her that most of his missions were under more peaceful circumstances and that he rarely found himself running from a band of rebels in the middle of an uncivilized jungle. But Tyler hadn't told her any of those things. He'd looked right at her and told her the truth—the unvarnished truth. And somehow she just knew that some of his missions were even worse than he'd just let on. Suddenly she found herself without anything to say.

"And now we need to get moving. We have hours of walking ahead of us, and I want to take it as slow as possible."

Tyler stood and reached out a hand to help Samantha up. He packed away the blanket and hooked the water canteen back through her belt loops. "Do you need some privacy before we take off?"

She refused to be embarrassed by his question but she felt her cheeks turn pink anyway. "Yes," was all she could manage.

Tyler lifted the fern and stepped out of their hiding place, giving her some privacy. She quickly attended to the business at hand and joined him, ready to be on the move. The closer they got to the village where they would spend the day, the better she would feel.

Tyler tried to take it easy but the jungle wouldn't cooperate. Even with the moonlight, it was still dark enough to have to watch your step. Samantha tripped more than once, catching her balance each time before falling to the ground. The night sounds were also enough to make her crazy. There were animal sounds that she couldn't place and didn't want to. There was constant rustling in the bushes that made her jump with fright. With each step she took she knew two things: one, that she was completely out of her element, and two, that Tyler was completely in his element. He walked and walked and walked and never seemed to tire or falter. He had reached into his backpack and taken out a long blade, which he used like a machete, hacking away at the foliage. He was strong, extremely well trained, and focused on his mission. And just watching him, Samantha didn't have a doubt that he would get them both home safely.

They stopped several times during the night to take a short rest and drink lots of water. Tyler was determined that Samantha not get dehydrated and he kept forcing water down her throat. Their breaks were less than twenty minutes at a time, and as the hours passed and they kept on walking, Samantha thought that she might not make it. Her legs were burning and her feet hurt like hell. But she wouldn't allow herself to give up, so with a determination she didn't knew she possessed, she kept on putting one foot in front of the other. Finally, after walking on-and-off all night, Tyler stopped at the edge of a small, isolated village.

"You rest here awhile and I'll go check things out."

She felt a spurt of panic at the thought of being left alone. "I'll go with you." Suddenly she wasn't the least bit tired.

"I won't be gone but a second, Sam. I want to find my contact and then I'll come back and get you."

Tyler had used his "I'm in command" tone of voice, but it wasn't working. And when he saw the look of fear on her face, he changed his tactic. "You'll be safe here for a few minutes while I check things out. And I'll be back before you know it." His tone was more gentle and a little coaxing. "Just sit on the blanket and you can watch for me from here." He retrieved the blanket and set it on the ground for her. "I need to make sure it's safe for us to go in."

It was only because Samantha didn't want to be a pain in his ass that she complied. She would much rather have gone in with him, but she knew that he was determined to make sure the village was a safe haven for them. And she was smart enough to know that he would be able to do that better without her plastered to his side.

"Please hurry back." She tried not to sound too scared as she sat down to wait.

"Listen, Sam." She was taken aback when he dropped his backpack and knelt down beside her. "Remember what I told you to do if for some reason I didn't make it out of the tunnel?"

"Oh God, Tyler. Please don't tell me—"

"Do you remember?" His stormy gray eyes were demanding a response.

"Yes. I remember." Her eyes met his and she couldn't have looked away if her life depended on it.

"Good. And do you still have the GPS device?"

"Yes."

"Okay. If I don't come out of that village in ten minutes, or if you hear any gunshots, take whatever you can carry out of the backpack, head out into the jungle, find a hiding place like we found today, and wait. Someone will come and find you as soon as they can." With that he reached into his trusty backpack and took out a handgun. "Have you ever fired a gun before?"

She sat and just stared at the thing. "Samantha, answer me. Have you ever handled a gun before?"

"Yes...yes." She had to stop herself from stammering. "I dated a cop for a few weeks and he took me to the shooting range once. It was a strange date, but by the end of the hour, I had done pretty well."

Tyler clicked off the safety and put the gun in her hand. "It's ready to fire, so be careful."

Before Samantha could recover from the shock of holding a loaded gun, Tyler was on his feet. He leaned down and placed a quick kiss on her lips.

"I should be back in ten minutes, so whatever you do, keep a close look out so you don't shoot me by mistake."

"Be careful," was all she could choke out before Tyler disappeared into the night.

Samantha sat, clutching onto the gun, counting down each minute. Her eyes were glued on the small village in the distance. She felt a fear so deep in her bones that it was a wonder that she was able to breathe. She was as much afraid for Tyler as she was for herself. If he didn't come back within the allotted ten minutes, she would be forced to do what he told her to do. And right at that moment she wasn't sure she'd be able to move, much less flee into the jungle and find a hiding place.

"Please God, please God," she kept repeating over and over. "Please God, let him be okay." Samantha kept up the prayer, right up until the time she spotted a lone figure moving toward her in the dark. She strained her eyes to try to make out if it was Tyler, but it was impossible to see that well in the dark. With a heavy heart, she lifted her hand holding the gun, and aimed it directly at the moving target. "Please God, please let it be him."

Samantha wrapped her other hand around the gun, trying to keep it steady. She was so nervous that she was actually shaking. Her eyes were focused ahead and her breathing was labored. She watched and watched, and wondered for one brief second if she would even be able to pull the trigger. If it was a rebel coming her way, could she actually pull the trigger and run? Her mind was trying to reassure her that she could, just as her eyes told her that the lone figure was in fact Tyler. She could tell simply by the way he was moving. His stride was long and purposeful, and he moved just like a panther.

Samantha lowered the gun as soon as she realized it was Tyler. Her hand was shaking so much that she was afraid she might discharge the weapon by mistake. She dropped the gun down onto the blanket and fought to hold back the tears, just as Tyler made his way to her.

"It's safe for us to go in." Tyler wasted no time in retrieving the gun. He clicked on the safety and tucked it into the waistband of his pants. "Believe it or not, the rebels have already checked out this village. They were here about three hours ago, looking for any signs of us. They should be long gone by now. I met with a missionary in the village who's willing to let us hold up in one of the huts for the day. They've even got plenty of food and water to spare."

Samantha shook off any remaining tears and stood up. She couldn't afford to fall apart now. She needed to stay strong.

Tyler didn't seem to notice the trace of tears. Or if he did, he pretended not to. He picked up the blanket and his backpack. He stuffed the blanket into the backpack before placing it over his shoulder. With his rifle held in one hand, he reached out his other hand for Samantha. And together they made their way into the village.

In less than five minutes Tyler found their hut and they were safely inside. He started to let down the cloth that acted as the door but stood for a while watching the sun come up. In a little under ten hours they would be on their way back to the Nigerian border and the American base. If all went according to plan, they would leave this hut and make their way to the extraction pickup without any trouble, and this mission would come to an end. He would put Samantha on a plane for home, and he would be sent to God knows where. And with that thought, he wondered what would become of his chances for a relationship with her.

Tyler wasn't stupid, and he knew that this entire experience affected Samantha deeply. She was kidnapped, held hostage, slapped around, forced into a dark tunnel, and dragged through a jungle. She was holding up better than most, but he saw the horror and the fear in her eyes. She was terrified beyond belief and he figured she'd never want to be reminded of this awful time in her life. And she probably wouldn't want to be reminded of what Tyler did for a living, now that she had seen it firsthand. So it was his guess that she'd probably prefer not to see him after this. It was just a guess mind you, but one he'd bet his house on. With a deep sigh of regret, Tyler let down the curtain. The hut was suddenly cast into semi-darkness. There was enough light coming though the cloth that made up the door and a cloth over one small window so that Tyler and Samantha could see their way around the hut.

On the floor of the hut was a straw mattress covered by a worn but soft-looking blanket, one large pillow, and a tattered old quilt. A scarred table sat in one corner, with a beautiful handmade bowl in its center. Next to the bowl was a plate of food covered with a cloth. A couple of chipped mugs and an old pitcher filled with what looked to be juice sat next to the food. A large barrel filled with water stood beside the table. One rickety old chair was the only other piece of furniture in the hut. Everything, except the exquisite bowl, was old, tattered, and well used. But to Samantha it was more beautiful than a room at the Ritz.

"Are you hungry?" Tyler's voice broke through her thoughts.

"Do you think I could clean up first? I desperately need to get some of this dirt and grime off of me."

Tyler reached into his backpack of never-ending goodies and pulled out the same cloth he'd used to clean them up yesterday.

"Here." He handed her the cloth. "Be my guest."

"Is it safe? Is it safe enough for me to take a little sponge bath?"

Tyler didn't realize how scared Samantha still was, and he chided himself for not putting her mind at ease as soon as they'd entered the hut.

"We're safe here until we leave, Sam. The missionary asked some men in the village to spread out into the jungle and stand guard against any returning rebels. They don't know why they're standing guard, but they're loyal men and readily agreed. If the rebels come anywhere near this village, they'll alert the missionary and we'll have plenty of warning. We can be back in the jungle and hidden away before the rebels get within half a mile of this place."

He could see relief wash over her face. "So go ahead and take your bath. And then I want you to eat and get some sleep. Some real sleep," he added. "We're as safe here as we can possibly be until we leave this village, so I want you to get some real sleep."

Samantha smiled her thanks at his reassuring words and took the cloth. Without hesitation she went over to the handmade bowl and dipped it into the barrel of water. She then placed her hands into the bowl, feeling the cool water run through her fingers. As she stood with both hands resting in the bowl of water, Tyler went to sit down. After a few minutes, Samantha lifted her hands and started to unbutton her blouse. Even though she was aware that Tyler was sitting Indian style on the straw mattress, watching her every move, she slipped out of her blouse and draped it over the table. She thought for a second about taking off her bra and rinsing it out but decided not to push her luck. So instead she dunked the cloth into the bowl of water and began to give herself a sponge bath. Being careful not to drip all over the hard-packed mud floor, she scrubbed and rinsed, and scrubbed and rinsed, over and over again. She started with her face. Then she washed her neck and her arms. Finally she rinsed out the cloth and washed her chest and stomach. She kicked off her shoes and bent down to wash her feet. Never in her life would she take a bath for granted, she vowed, as she dunked the cloth into the cool water one more time. She was thrilled at being at least relatively clean and would have started all over again, but she made the mistake of turning to look over her shoulder at Tyler, who still sat on the mattress watching her.

The looked that flashed across Tyler's face told her exactly what he was thinking. Even in the dim light she could see the desire in his eyes—desire he was trying hard to disguise. And in a heartbeat Samantha felt the same spark of desire. As she stood in her lacy, barely-there bra, she turned toward him so that he could take her in.

And with her eyes locked on his, she watched him and waited.

Tyler got to his feet ever so slowly, his eyes never leaving hers. He walked over to Samantha and stood before her. He lifted both of his hands and started to cup her face but stopped in mid-air. His hands were filthy dirty.

"I need to clean up." As he dropped his hands back to his side, he leaned down and gently laid his lips against hers. The kiss was warm, slow, and sweet, and to Samantha's thinking, way, way too brief.

"My turn," was all he said as he lifted his head.

Samantha was still trying to clear her own head when Tyler went over and dumped the bowl of dirty bath water out the door. Then he refilled the bowl with clean water and shrugged out of his shirt. And because she was still feeling a little lightheaded from his light, brief kiss, and because she didn't want to miss an opportunity to openly admire every inch of his bared body, she grabbed her blouse, put it on, and sat down Indian style on the straw mattress and watched him bathe.

Watching Tyler was like watching a beautiful sculpture of a man. The muscles in his strong back rippled as he washed his arms and chest. And when he leaned over to wash his face, his body looked smooth and tight, without an ounce of fat to be found. He dipped the cloth into the water again and washed his face over and over, giving Samantha a little more time to admire his masculine, efficient movements. She was enjoying the show immensely, especially since he was an absolutely perfect specimen to feast her eyes upon. But just like a man, Tyler was clean in no time at all and the show was over. He even managed to semi-wash his hair by running his wet fingers through it. And Samantha was immediately envious. She would have given an arm and a leg to wash her hair. It was long, dirty, and so tangled that she thought she would never be able to get it clean again.

Tyler must have read her thoughts, as he turned and spoke. "Let's eat something and then if you want, I'll help you wash your hair."

She was up on her feet in a flash. The thought of clean hair was enough to give her energy she didn't think she possessed. Tyler took the cloth off the plate of food to find several thick slices of bread, berries, two bananas, and two large oranges. It wasn't much, but it would more than do the trick. And it was bound to taste better than another MRE.

Together they sat on the straw mattress and ate. Samantha ate slowly, savoring every bite. She ate two slices of bread, half the berries, and a banana before she peeled the orange. She pulled off a slice of the fresh fruit and placed it between her lips. The fruit was so succulent that she sucked on the slice between her lips, letting the juice flow into her mouth. She had never tasted anything so good. When she finished with that slice she started on another. She placed a piece of the orange between her lips and sucked again, only this time some of the juice ran down her chin. As she took the orange slice into her mouth, she slowly ran her tongue back and forth over her lower lip, not wanting to miss even a drop of the sweet nectar.

As Tyler watched her eat the orange, he felt like he had been punched right in the stomach. He was instantly as hard as a rock, his body reacting to her of its own accord.

She just sat there with her eyes closed, sucking the juice out of the slice of orange, looking sexier than he'd ever seen her. And he knew that he had to do something quickly or he was going to forget that he was on a mission. No matter how much he wanted to make love to Samantha right now, he couldn't. He was not with her in the Nigerian jungle for personal reasons; he was sent on a mission to get her away from the rebels and to get her safety home. And because he was a Navy SEAL first and foremost, he would not take advantage of the situation. He'd never done that before and he was not about to start now. So with all the self-control he could muster, he got up, grabbed onto the little chair, and dragged it over to the table.

"If you're finished eating, I'll wash your hair." His voice was raspy and he had to clear his throat.

But Samantha didn't seem to notice. She finished off her orange and licked the juice from her fingers. Tyler had to bite back a curse.

"Come and sit here."

Samantha went over and sat down.

"Lean your neck against the back of the chair."

Again, Samantha did as she was told.

With her long hair hanging over the back of the chair, Tyler went to work. He took the bowl in one hand and held it so that her hair fell into it. Then he picked up one of the mugs, dipped it into the barrel of water, and slowly poured it over her scalp and down her hair. She sighed aloud with pleasure. Tyler repeated the process over and over again, until her hair was dripping wet. Then he set down the mug and ran his fingers through the long wet strands, gently working out the tangles.

"Please don't stop," she murmured. "Please don't stop. It feels so good."

Giving in to her softly spoken words, he reached again for the mug, filled it with water, and poured it slowly over her already drenched strands. After he had finally worked out most of the tangles, he wrapped her hair around his hand and gently squeezed out the water. Next he set down both the mug and the bowl. As he ran both of his hands and fingers through her hair, he brought his wet fingers against her temple and started to massage. His touch was light and relaxing, and finally he felt her start to unwind. Her eyes were closed and her breathing was deep and even. And while he watched the enticing rise and fall of her breasts, he wondered if she'd fallen asleep.

Since he liked the feel of her wet hair against his skin, Tyler didn't hurry through his task. He let her wet strands fall against his arms as he continued to tenderly message her temples. It took him a second to realize that she had opened her eyes.

"That feels wonderful." Her voice brought his eyes away from her breasts and back to her beautiful face. Looking down at her, the smile on her face told him that she'd noticed where he'd been focused. But he didn't care. He thought she had beautiful breasts, like the rest of her, and he wasn't ashamed that he'd been caught looking at them.

"Do you think you can sleep now?" As he asked the question he reluctantly drew his hands one last time through her hair.

"I think I could sleep for a month."

Tyler took a step back from the chair and fisted his hands at his sides. He had to fight back the urge to lean down and kiss her. Every cell in his body was screaming out to touch her again, but this time with a different intention. He knew that he had to keep his hands to himself, and washing her hair had not been the smartest thing he'd ever done. Now it was going to be even harder to keep away from her. But he swore to himself that he would and could keep his distance. And he'd start right now.

"Well, we'd better get some sleep. We need to leave here in about six hours. We have about a two-hour walk, before we're picked up at 1600 hours."

Even though Samantha's heart was still beating wildly from Tyler's touch, she knew that what they both needed was sleep. So she got up from the chair and went over to the makeshift bed. Tyler followed. The mattress was large enough for two but there was only one pillow. As Samantha lay down she scooted over next to Tyler, turned on to her side and laid her head down next to his. He was lying on his back, staring up at the ceiling. Because she couldn't help herself, she reached out and rested her arm over his stomach, placing her hand over his heart.

"Go to sleep, Sam." She noted that his voice sounded like a plea.

"Is that what you really want, Tyler?"

She could feel his body stiffen at her question, and she could also feel his heart start to accelerate.

"We both need to get some sleep. We really are safe here, Samantha, so close your eyes, and we'll be out of here before you know it."

Samantha knew that it was now or never. And before she could talk herself out of it, she took the plunge.

"You may need to get some sleep, but what I need right now is for you to make love to me."

This time Tyler's heart actually skipped a beat. At least it felt like it did beneath her hand. And as Samantha waited for his response, he rolled over onto his side, facing her.

"Tell me that again when we get home, and I'll take you up on your offer so fast it'll make your head spin." He reached out and softly caressed her cheek. But even as good as his touch felt, she wanted more, and she wouldn't be sidetracked.

"But I want you now, Tyler. And I want you to want me now." She was laying her heart on the line, but she couldn't seem to stop herself.

"My God, Samantha." He closed his eyes, took a deep breath, and then opened them. "I want you every minute of every day, and that hasn't changed just because we're in this stinking jungle. But this is hardly the most romantic place in the world, and when I make love to you for the first time, I want it to at least be in a real bed."

This time she reached out and touched his face. "I don't care about romance or comfort or anything else. I know that once we're headed out of here, it could be months until I see you again, and I don't want to waste any more time. I want to be with you now, Tyler. I want to be able to remember that we made love here, in this hut, on this straw mattress. I want that more than I've ever wanted anything, and I'm hoping you feel the same way."

"You may not care about romance or comfort, sweetheart, but what about timing?" At the look of confusion on her face, he continued. "I don't have any protection with me." He thought that his softly spoken words about protection would bring her back to reality, but instead she surprised him with her response.

"The timing is perfect, Tyler. I'm as regular as clockwork, and this is the best time in my cycle. I won't get pregnant."

Tyler was feeling himself weaken, so he took one more stab at being honorable.

"I'm on a mission, Samantha." He figured those five simple words said it all and that she'd understand that he couldn't make love to her now. But he should have known better.

"I know that. I really do." She paused, wanting to find just the right words. "But I was hoping that we could both forget about this mission for a couple of hours. Couldn't we put the rebels, where we are, and why we're here out of our minds and just think about us? Just for a while?"

"If this were any other time or any other place, we wouldn't even be having this conversation." His closed his eyes for a second and swallowed. "But this isn't another time or place, Samantha. And my orders are to rescue you and the other hostages and to get you safely back to base camp. I've never once been tempted to disobey my orders and make it something personal. I need to stay focused so that I can do everything possible to keep you safe." *There, that should do it.*

"But we're safe here for the next six hours. Didn't you say so? Didn't you tell me that we're safe in this hut until we leave?"

"We're safe here, Sam. I promise you. I wasn't lying to you about that."

Samantha knew she should give up, but she couldn't. She couldn't let it go—not if there was even the slightest possibility that she could convince Tyler to make love to her.

"I know that you're here because this is your assignment, Tyler. And I would never put your reputation or a mission at risk. So I promise you that whatever happens between us today will always be just between us. I will never, ever tell another soul."

"Sam…" He tried to interrupt but she wouldn't let him.

"I need you, Tyler," she spoke barely above a whisper. "I need you so much."

He closed his eyes and tried to remember all the reasons why making love to her right now was a really bad idea. It was just his luck that he couldn't seem to come up with another good reason why. And he knew it was because he didn't really want to. He wanted desperately to let her talk him into making love. And as if she could read his mind, she said the magic words.

"And I need to know what it's like to feel you inside me."

And those were the words that finally did it. In one split second Tyler could make himself forget that he was a Navy SEAL on a mission. He didn't care about romance, comfort, or timing. All he cared about was the woman lying beside him and how he was going to feel buried deep inside of her.

Tyler opened his eyes and searched her face for any signs of hesitancy. But all he saw was a look of warmth and invitation. So he wrapped his arm around her waist and brought her slowly up against his body.

Dumb idea, dumb idea, dumb idea. You're on a mission, you're on a mission, you're on a mission, screamed his brain. *Feels right, feels right, feels right,* screamed his body. And right or wrong, Tyler made the decision to listen to his body.

"Are you sure?" He asked the question as he bent his mouth toward hers, and one small part of him hoped that she would change her mind—the part of him that was still a SEAL on a mission trying to remember to obey orders.

"Yes." Her response was whispered against his lips, and in the next second her lips found his in a deep, soul-searching kiss. And Tyler was lost—totally and completely lost. And as he drank in the sweetness of her lips, he didn't think again about his mission, his orders, or the other hostages. He thought only about the woman he now held in his arms.

As Samantha sighed into Tyler's mouth, he took his time touching and tasting. He wanted to savor the feel of his lips on hers and refused to rush through the kiss. He opened his mouth, taking her with him, and slipped his tongue inside. He couldn't stop the moan that came from deep in his chest when the tip of her tongue played against his, touching and seducing him. The kiss that he refused to rush was now beginning to consume him, and his hold around her waist tightened.

Samantha had never felt more sexually alive in her life. She melted against Tyler, trying to keep up with the intensity of the kiss they were sharing. His mouth was hot, wet, and demanding, yet slow and almost unhurried at the same time. And the contrast between slow and demanding was driving her to distraction. As Samantha gave herself over completely to an overwhelming need, he pulled her up against his hard body, taking the kiss up another level. As he continued to kiss her more thoroughly than she'd ever been kissed before, his tongue swept almost lazily through her mouth, causing her to tingle all the way down to the tips of her toes.

As Tyler lifted his head so that he could place his open mouth against her neck, this time it was Samantha who couldn't stop a moan from escaping her parted lips. And all she could do was cling to him as his mouth started its decent, leaving a trail of wet kisses behind.

Tyler dragged his open mouth down her long throat, stopping only long enough to catch his breath. Then he gently turned Samantha onto her back. As he continued to nibble away at the side of her neck, his hand reached for the buttons on her blouse. And one by one, the buttons were slipped out of their buttonholes. He slipped one arm under Samantha, lifting her body just enough so that he could slide her blouse off of her. Next he easily managed to release and to get rid of her bra. And before she even had a chance to open her eyes, he lifted her up even more to his waiting mouth.

Loving the feel and taste of her, he took his time. Then he laid her back down on the mattress, causing her to call out his name.

With the sound of his name on her lips, Tyler proceeded to finish the job of undressing her. He lowered the zipper on her jeans and slid both her jeans and panties down her legs, tossing them aside. And what Tyler saw before him made him stop and stare in awe, because there lay Samantha, beautifully naked and waiting, lovelier than he could ever have imagined. At the sight of her looking up at him, his heart turned over in his chest, and he leaned down and kissed her again, and again, and again.

As Tyler made love to Samantha with his mouth, she brought her hands up and began the joyful task of taking off his clothes. With shaking fingers, she finally got his shirt open and off his magnificent body. But before she started on his fatigues, she needed to feel skin against skin. So she lifted her hands and laid her palms flat against his chest. And as she touched him she sighed.

Her hands and fingers explored every inch of Tyler that was not covered by clothes. She let the back of her fingers trail slowly through the dark hair on his chest, all the way down to the waistband of his pants. Then she reached around him and brought her hands slowly up his back, finally finding a resting place in the softness of his hair. She let her hands slide through his hair, loving the feel if it against her fingers.

Just as Samantha thought about getting Tyler out of his fatigues, he took his mouth away from hers and found her ear. He touched her earlobe with the tip of his tongue right before he began to whisper to her all the things he wanted to do to her in a low, raspy voice. And she couldn't wait another second to get him completely naked.

As Samantha helped Tyler out of his fatigues, her heart was beating a mile a minute. She was so aroused that she didn't know if she could stand it much longer. She wanted desperately to feel him inside of her, and before she could stop herself, the words came tumbling out of her mouth.

"I need you now, Tyler. I need for you to be inside of me now."

Tyler didn't hesitate. He leaned over her, and kissed her softy on the lips.

"Open your eyes, Samantha. I want both of us to watch each other. I want both of us to remember our first time together."

Samantha opened her eyes—dreamy green eyes latching on to lust-filled gray ones. And before either of them drew in another breath, Samantha almost went over the edge.

As Tyler joined their bodies together, he had to force himself to stay completely still, because he was afraid that if he moved he'd lose it; she just felt that good. And he suspected, even in his muddled brain, that she was already as close as he was. So he closed his eyes and mentally counted to ten, hoping to slow his body down. But even before he got to *five* he realized that it was a hopeless cause, because Samantha simply wasn't cooperating.

Tyler nestled his face into the crook of her shoulder just as she wrapped her legs around his waist, causing him to forget all about taking it slowly. And in the next second, they were making deep, penetrating, mind-blowing love.

With a great deal of effort, Tyler lifted his head, found Samantha's mouth, and kissed her. His body had taken over his mind. And before he gave in to his own burning need, Samantha dug her nails into his shoulders and cried out his name, bringing him right along with her.

Tyler had never experienced anything so powerful, and when it was over he all but collapsed. Careful not to hurt Samantha, he wrapped his arm around her and fell onto his back, taking her with him. She responded by curling up against his body.

"If it wasn't for the fact that we're still in this jungle hut, I'd think that I've just died and gone to heaven." He spoke into her still damp hair.

"I've never experienced anything so all-consuming. Being with you was even better than I'd imagined," was her honest reply.

"I wish it could have been under better circumstances for you, Sam."

She snuggled even closer to him. "It was incredible for me, Tyler."

"It was incredible for me too, sweetheart." And as he spoke the words out loud, he realized that he actually meant them, which scared him just a little.

"I felt my orgasm all the way to the tips of my toes."

"Yeah, I know what you mean." And he did, because he'd felt his own climax crash through every inch of his body.

"Do you think that maybe it was a fluke?" It took him a full second to realize that she was kidding.

"Could be." He responded with a smile, knowing what was coming.

"So do you think that we should try it again, just to see if it was really as good as we think it was?"

"I think it might take a couple of more times before we can come to a valid conclusion."

Samantha's sweet laughter enveloped both of them. "If you're up to a couple more times, Lieutenant, count me in." And his own laughter caught in his throat as she threw one leg over his outstretched body and drew herself over him. "One down and two to go," she whispered.

"Open your eyes, Tyler." She waited until he did as she asked. "I want both of us to watch each other. I want both of us to remember our second time together." She had remembered his own words and repeated them just as she glided herself down, taking him fully into her body. And as their eyes stayed locked together, they took each other further and further than either of them had ever dared to go.

Chapter Eleven

Samantha was wide awake, not even trying to get any more sleep. She knew that they'd be leaving the hut in less than an hour, and she wanted a little time to herself to think about what had happened between her and Tyler.

As she turned over, with touches of sunlight streaming into the hut, she watched him as he slept beside her. His breathing was deep and even, but she wasn't fooled. She knew that he was only partially asleep and that he would wake up, fully alert, at the slightest movement or noise. Because she didn't want to disturb him, she resisted the urge to reach out and touch.

Samantha was still overwhelmed by the intensity of what they had shared over the last few hours. Round two of their lovemaking had been even better than round one, which Samantha had found hard to believe. Afterward they had both fallen into an instant, exhausted sleep, only to have Tyler wake Samantha up again hours later. In her sleep she had tucked her bottom up against him, which he had decided to take full advantage of. And as she stirred from a wonderful, dreamless state, he had wrapped his arm around her waist and slipped into her. In almost slow motion Tyler had made love to Samantha again. And after they both reached fulfillment, he had snuggled up against her back, cupped his hand around one breast, and fallen back asleep.

Samantha had never imagined that lovemaking could be the way it was with Tyler. Granted, she had limited experience with serious relationships, but nothing could have prepared her for what she was feeling. Her heart was filled with love for this man she had known less than four months, and her body seemed to react not only to his touch, but to his voice and his glorious eyes. Even a half-smile from him could make her heart beat faster and her bones turn to mush. This was not a crush she was dealing with, or puppy love. This was a love that she knew would last her a lifetime.

The only problem with coming to grips with these new feelings was that Tyler didn't love her back. Sure, she knew that he wanted her; he'd just proven that three times. But wanting someone sexually and loving her were two different things. Samantha knew this and her heart ached because of it.

But there was something else that she also knew. She knew that even though Tyler wasn't in love with her, for right now she would take him any way she could get him. And if that meant that they would only have a sexual relationship, then so be it. Maybe down the road, if they stayed together, she would need something more from him, but for the time being she would live for today and try not to worry too much about tomorrow.

"What are you thinking about?"

Samantha had been so caught up in her own personal thoughts that she didn't even realize that Tyler was awake, watching her.

"I was thinking about you." She answered without thinking.

"Care to share?"

"I was just thinking about how safe I feel with you." That was the first thing that came to her mind. Never in a million years would she tell him what she'd really been thinking about.

Tyler leaned in and gave her a sweet, brief kiss. "I wish we had time for me to give you something else to think about, but we have a helo to catch."

Samantha leaned in and kissed him back, but her kiss was anything but brief. "I know," she sighed against his mouth. She didn't pull away from his warm lips.

"I wish we didn't have to leave right now." He ran his tongue seductively over her bottom lip.

"Me too." She ran the tip of her tongue slowly along his upper lip.

"It would be foolish for us to stay here any longer than necessary." He ducked his head and nibbled lightly at her earlobe.

"I wouldn't want us to do anything foolish." She pulled away from his playful mouth and found his earlobe, nibbling away on her own.

"Maybe…" Tyler stopped and sucked in a breath when her tongue stroked his earlobe. "Maybe we could stay a few minutes longer."

"That would be wonderful." She whispered against his neck and then she found his ear again and whispered something that was wonderfully wicked. The nasty words she kept whispering in his ear and her warm breath against his skin was his undoing.

"Five minutes, sweetheart. All we have are five more minutes." He barely got the words out. And because of what her tongue was doing to his ear, Tyler figured that he needed only two minutes, but he'd do his best to give her five.

And when two minutes turned into five, and five minutes turned into ten, both of them gave themselves up to the feelings they were sharing and the fulfillment of the moment.

As they both came crashing back down to earth, Tyler hated to break the spell of their lovemaking. But their time was running out and he needed to get things back into perspective. He needed to remember that he was still on a mission and that getting Samantha safely home was his priority—not to mention his direct orders. So with a light kiss on the tip of her nose, he wasted no time in getting out of their rumpled bed and back into his clothes.

Samantha followed suit, thankful for this time they had shared together and sensing that Tyler was slipping back into SEAL mode. In less than five minutes they were both dressed and ready to go. And like they'd done in Father Dominic's room, they straightened everything up, leaving no evidence behind that they had ever been there.

"We should reach our destination point in about two hours."

Yep, he is back to being Lieutenant Garrett, she thought. But she also thought that it was probably a good thing, because she knew that if it was up to her, she'd stay in this hut in this village with Tyler for a lifetime.

"Will the helo be waiting for us?" she asked.

"No. Once we get to our designated extraction point, we'll wait. The pilot will verify our location through GPS, and then he'll head in to pick us up. If we're on time, we won't wait longer than fifteen minutes."

Tyler gave the hut one more cursory look. "Ready to go?"

A small part of Samantha hated leaving the cozy hut. The interior was cast in soft shadows from the late afternoon sun, creating an intimate, romantic setting. She stood, looking down at the mattress, remembering every touch, every look, and every sigh.

"We need to go, Sam."

Tyler was trying to sound gentle, but she could hear a little impatience in his voice. He was back to being a Navy SEAL, and only a Navy SEAL.

"Yes, I'm ready." She tore her gaze away from what had been their bed.

"We'll be moving in daylight, so we need to be extra careful."

It suddenly dawned on Samantha how exposed they were going to be.

"Stay as close to me as possible, and it's important that we make as little noise as possible." Tyler lifted the cloth that served as the door to the hut. "I want to slip out of this village unseen, so we'll make our way out the same way we came in."

"Don't we need to say goodbye and thank the missionary who helped us?" Samantha stepped out of the hut behind Tyler.

"I don't want to put him or these people in any danger. And anyway, he knows how grateful we are for his help. I thanked him when I met him this morning."

As he spoke, Tyler led Samantha away from the hut, back into the surrounding jungle. And within seconds they were swallowed up by the protective foliage.

"Stay close," he said right before he leaned down and gave her an unexpected kiss. And before she could kiss him back, he took off. And Samantha, doing as she was told, stayed close and as quiet as possible.

They had been trudging through the jungle for well over an hour when Tyler came to a sudden dead stop. He turned and motioned with his finger to his lips for Samantha not to say a word. As Tyler stood and listened, Samantha stood and felt an all-too-familiar bubble of fear. Something was definitely wrong.

Very slowly and very quietly, Tyler stepped back toward Samantha. Then he took her by the arm, and as silently as possible led her over to an area where the grass was at least two feet high and there were low-hanging tree branches. He slipped off his backpack, took his M16 in hand, and laid down flat on the ground, taking Samantha with him. He slung his rifle around in front of him, positioning it so that he could look through the scope. One hand grasped the barrel of the weapon. His other hand he placed around the trigger.

Samantha lay next to Tyler in the tall grass, scared out of her mind. She tried to steady her breathing but was having difficulty with each breath she took. The only thing that saved her from hyperventilating was the fact that she didn't want to make any noise that would give them away. As she lay there, frozen in place, she finally heard what Tyler must have heard seconds ago. She heard men's voices—distant voices of men speaking in broken English. And she knew right away that they had to be a band of rebels.

The voices and footsteps of the rebels got closer and closer, but it was impossible to tell how many men there were. And Samantha wasn't about to lift her head to find out. In fact, she tried to bury herself as deeply as possible into the springy grass of the jungle, hoping to become invisible. Lying there, she forced herself to stay as still as a rock. The only part of her body that moved was her eyes, which she had focused on Tyler.

Tyler kept his eye trained on the scope of his weapon, with his finger resting lightly around the trigger. If need be, he was ready to fire.

"If we find the woman, remember that I get her first." The rebel's words could be heard loud and clear, as was the raunchy laughter that followed.

"But then you will share her? Yes?"

Lascivious comments followed that remark.

"Once I am finished with her you can have her if you want. As long as she is delivered alive, it makes no difference to me."

There was another round of lewd comments and loud laughter, and Samantha noted a small twitch of Tyler's trigger finger.

"Why does it matter if she is dead or alive when we find her? Wouldn't it be better to get rid of her now?"

Lying in the grass, listening to the rebels casually discuss Samantha's demise was like listening in on a bad dream. It somehow seemed so unreal to her.

"The captain said to bring all the hostages back alive. What he does with them is his business, not ours."

The band of rebels weren't even trying to be quiet as they made their way right by Samantha and Tyler's hiding place. They joked and laughed, and there was little doubt that she was still their main topic, which made her sick to her stomach.

One by one, the band of men passed by. Samantha felt somewhat safe tucked away as she was, but she couldn't get her heart to stop pounding as if it were going to jump right out of her chest. She knew that Tyler was at his most alert and that all of his attention was focused on the sound of the enemy. But she had to do something to still her wildly beating heart, so she started silently counting down the minutes. One minute turned into two; two minutes turned into three; three minutes turned into four. And just as she started to count away another sixty seconds, something terrifying happened.

One of the rebels broke away from his group and stopped less than a foot away from where Sam and Tyler were hiding. He was so close that they could actually hear the zipper being lowered on his pants. As Samantha lay frozen in fear, Tyler was debating whether or not he could take the rebel out with his hands without altering the others. Luckily, he didn't need to find out, because the rebel did nothing more than relieve himself. Within seconds he was zipped back up and joining the others. Samantha let out the breath she'd been holding, and Tyler returned his full attention to the scope of his M16.

The rebels were now stomping through the jungle, almost oblivious to their surroundings, and Samantha finally stopped counting away the minutes, thinking that the rebels weren't really looking for them very hard. Even though she couldn't see them, they just seemed way too casual about their search. So she drew in a steady breath and tried to will herself to relax. But just as she tried to assure herself that she and Tyler were going to get away unnoticed, she heard a rustling in the foliage right where they were lying. With the rebels still too close for comfort, Samantha watched in absolute horror as a huge, lethal-looking snake came slithering out of the bushes, heading straight toward them. And she had to swallow down a scream of pure terror.

Before she knew what was happening, she felt Tyler's hand clamp down over her mouth. Her frantic eyes looked up into his face and he mouthed to her "don't move." She just stared into Tyler's eyes, feeling the snake coming closer and closer. And against her will, and with what could only be called morbid fascination, she turned her eyes back toward the snake.

Samantha knew absolutely nothing about snakes, but she didn't have to. She could tell just by looking at the huge thing that it was deadly. It hardly moved, slithering barely an inch. But that inch was enough to cause her to start to shake all over. Tyler, feeling her reaction, tightened his hand over her mouth. As she watched the snake, he watched her. And when he was satisfied that she wasn't going to cry out or get up and run, he brought his hand and his eyes back to his weapon. And in that instant she knew that he trusted her enough to put both their lives in her hands. So she fought down the panic and remained perfectly still.

Samantha would never be able to tell if she was more afraid of the rebels passing by or the snake. Her eyes latched on to the reptile, watching as it came close enough for them to touch. Her heart was beating out of her chest, and she felt a cold sweat break out all over her body. She could still hear the men moving through the jungle, but their voices started to sound like they'd moved far enough away for it to be safe. But she didn't as much as move an inch.

Tyler, on the other hand, had carefully laid down his M16, and in slow motion he reached down and removed a long blade from a sheath attached to his belt. His eyes were now on the snake that was just inches away from Samantha. He was poised and ready.

"No matter what happens, do not scream."

His words were spoken so softly she wondered if she had imagined them.

She watched in a state of shock as the snake's tongue flicked out, and then back into its scaly mouth. It slithered a little closer. Tyler raised the knife. Samantha closed her eyes and prayed. But nothing happened. And as she continued to pray, she found the courage to open her eyes. The snake was completely still but Samantha could hear an awful hissing sound coming from it. And before she fainted dead away, the reptile surprised them both and simply turned its nasty head, flicked its tongue one more time, and then slithered away in another direction. And that's when Samantha felt herself start to fall apart.

As Tyler re-sheathed his knife, Samantha laid her face into her hands and gave in to the tears that had been threatening to fall. She was tired, scared, hungry, thirsty, and desperately homesick. And the awful-looking, frightening snake had been the last straw. But she was also still very aware of their precarious situation, so the tears that she cried were silent tears.

With the threat of the rebels finally behind them, Tyler laid a hand on Samantha's back and let her cry. With everything she'd been through in the last four days, he thought that a few more tears might actually do her some good. She had been brave beyond belief, and even though she'd cried in his arms two nights ago, he felt her tears now were well deserved. So he kept rubbing his hand slowly up and down her back while she cried her eyes out.

"We don't have much farther to go now, Sam." At the sound of his voice, she lifted tear-drenched eyes. "We should make it to our destination in about thirty minutes. Then we'll be able to hide out until the helo's in sight."

She turned, sat up and wiped her hand across her face, leaving streaks of dirt under one eye and across her cheek. And Tyler thought that she'd never looked more adorable.

"Think you can make it?"

"Yes." Her answer was direct, just as he'd expected.

Tyler stood and picked up his never far-from-reach backpack. Then he helped Samantha to her feet.

"Are you all right?"

"I don't know if I'll ever be all right again." She sounded drained and weary.

"Sure you will. This kind of adventure actually grows on you. You wait and see. Once you're home, in no time at all, you'll be longing for an escapade in some far away jungle." His was trying to joke her out of her exhaustion and she knew it.

"I won't let you down, Tyler. I've made it this far, and I can make it the rest of the way."

His response was rapid-fire. "Fact number one, Samantha James, you have *not* let me down. Fact number two, you *could never* let me down. And fact number three, you are one hell of a woman and if they ever decide to let women into the SEALs, I'd recommend that they start with you."

His words blew her away and she had to fight back a fresh batch of tears. But these were not tears of fear, frustration, or panic; these were tears of love—tears that she didn't want Tyler to see.

Luckily for her, Tyler had turned and was starting to make his way through the jungle. They had a schedule to keep to and they'd already been delayed because of the rebels and the nasty snake. And because his words had done the trick, she felt a surge of energy kick in. He moved a little faster than before and she had no trouble keeping up with him.

As promised, they stopped in less than thirty minutes and he found them a place that concealed them fairly well. As they shared a drink from the canteen, Samantha felt her spirits rising.

"How long do you think it'll take the helo to get here?"

"Not long."

"Are we the last ones to be picked up?"

Tyler suspected that she needed to talk to keep her mind off of what they'd been through. "The last two out will be Kid and Billy. David Cushman and the other hostages should've been picked up yesterday. You and I will be picked up today. Kid and Billy will catch a helo later tonight. Since the extractions were all planned for different times and different places, we won't see the team until we're back at base."

"And then what?"

"And then once we're all back at base camp, you and the others will be put on a plane for home."

"What about you? Where do you go from here?"

"Beats me, Sam. It would be nice to be sent home, but I can't say for sure that we'll be that lucky. More than likely they'll try to get one or two more missions out of us before they send us home."

Samantha was dying for Tyler to be sent home so that they could spend more time together, but she kept that thought to herself. She was afraid that if she said too much she'd give away her feelings for him, and that she didn't want to do.

"Katie and Brandon are getting married in two months. Will you make it home for their wedding?" That seemed like a safe enough topic.

"I've already put in a leave request, and it's been approved."

Samantha wanted to ask Tyler if he thought that they would see each other again before Katie's wedding, but she was too afraid of what his answer might be. So she purposely kept the conversation away from the two of them.

"Katie will be devastated if you don't make it to the wedding."

"I'll be there." There was no room for doubt in his voice. "But what about you, Sam? You still planning…"

Tyler stopped speaking as he heard the *click, click, click* of the chopper blades. He peered up into the sky and could see the helo far away in the distance. He knew from experience that it would be landing in about three minutes.

"Okay, Samantha. This is it." He stood and watched the approaching chopper. "As soon as the helo hits the ground I want you to bend low and run for it. The pilot won't shut the chopper down so you'll have to fight your way against the force of the air stream. I'll be right behind you, so whatever you do, don't stop. We only have a minute or two before the pilot will take off."

She looked at him with surprise. "What do you mean, before the pilot will take off? Surely he wouldn't leave without us?"

"There will be at least four other SEALs from another team in that helo and this extraction is timed to protect everyone on this mission. Those will be his orders. Two minutes, tops. If we're not on board, he'll take off."

Samantha could hardly believe her ears. It was beyond belief that they could come this far and then be left behind. *Well, they won't be left behind because of me*, she vowed. And she knew that as soon as Tyler gave the word, she would run faster than she'd ever run before.

The helo came in. The landing was quick but not quiet, and Tyler took hold of Samantha's hand, pulling her to her feet. "Go," was all he said, and because she knew that he was depending on her, she took off running. With every step she took, she felt that much closer to safety. *Just a few yards more,* she told herself as she kept running, *just a few yards more.*

Samantha could see two men in uniform at the open entrance of the massive helo. They both were kneeling on one knee, with weapons in their hands. "Just a few more steps," she repeated over and over. "Just a few more steps."

Because of the noise caused by the chopper blades, and because she was fighting against the force of the air stream, Samantha never heard the first shot that was fired. But suddenly, in a blink of an eye, everything changed. Both soldiers in the helo raised their weapons and started to fire. As she was just a few steps away from the entrance of the large bird, one of the SEALs jumped down while the other kept up a steady round of fire. The SEAL on the ground reached out for Samantha, just as she turned to make sure that Tyler was right behind her. And that's when her life flashed before her eyes.

Kneeling down, yards away from the helo and at the edge of what had been their hiding place, was Tyler. He was firing his weapon, providing cover for Samantha and the other SEALs. He was so focused on the rebels that came out of nowhere and so focused on the job at hand that he was not even trying to make his way to the chopper. In fact, he seemed to be making his way farther and farther into the protection of the jungle. But as he moved back he kept up a steady stream of fire.

Samantha's instinct was to take off after not only the man who had saved her life, but the man she was madly in love with. But before she could run toward Tyler, the SEAL on the ground grabbed her around the waist. The second she realized his intent, she tried to wrestle out of his hold. All she wanted was to make her way back to Tyler. Because she was so desperate and so determined, she was able to break free of the SEAL. She took off, stumbled, and fell to the ground. And before she could get up and run toward Tyler, the SEAL had her back on her feet, with a firm, iron grip around her waist.

With gunfire all around them, she looked over at Tyler and something inside her snapped and she stopped fighting the SEAL who had her locked in his grip. She was suddenly very aware that Tyler was doing the job he was trained to do, and she could hear him telling her over and over that his orders were to get her and the other hostages safely to base camp. She knew in that instant that she would not allow herself to become an inexperienced journalist who would put his mission at risk. She needed to be brave and not let Tyler and the other SEALs down. She needed to prove to him that she respected who he was and what he did. And she needed to be brave and prove it to him now. So she stopped trying to break away and she let the SEAL pull her over to the helo and lift her up and in. He quickly followed, covered by rounds being fired from not only the chopper, but from the lone SEAL who was making his way back into the jungle.

In a flash of a second, Tyler looked over at the chopper and his eyes clashed for one moment with Samantha's. Again, she felt the overwhelming urge to jump down and run to him but she stayed in place. And she saw a fleeting look in his eyes that told her that he approved. And as he continued to fire and move back even farther under cover of the jungle, she would have sworn that she read his lips and that he said to her "that's my girl" right before he disappeared from sight.

Two seconds after the SEAL followed Samantha into the helo, he pulled her away from the opening and the pilot started to take off. And that's when Samantha stopped being calm, stopped being brave, and started to scream.

"You can't leave him!" She shouted at the pilot. "You can't just leave him!"

It had never really dawned on her that they'd actually take off without Tyler. She remembered what Tyler had told her—that the pilot's orders were to take off in two minutes, regardless of who made it on board. But she hadn't believed it. She still didn't believe it. So she tried to make her way back to the opening but was stopped by several SEALs. As her calmness completely deserted her, she pushed, shoved, and scratched her way through them. "We have to go back!" She was now feeling frantic. "We can't leave Lieutenant Garrett! We have to go back!"

With tears streaming down her face and her voice getting more and more hysterical, one of the SEALs on board reached out to take hold of her. His hands clasped around her arms to keep her steady and to keep her away from the opening in the helo.

"Calm down, Ms. James. You need to calm down."

Samantha's wild eyes looked up into his. But all she could register at that second was that the helo was getting farther and farther away from Tyler. And she tried to jerk away from his hands. He held on tight.

"Please try to calm down. We're going to go back for Lieutenant Garrett."

There was a ringing in her ears, so she wasn't sure she had heard the SEAL correctly. So she stood still in his grip and looked at him with a question in her wet eyes.

"Did you hear me, ma'am? I said we're going to go back for the lieutenant."

Relief like she had never known before swept through Samantha at the words "we're going to go back for the lieutenant." But even as she heard the words, she didn't believe them, because the helo hadn't turned around.

"Are we going back now?" She knew the answer before he spoke.

"No."

For a moment Samantha was grateful that the SEAL still had his hands on her arms, because she felt like she was going to faint.

"When?" was all she managed to choke out.

"When it's safe."

"When it's safe for whom?" She didn't like his answer and because of her fear for Tyler, she felt some of her spunk returning.

"When it's safe for everyone involved in this operation." He dropped his hands from her arms and ran impatient fingers through his hair. "Lieutenant Garrett knows what he's doing, and he knows we'll be back. He's extremely well trained to survive in any situation. SOP on this mission is to wait another twenty-four hours before executing another extraction. We'll watch the clock, pick him up on GPS, and go in and get him."

The ringing in Samantha's ears got louder and louder, and she felt her knees start to buckle.

"Are you all right?" Two SEALs caught her and knelt down to steady her as she almost hit the ground.

"Ms. James, are you all right?"

Samantha was anything but all right. As a matter of fact, she had never felt more desperate and more frantic in her life.

The SEALs looked at each other over the top of Samantha's head, clearly bewildered by her reaction. The color had drained from Samantha's face and the tears had started all over again. She seemed totally despondent.

"Miss James, we can't help you if you don't tell us what's wrong."

"It's…it's not me," she sobbed. "It's…it's Tyler."

"Don't worry about Lieutenant Garrett, Ms. James. He'll be back before you know it."

"But you don't understand." She was trying not to get hysterical again. "You said you'll pick him up on GPS and then go in and get him."

"That's right. Like all SEALs, Lieutenant Garrett has a GPS tracking device with him. That's how we were able to pinpoint your exact location. We'll be able to find him with no problem."

As big tears splashed down onto her cheeks, Samantha reached into the pocket of her jeans. And as the SEALs watched her, she brought out her hand and opened her trembling fingers, which were clasped around a small, official-looking, Navy SEAL GPS tracking device.

"Lieuten…" She had to swallow back her tears and start over. "Lieutenant Garrett gave this to me in case we got separated." She looked and felt so forlorn. "He doesn't have any way for you to track him. He gave it to me and now you have no way to find him."

There was a heartbeat of silence.

"It's not as bad as you think, ma'am."

Samantha looked from one SEAL to the other. Her eyes were brimming over with tears.

"Does he still have his backpack with him?"

"Yes." That one word came out on a sob.

"Then he'll find a way to let us know where he is."

Samantha never did get a look inside his bag of tricks, but she was pretty sure that it contained more than just standard survival gear. There was no telling what he had stuffed into that thing. But it was never far from him, and more than likely he had planned for just this sort of disaster. He was so well trained that surely he wouldn't just give her his tracking device without keeping some sort of backup for himself. She couldn't believe that she hadn't thought of that before, and with that note of reassurance she felt a tiny flicker of hope.

"And there's one other thing, ma'am."

"What's that?" Her voice, although still emotional, sounded a little less strained.

"Lieutenant Garrett is one of us. And we will never leave one of our own behind. Every SEAL in Nigeria will volunteer to look for the lieutenant, you can be assured of that. So with his training and our commitment and dedication, with or without a tracking device, we will find him and we will bring him home."

Chapter Twelve

"Please, Commander Westinghouse. Please let me stay."

"I'm sorry, ma'am. But this base is not a place for civilians. We need to get you on a plane for home."

"But I promise that I won't be any trouble. I'll stay out of everyone's way and you won't even know I'm here."

"Again, I'm sorry, Ms. James. But I can't let you stay. It's against the rules."

"But you're in charge, so surely you can break the rules. Just this once can't you please make an exception?"

"You cannot stay here. The Nigerian jungle in not safe right now. "

Samantha hated to beg, but if it meant that she could wait at the base until Tyler was picked up, she'd beg until the cows came home.

"Please, Commander." Her voice was soft and pleading. "I can't go home until I know that Lieutenant Garrett is safe. He risked his life for me, and I..." She started to say that she loved him and thought better of it. How could she tell the commander such a thing when she'd not even told Tyler how she felt? "I need to know that he's been found."

"Lieutenant Garrett knew the risks of this mission going in. His orders were to get you out, which he did. He also knows that our orders are to get you and the other hostages safely home. So he'll expect you to be on the first plane out of here."

She wasn't getting anywhere with the man in charge, but she refused to give up.

"What can I say to get you to change your mind, Commander?"

"Ms. James, please try to understand. Because of the kidnapping and the rescue, there is an uprising going on around us in this jungle right now, and I can't free up any of my men to watch over you."

"Would you allow me to stay if I told you that I'm in love with Tyler and I can't bear to leave here without seeing him one more time?"

She hadn't wanted to confess her love to this man, but she felt she didn't have any other choice.

"Ms. James…"

"I'll keep an eye on her, Commander."

Samantha and Commander Westinghouse looked over to find Flyboy standing in the doorway. He was still dressed in jungle fatigues and he had a serious yet compassionate expression on his face—an expression that told Samantha that he'd heard her confession of love.

"This is not open for discussion, Lieutenant Thornton."

"Is it open for negotiation?" As Flyboy asked the question he walked into the room.

Commander Westinghouse looked exasperated but didn't dismiss Flyboy's question outright, which Samantha hoped was a good sign.

"I'm not in the habit of negotiating with subordinates, Lieutenant, even if they are officers."

"What if the subordinate officer can get his hands on a bottle of twenty-year-old Scotch? Would you negotiate then?"

Samantha watched the exchange between the two men and was amazed when a wide smile spread across the commander's face.

"And exactly when could I expect this bottle of Scotch?"

"As soon as I get back to the States, you get the Scotch."

Samantha held her breath, waiting for the answer. She didn't know what she'd do next if the commander refused to allow her to stay.

Commander Westinghouse walked over to his battered desk and sat down. He reached into a side drawer and pulled out a pack of cigarettes. He took out a cigarette, put it between his lips, and struck a match. He took two long drags before giving Flyboy an answer.

"Three days. I'll give you three days, Ms. James. We have a flight scheduled to take some soldiers to Germany in seventy-two hours. Whether or not Lieutenant Garrett is found, you will be on that plane. I will not discuss this with you again, nor will I renegotiate with you again, Lieutenant Thornton. Is that understood?"

"Yes, sir." Flyboy didn't hesitate to agree to the commander's terms; nor did Samantha.

"I promise I'll be on the plane, Commander. You have my word."

Samantha was absolutely positive that they would find Tyler before her seventy-two hours were up, so she happily agreed.

"All right then." Commander Westinghouse took another drag off his cigarette. "Lieutenant Thornton, I want you to take Ms. James over to the supply tent and see if you can find some clean clothes that will fit her."

It wasn't until the commander mentioned her clothes that Samantha even remembered that she was still wearing the same dirty, stained pants and blouse that she'd been wearing for the past five days. As soon as the chopper had landed on the base, she had been ushered out. Then there was a briefing with one of the higher-ranking officers. The briefing had taken close to three hours, and she told the officer everything that had happened to her from the moment she was kidnapped by the rebels until she landed on the base. Well, she told the officer almost everything. She left out the personal stuff that had happened between her and Tyler, because she figured that was no one's business but theirs. And she didn't want to get Tyler into any kind of trouble. She knew that making love to her was against the rules, and she'd never risk calling into question his code of conduct. And since she'd promised Tyler that she would never tell another living soul, she kept quiet about all the personal stuff.

After the briefing Samantha had been told that first thing in the morning they were going to put her on a plane for the first leg of her trip home. And that's when she went crazy. She tried at first to reason with the man in charge of her briefing, but when that didn't work she started to pitch a fit. She dug in her heals and refused to get on that plane. She tried to explain that she wasn't going anywhere until she knew that Tyler was safe and sound, but to no avail. And finally, after an argument that was going absolutely nowhere, she found herself escorted into Commander Westinghouse's office, where she had proceeded to state her position all over again.

And now here she was, allowed to stay on base for seventy-two hours, all because of the man before her whom the members of Team Mega One called Flyboy.

"I'll see that she gets a bath and some clean clothes, Commander." Before Commander Westinghouse could change his mind, Flyboy took hold of Samantha's arm to lead her out of the office. But just as they reached the door, the commander spoke.

"So tell me, Lieutenant, what's the plan for finding our wayward SEAL?"

Flyboy turned but didn't let go of Samantha's arm. "I'm sure you already know that Lieutenant Garrett is without his GPS tracking device?"

"Yes, so I've been told."

"He gave the device to Ms. James in case they became separated in the jungle."

"Which is exactly what happened, isn't it?" There was a certain amount of anger in the commander's voice. "And that is exactly why it is against regulations to give away your tracking device during a mission. To anyone, for any reason."

Samantha had no idea that when Tyler had given her his tracking device that he'd been breaking navel regulations, and she wasted no time in coming to his defense.

"Tyler…um, I mean Lieutenant Garrett was afraid that—"

The commander held up one hand, stopping her in mid-sentence. "Don't try to defend him, my dear. Lieutenant Garrett knows the regulations better than most. He's the leader of Team Mega One, and he'd not put up with this total disregard of the rules from anyone—not even a member of his own team."

"But—"

"I will deal with the lieutenant when he returns." He cut her right off and turned back to Flyboy. "So what's the plan?"

Flyboy spoke before Samantha could say another word. "We're going to send out a reconnaissance chopper starting tomorrow. We're not sure how far into the jungle Lieutenant Garrett had to go to get away from the rebels, so we're starting our search about five miles from where we picked up Ms. James. We don't want to fly in broad daylight for too long, and it's too risky to fly in the dead of night, so we're restricted to a few hours at the end of the afternoon, until dark."

"How are you going to make contact?"

"We know that Panther will be keeping an eye and an ear out for us. We all have flares in our backpacks, so we're sure he'll use that to signal us as soon as he knows it's safe and we're close enough to pick it up."

"Can I assume that Lieutenant Garrett did not give you his flares as well, Ms. James?"

Samantha could only imagine what kind of trouble Tyler was in. If she'd known about the regulation to keep your tracking device with you at all times, she would never have taken it from him. But it was too late now, and all she could do was respectfully answer the commander's question, even though she suspected he didn't actually expect one.

"He only gave me his tracking device, Commander."

Commander Westinghouse didn't respond to Samantha. Instead he spoke again to Flyboy.

"Keep me posted, Lieutenant Thornton. I want to be informed the moment you locate Lieutenant Garrett."

"Yes, sir."

"Dismissed."

Flyboy saluted his commanding officer before he steered Samantha out the door.

They were outside before either one of them spoke. And since Samantha's head was still spinning, she let Flyboy take the lead.

"We'll get you cleaned up and then we'll get you something to eat. The mess tent's open pretty much twenty-four hours a day."

He was walking at a pretty good clip and she did her best to keep up. In two minutes flat they were standing before a huge tented structure. It had a board hanging over the rickety wooden door with the words *supply tent* scribbled in black paint. It reminded her of something out of the old MASH TV show.

"How does a shower and some clean clothes sound, ma'am?"

Samantha didn't answer Flyboy's question. Instead she reached out and took hold of his arm before he could open the door to the supply tent.

"How can I ever thank you for what you just did for me?"

Flyboy looked down into her upturned face. "Did you mean what you said, Ms. James? Did you mean it when you told Commander Westinghouse that you are in love with Tyler?"

"Yes." Her gaze never left his. She wanted him to know that she was telling him the absolute truth.

"Then you've just found a way to thank me."

At first Samantha thought that what he'd said was an odd response, but then she caught on to his meaning. The men in Team Mega One really looked out for each other, and she knew that they only wanted the best for their fearless leader. She had picked up on that two months ago at Tyler's place, and Flyboy had just confirmed it for her. But what really made her feel better was that Flyboy was okay with her being in love with Tyler. In fact, his comment could only be taken to mean that he gave his approval without reservations.

"Let's get you something clean to wear." He opened the door and stepped back to allow her to go in first. "I'm afraid all we're going to find are fatigues, but at least they'll be clean."

"I'll be happy with anything, Lieutenant."

He stopped. "Why so formal? What happened to 'Flyboy'?"

She stopped beside him. "Why have you been calling me Ms. James? What happened to 'Samantha'?"

He smiled. "It's my training, Samantha. It kicks in every now and then when I least expect it."

Flyboy did two things. He went back to calling her Samantha and he put a small smile back on her face.

"Well, I like it better when you call me by my first name. And I think Flyboy fits you much better than Lieutenant Thornton."

"I agree." He laughed out loud. "But let's not tell that to the commander, okay? He gets kinda prickly when we forget to use our stuffy formal titles, salute, stand at attention, and shit like that."

This time it was Samantha's turn to laugh out loud. She was highly suspicious that Flyboy didn't dismiss those navel formalities as much as he'd like her to think he did. He was just too much a Navy SEAL for those things not to mean something to him. But she would never let on that she had his number, so she played along.

"Does Tyler make you stand at attention and salute him?"

"Are you kidding? Just because he's the highest-ranking lieutenant on our team, doesn't mean we give him that much respect. Hell, he's lucky we ever call him sir. And we only do that when we're forced to."

The glint in Flyboy's eyes told her that he was joking. He knew that she knew how much respect they had for Tyler, because she had seen it for herself.

"Well, good for you," she added. "You certainly wouldn't want him to get a big head just because he's in charge, now would you?"

"Oh you don't need to worry about that, Samantha. We'd never let Panther get a big head. At least not in this lifetime."

This time she offered up a genuine smile.

"Can I help you?" A petty officer who appeared out of nowhere interrupted their little exchange, and right before her eyes Flyboy became all business.

"I need some clean clothes for the lady and a pair of shoes if you have some small enough for her."

"Yes, sir."

"And after you find her some clothes, will you see that she gets a shower and a place to sleep?"

"Yes, sir. That'll be no problem, sir."

"Thank you, Petty Officer."

Flyboy turned toward Samantha. "I'm going to leave you in the petty officer's hands for now, Samantha. I need to check on a few things, but once you get settled why don't you meet me over in the mess tent and we'll get a bite to eat. Anyone can show you the way."

"Okay." Samantha suddenly felt awkward. In front of someone else she wasn't sure how to address Flyboy, and that uncertainty is what made her feel a little awkward. She noticed that, just like Tyler, he'd slipped right into SEAL mode, so she decided that her best bet was not to call him anything—and certainly not Flyboy—unless they were alone. The last thing she'd want to do was show him disrespect in front of a subordinate, especially since she owed him so much. So she played it safe and said as little as possible.

"I'll meet you in the mess tent as soon as I can."

"Take your time. I'm in no hurry." He was already headed out the door. "Take good care of the lady, Petty Officer. She's a very special friend of Lieutenant Garrett's."

"Yes, sir."

As Flyboy sauntered out the door, Samantha felt herself blush down to the tips of her toes.

"If you'll just give me a second, ma'am, I'll see what fatigues and shoes I can find that might fit you."

Samantha smiled and nodded her thanks. She was still too embarrassed by Flyboy's announcement that she was Tyler's very special friend to do much more than nod. And as she tried to find her voice, the young petty officer disappeared behind a counter and into the back of the tent.

One hour later Samantha was sitting next to Flyboy in the mess tent. She was clean, wearing fatigue pants, a pea-green T-shirt, and shoes that were a half-size too big.

"You didn't eat much, Sam."

"I'm just not very hungry."

"Why don't you try to eat a little more? You barely touched your food."

Because he was being so nice to her, she picked up her fork and forced herself to take another bite. But Flyboy wasn't that easily fooled.

"You do know that Panther will kill me if I don't take good care of you."

Samantha laid her fork down by her plate. At the reminder that Tyler was still out there in the hostile jungle, she felt her throat start to close up. If she'd thought that she was scared of the rebels and that awful snake, that was nothing compared to the fear she felt for Tyler. She was absolutely desperate to believe that he was going to be all right.

"Try to take one more bite."

She couldn't take another bite of food even if her life depended on it, so she just looked over at Flyboy sitting across from her. "Will you find him?" She surprised herself at how strained her voice was.

"We'll find him, Sam."

"Will you find him before I have to leave?"

For the first time she sensed some hesitation in Flyboy, and she felt her stomach start to cramp.

"I'm not going to lie to you. Tyler knows we'll be looking for him and he knows the drill. Because the flare he'll be using is easily spotted, he won't signal to us until he knows it's safe for us to go in and get him. And that may be tomorrow or that may be a week from now. He won't put SEALs or the chopper at risk, so he'll wait until he's absolutely sure there are no rebels in the immediate area before he sends up the flare. Even if that means we fly by, and he stays put."

She hated to ask the next question, but she had to. "And how long will you continue to look for him?"

"As long as it takes. We'll keep looking until we find him." Flyboy's answer was direct, firm, and without doubt.

"Do you believe in God, Flyboy?"

"Yes." He didn't seem the least bit surprised by her question or the abrupt change of topic.

"Do you pray to God?"

"Yes."

"Will you pray for Tyler?"

"I already have."

Samantha closed her eyes and said a prayer of her own. And as she prayed to God to bring Tyler back safely, she thought of the other men on the team and her eyes flew open.

"I can't believe that I completely forgot to ask." Her hand flew up to her throat. "Did everyone else make it back here safely?"

Flyboy pushed his empty plate away and took a drink of his coffee. "Everyone else is back, except Kid and Billy, and they were picked up twenty minutes ago."

"Thank God." And then she added. "So, Tyler is the only one that was left behind." She wasn't asking a question so much as making a statement.

"Listen to me, Samantha." When he said those words to her, she thought that he sounded just like Tyler. "You can't keep thinking that Panther's been left behind. I understand from the SEALs who were aboard the helo that picked you up, that you were frantic about them leaving Panther behind. You've got to believe me when I tell you that he's not been left. Panther knew exactly what he was doing. He spotted the rebels and his training took over. He provided cover for you to get aboard that helo, and then he assessed the situation. He knew that he couldn't make it aboard, and he would never put the mission at risk. So he did what he had to do, and then he took refuge back in the jungle. He also knows we'll come looking for him."

Samantha was a little ashamed of herself. She hadn't meant to infer that Tyler had been *left behind*—more like he hadn't made it back to the base camp like everyone else.

"I'm sorry, Flyboy. I didn't mean it the way it came out. I'm just so worried about him, and I'm afraid I'll have to leave for home before you're able to find him."

He reached across the table and took hold of her hand. "Tell you what, sweetheart. Let's just take it one day at a time, okay?"

"Okay."

Flyboy released her hand. "You're not going to eat any more, are you?"

She shook her head in response.

"Then let's get you to your tent so you can get some sleep. You must be beat."

She was totally wiped out but she didn't think that she'd actually be able to fall asleep. In fact, she was afraid that she wouldn't be able to sleep again until she knew that Tyler was found and safety aboard a helo. But because she didn't want to give Flyboy anything more to worry about, she kept that to herself.

Even in her exhausted state of mind, it didn't get past her that Flyboy had appointed himself as her guardian angel. He'd come to her rescue with Commander Westinghouse; he'd made sure she had clean clothes, a meal, and a bed. And he'd even made every effort to try to get her to forget her worries and smile. But most importantly, he'd made sure she believed that Tyler would be found. And she did believe that. She just didn't know when he'd be found or what shape he'd be found in. And even though she believed Flyboy, what scared her was not knowing if she'd get the chance to see him before she got on a plane in less than seventy-two hours.

But those were all of her worries, not Flyboy's, so she would just keep them to herself. And as he escorted her to her tent, she told herself over and over again that she would follow his advice and take everything one day at a time.

*   *   *

By the third day Samantha was riddled with worry and panic because they had still not found Tyler. She was now down to her last hour on base, and today's rescue mission had started less than two hours ago. So the chances that she would get to see Tyler, if they found him today were very, very slim. The transport plane, scheduled to take six soldiers to Germany, would be leaving in one hour and Samantha knew she was going to be with them. She had no choice. Commander Westinghouse had made it imminently clear when he'd granted her a seventy-two-hour stay that he would not discuss the matter with her again. And she believed him. Plus, she was too scared to ask him to reconsider and let her stay on, even though she'd been very tempted to do just that—so tempted that she had even broached the subject with Flyboy this very morning.

But Flyboy had been just as adamant as Commander Westinghouse had been. He'd noticed, like everyone else, that Samantha wasn't eating or sleeping, and when she asked if he thought she should go and talk with Commander Westinghouse about extending her stay, he had reached out, laid his hand over hers, and shook his head.

Samantha had known at that instant that her time had run out, and she fought hard not to cry in front of Flyboy. He was stressed out himself over the fact that they'd still not found Tyler, and she knew that he did his level best not to get her more upset than she already was. So when he had told her that it was time for her to go home, she knew that he thought it was for her own good. But even though today was day three, she still didn't give up hope that when the chopper took off it would come back with Tyler.

Every afternoon for the past three days, Samantha had stood at the edge of the rough-and-tumble airstrip and watched the reconnaissance chopper take off. And every evening, not too long after dark, she would stand in the same place and watch as the chopper would come back to base. She'd hold her breath as each man jumped down from the big bird, her heart cracking when Tyler wasn't among them. Usually there were four SEALs aboard. Except for today, Flyboy was always the pilot, and the other three SEALs were members of Team Mega One. It was one of their own who was missing and they would not leave his rescue to anyone else. So each day Tyler's men would set off on their search.

With her last hour ticking quickly by, Samantha had found her way to the makeshift camp chapel, waiting for either the sound of the chopper to return or the call for her to board the transport plane that would start her trip home. Her hands were clasped tightly in her lap, her head was bowed, and she was begging God to take care of Tyler and bring him back today. She knew that it was wrong to bargain with God, but she did so anyway. She was just so desperate that she couldn't help herself.

As Samantha sat in silent prayer, she had no idea that Flyboy and Mac had come looking for her. They found her sitting in a folding chair at the front of the chapel, and for a while both men were reluctant to disturb her. They both stood at the entrance and watched her with concern for a few minutes. Finally Flyboy made his way toward her. Mac followed closely behind.

Flyboy sat down quietly next to Samantha, while Mac slipped into the chair behind her. Without saying a word,

Flyboy reached over and laid his hand over hers. At his touch, Samantha turned tear-drenched eyes up to him.

"Please don't cry, Samantha."

Another tear dropped onto her cheek. "I'm trying not to. Really I am. But all I seem to do since you rescued me is cry."

Flyboy's heart went out to the woman he'd grown fond of. "We'll find him. It may take a few more days, but you have my word that we'll find him."

Samantha wiped away another tear. The last thing she wanted was to make Flyboy and Mac uncomfortable. They'd both been so terrific these past seventy-two hours, and she wanted to be brave for them; she really did.

"I'm sorry, Flyboy. I don't want to fall apart, but it's just that I'm so afraid for Tyler." Another unwanted tear slipped onto her cheek. She just couldn't stop crying.

"Will it make you feel better if I promise to find a way to get in touch with you back in the States as soon as we pick him up?"

She wiped away a tear with the back of her hand. "Can you do that?"

"I'll find a way, Sam. Just leave it to me."

Samantha knew that Tyler was already in trouble with his commander because of her and she didn't want to get Flyboy into trouble too.

"Please don't do anything you're not allowed to. I'd feel terrible if you broke the rules because of me."

Flyboy and Mac grinned. "We break the rules all the time, Samantha. The trick is not to get caught. And believe me, we're really, really good at not getting caught."

Samantha felt touched by his friendship and his concern about her. "Thank you, Flyboy. Thank you so much."

"You really love the guy, don't you?" Flyboy sounded almost amazed by that possibility.

"I never thought that I could love someone as much as I love Tyler. I am head-over-heels in love with him." She knew that she shouldn't be telling Flyboy and Mac something she hadn't even told Tyler, but it was important to her that they hear the words from her. They cared so much about Tyler and they'd done so much for her that she wanted to be honest with them about how she felt.

"You're good for him, Sam. He smiles whenever anyone mentions your name and I noticed that his eyes light up when he's around you. So you need to hang in there, if not for yourself right now, then for Tyler."

She knew what Flyboy was up to. He was giving her a pep talk so that she'd get on that plane without all the tears. She also knew that he and Mac had stayed behind today just to look after her. She wasn't fooled. She knew that they both would have been on the reconnaissance chopper, looking for Tyler, if they didn't feel responsible for her. And because of that she owed them more than tears.

"I won't cry anymore." She swallowed back the last of her tears. "I promise."

Flyboy sent her a smile of understanding before he stood up. Mac stood up behind him. "We promise that we will bring him back to you, Samantha. And we don't make promises that we can't keep."

With Flyboy's promise hanging in the air, Samantha sat and watched as both men turned and quietly left the chapel. There was nothing left to say. Flyboy had promised her that they would find Tyler and she just had to trust in her heart that they would.

"Excuse me, ma'am."

Samantha looked up to find the same petty officer who had helped her on her first day here. "Yes, Petty Officer?"

"I'm sorry to brother you, ma'am, but Commander Westinghouse would like to see you for a moment."

"Of course." Samantha stood up. She wasn't surprised by the summons. She had figured he'd want to see her today, if for no other reason than to make absolutely certain that she got on that transport plane. He had made it clear that he hadn't wanted her to stay, and if it hadn't been for Flyboy and a promised twenty-year-old bottle of Scotch, she wouldn't be here now.

Samantha and the young petty officer walked in silence to the commander's office. For some strange reason she felt as though she was walking to her own execution. And it crossed her mind that maybe this was like an execution to her because she was leaving here today without knowing that Tyler was safe.

"You can go right in, ma'am. The commander is expecting you."

She had been so caught up in her own thoughts that she hadn't even realized that they were standing in front of the commander's office. She smiled her thanks to the petty officer and knocked twice.

"Come in."

Samantha turned the knob, opened the door, and stepped inside.

"Oh, come in, Ms. James. And please, sit down."

Commander Westinghouse stood just as Samantha sat.

"Can I get you anything? Coffee, perhaps?"

"No, thank you. I'm fine."

The commander resumed his seat, placed both hands in front of him on his desk, and looked over at Samantha with what could have been described as sympathy in his eyes.

"You know that you have to be on that transport plane." His voice was kind and gentle.

"Yes, I know." Her reply was softer than she had intended.

"I wish that I could let you stay longer, Ms. James, but I'm sure you realize that it's not possible."

She didn't realize any such thing, but saying so wouldn't do her any good so she stayed silent.

"Are you ready to go? Have you packed up everything?"

"There is really nothing to pack, Commander. Everything I brought with me is still in the village where the Doctors Without Borders were working. It wasn't all that much anyway, so I'm leaving here with just what I have on. My other clothes—the ones I had on when Lieutenant Garrett rescued me—were so ruined that I threw them away."

"Then is there anything I can do for you before you go?"

Samantha almost asked him to please let her stay on a little longer, but she knew that it would be to no avail. So instead she reached into the pocket of her fatigues and pulled out a sealed envelope. She had completely forgotten about it when she was in the chapel. She would have preferred to give the letter to Flyboy, but now it was too late. He and Mac had taken off and her time had just about run out. So she held it in her hand for a second longer before sliding it across the desk.

"I wrote this letter today, and I was hoping that you'd give it to Lieutenant Garrett for me when he returns."

Commander Westinghouse picked up the envelope. "Of course I will. As soon as he gets back on base, I'll give this to him."

Neither of them brought up the possibility that Tyler wouldn't make it back. It was something Samantha refused to consider.

"I don't know how to thank you, Commander." And then she tacked on, "for everything."

"There's no need to thank me, Ms. James. I know how hard these past few days have been on you, and let me assure you that..."

The phone on his desk started to ring. "Excuse me." He picked it up and Samantha didn't know if she should go or stay. But the decision was taken out of her hands when he motioned for her to stay seated. He just sat and listened to the person on the other end of the line for about one minute.

"Thank God." His sigh of relief was audible. "What's the ETA?" His eyes found Samantha's. "Where the hell did they find him?" He listened intently. "Is he all right?" His unexpected smile told the story.

Samantha scooted to the edge of her chair, her heart beating a mile a minute, and waited impatiently for him to hang up.

"Well, my dear," he said as he hung up. "I have some good news for you. The copilot just radioed in that they located Lieutenant Garrett, and they're on their way back to base. They should be here any minute."

Samantha wanted to leap over the desk and kiss the man, but instead she closed her eyes and said a prayer of thanks. She had never felt such relief in her life.

"So now you can leave knowing that the lieutenant is safe."

Her eyes flew open. "Leave? You're still making me leave?"

Commander Westinghouse leaned forward and talked to her as if he were addressing a child. "Finding Lieutenant Garrett doesn't change a thing, Ms. James, other than to reassure you that he's been found and he's safe. The plane out of here is still scheduled to leave in a few minutes, and you are still scheduled to be on it."

"But finding Tyler changes everything, Commander!"

Commander Westinghouse got up and came around his desk. He sat on the edge, directly in front of Samantha, and leaned forward. "Staying here is not an option." She started to interrupt but he reached out and laid one hand on her shoulder. "As soon as that helo touches down, Lieutenant Garrett will need to be debriefed. He won't be able to see you until that process is complete, and with him gone so long, that could take a couple of days. And since I don't know when I'll be able to send another transport plane out of here, you have to go now. Today. Before the chopper with Lieutenant Garrett touches down."

Samantha didn't even realize that tears had started to drop from her eyes, because she didn't feel a thing. At the commander's words that she had to leave before seeing Tyler, she had gone completely numb. And as she sat, feeling all hope of seeing him drain away, the only emotion she felt was that of a broken heart. And as her heart shattered, her tears kept falling.

"Please don't cry, Ms. James."

It flashed through her mind that everyone seemed to be telling her that lately. And because she'd promised Flyboy that she wouldn't cry anymore, and because of the distress in the commander's voice, she tried to stem the flow of tears. She swiped at her eyes with trembling hands and drew in a deep breath. She had to get herself under control.

"I'm...I'm sorry, Commander." She looked up with a quiver of a smile. "I'll be ready to go whenever you say." Her voice was a little better but a few more tears escaped. *Dear God, will I ever stop crying?*

Samantha would have never known it, but Commander Westinghouse was a big softy at heart. And like most men, he would do just about anything to get a woman to stop crying.

"If you'll stop crying, I'll give you five minutes after the chopper touches down, but not one minute more. I'll hold the transport plane up to give you time to see for yourself that Lieutenant Garrett is safe and sound. Five minutes, Ms. James, and then you board the plane for home."

This time Samantha didn't care that he was the man in charge of this base and Tyler's commanding officer. She stood up, placed both her hands on his shoulders, leaned in, and gave him a kiss on the cheek.

"Thank you." She choked back the tears. "I will never forget you, Commander Westinghouse. You are a very kind man."

As she pulled away, she would have sworn that the man actually blushed. But she would never know for sure, because he turned away from her and picked up the phone.

"This is Commander Westinghouse. Hold the transport plane. New ETD will be five minutes after the reconnaissance chopper comes in. Have everyone on board and ready to go on time." He stressed the words *on time* more as a message to Samantha than to the person he was talking to.

"There you have it, Ms. James." He went around and sat back down at his desk. "You have your five minutes with Lieutenant Garrett."

Samantha was so overwhelmed that she just stood there, not sure what to say. She knew that Commander Westinghouse didn't like the fact that he'd shown someone his soft side. And because she respected him and didn't want to embarrass him, she thanked him again and turned to leave. It was just as her hand reached out for the doorknob that he spoke again.

"Ms. James."

"Yes, Commander." She looked at him over her shoulder.

"Lieutenant Garrett is a very lucky man."

Samantha was taken aback, but only for a second. And then she spoke from her heart. "I am the lucky one, Commander. Tyler is safe, and that makes me the luckiest woman in the world."

He smiled and so did she. And before they started to debate who was the lucky one, Samantha heard the distant sound of the approaching chopper. And without so much as a backward glance, she flew out of the commander's office and headed in the direction of the *click, click, click.*

Samantha stood at the edge of the airstrip, looking up into the sky. She could see and hear the chopper, which surprised her considering that she didn't think she'd be able to hear anything over the loud pounding of her heart. Standing with her were the three members of Team Mega One who hadn't gone on this rescue. Other than Flyboy, who had insisted on flying every day except for today, the other guys had traded off—three one day and three the next. So now here they stood, waiting and watching.

It took the longest five minutes of Samantha's life for the chopper to land. It landed about twelve yards away from where she was standing, and it took all of her willpower not to go running the instant it hit the ground. But she stayed put with the other member's of Tyler's team.

The chopper landed. Samantha held her breath. The blades stopped whirling. Samantha let out a breath. Medicine Man jumped out of the helo and onto the tarmac. Billy followed Medicine Man. Scotty was close behind. Samantha's hand came up to clutch at her heart. Kid was the next one out. Then Scotty caught a backpack that was tossed out of the helo. Finally a tall, tired, dirty Tyler jumped out of the chopper. And Samantha couldn't stop a little cry of relief.

She watched from a distance as Scotty handed Tyler his backpack, which he slung over one shoulder. Even from where she stood she could see that Tyler's hair and clothes were filthy. And just by the way he was standing she could tell that he was dead tired. Her heart caught in her throat.

For some reason Samantha couldn't move. Her eyes were transfixed on Tyler. She looked on as some other soldiers walked over to the chopper. The men saluted and Tyler and his men saluted back. Medicine Man, who was standing behind Tyler, said something that caused Tyler to turn in his direction. But just as he started to turn, Samantha watched as his eyes scanned the area and looked toward where she was standing. And just like her, he seemed to freeze in place.

Tyler stood staring at Samantha with a look of total disbelief on his face. Samantha stood staring back with a look of love in her eyes. Everyone else seemed to stop what they were doing, with looks of amusement on their faces. All eyes were now on the two of them. Samantha was scared out of her mind that he would be mad that she was here instead of on a plane for home, but she held her ground. She kept her eyes on his and finally a slow, wide grin spread across his face. And before she knew what she was doing, she took off like a flash.

Tyler barely had time to drop his backpack to the tarmac. But just as it hit the ground, he opened both arms and Samantha came flying toward him. And without caring that they were surrounded by team members and other soldiers, Samantha flung herself into Tyler's arms, wrapped her own around his neck, and kissed him for all she was worth. And Tyler did what he did best: He kissed her right back.

Samantha completely forgot where she was as she leaned into Tyler's kiss, but Tyler, being Tyler, didn't forget. And much too soon he lifted his head. With a wink and a smile, he put his hands on her waist and eased her body away from his.

"My God, Samantha, look at you. You made it into the SEALs after all."

For the first time Samantha looked down at her military attire. She was dressed just like Tyler, except for the jungle boots. She still wore fatigues and a green T-shirt, and she thought she probably looked like a sight to behold.

"What are you doing here? Why aren't you home?"

If he could ignore their audience, then so could she. "I needed to stay until you were found."

"Well, I'll be damned. The commander actually let you stay?"

She didn't even hesitate to tell the truth. "The commander didn't want me to stay at first. But Flyboy promised him a bottle of special Scotch if he'd let me stay long enough to be sure you were safe."

"It took awhile, Sam, but I'm safe." His voice softened and his eyes never left her face. He seemed to be eating her up alive. And she wanted to kiss him again.

"Are you all right? Are you hurt?" Even though he looked unharmed, you could never be sure. And he looked so weary that she had to ask.

"I'm fine. I just need some hot food, a shower, and about twenty-four hours of undisturbed sleep."

"I've been so worried about you." She couldn't help it; the words just slipped out. But before Tyler had a chance to say another word, they were interrupted.

"Excuse me, sir."

"Excuse me, ma'am.

A very young soldier spoke to Tyler at the same moment the petty officer spoke to Samantha.

Tyler reluctantly drew his eyes away from Samantha. "We…um…we need to go, sir. Intel is waiting for you, sir."

"I'm sorry, ma'am, but I've got my orders to put you on that plane to Germany, and it's getting ready to leave." The petty officer was talking to Samantha but was looking at Tyler.

Samantha knew that her time was up. She had her five minutes and now she had to leave. It was what she had agreed to. But even though her head told her that it was time to go, her heart told her to stay—at least for one more minute.

"Please, Ms. James. The plane is waiting."

Samantha took one long, last look at Tyler. His intense gray eyes appeared to look deep into her soul. He seemed to be having as much trouble moving away as she was.

"Sir?"

That was all it took. With just the one word Tyler was reminded where he was and was drawn back to being a SEAL. He leaned down and picked up his backpack, nodded to his teammates gathered around him, and glanced back at Samantha.

"I really am fine, so don't worry about me anymore, okay? You need to get aboard the plane now so that you can get home. I…" He started to say something and then changed his mind. "Have a safe trip, Sam" was what he said to her instead.

The petty officer took those words as his cue to get Samantha on that transport plane. He took her by the arm and started to lead her away, just as Tyler turned reluctantly away to follow another young soldier. And something in Samantha snapped. She had already made a complete fool out of herself, so why stop now? She had begged to stay on base until Tyler was found; she had confessed her love to Commander Westinghouse, Flyboy, and Mac; she had cried more tears than she thought were possible; she had flung herself into Tyler's arms; and in front of an audience she had kissed him blind. But given all of that, there was still one more thing that she needed to do.

As gently as possible, Samantha pulled her arm out of the petty officer's grasp and turned around.

"Tyler!" Her voice was loud enough for him to hear. He turned around, and so did everyone else.

For a blinding moment, doubt flashed through her mind—doubt that she was doing a smart thing. But when that moment passed she followed her heart.

"I love you Tyler. I love you more than I thought it was possible to love anyone. And like I told you back in San Diego, I will wait for you."

No one in her right mind would confess such a thing in front of so many people, but what choice did Samantha have? She hadn't a clue when she'd see Tyler again and she wanted him to know how she felt. She wanted him to know that for her the time they had spent together making love was more to her than just sex. It was important to her even if it wasn't important to him. And she wasn't going to get on that plane without telling him, which she did with way too many people looking on.

For what seemed like a lifetime, everyone, including Tyler, was completely silent. No one moved either. They all just stood and watched. And Samantha felt her heart turn over in her chest, because Tyler seemed completely at a loss for words. He stood rooted to the spot, not smiling, not frowning, not anything. His expression was completely blank. And that alone told her all she needed to know. He didn't love her back, and he probably wasn't thrilled that she'd fallen in love with him. And to top it off, he was probably embarrassed that she'd chosen this moment to tell him.

Swallowing back another onslaught of tears and trying to gather what little composure she could, Samantha refused to back down. She had said she loved him because she did, and if he couldn't or didn't want to return her love, then that was just tough, because she would not take the words back. Never would she take the words back. And she would wait for him, whether he wanted her to or not, because when Samantha loved, she loved with all of her heart and soul.

Willing herself not to give in to the unwanted tears, with a tilt of her chin she gave Tyler one more look. But all he did was blink his eyes as if he were trying to wake up from a bad dream. *Crack* went her heart. And as it broke in two, she had no choice but to turn and walk away—away from the man she loved and toward the plane that would take her home and most likely out of his life forever.

Chapter Thirteen

Three Weeks Later

Samantha would always think of the past three weeks as the most painful three weeks in her entire life. Sure, she had felt pain and panic when Tyler had been missing in the Nigerian jungle, but it was nothing quite like this. For the past three weeks, she'd felt pain, panic, sadness, depression, and loneliness. And it was all because of Tyler and the fact that she hadn't heard a word from him—not one lousy word.

Every time the phone would ring Samantha's heart would skip a beat. She had convinced herself every day that the only reason he hadn't called was because he was still in Nigeria, or Iraq, or on some other faraway covert mission. But as one day slipped into another, her brain and her heart knew better. Her brain just knew that he was probably home, standing on his deck overlooking the ocean, never planning on calling her again.

No matter how long she lived, Samantha would never forget the look on his face when she'd told him that she loved him. She'd played it over and over in her mind until she thought she would go mad. And still she didn't regret her words, because they came straight from her heart.

Samantha spent the past three weeks trying to convince herself that not accepting her love was Tyler's loss, not hers. She'd wander aimlessly around her apartment, telling herself that she was better off without him in her life. She would remind herself that even if they had a relationship, he would always be dropping in and out of the country—and most likely more *out* of the country than *in*. And she didn't want that. Or did she?

Finally, as day twenty-one arrived with still no word from him, Samantha knew that she still wanted to be with Tyler, in or out of the country. If he would have given her half a chance, she would have made every effort to have a life with him—a good, solid, loving life. But he hadn't given her any chance at all, and it was time that she accepted that fact and tried to get on with her life.

So as the sun started to set on day twenty-one without a word from him, Samantha grabbed her purse and decided to take a walk. She'd walk through her neighborhood, where she knew it was safe, and she'd walk Lieutenant Tyler Garrett right out of her life. And when she returned to her apartment, she vowed that she would be a new woman and that she would buy into the old saying that *today is the first day of the rest of your life.*

Numb from sadness and a feeling of loss, Samantha walked for over an hour. The sun had set and there was a slight breeze blowing through her hair. She reached her apartment building, walked up one flight of stairs, and turned in the direction of her apartment down the hall. And as she took one step closer to her apartment, her heart lodged in her throat and she had to blink her eyes to be sure she wasn't seeing a ghost. Because sitting in the hall, with his arms draped over bent knees, hands clasped, and with his back resting up against her apartment door, was Tyler.

Samantha simply could not believe her eyes. After twenty-one days and after giving up and believing that she'd ever see the man again, there he sat, right in front of her apartment. In somewhat of a trance she took another step. Tyler, who was watching her with a cautious look in his eyes, stood up. She stopped. He smiled.

"Hi, beautiful."

His voice was so relaxed that it bordered on nonchalant. And because Samantha was feeling anything but relaxed and nonchalant, she didn't know whether to step up and slap his handsome face or throw herself into his arms. She did neither.

"What are you doing here?" That was not exactly what she'd daydreamed her first words would be upon seeing him again, but she was so taken aback by his presence that the question just popped out.

"I came to see you."

"How did you know where I live?"

"Katie told me."

"Why didn't you call first?" *What's the matter with me?*

"I didn't call because I don't want to talk to you over the phone. I want to talk to you in person."

"Oh," was her only response.

"And it would be nice if we could go inside and talk. I'm pretty sick of sitting in this hallway."

"How long have you been waiting?"

She couldn't figure out for the life of her why she kept asking one lame question after another instead of opening up her apartment door. But she couldn't seem to help herself.

"Long enough for the manager of this building to come over and check me out. I had to do some pretty fancy talking so that he wouldn't throw my ass out of here."

"What did you tell him?"

Tyler let out a long, exasperating sigh. "Okay, Sam. Stop stalling. You don't want me here, just say so."

His words and the look on his face had the desired effect and she shook herself out of her trancelike state. She reached into her purse and then moved toward her apartment door, with key in hand.

"Don't be ridiculous, Tyler. Of course I want you here. I'm just surprised to see you…that's all."

She opened her door and stepped inside, with him right on her heels. She set her purse down and turned toward Tyler, who was standing in the middle of her small living room, checking out the place.

"Nice," was his only comment.

"Thanks."

"How long have you lived here?"

"About two years."

"Did you decorate the place yourself?"

"Yes."

"I like it."

"Thank you." *My God, is this all we can come up with to talk about?*

Tyler walked over to the couch and sat down, making himself right at home.

"Would you like a beer?"

"No thanks. I'm driving."

And Samantha guessed right then why he was at her door and why he hadn't called instead. He came to do the honorable thing. Her heart told her that he came to L.A. so that he could tell her to her face that he didn't want her to be a part of his life. That was just so like him. He would never take the coward's way out and break up over the phone. He would be grownup about the whole thing and deliver his news in person. And after he broke up with her, he would be on his way. And since he didn't want a beer, she surmised that he planned to deliver the news as quickly as possible and then be on his way in a flash.

"Well, I think I'll have a drink, if you don't mind." She needed something to help her get through what she knew was coming.

Samantha went into the kitchen and Tyler got up and followed her. As she poured herself a glass of cool white wine, he pulled out a barstool and sat down at the kitchen counter.

"Sure you don't want anything?"

"I want lots of things. But nothing to drink, thanks."

For a fleeting second she wondered if there was a double meaning in his response. But then again, maybe not. Maybe his reply meant nothing more than what it was.

"So, how've you been, Sam?"

She placed the bottle of wine back in the refrigerator before answering. "I've been…" She stumbled over her words but quickly recovered. "I'm fine."

He watched in silence as she took a long sip of wine.

"How have you been?" As she asked the question she walked around the kitchen counter, pulled out a barstool, and sat down next to Tyler. She felt a sudden need not to shy away or allow Tyler to intimidate her. This was her apartment and she refused to feel ill at ease in her own home. So she sat down and faced him head on.

"Not bad…considering," he said, and he turned in her direction, his eyes latching on to hers.

Now this was the man that she knew, and she couldn't help herself as a small unwanted smile slipped into place. He was back to being the king of vague. But since she wasn't interested in vague responses, she asked another question—a very direct question.

"What happened to you after I left Nigeria?"

"What do you mean?"

"Well…" She paused but only for a brief second. "I got the feeling before I left that Commander Westinghouse wasn't very happy with you."

She knew he couldn't get away with a one-word answer. But even so, he tried to evade her question.

"I'm still not sure what you mean?"

"I mean, Tyler Garrett, that Commander Westinghouse was pissed as hell that you gave me your tracking device. And when I tried to explain to him why, he didn't want to hear it. He told me in no uncertain terms, that he'd deal with you when you got back."

"Oh, that."

"Yes, that."

Tyler reached over for her glass of wine. He started to take a sip and then thought better of it.

"Yeah, well, after my debriefing he and I had a little discussion about that. And you're right, he was pissed as hell. And he reamed out my ass over it too."

"Did you get in trouble?"

"It all depends on what you define as *trouble*."

"Don't get cute with me. Answer my question." She was tired of playing his word games.

"Listen, Sam, here it is in a nutshell. I blew off standard regulations and gave away my GPS device. There are good reasons for following regulations, but I didn't care. In doing that I jeopardized not only my own rescue, but the safety of the men trying to find me. It was stupid and irresponsible, and I got reprimanded for it. But I'm going to tell you what I told Commander Westinghouse. I told him that if I was faced with the same decision again, given the same circumstances, I wouldn't do anything differently."

Wow, that was a mouthful. "And how'd he react to that?"

"As expected, he blew his top. Then he proceeded to send me out on two so-called reconnaissance missions that turned out to be nothing more than a waste of time and a major pain in the ass. He sent me back out into the jungle, with a couple of green recruits, and he made sure we were gone for days at a time. He just wanted to punish me. It's a damn good thing he didn't know about the other rules I broke on that mission. If he did, I'd still be stuck in that shithole jungle."

She ignored his subtle reminder of the time they spent together in the hut and took another drink of wine. "What about your teammates. Were they punished too?

Tyler started to chuckle. "Hell no. They'd followed orders and had nothing to worry about. They'd completed their part of our mission without losing a hostage or any of their equipment. So, after my debriefing, they were all sent home on the first plane out of there. I was the only one held back. Flyboy and the rest of the guys laughed all the way to the plane. They pretty much knew what was coming my way, and they thought it was hilarious."

"They may have loved laughing at your predicament with Commander Westinghouse, but while you were missing they were worried about you, Tyler. They didn't want to let on for my sake, but I could tell that not one of your men was going to draw a calm breath until you were found." She knew that he already knew this, but she told him just the same.

The look in his eyes turned serious. "Yeah, I know. I put them in one hell of a bind by giving you my GPS. I knew that they'd look for me, and not give up. And without my GPS I knew I'd be hard to find. I also know I've mentioned to you before that my team specializes in rescue missions, but it's different when it's one of our own. Those guys never gave up, and because of that they saved my life."

Samantha reached over and laid her hand on his. She knew that it probably wasn't a good idea to touch him but she didn't care. She just couldn't seem to stop herself. "And you saved my life," she whispered. "And amidst all the excitement in Nigeria, and with my surprise in finding you here now, I've forgotten to thank you."

Taking her completely by surprise, he turned his hand over and laced their fingers together. "It's what I do, Samantha."

Without even thinking about it, her fingers tightened around his. "Don't make light of what you did, Tyler. I realize that you and your men rescue people for a living, but I also know that you don't just give away the tracking device that's meant to help keep you safe. You not only saved my life, but you did so at the risk of your own. I don't even know how to thank you for that."

Tyler released his hold on Samantha's hand and reached over to grab her wine glass. This time he did take a drink.

"So, how's your job?"

It didn't get past her that he was uncomfortable with her words of thanks so he simply changed the subject. And that was very typical of Tyler. If he didn't want to talk about something, then he would either give vague responses, ignore the question altogether, or do what he was doing now: change the topic of conversation. It was only because she didn't want him to feel even more uncomfortable that she let him get away with it.

"I've changed my focus." She replied matter-of-factly, and it got his attention.

"How so?"

"I learned one very important thing out there in the jungle." Well, she'd learned a lot of things, but only one she would share with him right now. "I discovered that I'm not really cut out for a life of adventure. I was scared out of my wits from the second the rebels entered our village, right up until the time I saw that you'd been rescued safe and sound. And even though I ended up fine and on my way home, that was enough of an adventure to last me a lifetime."

"I don't know about that, Sam. You were pretty terrific out there. Even under fire, you held your own. And when you got on that chopper without me, I was never more proud of you. You did exactly what I asked you to do, without question."

"That was the hardest thing I've ever done in my life, Tyler. And if I had to do it again, I'm not sure I'd be able to leave you behind a second time." She hadn't meant to tell him that. But it was too late now, so she finished her thought. "I don't think I'll ever forget what it felt like watching you make your way farther and farther into the jungle, fighting to keep me and the other SEALs safe."

"Well that's something I'm trained to do, Sam. But you aren't. And that's what makes you even braver. I mean it when I say you held your own out there, every step of the way."

His praise filled her with pride, but not enough to sway her. "Well, be that as it may, I was still scared out of my mind. And now I know that I'm really not cut out to be a hardcore foreign correspondent. And besides, there are plenty of serious issues I can write about right here at home. There's the plight of the homeless, Americans without healthcare, aliens crossing our borders looking for a better way of life, drugs in the schools." She took a deep breath. "I will never run out of good, important things to write about, and if I do, I can always do a follow-up article on flying." This she added with a smile.

"Ah, speaking about flying. Flyboy said to say hello."

Again, he masterfully changed the subject. But she didn't mind, because she loved getting a message from Flyboy.

"And how is Flyboy?"

"He's fine. Even if he is pissed at me."

"Why in the world is he mad at you?" She found it hard to believe that he was serious, but she asked him just the same.

"I'll tell you about that later, 'cause the real issue here is that I should be madder than hell at him."

She knew that she shouldn't ask. She could hear the little voice in her head telling her not to ask. But when did she ever listen to herself?

"Okay. I give up. Why should you be mad at Flyboy?"

Even though she braced herself, she was not prepared for his answer.

"I'm pissed because I think that Flyboy's more than a little in love with you."

She was taking a sip of wine when he spoke and she nearly spilled the rest of it down the front of her. "What!"

"You heard me. I said that I—"

"That's ludicrous." She interrupted him and waved off his outrageous suggestion with a flick of her hand.

"It's not ludicrous. He actually had the nerve to tell me that if I was stupid enough not to ask you to marry me, then he'd be more than willing to ask you himself."

She sat looking at him with her mouth gaped open until he placed the tip of his finger under her chin to shut it. Again, there was that little voice in her head that said *let it go, Samantha,* but again she didn't listen.

"And what did you say to that?" She finished off the rest of her wine in one gulp.

"Not much."

And that was his only response, which made her want to cry on the spot because she now knew for sure that he didn't love her. For some stupid reason, Samantha had been holding on to the slim possibility that he'd shown up at her door unannounced because he loved her and he didn't want to tell her such an important thing over the phone. But now she knew that wasn't the case. He wasn't in love with her and there was nothing she could do or say to make him change his mind. So she didn't even try. And because she wanted to hang on to as much dignity as she could, she didn't say another word and waited for Tyler to break the silence.

"Wanna go for a ride?"

Again there was an abrupt change of topic, so it took her a second for his question to register. But when it did she shook her head. "I don't think so." All she wanted now was to get rid of him so that she could be alone with the tears that she was desperately holding back.

"Oh, come on, Sam. I just got my bike out of the shop and I need to put some more miles on it. So let's go for a spin."

"You've got a motorcycle?" she asked with semi-amazement.

"Yeah. I rode it down here to see you. I wanted to see how it's running after my mechanic tinkered with the engine, and so far so good. But I want to run it some more, so come on. It's the perfect evening for a spin around the block."

"You came all the way to see me just so you could take your bike out on a test run?"

"I came to see you for lots of reasons, one of which is to try out my bike."

Samantha got up from her barstool. She needed to get him out of her apartment before she fell completely apart. She didn't need to be hit over the head with a sign that read *I came to see you to try out my bike, not because I love you.*

"Listen, Tyler—"

"No. You listen, Sam." He reached out and took hold of her hand. "Let's go for a ride. You'll love it. I promise."

Short of digging in her heels and forcing him to drag her across the room, there was little Samantha could do. He was tugging on her, laughing out loud.

"Okay, okay, you win. I'll go for one quick spin around the block." She gave in as gracefully as possible and let him lead her out the door. He was being so charming and so persuasive that she didn't really have a choice. She grabbed her purse to take it along, but he stopped her.

"All you need are your house keys. No point in dragging along the purse."

She threw her purse back inside the apartment and turned in the hallway to lock up. Tyler was standing so closely behind her that she could feel his warm breath against the back of her neck. Forcing herself not to give in to the ripple of awareness she felt down to the tips of her toes, she stepped away from him and hurried down the hall. He followed.

Samantha tucked her keys into the front pocket of her jeans as they walked outside and over to a motorcycle that was parked across the street.

"Wow, Tyler. This is beautiful." The words just popped out.

In response, he ran a hand almost lovingly along the seat of the bike. "I treated myself to it last year. I bought it secondhand from a fellow SEAL who decided that jumping out of planes at low altitude was all the excitement he needed. I really love it, but unfortunately, I'm gone so much that I don't get to ride it as often as I'd like."

She glanced at Tyler and again at the bike, realizing that he was just the type to ride such a thing. Jumping out of a plane, even at low altitude, would never be enough excitement for this man. The bike was perfect for him.

"Ever been on a bike before?" His voice brought her eyes back to him and she shook her head, uncertain as to whether or not she really wanted to do this. "No problem. Riding on the back is a piece of cake." With that he unsnapped two helmets that had been strapped to the handlebars. He put one on her head, securing the strap under the chin. Then he plopped the other on his own head. And she watched as he flung one jean-clad leg over the seat of the bike. He settled in, turned to Samantha, and tilted his head toward what she presumed was the back seat.

"Hop on." He was grinning from ear to ear.

Deciding to throw caution to the wind, and because she couldn't resist his infectious smile, Samantha did as she was told and *hopped on.*

"Put your arms around me, Samantha, and try to move with me. And when I make a turn, lean with me. It's easy, you'll see."

She had no trouble complying with his instructions. Putting her arms around him was like a little piece of heaven.

"Okay, sweetheart. Hold on." With that he started up the engine, pried up the kickstand with his boot, straightened out the bike, and took off.

What was intended to be a little spin around the block actually turned into a forty-five minute ride. Tyler was in full command of the bike and Samantha felt her confidence grow with each spurt and turn. She loved the feel of the wind against her face, loved the free-flying feeling, and especially loved hanging onto Tyler. She would tighten her hold and lean into his back whenever she got the chance.

Before Samantha knew it, Tyler was heading into a public parking lot located at Huntington Beach. *Leave it to a SEAL to head for the beach*, she thought as he found a parking spot and turned off the bike. He got off, helped Samantha off, and assisted her with her helmet.

"Have fun?"

She hated to admit it, but she'd had a blast. "It was wonderful. But do you think on the way back, I could drive for a while?"

Tyler threw back his head and laughed. "We'll see." He took her hand in his and they headed in the direction of the ocean.

It was an incredibly beautiful summer evening. The sun had set but the moon cast a glow on the sand and on the water. Because of the warm evening, there were families, kids, and lovers all out on the beach. Some were using the barbeques, others were sitting around bonfires, and others were just strolling hand in hand. It was a prefect night: breezy, soft, and sensuous.

Keeping her hand tucked securely in his, Tyler led the way across the sand and closer to the water. He stopped on the dry sand and sat down, taking Samantha with him. They sat, side by side, still holding hands and looking out over the water. For a while neither one of them felt the need to speak. But after a few minutes, Tyler broke the silence.

"Do you still want to know why Flyboy's mad at me?"

She'd completely forgotten that he'd even mentioned it. But she figured there was a reason for his asking, and she now was too curious to let it go.

"Sure."

He didn't meet her gaze. Instead he kept his eyes focused on the ocean. "Flyboy told me in no uncertain terms that I was a complete jerk for the way I acted in Nigeria. He said you spilled out your heart to me, and I just stood there like a complete jackass. Those are my words, not his. His description of me was a lot more colorful. The guy really let me have it, and to make matters even worse, he's still pissed at me over it."

Samantha wanted to die. She'd hoped that they would get through the evening without bringing up her declarations of love. But she should have known better, because this was the perfect segue for Tyler to bring up the matter of breaking things off with her, although holding her hand in his and coming all the way to the beach didn't quite fit the mold of the perfect break-up. But what did she know? Maybe it did make perfect sense. Right now she was more confused than ever. And because she felt uncomfortable by what she was sure was going to happen, and because she didn't want to appear to be a complete fool, she tried to head him off at the pass.

"Please, Tyler. Before you go any further, I want you to know that I don't think you acted like a jackass at all." Her words drew his eyes toward her. "I'm sorry if I embarrassed you in front of everyone in Nigeria. I didn't know when I'd see you again and I couldn't leave without you knowing how I felt about you. It was impulsive and selfish, and I realized too late that you didn't feel the same way about me. I just wasn't thinking."

"How do you know what I was feeling?" His question surprised her. But then again, he always seemed capable of surprising her.

"It was pretty obvious, Tyler. The look on your face said it all."

He took that in for such a long time, and she wondered if he was thinking back to that dreadful day.

"Did you mean it?"

She didn't even try to pretend that she didn't understand what he was asking. And because she still loved him, she could never lie to him. So out came the truth, no matter how painful it might turn out to be.

"Yes."

He thought that over for a second. And then he reached into the pocket of his sweatshirt and pulled out a crumpled letter.

Samantha watched in horror as Tyler opened the letter and straightened out the wrinkled paper with his hand. Samantha felt her throat start to close up, and all she could do was to sit and stare down at the familiar letter. She was completely speechless. But Tyler, obviously capable of speech, began to read.

"Dear Tyler." His voice was low and a little husky. "Commander Westinghouse is sending me…"

She tried to stop him from reading any further. "Please, Tyler. You don't need—"

He halted her in mid-sentence with one long look—a look that she hadn't ever seen in his startling gray eyes before. And because she read a look that seemed to say *I really need to do this,* she remained quiet, swallowed what little pride she had left, and let him finish.

Tyler started over again. "Commander Westinghouse sent me away today, without knowing if you've been found. But I believe in my heart that it is only a matter of time until you're picked up, and I didn't want to go without telling you this." He stopped and glanced over at Samantha briefly. Then he turned his eyes back to the letter he held in his hand, and continued reading. "I want you to know that I have more respect and more admiration for you than for anyone I have ever met in my life. I feel privileged to know you, and I feel safe and protected when I'm with you. These past few days have been life-changing for me, in more ways than one. I've learned a lot about myself as a person, and I've learned that life is not something we can ever take for granted. I've also learned that we should never take our feelings for granted, or our feelings about other people. Life is just too short. So, Tyler, I simply want to tell you that I've fallen in love with you. And that I'll love you until the day I die." This time Tyler took a deep breath before continuing. "I'm not sure how you feel about me, but my heart and soul told me to tell you how I feel about you. Please hurry home, stay safe, and know that you are in my prayers every minute of every day. I love you, Sam."

Samantha didn't say a word. She couldn't think of anything to say that wouldn't make matters worse, especially since she wasn't sure why he read her the letter now. She'd thought about that letter hundreds of times over the past three weeks, finally convincing herself that Commander Westinghouse hadn't even given it to him. Since he'd let her stay and she got to see Tyler and say goodbye, she figured that the commander had probably tossed the letter in the trash—at least that's what she had hoped. But now she knew better.

"Do you still mean it?"

She thought again that there was really no reason to lie to Tyler, so she answered him truthfully. "Yes."

Once more he took in her response, not replying for what seemed like forever. His gray eyes looked out over the ocean one more time before returning to Samantha.

"You told me earlier that you discovered that you weren't cut out to be an adventurous foreign correspondent. Can I ask you a personal question?"

"Of course." She had absolutely no idea where this was going. But because she desperately wanted to change the subject and not talk about her letter anymore, she didn't really care, that is until he spoke again.

"Well, given your lack of enthusiasm for the adventurous life, do you think that you might be cut out to be the wife of an adventurous Navy SEAL?"

"I...What did you say?" She wasn't sure she'd heard him correctly.

Tyler looked so deeply into her eyes that she was lost. "I didn't mean to stand around like a jackass when you told me in Nigeria that you loved me, Sam. I was just so stunned and a little off balance. I'd been awake for almost forty-eight hours, and I was still trying to convince myself that you were not a dream. I knew that I felt our kiss through every part of my body, but I just couldn't believe that you were in Nigeria, standing right before me, telling me and everyone within earshot that you loved me. And before I knew it, you were being whisked away to catch a plane."

Samantha could hardly believe her ears and she felt hope well up in her heart.

"If I had to do it all over again, right there in Nigeria, I would drag you back into my arms, kiss you again, and tell you how much I love you."

Samantha was afraid to breathe, because now she felt like she might be dreaming.

"It's almost funny, Sam, but I suspected that I loved you the second I dropped through the window of that building where you were being held hostage, and found you tied up on that dirty, filthy floor. But I refused to admit it to myself. And I knew—really knew—that I loved you when I knelt down in front of you to clean away the dirt and blood from your face. And that's what makes my behavior that day in Nigeria almost comical. How I could let you get on that plane, and act the way I did, is beyond me."

Don't cry. Don't cry.

"And then, after you left, I tried everything I could think of to convince myself that I wasn't in love with you. I wasn't prepared to fall in love, Sam, and you, better than anyone, know how stubborn I can be."

Don't cry. Don't cry.

"But I've been miserable as hell thinking about my life without you. And hearing Flyboy tell me every day that he's nuts about you, has driven me crazy. Even though I knew he's only pushing my buttons, I've had a tough time dealing with this insane jealously. I can't stand the thought of you with another man, Samantha. So the second I got home from Nigeria, I called Katie to find out where you live, jumped on my bike and headed up here to find you."

Don't' cry. Don't cry. Now is not the time to cry.

"All the way up here, I just kept praying that I wasn't too late. I am crazy in love with you, Samantha, and I'm sorry as hell that it has taken me so long to tell you."

One tear, and then another, slipped onto her cheek.

"You're awfully quiet." He sounded so uncertain and very much *not* like the Tyler Garrett she knew.

"I'm..." she gulped. "I'm trying very hard not to cry." A soft sob escaped.

"Why are you crying, sweetheart?" He draped an arm across her shoulders and pulled her close. There was a hint—just a hint—of laughter in his voice, but she decided to give him a serious answer anyway.

"I suspected that I loved you the night you were called away, and we said goodbye at your house in San Diego. But I knew—really knew—that I loved you when we were crawling through that tunnel, and there was the possibility that you wouldn't be coming out of there with me. My heart told me loud and clear that I had fallen head-over-heels in love with you, and that hasn't changed. I love you so much, Tyler."

He pulled her close and leaned down to whisper into her ear. "Do you love me enough to take a chance and marry a guy who will get called away in the middle of the night, and who could be gone for months at a time? And do you love me enough to live with me in my little beach house in San Diego? And do you love me enough to have my children? And do you love me enough to stay with me for the rest of our lives?"

Samantha didn't even hesitate. Not for one second did she hesitate.

"I can't even imagine my life without you, Tyler. So if you're asking me to marry you, and to have a family with you, my answer is yes."

"I'm asking," was his reply right before he lowered his head and brought his lips down to hers. His lips touched hers lightly before he lifted his mouth barely an inch above hers.

Samantha laughed softly against Tyler's mouth. And because she wanted a kiss—a real kiss—she reached up, wrapped her arms around his neck, and pulled him back down to her waiting mouth. This time the kiss wasn't brief or light; it was packed with all the emotion and passion of two people who were desperately in love. Samantha melted into Tyler's arms and he deepened the kiss. Then, all too soon, Tyler lifted his head.

"If we're going to get married, I guess I can give this to you now." He reached deep into the front pocket of his jeans and fished around. And what he pulled out made tears well up all over again in Samantha's eyes. "If you start to cry I won't give this to you."

Tyler swiped away at a tear that had fallen against one of Samantha's cheeks while she lifted a hand and swiped away at another. With a sniffle and a smile, she extended her left hand.

"See. I've stopped crying."

Tyler softly whispered her name, took her hand in his, and slipped onto her finger a beautiful solitaire diamond engagement ring.

"We'll probably disagree a lot," he said, with his eyes never leaving hers.

"Yes. I know."

"But we will love a lot, too."

"Yes. We will."

"And we should have beautiful children."

Her heart melted at his words. "I can't wait to have children with you, Tyler."

"I promise that I'll be a good husband."

"And I promise that I'll be a good wife."

"I promise that I will love you forever, Samantha James."

"I promise that I will love you forever, Lieutenant Tyler Garrett."

And with those words, they both leaned toward one another. And there on the beach, with the moon shining down on them, all of their promises were sealed with a kiss.

Epilogue

One Year Later

Lieutenant Tyler Zachary Garrett stood *at ease* with the seven other men who made up SEAL Team Mega One. Once again they were crammed into another hastily erected tent, in another godforsaken Middle Eastern desert, standing before Commander Jackson R. Pearl, waiting for orders for one more highly covert mission.

"Well, Lieutenant Garrett, I'd say welcome back, but instead I'll just say that it looks like we've been through this drill before."

As Commander Pearl addressed the leader of Team Mega One, he recalled the mission he had sent them on almost eighteen months ago. And he remembered how when he had asked for a few volunteers last time around, he'd gotten the entire team even though he only needed four men to step forward. This mission was different in that it was going to be a rescue mission at sea, but his request was going to be pretty much the same. He'd ask for three volunteers, four tops, but he'd bet his retirement pay that he'd get all eight. And as he looked down the line of men standing before him, he felt a sudden burst of pride, for these men were the best the navy had to offer. They were the best of the best. They were the best trained, the most dedicated, the tightest-knit team, and the best of friends. And for this delicate mission, they were all his.

"Here's what we've got, gentlemen. We've got a deserted oil tanker out in the Indian Ocean, that's been taken over by a small terrorist cell. Even though it's a small cell, they've got more initiative than most. Intel has been keeping a close eye on these guys, and now they tell us that the cell members have been busy getting real friendly with a group of Nigerian rebels."

"Isn't that a bit odd, Commander?" Tyler couldn't keep quiet. "Terrorists mixing with Nigerian rebels? What's the catch?"

"It seems that it's a trade-off of sorts, Lieutenant. The rebels seem to have gotten their hands on some high-powered weapons that the terrorists want. And the rebels, who seem to be growing in force, now need some formalized training—the kind of training that the terrorists specialize in and the kind they are willing to provide, at a cost. So they've struck up deal—weapons for training. But from what information intel was able to provide, the rebels wanted to conduct a little loyalty test before shaking hands with the devil, so to speak."

Tyler felt his stomach tie up in a knot, because he had a sick feeling he wasn't going to like what was coming.

When Tyler and his men stayed silent, Commander Pearl went on. "Looks like the rebels want to get rid of a missionary who runs a small Nigerian village, because they suspect he has connections with the U.S. military. They suspect that he's helped us out on more than one occasion, and because of that they want to see him disappear. And they're right. This missionary has helped us out of a bind several times. So they've asked the terrorists to nab the guy, stash him away on the tanker, and then blow the thing to hell and back. The rebels figure this hit accomplishes two things. They get rid of the missionary with ties to the U.S., and it proves that the terrorists are loyal to their cause."

"And what about loyalty to the terrorists? What do the rebels need to do in return to demonstrate their loyalty to the terrorist cell?

As usual, the men of Team Mega One let their leader do the talking.

"The terrorists don't give a shit about loyalty from the rebels. All they want are the weapons."

"So, who is this missionary, and has he been nabbed yet?"

"You do get right to the heart of things, Lieutenant Garrett."

Tyler didn't say anything further. He wanted to hear more from the commander about this mission.

"As it turns out, you know this missionary. His name is Father Dominic. And his disappearance happened about six hours ago."

Oh shit, was Tyler's thought right before he looked down the line at his men. They all knew the story and how Father Dominic had risked his life to help him and Sam get out of the Nigerian jungle last year. Tyler would never forget lying in that dark tunnel, listing to Father Dominic lie to the rebels so that he and Samantha could make a clean getaway. He would never forget it no matter how long he lived, and he didn't need to hear any more from

Commander Pearl. He'd be the first one in to go and get the missionary out.

"How many of us do you need, Commander?"

"Three of you should probably be enough for this mission, Lieutenant. You'll be dropped into the water a good ten miles from the tanker. We want you to raft in as stealthy as possible. We also want you to slip aboard that tanker and slip out with Father Dominic completely unnoticed. We do not want it to appear as if Father Dominic was rescued. We want it to look like the terrorists screwed up their part of the bargain. Once we get Father Dominic safely home, we'll find a way to leak it back to the rebels that he is back in the states. That alone should pit the two forces against each other. The terrorists will flunk the loyalty test because it'll look like they reneged on their part of the bargain, and if you do your job and get the missionary out, sight unseen, then they won't be able to prove otherwise."

"When do we leave?"

"You leave as soon as you gear up. I suggest you take two men with you."

"I'll take the men in this time, Panther. You've earned a reprieve."

It was Flyboy who spoke up. He looked briefly at Commander Pearl and then turned his gaze onto Tyler. And there it was: the silent communication between the two of them that the married guys should stay behind and let the single guys take on the mission. But Tyler wouldn't have any part of staying behind, even if he was the newest married member of Team Mega One. Father Dominic was a man he owed his life to, and he would lead the team that would go in and get him off that tanker.

"Thanks, Flyboy, but I'm going."

With those words, Commander Pearl stood back and witnessed a repeat of what he'd experienced with these men eighteen months ago. One by one, they stepped forward. One by one, each man voiced a reason why he needed to go along. And one by one, they made it clear that they would go as a team.

Commander Pearl couldn't stop the grin the spread over his face. Even though he had expected exactly this, he was still pleased that this team of men hadn't disappointed him. "It's your call, Lieutenant Garrett."

"We'll all go."

No surprise there. "Very well," was the commander's only comment as he saluted the men who were now standing *at attention* before him. And he watched as one by one they exited the tent to go and do what they were trained for and what they did best: rescue someone who needed rescuing.

Now less than twenty-four hours later, Tyler, Flyboy, Mac, Billy, Medicine Man, Scotty, Brian, and Kid were on a transport plane headed home. The mission had been highly successful. Father Dominic had been found with no problem and taken off the tanker with no trouble. And best of all, the SEALs had left absolutely no clues behind that they'd even been there. Mission accomplished.

Tyler sat back in the plane and closed his eyes, thinking about how anxious he was to get home and see his wife of six months. He and Samantha had managed to make it through a six-month engagement before coming to the conclusion that being engaged wasn't all it was cracked up to be. What really mattered to them was to be together. So one weekend they'd packed a couple of bags, headed up to Lake Tahoe, and tied the knot, just like that. In a matter of hours they were husband and wife. And neither of them could have been happier.

A smile of satisfaction crossed Tyler's handsome face. He couldn't believe how the past six months had changed his life—and all for the better and all because of Samantha.

Right after they had returned from an all too brief honeymoon in Lake Tahoe, Samantha had packed up her clothes and moved into Tyler's little house in San Diego. She told him just about every day how much she loved living by the ocean and how she could write from just about anywhere. So without any further discussion, they had made the small house on the beach their home. And what a home it was.

More times than not, the house was filled up with the guys from Team Mega One. The single guys were always hanging around, and even the married ones showed up with their wives in tow. Throughout the house one could always hear lots of laughter, as well as the ever-present, ongoing argument about who was the best pilot on the team. Samantha had had absolutely no trouble blending right in, and Tyler's best friends had become her best friends as well. And for this Tyler was eternally grateful.

As the transport plane got closer and closer to home, Tyler got more and more excited. It'd been almost a month since he'd last seen Samantha, and he wanted to make every second that they were together count. He was already thinking about the best way to go about ditching the guys and locking himself away with his wife for no less than a week. They had a lot of catching up to do, and he was eager to get started.

“Five minutes to landing.” Those words to Tyler were like manna from heaven. And he and the rest of the guys got ready to touch down at home.

As the door to the transport plane sung open, the men from Team Mega One came down the steps. Tyler was the last one out, stopping at the top of the steps to look out over the landing strip. His gray eyes scanned the area and his heart kicked up a notch as he found the woman of his dreams standing at the end of the airstrip, waiting with a smile on her beautiful face.

With his eyes latched on to hers, he started down the steps. When he reached the bottom he adjusted his backpack and his mind flashed back to the time at the Nigerian base when he'd spotted her waiting for him. Even though after every mission he could count on her being there waiting for him, he always remembered that first time—the first time that she had told him that she loved him.

And like that first time and every time since, he looked over to see her take off like a flash. As he dropped his backpack onto the tarmac, he opened his arms. And with everyone looking on, Mrs. Samantha Garrett flung herself into her husband's waiting arms, kissing him like there was no tomorrow. And both of them knew that the kiss they were sharing was a kiss filled with promise, love, and a long and happy future together.

THE END

Printed in the United States
72839LV00001B/7-24